# The Cooke Brothers

PRAIRIE BRIDES    BOOKS 1-3

HARRISON

COLIN

DUNCAN

BESTSELLING AUTHOR
# KIT MORGAN

ANGEL CREEK PRESS

**Prairie Brides: The Cooke Brothers**

His Prairie Princess (Prairie Brides, Book One)
Her Prairie Knight (Prairie Brides, Book Two)
His Prairie Duchess (Prairie Brides, Book Three)
©2013, 2014 Kit Morgan

Cover Design and Interior format by The Killion Group
http://thekilliongroupinc.com

# THE PRAIRIE GROOMS SERIES

# TABLE OF CONTENTS

Pat —

Happy Reading!

Liz Morgan

"There's just something about a western. They're so simple. Good versus evil. The cowboy or lawman has to save the girl then gets the girl. You don't need to dress them up; their purity alone tells a simple story that always satisfies. That's why I love westerns."

~ John Terleski

# His Prairie Princess

# ONE

*Oregon Territory, March 1858*

"Let's just kill her and be done with it!"

Sadie Jones cringed. Kill her? What did they mean, kill her? The idiots just tied her up – why bother if they were going to kill her anyway?

"Ah, now why wouldja wanna kill a purty thing like this fer? I know a *much* better use fer her! After all, it's why we took her in the first place, ain't it?"

Two of her captors laughed and leered in her direction. Oh, no! Not *that!*

"I still say killin' her is our best option."

"But Jeb!" complained another. "Think of the horrible waste! Ya gotta admit, she's mighty pretty!"

Now all four of them leered, including Jeb.

Her eyes widened. *No, no, please!* She didn't want to end her life like this – raped and murdered by a gang of dirty, stinking, halfwit outlaws!

Thankfully, one of the men's stomachs growled, loudly. They looked at each other, then at their bellies. If Sadie's guess was right, her life was about to be spared by a pot of beans.

"Well, I dunno about y'all, but I can't think on an empty stomach," one moaned, confirming her assumption. She slumped in her chair in relief. "And I'm plumb tired of wearin' this here mask!" he added, adjusting the bandana that still covered the lower half of his face. They'd been wearing them ever since they robbed the stage several hours ago.

"Cain's right. I'm starved, and she can't see us if'n we're in the other room eatin'. Let's go."

Jeb, the leader of the gang, studied her a moment longer before giving in. "All right, let's get some grub. She ain't going anywhere. And later, it won't matter if she sees us. As soon as we're all done with her, she'll be half-dead anyway – we can draw straws to see who gets to finish the job."

They laughed, slapped each other on the back in a congratulatory manner and, spurs jangling, headed into the main room of their cabin hideout.

Sadie Jones took a deep breath through her nose, and grimaced. The odor from the gag they'd placed on her was atrocious! She continued to make a face at the awful smell and let her breath out slowly.

Trussed up, gagged, and stuck with four lecherous outlaws. Lovely. How was she going to get out of this? She should have listened to her father and never set foot outside her door! Why had she gone off by herself? *Why?*

Because she was a headstrong, stubborn, fiercely independent girl, that's why – traits her father said would get her into a lot of trouble. And now they had. Whatever was she to do?

When the outlaws had robbed the stage, she'd figured that was that – her money would be gone and her quest cut short. Worse, she'd have to contact her father and face his wrath over her brash behavior. She was supposed to be heading to her aunt and uncle's ranch for a visit, not gallivanting across the prairie in the opposite direction, in search of her mother.

Guilt suddenly assailed her. Her father didn't suspect a thing. Days, even weeks could pass before he got word from her aunt that she hadn't made it. Sadie had set off on the four-day journey just as she had on past visits, but when the stage caught up with a wagon train, the temptation was too much. She left the stagecoach and paid one of the families in the wagon train to take her along, at least until they came to a point where she could catch a stage to the little town of Clear Creek in the Oregon Territory. It worked, too, until said stage had been held up. But Sadie had never expected to be taken along with the rest of the loot. Being abducted was the last thing on her mind that morning.

Unfortunately it was the foremost thing on it that afternoon.

Sadie again tried the ropes used to lash her hands behind her back and tie her to a chair. No use. They were too tight. She was a helpless captive. So helpless, in fact, that she did something she hadn't done in a very long time. She began to cry.

It wasn't so much out of fear, though she was sure she'd succumb to it when the men came back. No, these tears were out of anger: anger at herself for not heeding her father's advice to wait for him to wrap up a business deal before he could help find her mother. Her *real* mother. But she knew that once her father got around to finishing things up and making their travel arrangements, her mother would be out of time, and out of luck. Death usually didn't give second chances. And, according to a letter her father had received, death was obviously closing in on her. Not the same way it was closing in on Sadie now, but once you're dead, what did it matter?

Sadie closed her eyes. It was her fault for taking off in the first place. She wanted to meet her mother before she died, but it looked like that wasn't going to happen. Her mother would be taken to glory by whatever sort of disease was slowly eating away at her. And Sadie would meet a similar fate, at the hands of four men who thankfully had more interest in a pot of beans at the moment than in her. But those beans weren't going to last the scoundrels much longer ...

So Sadie, being a practical girl, did the only thing she could think of considering her current predicament. She sniffed back her tears, bowed her head and prayed that she'd be ready for whatever happened when the beans ran out.

Harrison Cooke crawled out of his hiding spot underneath the cabin's porch and crouched beneath a window. He'd followed the outlaws' trail for hours before finally catching up with them. The driver of the stage was badly injured, and it galled Harrison to have to fetch a nearby farmer to tend him. But he couldn't leave the man – then he'd be no better than the thieving scoundrels who'd beat him half to death.

He pushed the thought aside as he slowly stood to peek in the window. The outlaws were all inside as far as he could tell, their horses unsaddled and put in a makeshift corral. He figured they'd been here at least an hour and had possibly settled in for the night. He could smell beans cooking and hear laughter. The scum were probably slugging down shots of whiskey and counting the minutes until they opened the strongbox and mailbag they'd stolen. That is, if they hadn't already.

But he hadn't heard any shots fired or sounds of forcing the lock – and he'd been under the porch for at least half an hour. The strongbox must still be intact. He hoped the mail fared as well, since that was what he was after – specifically, letters from Washington regarding his brothers' pardons. Harrison was prepared to do whatever he had to in order to get them. His two brothers were not going to spend another minute in that rancid, disgusting prison if he could help it!

He took a deep breath and carefully looked again through the dirty window. "What the bloody...," he whispered in shock. "No, it couldn't be."

He turned from the window, shut his eyes tight, then opened them and peeked through the glass again. They had a *woman* tied up in there! Now what was he going to do? His only goal was to retrieve the mailbag; he wasn't equipped to deal with a hostage!

Granted, the stagecoach driver had mentioned a passenger. But Harrison and the farmer had figured that if there was one (unlikely, for who on Earth *wanted* to come to Clear Creek?), the fool must have wandered off after the stage was robbed. That being the case, the passenger could fend for himself; the driver had a more pressing problem. Besides, come suppertime the missing passenger would likely find his way to the farmer's house, as it was the only one in the area. It was amazing how an empty stomach could help a man's sense of direction.

The passenger's real problem, as Harrison saw it now, was that *he* was actually a *she* – and she had been taken from the stage along with the strongbox and mail. With women being exceedingly scarce in these parts, and these outlaws not exactly being church deacons, it didn't bode well for her. He closed his eyes and said a quick prayer that he would get to her before the outlaws did, not to mention get them both out alive and unharmed.

He looked at the closed door leading to the cabin's main room. Voices and raucous laughter could be heard coming from the other side. The mailbag was more than likely there. Then he looked at the woman. Even in the dim light from a nearby lantern he saw she was young, and frightened. Her eyes, a dark blue, were wide over the gag and filled with tears. She wore a simple white bonnet, from which her hair had escaped in tiny dark tendrils about her face. The rest of her ensemble was a white blouse and dark wool skirt – any coat, shawl, or other covering must still be on the stage with her belongings. She had to be half-frozen from the ride to the ramshackle cabin.

Her boots were practical and dirty – they looked like she'd done a lot of walking in them. He briefly wondered if she'd come from one of the wagon trains that passed through to the south. They were also tightly lashed together at her ankles. *Crumbs!* He certainly hoped she had some feeling left in those tiny feet and ankles. She was going to need them in a moment, to run for her life.

Harrison pulled a Bowie knife from the scabbard on his belt. It was the only weapon he had on him. He'd been in such a hurry to meet the stage, he hadn't bothered to change out of his dirty work clothes or put on his gun belt. Despite being an excellent shot he didn't wear a gun often; pig farming didn't much call for it. But he'd gladly carry one from now on if he managed to get out of this.

He took one last look at the woman. Her head was bowed and her body shook, either with silent sobs or from the cold. Either way, it didn't matter – the sight still made his gut twist. He gritted his teeth and quietly backed away.

Now he needed a diversion, something to draw the outlaws away from the cabin long enough to rescue the woman and retrieve the mailbag. He looked at his surroundings. It was already dark, and getting colder by the minute. The bit of snow on the ground, coupled with the scant light from the crescent moon, would help, but it was still going to be difficult to get himself and the woman to his horse without a lantern to light the way.

Harrison took in his surroundings for another brief moment before he suddenly smiled. Of course, why hadn't he thought of it before? He had just the thing to use for a distraction ...

Sadie's head hung low, her chin on her chest. She watched her tears fall into her lap and tried to keep from shivering. It had been easy to stop crying when she was angry with herself. But the sound of chairs being pushed away from a table, deep male laughter and plenty of belching told her that she was about to be served up on a silver platter – or in this case, probably the dirty wooden floor her chair sat on.

The only furniture in the room she occupied was the chair she was tied to and a small wooden barrel with a lantern on it. Was there was a third room with an actual bed inside? It might be nicer to die on a bed and not the floor, or the kitchen table. Perhaps the third room was through the door directly behind her. She'd noticed it when they shoved her into the chair and tied her up.

Oh, what was she thinking? *Stop it, Sadie, stop it!* She was the daughter of a cattle baron, for Heaven's sake! She'd come north from Texas with her father when she was five, when the war with Mexico started, and had helped him settle in the Oregon territory after her stepmother had died. He'd become one of the major names in the beef industry, had brought commerce to the wilds of Oregon, supplied the wagon trains and helped tame the prairies.

And the whole time, she'd been right by his side, working almost as hard as he had. She could shoot a gun. She could brand a steer. She'd been on a cattle drive. And, by God, she wasn't going to go down without a fight and have her father think of her as some weak, stupid female who couldn't take care of business!

Of course, if she survived this, she'd still have to hear about not listening to him. And taking off by herself across the prairie. And getting abducted, of course. But it would be a small price to pay ...

Her head snapped up. A sound suddenly caught her attention. A horrible howl carried on the wind sent a chill up her spine. *Wolves?* Her eyes darted to the door. Her captors heard it too, if the dead quiet in the other room was an indication.

Another sound caught Sadie's attention, this one much different. A horse was running past her window – she could hear the hoofbeats loud and clear.

Another wolf howl rent the air, closer this time.

"The horses! Those stinkin' varmints are goin' after the horses!" one of the men cried. There was a mad scramble on the other side of the door. She heard their cursing along with the sound of booted feet stomping every which way but out the front door. They weren't the most organized lot, and she thanked the Lord for that. It might buy her some time.

Finally, after several more sets of racing hoof beats, further stomping and cursing, and the sound of a door being thrown open, the cabin went silent.

"Don't move a muscle and don't make a sound," a deep, accented voice hissed in her ear from behind. Where did he come from? She hadn't even heard him enter the room! She saw a flash of steel out the corner of one eye. A knife – a really *big* knife! *No! Oh, no, please!* One of them had stayed behind, and was going to take her before the others had a chance.

"I hope you've enough strength in you for what's to come," he whispered as he began to saw through the ropes used to tie her to the chair. "But don't worry, we'll be quick about it. They won't know until it's too late."

Sadie's tears fell in force, blurring her vision. Where had her bravery gone? And oh! – the man stunk to high Heaven. He smelled of mud, straw, and ... was that pig?

He grabbed her from behind and yanked her out of the chair.

*Nooooo!* Sadie's entire body shook with terror. She couldn't breathe, couldn't see and, for the first time in her life, couldn't stay conscious ...

# TWO

The woman landed on the floor like a sack of potatoes. Harrison had barely let go of her to untie her ankles when she toppled over in a dead faint. He glanced quickly around. Blast it, the outlaws could be back any minute!

There was only one thing to do. He picked her up, threw her over his shoulder and – since he couldn't very well use the bedroom window he'd crawled through to get into the cabin – headed for the back door. But to get to it, he realized, he'd have to go through the main room ...

He carefully opened the door and looked for any sign of the mailbag. Nothing! Where could it be?

A horse ran past the open front door. A shout soon followed.

Harrison had no choice. He had to escape! Tightening his hold on the woman, he made for the rear door on the other side of the room, checked for any signs of the outlaws, and then ran into the cold night.

He almost slipped on an icy patch of snow, but managed to keep his feet under him. The woman was blissfully light, thank the Lord for that! But even so, he would have to carry her a good distance, and over time he would eventually tire. Especially if it took him a while to find his own horse in the dark ...

He had begun to wonder if the woman had regained consciousness when he heard another shout in the distance. He pushed himself harder, stumbled again and ran sidelong into a tree, shoulder first. He grimaced as he hit, and hoped the audible *thud* he'd heard wasn't the woman's head. But then, what else could it be? If she had woken up, that blow would have put her right out again. The only consolation was that it was certainly a better fate for her than what the outlaws had planned. Regardless, once they were safe he could take her straight to Doc Waller in Clear Creek.

Harrison kept moving until he heard the sound of water and headed for it. He'd hobbled his horse near a small stream, and the animal couldn't be far off. He carried the still form down to the bank, stopped to catch his breath, then risked a low whistle. His mare Juliet nickered in return. It was faint, but it was enough, and he took off downstream toward the sound. After a few moments he found Juliet right where he'd left her.

Just in time, too. It was starting to snow.

"OK, darling – you're going to have to take it from here," he whispered to Juliet as he hefted his load across the saddle. It was a horrible way to transport the woman, but he wasn't sure he had time to untie her and bring her around. Who knew how close those outlaws might be? He quickly mounted, lifted her body to slide into the saddle himself and laid her across his lap as best he could. It was going to be a rough ride with her body wedged between his torso and the saddle horn, but at least she would stay put.

With one hand on the woman and the other holding the reins, he kicked Juliet into action and they were off across the stream, through the woods and, none too soon, heading for the open prairie. This was the one place he feared they might be caught. A couple inches of snow covered the ground, and even though the crescent moon gave little light, it would probably be enough for the outlaws to track them. He needed to get some distance from them. With luck, it would snow enough soon to hide any trail he'd left.

Harrison slowed Juliet and turned to check the landscape behind them. Nothing. No light in the trees, no dark forms coming across the snow. By now the outlaws must've caught their horses and discovered that the woman was gone. Even if they had been dumb enough not to guard her, they weren't so dumb they wouldn't notice her bonds had been cut, the "wolf pack" nothing but a diversion.

But after a few more minutes, he took another quick look at the dark line of pine bordering the prairie. It was snowing harder now, but not so hard he couldn't see the light of a lantern flashing through the trees.

They were coming.

He had a good head start, but was it enough? They might still see him. Taking the woman straight to Doc Waller, then, was out of the question – Juliet would never make the extra miles to town if he pushed her much harder. He wished he'd taken his brother's stallion, Romeo – a race across the open prairie would be no problem then – but he'd only planned to get the mail, not rescue a damsel in distress! He could still lose them in the gentle rolling landscape of the prairie – the outlaws wouldn't be able to keep a steady eye on him. Unfortunately, he wouldn't be able to keep an eye on them either.

He stopped briefly to take in his surroundings. The farm was closer. Juliet could make it with no problem, and at least his stepbrothers and father would be there. They could help protect the woman ... maybe. It would depend on how much they'd been drinking. In fact, the more he thought about it, he might have to protect her from his stepbrothers and father as well. None of them had been around a woman in a long time; the only "soiled dove" in the area was indisposed, and not a very good one at that. The others had been run out of town.

That left only one choice.

Harrison groaned at the thought and took off again, this time toward home. He prayed as Juliet naturally picked up her pace: *Father, please forgive me for what I must do. And please, Lord, may this woman forgive me, too.*

Sadie tried to open her eyes. The effort was painful. In fact, every part of her body hurt – her limbs ached, her head felt like it was about to explode, her stomach was cramping. Where was she? The last thing she could remember was ...

She didn't seem to have any memory at all! Maybe it was because the effort it took to think hurt too much.

She decided to try and figure out where she currently was instead of where she'd been. But when she attempted to move, she found she was held in place. She was on her back, that was certain, and it was dark, and she could smell hay. In fact, she was not only lying on a bed of hay, she was covered with blankets of it.

Sadie tried to roll over, move, anything, but couldn't. Finally she realized she was still bound and gagged.

*Oh, Lord, no!* Memories came trickling back: the stagecoach, the outlaws, the ... *rescue?* Is that what happened? Where was the man who freed her from the chair? She must have fainted, but how long does a faint last? And where was she now?

She vaguely remembered being carried through the dark. She remembered the cold. In fact, she was still cold, but not like before. But if she'd been rescued, why was she still tied up? And why did her head feel like it was about to shatter like glass?

A door creaked and groaned. Sadie froze. *If I'm about to die, Lord, let it be quick. I feel terrible enough as it is.*

Booted footsteps. A man. There was a rustle of hay and before she could even scream into the gag, he was almost upon her!

But he didn't grab her as she expected. Instead, he was very gentle, removing the hay that was covering her. Then he stood and lit a lantern.

His back to her as he hung the lamp on a peg, she quickly studied him. He was as tall and broad as some of her father's cowhands; she could tell by his frame that he'd known hard work. His hair was a sable brown, much like hers, and just reached the collar of his coat. When he turned, his dark eyes widened as he looked at her. No, not at her – *into* her, right into her very soul. It made her feel incredibly vulnerable. Being helplessly bound certainly didn't help, either.

"Oh, good – you're awake," he whispered. "I wasn't sure if you would be. Your head ... I'm so sorry, but it took quite a blow."

Her eyes widened. He had an accent ... English, maybe, or perhaps New England. Who was this man? She struggled briefly in her bonds, but the pain stopped her.

"Oh, dear! I'm so sorry – let me help you." He reached behind him and pulled out a huge knife. Sadie automatically shook her head.

"No, I won't hurt you, I promise. I'm here to help. I do apologize for not untying you earlier – I was in a bit of a hurry ..." He gently pulled her up to a sitting position.

Her head swam, and she fell against his shoulder as he reached behind her and began to cut the rope binding her wrists. She belatedly realized she was wrapped in several blankets – of cloth, not just straw. No wonder she wasn't as cold as before.

"I'll free you, but you must promise me to stay calm. I cannot help you if you start to scream and panic. Do you understand?"

He was warm, and didn't smell as bad as before. He had to be the same man who took her from the outlaw's cabin. He spoke with the same odd accent and still had the scent of livestock on him, particularly pig. She knew that smell – they had kept pigs at home.

The ranch. Her father ... Sadie moaned.

"There, there. You'll be all right." He tossed the rope aside and took a moment to study her in the soft lantern light. His eyes widened and his breath caught. He collected himself, and quickly began to untie her ankles.

Sadie let herself fall against him as he worked, too tired to care about the contact. He was wonderfully warm. The sensation brought comfort and eased the pain that throbbed throughout her entire body.

He returned her to a sitting position. "You promise you won't scream?"

She nodded. It hurt.

He reached behind her head and untied the bandana. She nearly choked when he removed it, her stomach suddenly sick.

She must have looked ill, for he quickly took her in his arms and cradled her against him, beginning to rock gently. "You're going to be all right," he said as he looked down into her eyes. "I'll take you to town to see the doctor. Then we can find the sheriff – he should be back by now. He's been hunting an outlaw gang, possibly the same ones who abducted you. Would you like some water?"

She stared back. His face was bent over hers, his eyes conveying a warmth no number of blankets could produce. It was a look she had never seen before and couldn't quite put a name to. She licked her dry lips. "Water ..."

Without taking his eyes off her, he reached behind himself and grabbed a small canteen. He opened it and held it to her lips. "There, there, not too much. Take small sips."

She took little gulps instead. It was a mistake – she immediately turned and retched into the hay.

"Not to worry, not to worry! Let me help you." He pulled a handkerchief out of his back pocket, poured some water onto it, and cleaned her face as if it was the most natural thing he could do. "I dare say, but you're in a bad way. I've got to get you to Dr. Waller."

Sadie looked at him. "Who are you?" she croaked.

"Oh! I'm terribly sorry – Harrison Cooke, at your service. And you are?"

A raspy whisper. "Sadie Jones."

"Would you like to try some more water, Miss Jones? Perhaps just to rinse your mouth this time? Or a little sip?"

She did one, then the other. It was better. The water stayed down.

"You've been through a horrible ordeal, Miss Jones. I'm terribly sorry you've suffered so."

She looked him over with what strength she had left. "What are you doing here?"

"I've come to help you, of course."

"No. I mean, what are you doing here in Oregon Territory? Where are you from?"

Oh ... yes, well. I hail from Sussex originally. My family came here in 1846, when this was still British territory – or at least disputed," he added with a wry smile.

"An Englishman?" Sadie whispered, and put a hand to her head in an attempt to still the throbbing.

"Here now, lie back. There's a good girl. I'm going to get the wagon ready and take you to Dr. Waller."

"What happened to me?" she asked as the room began to spin.

"You were abducted by outlaws. I rescued you and brought you here."

"To a ... *barn?*"

"Er, yes. A barn. Trust me, it's much better than the alternative. We'd best see to your head now." He gently covered her with the blankets again, then poured more water on the handkerchief, folded it, and placed it on her forehead.

The cool cloth felt good. Sadie closed her eyes, her body heavy with exhaustion. Sleep began to pull at her. And his voice was like soft silk against her raw nerves. "Now, dear princess, let's see about getting you to the doctor ..."

# THREE

Harrison wanted to kick himself for such a forward statement. "Princess? Really?" he mumbled as he tucked the blankets around her. She had fallen asleep quickly – perhaps too quickly, considering her ordeal. He knew a little about this sort of thing, enough to know that it was dangerous for someone to drift in and out. He'd watched it happen to his own father. But when his father had fallen asleep after hitting his head in a carriage accident, he'd never woken up again.

In short, he had to hurry.

But despite his need to get the woman to town, he couldn't help but take a few seconds to study Miss Sadie Jones. Her dark lashes were long and beautiful against her pale skin, her lips a delicate pink. A lock of hair had fallen across her face, and he gently brushed it away, reveling in the softness of her cheek. She was beautiful. Perhaps calling her "princess" was appropriate – she certainly looked like one. A sleeping beauty he could awaken with a kiss ...

*Get a hold of yourself, man!* He tore his gaze away. His stomach knotted with a pang of unfamiliar emotion, one much different from when he'd seen her tied to a chair. That was righteous anger over the outlaw's cruel treatment of her. This was desire, a deep, possessive desire that rose up with incomprehensible force as he knelt beside her. It scared him.

The outlaws had intended to harm her in the worst possible way. If he hadn't gone to meet the stage, then set out after the mailbag, she'd likely be dead. That scared him even more.

He chuckled to himself as he stood. His sleeping princess hadn't been saved by a kiss, but by a piece of mail intended to save his brothers – a piece of mail he still needed to find. But he had to take care of Miss Jones first. She was still in danger from her injury, not to mention the outlaws until they were safely behind bars. He vowed to make sure the scum wouldn't get anywhere near her in the meantime, even if it meant putting them behind bars himself.

But it wasn't only the outlaws he needed to protect her from. He had to hurry and get her to town before his stepbrothers and stepfather discovered her in the barn. They were just as bad, maybe even worse – as he'd suspected, they'd been drinking.

Harrison walked to an old trunk where his gun belt lay, picked it up and put it on, then went to hitch up the wagon to take his sleeping princess to safety.

Sadie awoke to the jangle of harness, and hoof beats crunching on the snow. It was cold, bitterly so, at least on her face. The rest of her was wrapped snugly in a pile of quilts and blankets from the barn.

She had to blink her eyes a few times against the morning light before she could see. The sun was coming up to her left, the sky a dark blue. They had to be heading north, presumably to Clear Creek and the doctor.

She again lay on a bed of hay, and was glad for it – its softness helped to cushion her aching body from the ruts in the road. She took some time to figure out what to do once they got to town. She'd have to talk to the sheriff, of course, and let the doctor tend her – those things came first. But then she needed to inquire about her mother. She must still be alive, she had to be!

And after she found her, she could send word to her father. That wasn't going to be pleasant no matter how she looked at it. At least she would have time with her mother before the famous Horatio Jones came riding into town like a tornado to whisk her back to his cattle kingdom. But she would insist they take her mother with them. She couldn't bear it if her mother was still deathly ill and her father turned his back on her. He'd done that once already.

Sadie knew the story – a few months ago, Maria, the family cook, had told her everything. Maria had been with the Jones family since Sadie's father was a boy and remembered his trip to Paso del Norte before his engagement, to sow his wild oats before he got hogtied into matrimony. A few years later, however, it became evident that his new wife was barren.

It was also quite evident that Horatio Jones had a daughter – or so said a letter he'd received, saying to come get the babe if he had any interest in her. The note had come from an El Paso madam named Bess, who was planning to head to the Oregon Territory.

Horatio, as it turned out, had bedded down with a Mexican merchant's daughter. The act had ruined her, and cast out by her family, she'd had only one option to stay alive. She quickly became a fine addition to Bess's establishment, a radiant beauty and very popular with the gents, but it wasn't long before they found out she was pregnant.

Had she not been such a beauty, Bess might've thrown her out on the streets. But the madam was already planning her trip north, and knew she'd be worth her weight in gold along the trail and into

Oregon, where women – especially exotic-looking women like herself – were few and far between. Men would pay good money to have her, and lots of it. A child would only complicate things.

Thankfully, Bess had a soft spot for the tyke, and knew who the father was. But out on the frontier, you had to be practical. The upshot was that Bess would let her "girl" keep the baby until it came time to leave, but she wouldn't be allowed to take it along. If she wanted to hang onto her job, she'd have to get rid of it.

Of course, Horatio Jones had no idea that Sadie knew. Both he and her stepmother, Ellie, had told her she was orphaned by her birth mother when she joined a wagon train to Oregon, that Horatio had rescued her and brought her home to be raised by the childless couple. That was true – or more correctly, half-true. They left out the part about her mother being a whore, and her father being her actual father.

"We're almost there. Are you feeling any better?"

Sadie turned her head slightly. Her own rescuer was out of her line of vision, but she heard him well enough. "A little. Can we go to the sheriff first?"

"Good Lord, no! You're in no shape to see the sheriff just yet. I'm taking you straight to Dr. Waller. Everything else can wait."

His manners surprised her, and his accent was charming. He was a delightful contrast to the rough and dirty cowhands around her father's ranch; half of them didn't even speak English, and the other half only did so punctuated with crudities. Harrison Cooke looked the part of a rough cowhand or farmer, but he certainly didn't act or speak like one.

He stopped the wagon in front of a small, two-story, whitewashed house at the edge of town. She looked over the town of Clear Creek as he carefully helped her out of the wagon and carried her toward the house. There was only one street, with three or four buildings on either side, a livery stable at the far end, and a few small houses at the near one. There wasn't even a church or schoolhouse that she could see.

It was a far cry from El Paso, she thought. Granted, El Paso only had a few hundred people, but there was still the river traffic and merchants coming over from the much larger town of Paso del Norte on the Mexican side of the border. On the ranch, "going to town" meant at least a little taste of civilization. She'd assumed she'd given that up in coming to Oregon, but she had expected more than ... this!

Her rescuer carried her to the door and tapped on it with his boot. She heard footsteps approach from the other side, and the door opened. "Harrison Cooke! What have you got there?" a tall, thin older woman asked. "Quick now, bring her in before the wind gets into my bones."

He brought Sadie into the house. Warmth immediately wrapped around her, bringing with it the delicious smells of fresh-baked bread, bacon and coffee. Her stomach rumbled louder than the outlaws' had the night before, much to her embarrassment.

"Heavens, what a sound! When was the last time you ate, child?"

Harrison gently set Sadie on her feet but didn't let go. "If my guess is right, not since yesterday morning," he answered for her. "She was on the stage when it was robbed."

The woman gasped and took her from his arms. "Are you hurt? What happened?"

"I think I'm all right now. But I am terribly hungry, and cold."

"Let's get you some food, then. I just took some bread out of the oven, and the kitchen's nice and warm." She began to steer Sadie toward the wonderful smell of food. "You'll find Doc out back, Harrison. Best go fetch him."

He tipped his hat and hurried out the door.

The woman led Sadie down a short hall to the kitchen, settled her at the table and got her a cup of coffee. Sadie took it gratefully and held the cup between her hands to let the warmth sink in. It was heaven.

"Your name, child," the woman stated rather than asked as she began to slice some bread.

"Sadie. Sadie Jones."

"Sarah Waller. But everyone around here calls me Grandma."

"Everyone?"

"Oh, yes. I'm the oldest living soul in town, even older than Mr. Waller. Settled here when our wagon broke down, along with a few other families – including Harrison and the rest of that brood of Cookes. Been here a good eight years now."

"What brought an English family out west?"

The woman stopped slicing a moment. "Well, Harrison's father died in St. Louis. He and his wife and sons were coming out west to raise cattle, but he had some sort of accident. The mother remarried to survive, I suppose, and brought her three sons out here along with her new husband and his two boys. Harrison was probably seventeen at the time."

"Where are you from?"

"Kansas – a little town called Lawrence. Mr. Waller got it in his head to do his doctoring in Oregon City, but this is as far as we got. We both fell in love with the prairie and the nearby mountains. It's not like Kansas prairie, mind you, but we knew we belonged here. Besides, from what I've heard since, Lawrence isn't exactly a hospitable place anymore. Here, have some bread and bacon – you must be half-starved, and here I am flapping my gums!" She set a plate in front of Sadie.

The only thing that kept Sadie from wolfing down the food that moment was Harrison returning with the doctor. They headed straight for her, but Doc Waller, a wiry little man with white hair, stopped up short, his mouth half opened, and stared.

Sadie looked from one man to the other. What could be wrong? Harrison wasn't looking at her so strangely.

Doc Waller glanced at his wife, then back to Sadie, and now both studied her with interest.

"It's her head I'm concerned about, Doctor," Harrison said, interrupting their scrutiny. "She took a frightful hit."

"For Heaven's sake, child," Mrs. Waller began as she handed Harrison a cup of coffee. "Why didn't you say so? A head injury can be dangerous!"

"I don't think it's so bad. I feel much better than last night," Sadie volunteered.

"I'll be the judge of that," Doc Waller said firmly. "Take off that bonnet. It looks like it needs a good washing anyway."

"Yes, sir," said Sadie, setting the half-eaten bread on the plate as he came around the table. When she complied, her hair spilled out of the bonnet in a dark cascade, loose pins tinkling onto the floor.

Harrison had just taken a sip of his coffee, and almost choked.

"Steady there, son," Doc Waller commented knowingly and began to examine her head.

It didn't take long to find the spot. "Oh!" Sadie exclaimed when he touched the large lump.

"Ooh, that's a doozy – maybe the biggest lump I've ever come across. How'd you get it?"

Now Harrison did choke.

"I don't remember."

"Hmmm," Doc began. "You wouldn't happen to know anything about it, would you Harrison?"

Harrison set his coffee down. "Ah, yes. Well, as it was, Miss Jones ... she ... well, I had to ... what I mean to say ..."

"Spit it out, boy!"

Harrison looked at Sadie. "I do so apologize." He turned to Doc Waller, his face reddening. "I accidentally ... ran her into a tree."

"You ... you did *wha-a-a-at?*" Doc Waller sputtered.

Sadie sat and stared at him, eyes wide.

Harrison squared his shoulders. "I had to carry you after you fainted. As I was fleeing, I slipped on some ice, and fell against a tree. I'm afraid, Miss Jones, your head hit it harder than I did. Please, dear lady, accept my most humble apologies."

"That'd do it," Doc Waller mumbled as he began to feel around the injured area again.

Sadie continued to sit and stare. So he really had rescued her – okay, clumsily, but rescued her nonetheless. She knew she was delirious last night, and thought she might have imagined parts of it. But she hadn't. It must have been horrific for him to carry her while running for his life as he escaped to his horse, or wagon, or ... oh, the details didn't matter! What did matter was that he had risked his life to save her, and succeeded. A bump on the head was a small price to pay. "Thank you," she told him softly.

Harrison gave her a single, nervous nod and smile. "Well, then ... I'd, um, best go see if I can find the sheriff." He quickly darted from the room.

Sadie could only nod at his retreating back as Doc Waller continued to poke and prod her skull. The enormity of her recent ordeal was hitting her full force. She would be forever grateful to the broad-shouldered Englishman who'd saved her life.

Not only that, but he'd also saved her quest. "Dr. Waller? Do you know a woman here in town by the name of Teresa Menendez?"

"I don't know of any Miss Menendez. There is a woman in town named Teresa, but ..." He trailed off.

Mrs. Waller's mouth formed into a thin line. "Here now, girl – what business do you have with the likes of her?"

Sadie ignored her tone. "Do you know her?"

The Wallers exchanged a quick glance as Doc came around the table to stand next to his wife. "We both know *of* her," he answered.

"But what would you want with her, dear?" Mrs. Waller importuned. "She's a harlot, child – a harlot! You've no business even going near a woman like that!"

"Sarah, hush now!" Doc Waller ordered.

Mrs. Waller's words stung, but Sadie's resolve was firm. She took a deep breath. "Is she alive?"

"Yep, I reckon so," he began. "That is, the last time I checked. But ... why? What's she to you?"

"Perhaps to you, she's nothing more than a harlot. But to me ..." Sadie looked them in the eye. "... she's my mother."

# FOUR

"Your mother?" Mrs. Waller gasped.

"Blazes, Sarah, of course! I knew she looked familiar – I just didn't know why. Now that you mention it, you can see it plain as day ..."

"Well, yes, I can see it! But did she know her mother was a ... a ..."

Sadie was getting close to having had enough of this. "An adventurous woman, Mrs. Waller?" she finished the sentence. "A prostitute? A courtesan? A whore? Yes. Yes, I know."

Mrs. Waller stood and stammered as she searched for the best way to apologize. Finally she said, "I'm sorry if I offended you. Guess it don't much matter what she's done – she's still your mama. And it's none of my business, anyway – it's just that ... well, decent folk around here ran the rest of those women out of town. They left your mother behind on account of her being ill. Only a matter of time before she'd be run out, too, only no one wanted to be responsible."

"Responsible for what?"

Mrs. Waller closed her eyes a moment. "Her passing on."

Sadie stood. That made sense – driving a sick woman out of town in this cold would be a death sentence. "Can you take me to her?"

"Well ..." Doc Waller was clearly reluctant. "After that knock to the noggin, you really should be resting. But if you feel you're up to it ..."

"I do," Sadie interrupted.

"Then we can go right now if you like."

"Or at least after you finish eating," Mrs. Waller added.

"Thank you. I would appreciate it. And no offense taken – I know what my mother is." Sadie took another bite of bread and tried to collect herself. How could people be so cruel to another human being? The townspeople here had no idea what had made her mother sink to such desperation. *But I know*, she thought to herself. "More than anything else, I want to be able to tell her I love her before she dies. She is dying, isn't she, Doc?"

Doc Waller slowly nodded.

Tears stung the back of Sadie's eyes, but she refused to let them have their way. "Let's go, then. I can eat on the way."

Within minutes, Sadie was on her way to meet a woman she could not remember. She had no idea what she looked like – except vaguely like her, according to the Wallers – or what kind of person she was before her ruin, or if the woman even loved her. But one thing she did know was how much it could mean to someone to let them know they were loved. And even if her mother would not, or could not, tell her how she felt about her, she desperately needed to tell her mother she loved her. And forgave her, if anything needed to be forgiven.

Perhaps then, Sadie could find it in her heart to forgive her father.

Harrison hurried down the street to the sheriff's office, the look on Miss Jones's face still fresh in his mind. It had changed from accusatory to admiring as she realized what he'd done. He was right – a bump to the head was much better in her eyes than being dead at the hands of outlaws.

He smiled as he stepped up to the sheriff's office, and it broadened as he remembered her dark hair, freed from the confines of her bonnet, spilling down around her shoulders. He'd never seen such a beautiful sight. Such a beautiful woman. Such a ...

The door was locked, the sheriff's office empty. "Blast!" The posse was probably still out searching for the outlaws.

He focused himself back on the business at hand. He had to find out if the posse had retrieved the mailbag, not to mention those no-good outlaws – but short of riding out alone trying to find them (which would be foolhardy even if it wasn't the middle of winter) he had no way of doing that. Therefore, there was no sense in waiting around. He might as well head back to the Wallers' and see how Miss Jones was faring.

"You're up early, ain't ya?" a voice called.

Harrison turned. His stepbrothers, Jack and Sam, stood on the other side of the street. Great. This was all he needed. He sighed. "I'd say the same for you – you two are never up this early. Is Mulligan giving away free drinks this morning?"

His brothers both sneered at him. "If'n he was, we never woulda come home last night!" Jack called back. Both brothers laughed boisterously at the remark.

Harrison rolled his eyes. It didn't take much to send them into hysterics. "Are you telling me you've actually come into town for a *purpose*?"

Sam settled himself somewhat. "We came for coffee, an' a few other things. Seems *someone* ain't been keeping up on the supplies like he oughta."

"Why else would I be here?" Harrison countered.

"Then how come you're hangin' 'round the sheriff's office? And why's the wagon over by Doc's?" Jack asked, a challenge in his voice.

"Why don't you come across the street and talk to me, instead of doing all this yelling?"

Sam spit. "Worthless piece of ..."

"I've heard the posse will be back soon," Harrison said, changing the subject. "I was wondering if they'd found out anything before I got supplies. You haven't seen them, have you?"

"What do we care?" Sam asked.

"I thought you might be curious, like everyone else. There's been too much thievery of late, don't you think?"

Sam and Jack both spit. "Don't pay it no mind," Sam said. "Get the supplies, then get on home. You got pigs to feed and a barn to clean, boy." He shoved Jack, and they headed down the street toward the livery stable.

Harrison watched them go. Mulligan's was closed, and his lazy brothers never came to town to actually take care of any real business. That was Harrison's job. The only business that brought the other Cooke men to town was drinking. So why were they here at this hour? Hadn't they noticed the wagon was gone? That alone should have indicated he'd come to town to tend to things. And if one of those things had nothing to do with keeping them and their equally unindustrious father provided with caffeine and food ... well, he didn't see that it was any business of theirs. He headed back to the Wallers' and continued to puzzle over his brothers unusual presence.

It wasn't long before he saw Miss Jones walking toward him, the Wallers along with her. He stopped short and watched her approach. He was glad she had an overcoat on – probably the doctor's, as her hands barely peeked out from the long sleeves. She'd not bothered to re-pin her hair, but instead wore it long and loose. By Heaven, she was the most beautiful thing he'd ever seen.

He swallowed hard as she walked up to him. "Mr. Cooke, did you find the sheriff?" she asked.

Harrison's eyes locked on hers. The deep cornflower blue was mesmerizing. "I'm afraid he hasn't returned," he rasped. He hadn't wanted to sound like a blithering idiot, but his mouth had gone dry, and he had to fight the urge to lick his lips. Good God, had it been that long since he'd been around a beautiful woman?

Actually, now that he thought about it, yes, it had. And he wasn't sure he'd ever been around one *this* beautiful before yesterday ...

Dr. Waller eyed him and smiled a lopsided grin. Grandma Waller also looked, smiled and quickly glanced at Miss Jones. Egads, was he being *that* obvious? Inwardly, he groaned.

Miss Jones, if she had noticed his starry-eyed expression, was either too polite to comment or too intent on other things. "Just as well. I was going to visit my mother."

Harrison opened his mouth to speak but nothing came out for a moment. There were only so many people in Clear Creek ... "Who is your mother?" he finally asked.

"Teresa Menendez. And before you say it, yes, I know." Miss Jones walked on, the Wallers trailing behind.

Harrison turned and watched them go, his mind ticking off a mental list of people he knew in Clear Creek. Which, in this case, was practically everyone. But he didn't recall a Teresa Menendez. Unless ... "Do you mean to tell me your mother is Tantaliz–" He snapped his mouth shut, and covered it with his hand. Oh dear ...

Miss Jones spun on her heel to face him. Her voice was unraised, but with an edge. "I'm sorry – what did you call her?"

If he had any sense, Harrison thought, he'd pull his gun out and pistol-whip himself with it – or perhaps shoot his own tongue off. Probably the latter, as it would keep him from making such an error again. "I did not mean to offend, I assure you. But the only person I know of here named Teresa is ..."

"The town whore. Yes, I've been informed," she replied darkly.

Harrison's eyes widened slightly. "Tantalizing Teresa ... is your mother?"

"Tantalizing. An interesting nickname." If words were knives, she would have just pinned him to the nearest wall.

"It's ... what the men here call her."

"Really? And what have you called her, Mr. Cooke?"

Harrison sighed. She automatically assumed he'd used the services of the only "soiled dove" remaining in Clear Creek. After all, there weren't any other unmarried women in the area. There were blessed few *married* women – Grandma Waller; Irene Dunnigan, who ran the mercantile with her husband, Wilfred; a few farmer's wives; and Mrs. Van Cleet, who had come to Clear Creek with her husband, Cyrus. They planned on building a hotel in the spring, when everything thawed out. The stage came through once a month, but word was it would come more frequently in the very near future. Especially with a hotel in town ...

"Well, Mr. Cooke?"

Sadie's voice brought Harrison out of the reverie to which he'd attempted to escape. If he wanted to live, he decided, he had better choose his next words carefully ... "To be perfectly frank, I've never made her acquaintance."

Miss Jones sighed in relief. "Well ... I suppose that's for the best, don't you think?" She quickly turned and started off again. The Wallers followed.

Harrison walked quickly to catch up as a disturbing thought crossed his mind. There were at least ten men for every woman in the area, and almost all of those women were married. Tantal ... er, *Miss Menendez*, was the only "working girl" that hadn't been chased off, and there were no virgin daughters around that he knew of. He had a sudden urge to take the beautiful Miss Jones and whisk her away to safety, to protect her from the potential riot once the men of the region found out an eligible female had arrived!

It wasn't long before they reached the saloon. "According to Mr. Mulligan, Mrs. Dunnigan insisted that, um, Teresa move to the shed out back," Doc Waller informed Sadie. "More privacy. Follow me."

They went around the side of the building to the rear yard. Harrison had never been behind the saloon and was surprised to find a small fenced area that looked like it was used as a vegetable garden. Beyond that area was a tiny shed, no more than seven feet to a side. It had a door and a small window. Many of the shed's boards had knotholes which the wind probably blew right through. Dear heavens, the poor woman had to be freezing in there!

Miss Jones must have thought the same thing. She raced to the shed's door, her face stricken, and softly knocked before entering.

Harrison and the Wallers quickly followed her in. Just as Harrison had guessed, the temperature inside wasn't any different from outside. There was a small pot-bellied stove, but it was stone cold. "I'll start a fire right away," he offered.

"No need, Harrison," Dr. Waller told him, and bent over the cot against the wall.

A thin form was buried beneath several ragged quilts. He gently shook the woman who, in reply, fell into a horrible coughing fit. She poked her head out from under the quilts and spit blood into a nearby bucket, then took in the faces staring down at her. "What do you want?" she rasped.

Miss Jones approached slowly, and the others moved out of her way. She pushed the bucket behind her and knelt beside the cot. "I ... I've come to help you."

The woman's glazed eyes narrowed. "Help me?" She coughed again. "Help me out of town, you mean. What's the matter? This shed still too close to Mrs. Dunnigan? I suppose now she wants to send me out onto the prairie to die."

Miss Jones shook her head. "No, no – nothing like that. We're here to take you to Dr. and Mrs. Waller's home. You can get better there. They have a room you can use."

The Wallers exchanged glances. This wasn't part of the plan! And yet ...

The woman looked at her and began coughing again, finally spitting more blood into the bucket Miss Jones had been quick to grab. Exhausted, she fell back on the cot. "Who are you?"

Harrison watched as Miss Jones took a deep breath, and said, "I'm your daughter Sadie, and I've come to get you out of here."

# FIVE

Sadie held her breath.

Her mother stared at her in shock and disbelief before she clawed her way to a sitting position. Once she managed that, she again began coughing uncontrollably. Doc Waller stepped forward. "We'd best move her before the cold takes its toll. It's freezing in here." He turned to his wife. "You run on ahead and get the bed ready."

Grandma Waller shook off her shock and hurried out the door as the coughing continued.

Sadie extended a hand and began rubbing her mother's back. The woman looked like she was trying to wave her away as her body jerked and heaved from the force of her coughs, but Sadie wouldn't stop. Even if she wasn't her mother, no one should suffer so. "Let's get you out of here. You'll be much more comfortable at the Wallers'."

"Why … are you … doing this?" her mother rasped between spasms.

"I told you. I'm your daughter. You won't get well in this drafty shack. What are you doing out here, anyway?"

The woman hugged herself to get her heaving body under control. "Don't you know? I ain't fit enough to be inside. I'm no better than a filthy animal in this town's eyes."

Sadie motioned to Doc Waller to help get her mother off the cot. She'd deal with the remark about the town later; getting her mother warm was more important.

"Please, let me help," Harrison said. He bent to the cot and, in one swift move, lifted her mother into his arms, quilts and all.

"Mr. Cooke!" Sadie said. Surely he wasn't going to carry her all the way back to the Wallers' home? But then … he'd carried her, for a greater distance and under much more difficult circumstances. She felt an odd flutter in her stomach at the thought of his race to save her from the outlaws.

He looked at her, an eyebrow raised in question, and smiled. "Don't worry. I'll make very sure to avoid trees, I promise."

The joke served its purpose – it made her feel better. "I don't think there are any along the way to worry about, Mr. Cooke." She wanted to call him by his first name, but wasn't sure it would be proper.

His face split in a great, glorious warm smile that sent Sadie's heart into a backflip. "We really should go. Their house is on the other side of town." He looked at the woman in his arms, who now had her head against his shoulder, her eyes closed. She hadn't put up a fuss when he picked her up – all her strength was spent for the moment.

They left the shack and headed back to the Wallers'. Sadie walked beside Harrison, watching her mother for signs of discomfort. Or worse – her body was so still, she almost looked like she had died after he picked her up. But Sadie could hear her moan softly now and then, confirming that she was still quite alive.

Sadie was glad he'd taken the initiative and gathered her up. She had previously planned to support her mother and walk back to the house with her, or even walk back by herself and ask if she could borrow the Wallers' wagon. This was much quicker. She smiled at him gratefully.

"In the street there! What are you about?" a woman's voice called.

Sadie turned toward the sound. A plump woman stood on the porch of the mercantile, looking perturbed. *Dunnigan's* was painted on a small board that hung above her head by the door.

Doc Waller stopped. "Good morning, Mrs. Dunnigan! Afraid I can't talk – got sickness to tend to!" He trotted to catch up with his wife and Harrison, who hadn't slowed for a second.

"You there – young lady! What are you doing with her? Is she dead?" The woman actually sounded hopeful.

Anger ignited within Sadie. "She most certainly is not! In fact, I plan on seeing she makes a full recovery!" She turned back before she said something harsh, and pointedly ignored the huffing and puffing of the woman launching herself off the porch and following them.

They reached the Wallers' house and quickly went inside. Mrs. Dunnigan shoved her way in before Sadie could shut the door. "Why has that woman been brought here? No decent Christian would be caught dead touching such a disgusting creature!"

Sadie spun to face her. "How dare you! She's sick, and the doctor is going to treat her! No *decent* Christian would do less!"

Harrison was already following Doc Waller upstairs. He slowed at the exchange, but Grandma Waller appeared at the top of the stairs and quickly motioned him up. Sadie watched as he reluctantly continued.

"I don't know who you are, young lady, but you have no idea what you've done, bringing that woman into this house! Not to mention that Cooke boy – what's he doing hauling her about?"

Sadie bit her tongue to stay civil. It worked, but only partly. "I can only conclude by your obvious disdain for my mother that you are disgusted to even be in her presence. That being the case, I strongly suggest you leave." That wasn't so bad, considering how angry she felt. She opened the door for the woman, her jaw set and chin high.

Mrs. Dunnigan's mouth dropped open. "Your *mother*?! Well, I might have known, the way your hair is loose like a strumpet's! Like mother, like daughter, I always say!"

Sadie's hand had just balled itself into a fist, with the intention of burying it in Mrs. Dunnigan's haughty face, when Harrison rushed down the stairs. "Leaving so soon, Mrs. Dunnigan? Well then, may I escort you back to the mercantile? Those *outlaws* are still at large, you know."

Mrs. Dunnigan looked like she was going to let him have it with both barrels – until the word outlaws registered on her consciousness. Her eyes widened and she quickly looked to the door. "You can come back with me, and pay your pa's bill." She turned to Harrison in a huff. "It's overdue. I'll not sell you another thing until it's paid in full."

"By all means! Shall we?" Harrison motioned for her to precede him and she stomped across the front porch and into the street. He winked at Sadie as he walked past. "I'll return shortly. Thank you for not striking her, no matter how much she deserved it." He then stopped on the threshold, turned and whispered. "And your hair makes you look like a magical fairy princess. Never let that old hag tell you otherwise." He smiled the same warm smile as before, gave a small bow, and headed out the door.

Mrs. Dunnigan huffed, puffed and snuffed all the way back to the mercantile. Harrison followed along, his jaw tight. The old bat had really gone too far this time. Her hatred of anything sinful – which, in her mind, was anything not to her standards – got on most people's nerves. But most people had credit at the mercantile and appeased her in order to survive. Thankfully, he had money with him, and, if he was lucky, it was enough to pay his stepfather's bill.

He would have to explain to Miss Jones about Mrs. Dunnigan's view of the world and how she was, of course, the only decent upstanding citizen in it. Though Miss Jones had probably figured it out already.

Mrs. Dunnigan waddled behind the counter and pulled out a cigar box. She sifted through varying bundles of receipts until she found the one she wanted. "Twenty dollars and seventeen cents! I'll not take a penny less!"

"Has anyone ever told you how lovely your skin looks when you're collecting money, Mrs. Dunnigan?" He shouldn't have said it, but her treatment of Miss Jones gnawed at him.

Mrs. Dunnigan's eyes narrowed. "Was that an insult?"

"Of course not!" he replied, pretending to be affronted. He reached into his pocket and pulled out the money. A good thing he'd been able to sell some livestock that week. He counted out the amount and handed it to her.

She took it, shoved it into another box, and then handed him the bundle of receipts, never once taking her eyes off him.

He took the receipts from her and turned to leave.

"You no longer have credit with me, Harrison Cooke. You and that pack of filth can pay cash from now on."

Harrison turned back and studied her. He'd never seen her so riled up before, and made sure not to join her in high dudgeon. "Tell me, Mrs. Dunnigan ... what makes a woman like you hate God's creation so very, very much?"

She started at the question, truly taken aback for a moment, then squared her shoulders. "I don't hate God's creation – only the disgusting filth in it. Like that woman you toted over to Doc Waller's house. She's better off dead. Then maybe this town can start to grow and some decent folks will settle here."

"But there are decent folks who've settled here, aren't there?" His voice was calm, level, but he was keeping it so with an effort.

"Decent? Like you, I suppose – a dirty pig farmer without a penny to his name? Your thieving brothers in prison? Your mother dead not a year on account of your pa's drinking? Decent? The apple doesn't fall far from the tree! Don't tell me folks here are decent! They're no better than you are!"

Harrison should have been angry, but all he felt for her now was pity. What could have happened to make her this way? "You are, of course, entitled to your opinion, Mrs. Dunnigan. But your opinion is just that. It doesn't make you right. Scripture says that we are all created in God's image – even myself, even my stepfather, even Teresa ... and even you. And if I hear you disparage God's image again as you did at Doc Waller's, I assure you that an extension of credit will be the least of your worries." He paused to let that sink in. "Good day." He tipped his hat and left.

He walked quickly back to the house. Mean spirited as she was, Mrs. Dunnigan would hold to her threat of not allowing his family any more store credit. He'd have to make sure he had the cash to work with when he needed supplies – which, unfortunately, would be later that day. But before that, he needed to take care of Miss Jones and her mother – he wanted to get them settled before he headed back to the farm.

And meanwhile, there was the issue of his brothers' pardons. He had to find out what was in that letter – for all he knew, they had already been released and were on their way home, or the pleas had been rejected and he needed to find more evidence. But he had his suspicions about where to look ...

As it turned out, when he got back to the Wallers', there wasn't much settling left to do. Dr. Waller had agreed to let the two women stay there for the time being. He was going to have his hands full nursing Miss Menendez back to health, so he asked Harrison to contact Miss Jones's family, and Harrison agreed

He entered the extra bedroom Grandma Waller had prepared, stood quietly and took in the sight of mother and daughter as the doctor pulled the curtains shut to help keep the room warm.

Teresa Menendez was propped against several pillows, and looked better already just from getting out of the weather. Miss Jones sat in a rocking chair at one side of the bed, with Grandma Waller on the other attempting to spoon broth into the sick woman's mouth. "It'll make you feel better, dear. You haven't had a thing in days. It's a miracle you haven't starved to death!"

Teresa looked at the spoon in front of her, then around the room. "I ... I can't pay you," she began, her bottom lip trembling. "I don't have money."

Miss Jones left the chair and sat beside her on the bed. "You don't have to worry about a thing. You won't need money ever again, I'll see to that. Just concentrate on getting well. Now have some broth. It will warm you up."

Teresa's eyes locked with her daughter's. "Who are you again?"

"I'm your daughter," came out a whisper.

"I have ... a daughter?"

A single tear blazed a trail down Miss Jones's left cheek. It nearly tore Harrison's heart out. "Yes, of course you have a daughter, and she's here to take care of you."

The woman again looked around. "This sure is a ... a fine room. I'm not dead, am I?"

Miss Jones gently hugged her. No, Mama, you're not dead."

Teresa's eyes widened. "You ..." she began then coughed. "You called me 'Mama'. If'n I'm your mama, then who's your papa?"

"Horatio Jones."

"Oh my ..." Teresa's eyes grew even larger just before they rolled upwards. She fell against the pillows in a dead faint. Everyone looked on in shock.

Dr. Waller waved Miss Jones off the bed and began to examine Teresa. After a moment, he turned to her. "Does the mention of your father always have such an effect on women?"

Miss Jones rolled her own eyes at the lame joke. "She must have remembered."

"Just what happened between your ma and pa, child?" Grandma Waller asked.

"Well ... that's what I hope to find out."

And Harrison silently vowed to help, especially if it meant getting to find out more about the lovely Miss Jones.

# SIX

Nearly a week passed. Harrison Cooke still had no word from the sheriff. And neither Harrison, nor Sadie, nor the Wallers had had much word from Sadie's mother. She'd hardly spoken to anyone since the mention of Horatio Jones.

Sadie had sat with her several times a day at first, but eventually left her alone at Doc Waller's suggestion. Her mother slept most of the time anyway, which she desperately needed for her recovery. But Sadie needed to make her understand that everything would be all right, that she wouldn't have to worry about taking care of herself ever again. She couldn't stand the look of distrust in her mother's eyes, even though she understood where it came from.

"Give her time, dear – she'll come around once she feels better." Grandma Waller took a loaf of bread out of the oven and set it on the table. "It must be quite a shock to have your child suddenly turn up after eighteen years. Hand me those pies, will you?"

"Sure, Grandma." Sadie had taken to calling her "Grandma," just like everyone else in town. She handed her the apple pies one at a time. They had been baking bread all morning, and the pies would take up the afternoon. It felt nice to work in the kitchen with Grandma.

It was even nicer to know the meal being prepared today was special. Mr. Cooke was coming to supper.

Sadie felt herself blush at the mere thought of him. He'd been over every day, twice a day, to see them, but never stayed longer than was proper – and never stayed to eat. Today was a first.

She absentmindedly smoothed her dress. Mr. Cooke – correction, *Harrison* (Grandma had them on a first-name basis) had brought her trunk the second day of her stay. She wanted to look nice for him and had ironed her best blue calico.

"I know she must be thinking about things. A lot of things," Sadie replied to distract herself from thoughts of the soon-to-arrive guest.

"Of course she is, child. Good heavens, it's a lot of regret to have to wrestle with. And she's doing it alone. Most folks don't come out of a fight like that, but I have a feeling your mother will."

"I know she will."

Grandma smiled. "I suspect the good Lord is having a word or two with her. She asked for a Bible the other day, so I gave her mine."

"Yes, I noticed it on the bedside table. Thank you. In fact ... thank you for everything. I promise to repay you for all your kindness. You've gone far beyond what a lot of people would do."

"Hush, now – almost anyone in town would do the same. Besides, there's no hotel in town yet. Where else would you stay?"

They both laughed, but for only a moment. Sadie suddenly sobered. "I know one person who wouldn't show the same generosity."

Grandma's face soured. "Irene Dunnigan. Now there's someone who needs either a good dose of Christian charity or a good knock on the head. Or maybe both."

"Maybe we ought to let Harrison have a go at her?"

Grandma looked shocked for a moment before she burst into laughter. "I hope you haven't brought that tree incident up again! Leave it be, child – the man has his pride, after all."

Sadie smiled. She'd been teasing Harrison all week about it. "I don't know ... it might do Mrs. Dunnigan some good."

Grandma snorted. "You can't let things get to you like that. You've got to be strong. Especially out here in this wilderness."

"What do you mean?"

"What I mean, child, is that Mrs. Dunnigan let something get the best of her years ago, and now look at her. She's a bitter old woman who hates the world, and hates herself even more."

"What happened?"

"Well ..." Grandma Waller seemed to be having an internal debate. "Aw, after how she treated you and your mama, you have a right to know. But most folks don't know this, and I'm not one to get wrapped up in gossip, so this doesn't leave this room."

"I understand."

"Okay. To hear her husband Wilfred tell it, Irene's pa got into gambling, drinking and women. Ruined the family. Killed himself besides – he got himself shot in a poker game back in Iowa. The mother couldn't cope, and she drank some poison and killed herself, leaving poor Irene behind. All that drove Irene a little crazy, Wilfred says."

Sadie poured them both a cup of coffee. "How did they end up out here?"

"Wilfred was betrothed to Irene by then," Grandma began as they sat with their cups. "Married her to please his family and, at her urging, came out west. She didn't want to stay in Iowa, not when she had so many bad memories of the place."

Sadie sighed. No wonder Mrs. Dunnigan was so venomous toward her mother. "She hates anyone having to do with the vices that dragged her father down."

"Yes, she does. But she compounds it by condemning everyone around her, and always having to get the last word. Lord knows we've all prayed for her. But she's the one who has to want to change."

"I know what … *cough* … what you mean." Sadie and Grandma turned to find Teresa standing in the doorway. "Is that coffee? I'd sure like some," she rasped.

"Mama," Sadie whispered. "Of course! Come, come sit with us." She got up and pulled a chair out for her mother, who sat carefully, still weak.

"Look at you all up and about!" Grandma said as she got up and busied herself at the stove. "But you best not stay down here long – you do still need your rest." She stirred the pot of stew she'd made for supper, poured Teresa a cup of coffee, and then refilled the other cups. The three women sat silently for a few moments, the only sound the occasional pop from the fire in the cookstove.

Teresa finally spoke. "I wasn't always the kind of woman I am now." She stared straight ahead, her cup in her hands, and took a slow sip. "I was a respectable girl. Just like you." She nodded to Sadie.

Sadie had to fight to keep quiet. She wanted to tell her mother it didn't matter, that her old life was behind her now, that she could start over. But letting her speak was more important.

"I was betrothed to a man that I hated. My father had arranged it – he was one of Papa's business partners in Monterrey, where we lived. He was a good thirty years older than I was, and rich." Teresa snorted in disgust. "Oh, he was plenty rich. But I didn't care. I refused to marry a man I cared nothing about, and who repulsed me."

Sadie closed her eyes at the words. How could anyone do that to a child? "Did your father want you to marry him just because he was a wealthy man?"

Teresa held her cup to her lips again, "Yes." She took another sip. "I had to do something. But I wasn't brave enough to run away. So I did the only thing I could think of – I found another man."

"My father?"

"I figured if I was already married, my folks couldn't make me marry someone else. But I went about it all wrong." She looked at Sadie, tears in her eyes. "I'm so sorry ... so very sorry."

"What did you do?" Sadie asked in a whisper.

"I had to get married quick. I figured – fool that I was – that if I got pregnant, the man would have to marry me. But I was wrong."

"What are you saying?" Sadie asked, though she already had a guess.

"I ran. I ran all the way out of the state, all the way to Paso del Norte. And when I got there, I met – and seduced – your father. And my plan worked ... except for the part where he married me. By the time I knew I was expecting, he'd gone back to his ranch. I never saw him again."

Sadie took the cup from her mother's hands and held them. They were very cold, and she rubbed them as she spoke. "I don't care what happened – I'm just glad I found you. Someone here in Clear Creek sent word you were sick. I had to come."

Teresa smiled, and then began coughing.

Grandma immediately got up and went around the table. She rubbed Teresa's back before she helped her out of the chair. "Best get you back to bed."

Teresa stopped her and turned to Sadie. "Miss Bess. She must've done it before they got chased out of town." She began to cough again.

"No argument this time," Grandma said sternly. "Back upstairs you go."

A knock suddenly sounded at the door.

Sadie got up, but instead of answering the door, she went to her mother and hugged her. "I love you."

Grandma let go, and her lower lip quivered as she watched mother and daughter hold each other at last. "I'll just ... go get the door. It's probably Harrison."

As soon as Grandma was gone, Teresa weakly pulled back. "Don't make the sort of mistakes I've made. Promise me you won't. You're the only right thing I've ever done."

"I promise, Mama," Sadie said as her tears began to fall, unable to hold them back.

"Promise me you'll marry a man who truly loves you."

Sadie sniffed and nodded. "If I ever find one, I will."

"One may be closer than you think. You see him, you go get him." Her coughing started again. Sadie pulled her back into her arms.

Harrison and Grandma entered the kitchen. "Miss Menendez! So good to see you out of ... bed." Harrison said, slowing as her hacking interrupted him. He pulled a clean handkerchief out of his jacket pocket and handed it to her. She took it gratefully and held it to her mouth.

"I was just taking her upstairs," Sadie said as she guided her mother toward the hall. "If you could excuse us for a moment?"

"By all means. I'm glad you're beginning to feel better, Miss Menendez."

Her coughing stilled, she nodded and let Sadie lead her up the stairs. Once in the bedroom, Sadie hugged her again before helping her into bed.

"That young man down there ... he has taken a liking to you."

Sadie pulled a quilt over her. "Nonsense, Mama. He's just ... just looking out for us while we're here."

"Mark my words, girl – he is not 'just looking out' for you. Trust me, I can tell the difference between a man who just lusts after a woman, and one who actually feels something."

Sadie tucked the quilt around her and smiled. If only her words were true. Though even if they were, what did it matter? It wasn't as if she'd completely set her cap for him. Or had she? He *was* very attractive. Yes, that was probably it – she was just a little lonesome and attracted to him. Besides, as soon as her father found them, both she and her mother would be gone, whisked away across the Oregon Territory to home. "You get some rest, Mama. I'll bring you something to eat later." She kissed her mother on the forehead and left the room.

But as she descended the stairs, she began to wonder. Would her father even allow her to marry a poor, dirty pig farmer in a nothing town in the middle of the prairie? Before she got halfway down the stairs she knew the answer – Horatio Jones would never let the heiress of his ever-growing cattle empire marry a dirt-poor anything. No matter how well mannered he was. It just wasn't done.

Harrison sat in the parlor and held his hat in his hands. He'd worn his Sunday best, but wasn't sure it was good enough. The trousers were too short, the jacket patched at the elbows, and it had taken a good while to find the tie; it was in the barn, of all places, being used to hold a bridle together. He suspected his stepbrothers had something to do with it. They often did. He would've found the tie sooner, but it really had been a long time since he'd had a reason to wear his Sunday best ...

Well, now wasn't the time to worry about it. He had more important matters on his mind, one in particular. And he wished she would hurry up and come downstairs.

"Now, Harrison Cooke – if I didn't know any better, I'd say you were nervous."

Harrison turned to see Grandma Waller smirking down at him. "Not at all, I assure you," he replied, then caught himself twisting his hat in his hands.

Grandma nodded knowingly. "I'll just take that hat ... before you tear it up." She held out her hand.

He returned her stare boldly. But he also handed her the hat.

"That's better. And I hope you like apple pie. There's a little lady upstairs who fussed for hours over the baking ... once she found out we were having a guest." Grandma winked and left.

Harrison suppressed a smile and wiped his hands on his trousers. Perhaps Sadie Jones felt something more than gratitude toward him. It would certainly make the afternoon go more smoothly. He was nervous enough with what he'd planned, and didn't want any interruptions when it came time to speak with her.

*Blast it, why were his hands so sweaty?*

He took a deep breath. This must be what it feels like to ask a girl to marry you. But he wasn't going to ask for Sadie's hand in marriage, though the thought had entered his mind earlier and stuck there. No, this was something else, something that would help all of them. And he was positive she would be pleased with his proposal ...

"Harrison, I hope you didn't mind waiting," Sadie said as she entered the parlor. "Doc isn't home yet, but as soon as he gets here we'll eat."

"That's quite all right. I came early because I wanted to discuss something with you."

"Oh?"

He nodded, unable to speak. Good Lord, but she was beautiful. Her eyes were brightened by the afternoon sun shining in through the lace-curtained window. She wore a beautiful blue dress and had braided her long hair and wrapped it around her head like a dark, glistening crown. Her apron was fresh and white with a spot of something here and there, probably cinnamon from the pies he could smell baking in the oven.

Harrison swallowed hard and resisted the urge to wipe his hands on his trousers again. The thought of marriage suddenly unstuck itself and raced to the forefront of his mind. If she were his wife, he'd never let her out of his sight.

Which brought him to the matter at hand. "I know you will need to be returning home. Your family must be worried sick about you, and there's been no word from the sheriff since he took off after the outlaws almost two weeks ago. He's determined to catch the men responsible for the stage robbery, but I dare say he likely doesn't even know you were abducted. But outlaws have struck in these parts before, and I imagine the sheriff suspects they are one and the same gang."

"I suppose they could be. But what did you wish to discuss?"

"I wish to offer my services as escort for you and your mother."

"Escort?"

"Protection."

"Protection ... from what?"

"The outlaws, of course. I wish to escort you home."

Sadie's eyes widened. She opened her mouth to speak but nothing came out. If Harrison didn't know any better, she looked like she wanted to say something that shouldn't be spoken in polite company. He'd seen that same look on his mother's face upon occasion. And so what she did next, he assumed any lady would do.

She fled from the room.

# SEVEN

Sadie retreated to the kitchen, which thankfully was empty. Grandma must have gone upstairs to check on her mother. She absently took the lid from the stew pot and gave the contents a stir.

Why in Heaven's name was she so upset? Harrison had only offered to take her back to her ranch. Her home. Her father ... all right, she admitted, that part was upsetting. It would mean seeing her father sooner than expected.

*And parting from Harrison sooner than she wanted.* She did so enjoy his company, and had come to know him better over the last week. His descriptions of the English countryside fascinated her, and she loved to hear him talk of London and his family there. But she dared not let herself feel anything for him – her mother was more important, and she still had to convince her father to let her come live with them at the ranch. She would *not* leave her behind in Clear Creek!

She stirred the stew one last time and checked on the pies before returning to the parlor. Harrison stood as she entered, confusion on his face. "I ... I thought I smelled supper burning," she stammered. "And I needed to check on dessert."

Harrison's face broke into a warm smile. "Oh, of course. It all smells wonderful, by the way. Come, do sit down."

She went to the settee and sat. He joined her and they enjoyed a companionable silence for a few moments.

"Sadie ..." Harrison's whisper was deep and throaty.

She looked at him and swallowed.

He cleared his throat and scooted closer. "I don't wish to frighten you, but you do need a man's protection out here. I rescued you, and I feel I am responsible for you until your father comes. If he does not come to fetch you, it could mean that he fell victim to the outlaws as well."

Sadie shook her head. "No ..."

"I'm sorry if that upsets you, but if he doesn't come soon then I feel it's my duty to see you home." He turned to the window, moved a lace curtain aside, and looked out to the street. "You cannot plan to stay here forever."

*Forever.* The word seemed to hang over them. Sadie had never thought about where she would spend the rest of her life, or with whom ... until now. She studied him as he continued to look out at the street. A wagon rolled by, and his eyes latched onto the horse being pulled along behind it.

He was so different from the other men she was familiar with. His looks were striking, of course, but she'd met handsome men before. No, Harrison Cooke had something the others didn't. It was a quiet strength, wrapped up in polite manners. His English mother had no doubt taken her job of teaching her sons proper deportment very seriously. It was hard to imagine his brothers being falsely accused and locked in prison.

But at the same time, she knew these men wouldn't hesitate to do what was necessary to protect her. This was not some fancy English fop she'd read about in a novel. This was a man who'd spent the last eight years taming the Oregon prairie with other men of his ilk, pioneers who wanted a better life and were willing to pay the price to get it.

"I have no doubt my father will turn up eventually. Until that time, I plan to take care of my mother and see that she gets well."

Finally he turned back to her. His eyes focused on her mouth, and he swallowed hard. "I shall continue to look after you, then. And check daily on you both."

Sadie's stomach did its little flip. Only this time it was more of a flop, as something seemed to sink deep into her. When she finally recovered from the odd sensation, she found herself staring at Harrison's mouth with the same intensity he stared at hers.

"Erm, sorry to interrupt ..."

Sadie had to fight to tear her gaze away. That felt even stranger.

Doc stood out in the hallway. "Is supper about ready?"

Sadie glanced back at Harrison, and realized they had been leaning toward one another. To Doc Waller, it must have looked like they were about to kiss.

"Well, it sure smells good! I think I'll just go see what's in the oven." Doc chuckled and turned to head down the hall.

Sadie swallowed as she watched him leave. Why couldn't she speak? What was wrong with her? Did she *want* Harrison to kiss her?

She turned to him again, and again his eyes immediately darted to her mouth. Yes ... yes, she did – and apparently he had the same idea. But what should she do?

*You see him, you get him,* her mother's words echoed in her mind. But how could she? What if he only wanted to kiss her because she was the one eligible woman in town *to* kiss? She'd seen how the other men stared at her when she went out with Grandma to run errands over the last few days. Harrison had warned her not to leave the house unescorted, and she'd soon found out why. And Doc Waller had mentioned he suddenly had a lot more men coming to be tended since she'd arrived. Was Harrison different, or, like all the others, simply in desperate want of a female?

Well, probably not quite like the others – he'd never even *met* "Tantalizing Teresa." Or so he'd said ...

His gaze was still locked on her face. "What's ... for supper?" he asked as if in a daze.

"I don't remember," she sighed, her mouth now inches from his. He had one arm across the back of the settee, the other hand coming up under her chin as she stared at him. When he took her chin in his hand and tilted her face up, she thought she might faint. His fingers were warm, his breath on her face even warmer.

He bent his face to hers, and it was as if he was swallowing her up. "You have my protection, Miss Jones," he whispered. "But ..."

"But what?" she whimpered.

"But ..." Suddenly he pulled away, his eyes downcast "But I don't know how much longer I can protect you from myself." And like a proper gentleman, he stood to his feet and, clearly abashed, left the room.

Sadie was left staring after him, in shock at his abrupt departure. She hadn't wanted him to go. But, thinking about how she had broken and run for the kitchen just a few minutes before, she understood. And slowly, she smiled.

No, Harrison Cooke certainly wasn't like the other men.

Harrison rushed into the kitchen so fast he nearly knocked Doc over. "Blazes, boy! What's the trouble? The house on fire?" He watched Harrison glance down the hall toward the parlor, and nodded in understanding. "Oh, I see. The house isn't on fire, but you sure are!"

"Dr. Waller, please ..."

"Did you kiss her?"

Harrison straightened. "Good Heavens, no!"

Doc slammed the lid back on the stewpot, from which he'd been sneaking a bite. "Well, why not? What's the matter with you? The prettiest girl around for fifty miles and you're telling me you don't want to kiss her?"

"Please, she'll hear you ..."

"Well, I should hope."

"Kissing her would have been a, a, a travesty."

"A what?"

"A mistake."

Doc stared at him a moment. Then they both heard the sound of Sadie squeaking in outrage and stomping up the stairs, followed by a door slamming.

"Well, you can bet she heard that," Doc scolded.

Harrison sank heavily into the nearest chair. "It's not that I didn't wish to. But I ... I don't want her to get the wrong impression."

"Son, this isn't London – this is Clear Creek. Eligible young women aren't just scarce – until last week they were non-existent. I'm telling you right now, if you fancy that little lady, you'd best stake a claim to her before someone else does."

"But when her father comes ..."

"... then we'll deal with her father," Doc finished. "I saw my Sarah for the first time and two weeks later we were married. And that was in Philadelphia, which isn't exactly the back of the beyond. After we settled in Kansas, I brought more than my share of babies into the world, a lot of which came out west with us. Those folks went on to Oregon City, and most of them are probably married by now. But in Clear Creek, what are your chances of finding a woman to wed?"

*Slim indeed*, Harrison thought, and not for the first time.

"And the good Lord saw fit to drop one right in front of you. Don't you think you owe Him at least the courtesy of accepting the gift?"

Harrison felt like a cad. He'd wanted to kiss her all right – kiss her until she swooned. But he wanted more time with her, and he'd thought that escorting her back to her ranch with a few of the sheriff's men would give him that time. Not to mention, now that he thought of it, it would give him time to think of a good reason Mr. Jones should let him marry her. And furthermore, Mrs. Dunnigan had the town thinking Sadie was no better than her mother. He'd like more time for the old biddy's tempest-in-a-teapot to blow over.

Dr. Waller was right – if he wanted her, he needed to do something about it. But there were so many obstacles: his wastrel stepfather and stepbrothers, his concern that he wouldn't be able to provide for her in the manner to which she was no doubt accustomed, Mrs. Dunnigan's great fat mouth.

But first he had to deal with his current dilemma – that after his *faux pas* in the kitchen, she probably thought he didn't care a whit about her. Or worse, that he just wanted her body. He did want it, mind you, but with a wedding ring attached and her heart committed to his. He would simply have to explain it to her. In fact, he ought to march up there right now and do so!

Doc saw the steel in his eye, and grinned. "That's it, son – go get her. Keep those fancy manners your mama taught you, but don't let them spoil a good thing. She'll be more of a mind to let you court her if she knows how you feel."

"Court her? What happened to 'staking claim'?"

"All women want to be courted a least a little. Even out here."

"I wouldn't know about that – I have yet to see anyone get married out here."

Doc laughed as Grandma walked in. "What's going on? Sadie's upstairs mad as a rattler. Harrison, what did you do?"

"A misunderstanding, which I will be correcting shortly." He marched down the hall to the stairs. But just as he was about to set foot on the first step, Mr. Mulligan burst through the door. "Doc, Harrison! The sheriff's back! And he's got one of them outlaws!"

Sadie sat on Doc and Grandma's bed. She'd been sleeping on a pallet in her mother's room, but didn't want to disturb her. Instead, she'd walked in on Grandma – and then had to apologize for slamming the door. Now that Grandma was downstairs, she let the tears fall.

First, Harrison acted like he was clearly attracted to her, and just wanted to be gentlemanly about it. A minute later, he called the possibility of kissing her "a travesty." What sense was she supposed to make of that?!

Maybe she and her mother were becoming a burden for him. He was coming by twice a day, and she couldn't imagine how he managed that and worked on his farm too. Maybe she was confusing him by her presence. She was certainly becoming a temptation for him, and she didn't want to do that.

She didn't want to be just an appetizing morsel waiting to be eaten, the way men had treated her mother. And around here, if Mrs. Dunnigan had her way, that's the way everyone would see her. Harrison's desire to protect her was flattering, but he also seemed desperate to get her out of town. Perhaps the temptation was too much.

Sadie went over their conversation again in her head. His resolve to protect her body was admirable, but what about her heart? She sighed – that was something she should have seen to herself. She hadn't realized until that afternoon that her heart had allowed the Englishman in. Worse still, she didn't know how to get him out.

There was a logical solution, however – pack up her mother as soon as she was able, and leave town. She'd gotten herself out here, albeit with a little help from Harrison, and she could get back. Surely someone here could contact her father and see she was returned safely.

She didn't want Harrison to have to escort her across miles of prairie in order to rid himself of the temptation she represented; she'd already done enough damage. What if he couldn't hold out? What if *she* couldn't? Until that day, she'd never felt this way around a man, never had an inner longing pull at the deepest part of her soul when she was with one. What *was* it? Was this what it felt like to fall in love?

If so, they could keep it, thank you very much indeed!

Sadie wiped her tears. She wanted a man to marry her because he loved her, not because he needed to use her body to slake his lust. And if Harrison wasn't even sure which he felt, it was probably better to not befuddle him further ...

A commotion downstairs interrupted her thoughts. She stood just as Grandma burst back into the room. "The sheriff's back! He'll want to see you – he and the posse managed to bring back one of those no-good outlaws!"

Sadie's eyes widened, and cold slipped up her spine. Which one could it be? And would she be able to identify him? They were wearing masks the entire time she'd been in their company.

"Best get your coat. Supper will have to wait until after you've talked with the sheriff. Harrison'll take you."

Sadie nodded numbly as she left the room, went downstairs and donned her coat.

Harrison came out of the kitchen, where he'd been speaking with Doc Waller and another gentleman. "Are you all right?" he asked.

She looked up at him. His face was full of concern.

Without warning he pulled her into his arms and held her tight. "I'll be right there – you have nothing to fear. They only want to know if the scoundrel is one of the men who seized you."

"Thank you," she gasped. His embrace was like Heaven: warm, strong, safe. His voice was a soothing balm, wondrous. If she was still intent on leaving, it was going to be harder than she thought.

Harrison pulled away just enough to take her hand and lead her from the house. Once outside – ever the gentleman! – he offered her his arm. She took it, and they made their way to the sheriff's office.

Sadie had never seen Clear Creek so lively – half the town must've been part of the posse. Horses were tethered outside the sheriff's office and Mulligan's saloon across the street. She saw more people in several minutes than she'd seen the entire previous week. Mrs. Dunnigan was charging around, yelling about wanting to see "the criminal" and brandishing a hatchet. Apparently the outlaws had caused quite a few problems for the townsfolk, and everyone wanted a piece of their hides.

Sadie didn't feel one bit sorry for the man.

"Go on home, everyone!" The sheriff was tall, middle-aged and kindly-looking, even as he hollered at the closest Clear Creek could come to a crowd. "We'll let you folks know, just as soon as we find out anything."

"Find out if them's the ones that stole my cows!" a voice yelled.

"And mine!"

"What about the stage robbery?"

"Folks, we just got back – me and the boys need a rest. Then we'll find out if this fellow is connected to any of your missing livestock."

"You mean you're not going to do anything?" Mrs. Dunnigan huffed as she shoved her way forward.

The sheriff sighed and rolled his eyes. "Good afternoon, Mrs. Dunnigan."

"Don't you 'good afternoon' me! Is this one of the outlaws or not?"

"That's what I hope to find out. We need to question him, and gather evidence."

"Evidence? What evidence? There are only so many people in town! I would think process of elimination would be sufficient!"

"Mrs. Dunnigan, we still need proof. You can't go accusing folks of being outlaws without proof."

"What about a witness?" Harrison called out as he led Sadie to the front.

"Now who do you have there, Harrison?" the sheriff asked.

"Miss Sadie Jones. The passenger the highwaymen abducted when they robbed the stage."

Mrs. Dunnigan gasped. The rest of the crowd whispered amongst themselves.

And two figures silently backed away and slipped out of sight. If this so-called witness could identify the captured outlaw, she might be able to identify them as well.

# EIGHT

"Abducted?" the sheriff exclaimed. "She's the missing passenger? But I thought she made her way into town on her own. One of the boys told me when they brought us supplies a few days ago."

Harrison drew Sadie against him. Mrs. Dunnigan snorted disgustedly behind them, which he ignored. "No, sir. I left to meet the stage on account of some mail I was expecting. When the stage didn't arrive, I went searching for it, and discovered it had been robbed. I took care of the wounded driver, then followed the outlaws' trail in the snow to a cabin north of the first ridge." He looked at Sadie with the same concern as before, and her insides melted like fresh-churned butter. "Thank the Lord, it also snowed during our escape, and made it much harder for them to track us."

The sheriff looked, open-mouthed, from Sadie to Harrison and back again. "Is this true?"

"Yes, sir," Sadie replied. "The stage was held up where the road forks. Four outlaws took the strongbox, the mailbag, and me. We rode for hours to a cabin, just as Harrison said."

The sheriff took off his hat and slapped his leg with it. "Well, I'll be hornswoggled. How did you manage to get away?"

Harrison blushed and went silent. Sadie looked at him and nudged him gently.

"Well?" the sheriff urged.

Harrison sighed. "I performed a few ... animal calls."

"Animal calls?"

Raucous laughter erupted from some men in the crowd. "Did you scare 'em off imitatin' a hoot owl?" a man shouted.

Harrison's pride was pricked, and right then and there he did a wolf howl, one good enough to silence his erstwhile critics.

Sadie was also impressed. "That was awfully good," she said, smiling in gratitude at his inventiveness. She didn't really care if he had mimicked one of his pigs; it had gotten her free of the outlaws.

He looked at Sadie and blushed again. "It seems a silly talent to have. But I've been able to imitate animals since I was a child."

"Well, it got the job done, and that's what counts," the sheriff replied. "Come inside, young lady. We need to talk." He turned and went into his office.

Harrison and Sadie moved to follow, but Mrs. Dunnigan grabbed her other arm before she could cross the threshold. "You mean to tell me you were taken by those outlaws and holed up in a cabin with them? Why, the disgrace! No doubt they took their pleasure with you!" She turned to the crowd. "And she nary bats at an eye at the ordeal!"

Several men in the crowd suddenly looked at Sadie like she was a freshly-baked apple – with a worm in it. Mrs. Dunnigan gave a little triumphant smirk.

Harrison was having none of it. He backed out of the door, while at the same time gently coaxing Sadie through it, then shut it behind her. "For your information, Mrs. Dunnigan, I rescued Miss Jones before any such debauchery occurred, which accounts for her surviving the ordeal so admirably. The only disgrace involved seems to be within your own wicked mind. Kindly keep your thoughts to yourself from now on." He turned to go inside.

"Or what?"

Harrison stopped up short. "Pray, dear lady ... or should I say, dear *woman*. Pray you never find out." He turned his back to her and opened the door.

Mrs. Dunnigan was about to retort, but the sheriff's voice from inside was loud, and excited, enough to override her. "Sakes alive – your daddy owns the Big J? He'll be riding in here any day now with guns blazing if he's anything like folks say!" He pushed Harrison out of the way as he hurried onto the porch. "Charlie, Tommy! Get some food and fresh horses – I got a message for you to deliver!"

He spun on his heel to go back inside, but Harrison stopped him. "What's wrong?"

"Nothing's wrong, son! You rescued the daughter of one of the biggest cattlemen in the West! In these parts, that makes her royalty!" He hurried back inside and slammed the door closed behind him.

Harrison stood in shock for a moment. Then he stole a glance at Mrs. Dunnigan, whose jaw hung like a broken gate ... and the opportunity was irresistible. "Well, Mrs. Dunnigan. It seems that the young lady you've been so quick to condemn is the daughter of a king of sorts. A princess, you might say."

The men in the crowd leaned forward and watched the spectacle. They'd never seen Irene Dunnigan at a loss for words before. Her face turned a few shades of red as she noticed the attention now focused on her. With an outraged squeak, she took her hatchet and stomped off toward the mercantile, the crowd breaking into guffaws as she retreated.

"It's all right. He can't hurt you while he's locked up in there." Harrison whispered in her ear from behind her. "Is this one of them?"

His voice calmed her, but Sadie still had to force herself to look at the man sitting in the jail cell. He wasn't wearing a hat, nor a bandana over his lower face – how could she possibly recognize if he had been one of her kidnappers? "I'm not sure."

The man in the cell was reclining on the cot in the cell, smirking. If he recognized her, he certainly gave no indication.

This was terrible. Everyone was counting on her to identify him ... but she'd never seen any of their faces. She turned to Harrison and the sheriff, thinking furiously – and then it came to her. "Make him say something," she whispered.

"What for?" the sheriff whispered back.

"Their faces were covered while I was with them. But they talked in front of me a lot. I might recognize his voice."

The sheriff eyed the outlaw, who eyed him back and then spat. "I don't suppose we can let our new prisoner starve ... you hungry?"

The outlaw's entire demeanor changed. "Now, Sheriff, y'all know I ain't had a thing today! I'm so famished, I can't hardly see straight!"

Sadie tried her best not to let her face show anything to the prisoner. Instead she turned quickly to Harrison and whispered, "I think his name is Cain."

The sheriff overheard her, and nodded at Cain. "Well ... I'll see we get you something."

"Much obliged, Sheriff. I ain't worth being accused of nothin' on an empty stomach."

All three looked at Cain, who had no clue he'd just been found out. Harrison took Sadie by the hand and led her to the front office of the jail, with the sheriff right behind.

Once he'd closed the door to the cell area, he sighed in relief. "I can't thank you enough, Miss Jones. I've been after this gang for a long time now. What else can you tell me?"

"I'm sure they called this one Cain. There was another man, Jeb – I think he was the leader. The other two, I have no idea."

"Well, this is a mighty big help, Miss Jones. A couple dozen missing cattle probably don't seem like much to you, but around here it can be life-changing. Folks will be happy to know we caught one of the rustlers, and this'll help us catch up with the rest. I sure hope it's only the one gang."

"Be it one or several, let us hope they don't leave the area before you have a chance to apprehend them," Harrison commented.

"I can agree with that! As soon as the boys and I rest a spell, we'll set out again. The sooner we round up the rest of these good-for-nothings, the better. Your daddy's gonna be mighty proud of you, Miss Jones."

Sadie slumped slightly at the mention of her father.

"I sent word to him, so he should be here within a week at the most. It all depends on where he is now."

Sadie had to sit. She didn't have to worry about Harrison falling into temptation while escorting her across the prairie now. Instead, she had to avoid him until her father arrived, to keep from losing her heart to him – if she hadn't already. She wondered which fate was worse.

Mr. Mulligan poured two shots of whiskey. "Looks like your little brother's a hero."

Jack and Sam Cooke grabbed their shots and slugged them back. Sam growled and slammed his glass on the counter. "Worthless whelp. Now we know why he's been comin' into town so much."

"Sneaky cuss. Wait 'til Pa finds out." Jack added.

"Pa ain't gonna find out nothin'!" Sam snapped. "Last thing we need is fer Pa to ease up on him. Then *we* might have to do some of the work, an' that don't sit well with me."

Mr. Mulligan laughed, poured them each another shot, and moved down the counter to serve his other customers.

Jack leaned into the bar, his head low, his voice lower. "Jeb's gonna kill us."

Sam glanced around before he spoke in the same low tone. "We ain't done nothin' wrong."

"It was Harrison took her from us! What if she recognizes Cain and tells the sheriff? You know that's what's going on 'cross the street right now!"

"Shut up. I can't think with all yer babblin'."

"What happens if'n she sees one of us?"

Sam grabbed him by the collar. "I said, shut up. We'll just have to make sure she doesn't see us, you got that?"

Jack slapped Sam's hand away. "If Jeb finds out she's here, he might cut us out of the deal."

"He can't! It's our deal!"

"You think Jeb cares?" Jack snorted in derision.

Sam growled again. "Well, if he tries to cut our deal, I'll be cuttin' somethin' too – his mangy throat!"

"If'n he don't cut our hearts out first." Jack grabbed his shot and slugged it back.

Sam stared at his own drink and watched the amber liquid swirl as he moved the glass. "Which means we need to cut that girl out, quick-like." He gulped his whiskey down and set the glass on the counter. "Best we figure out a way to get her off by herself."

Now Jack glanced around. Mr. Mulligan was still at the other end of the bar, talking and laughing with several men from the posse. "What about Harrison?

He's always in town now. Prob'ly been seein' her this whole time!"

"Just have to make sure he don't get in the way. I'm sure there's all kinds of work Pa wants that boy to do the next few days."

"Nah. He's already done all the work there is to do."

"Not if we make sure he has to do it again," Sam said as he signaled to Mr. Mulligan for another round. The brothers chuckled as the bartender headed their way, whiskey bottle in hand.

# NINE

"What do you mean, 'keep an eye out'?" Sadie asked. "Surely the rest of the outlaws wouldn't be foolish enough to come into town, would they?"

"They might wish to free their comrade," Harrison explained. "In which case, now that he's seen *you*, you could well be in danger."

"I don't want to risk it," the sheriff added. "It's best we have someone look after you until your daddy gets here. He'd probably try to hang the whole lot of us if something ever happened to his only daughter."

"But I'm already staying with the Wallers. I'm never alone."

The sheriff shook his head. "They're both getting on in years – neither one would be much help in a shootout. No, I'll have one of my men watch the house."

"I'd like to volunteer, Sheriff. I can see to it Miss Jones is kept safe."

Sadie's eyes widened.

"That's mighty kind of you, Harrison. Can you spare the time away from your farm?"

"I'll make the time. I have no doubt that if the outlaws find Miss Jones is here and has identified their man, they'll come after her." He looked at Sadie. "I can't have that. I'll not see you put in harm's way."

Did he have to look so handsome when he said it? And as his voice dropped in pitch, his eyes looked like hot dark cocoa, a luxury in these parts. How was she supposed to keep from falling for him? His insistence on protecting her didn't help on that score.

Harrison helped her up from the chair and turned to the sheriff. "We must be going. Doc and Grandma have prepared supper for us and are waiting."

"Sure, you go on. I'll finish up here and drop by later this evening – if that's all right, Miss Jones?"

Sadie could only nod. Harrison had already wrapped her arm around one of his and was heading for the door. How did she manage to go from *Surely, I can avoid the man for the next week or so* to Harrison being her self-appointed protector? Although he volunteered for the job, and the sheriff certainly didn't put up any fuss over it. Wasn't it improper for Harrison to be glued to her side? She was sure Mrs. Dunnigan would say so, loudly and at length.

Harrison pulled her along as they went back to the house. "I'll find out who's to take the first watch and how often they plan to change."

"Change?"

"The sheriff won't allow just one man to do the job. They've been looking for these outlaws for weeks. They're tired and hungry, and can only stand watch a few hours at a time. I'll take a shift myself to ensure you're safe for tonight. At some point I can head back to the farm and take care of a few things. And tomorrow, we'll come up with a definite plan for the rest of the week."

Sadie gave him a half smile before she looked away. He looked exceedingly pleased about something, but she couldn't tell what. An hour ago, she was a potential "travesty" and he couldn't wait to get rid of her. Now he couldn't stand to let her out of his sight. Maybe protecting her from the outlaws made it easier for him to protect her from himself. Or something.

They reached the house and went inside. Sadie was delighted to find her mother sitting at the kitchen table with Doc and Grandma. "You're up! Do you feel strong enough to eat with us?"

Teresa took in the sight of Sadie still on Harrison's arm and smiled. "It's why I came down. I'm stronger every day, thanks to you. I only needed a little rest before supper."

Sadie detached herself from Harrison and gave her mother a hug. "I'm so glad!"

Teresa smiled, took one of Sadie's hands and gave it a squeeze.

Grandma got up and began to pull linens from a sideboard. "I'll just go set the table then. We'll eat in the dining room – this is a special occasion, after all. Sadie, you'd best take those pies of yours out of the oven."

"Allow me to help you, Grandma." Harrison offered and followed her into the dining room.

Sadie watched him go. The Wallers' house was modest – a simple dining room and parlor were separated by the center hallway and stairs, with the kitchen in the back and two bedrooms upstairs. It was so much smaller than her father's ranch house, but she loved it and wondered what it would be like to have one of her own someday, especially if it came with a husband and a family.

*Harrison ...*

Sadie shook herself, and set about taking her pies out of the oven. She placed them to one side to cool before checking the stew. While Grandma and Harrison finished setting the table, she sliced the bread.

Soon the table was ready and the meal laid out upon it. Doc and Grandma beamed as they looked at their guests. Harrison sat at one end of the table, and Doc at the other. Sadie and her mother sat side-by-side, with Grandma opposite them. "We haven't used this table in a long while – the kitchen has been enough for the two of us," Doc said. "But this is much nicer. Harrison, you say the blessing."

When Harrison held both his hands out, Sadie stiffened. She was going to have to hold his hand for the blessing?! She slowly took her mother's hand and stared at the one Harrison offered. He waited, with that same warm smile on his face.

Sadie's mouth went suddenly dry as heat seeped into her bones from some unseen source. She gritted her teeth, took his hand ... and the heat positively exploded.

"Dear Lord, we thank you for this day and those in it. We also thank you for helping our sheriff apprehend one of the outlaws, and pray the others will be taken into custody soon. I thank you for the safety of everyone here. For what we are about to receive, may we be truly thankful." He gave Sadie's hand a squeeze, then looked her right in the eye.

She thought she was going to slide from her chair and into a puddle on the floor. His eyes had a look she'd never seen before – one of determination and strength, as if saying he would not be letting her out of his sight anytime soon. It was so profoundly primal, masculine ... possessive. Even someone as inexperienced as she could recognize it.

*Oh, no*, she thought. *I'm a dead woman–*

"Sadie! Sadie? Pass the bread, would you?" Grandma requested.

Sadie pulled herself out of her stupor and reached for the plate of bread next to her. Doc chuckled as he began to dish up stew, while her mother patted her leg reassuringly and took a sip of milk.

Apparently she wasn't the only one who'd recognized the look on Harrison's face. And nobody was saying or doing anything to oppose it.

Yep, she was a dead woman, all right ...

After the meal, they took their pie and coffee into the parlor and chatted about the sheriff, the posse and their hunt for the outlaws. Harrison said nothing about a guard being posted, and Sadie figured he didn't want to worry the others.

But even if her mother and Doc were blissfully ignorant of what was happening, Grandma wasn't. Sadie watched as she peeked past the lace curtains to the street for at least the sixth time.

"What in tarnation are you looking at?" Doc finally asked.

"I was just wondering why Henry Fig is sitting across the street twirling his revolver. Boy's been there for the past hour – he should be home having supper with his wife." She turned from the window to Sadie. "Henry's one of the few menfolk around here that has a wife. You'd think he'd rush home to her after being gone more than a week."

"Perhaps he's ... waiting to get orders from the sheriff," Harrison offered. "I heard him ask several of the men to stay behind in town and await further instructions."

"Further instructions?" Grandma became irritated. "The only instruction any of those boys wants to hear after all they've been through is "eat up!" I'd best fix him something – he's looking awful hungry sitting over there."

"I'll help you, Grandma," Sadie said as she stood and began to gather up the dessert plates. Teresa stood also, but Sadie held up a hand. "No, Mama, you stay here unless you'd like to go upstairs. I don't want you to tire."

She smiled and sat. "I think I will sit a while longer before I go up. This has been the nicest day I can remember."

Everyone looked at her, realizing it was true. How many evenings, over how many years, had it been since this woman enjoyed such a simple thing as pie and coffee in a cozy parlor with folks who cared about her? Probably not since childhood, Sadie mused. "I'm glad you enjoyed it, because you're going to have this every day!"

Teresa's bottom lip quivered as her tears started.

"Oh, now don't go starting none of that!" Grandma choked out. "I gotta fix something for Henry and take it across the street! Boy'll be wondering who died over here if I hand him a dinner plate all teary-eyed." Everyone laughed as she stomped into the kitchen, wiping her eyes as she went.

Sadie went to a table and picked up a small book. "Here, this will entertain you. It's Grandma's."

"What is it?"

"It's called a 'penny dreadful.' Harrison's mother brought some from England when she came to America, and after she passed Harrison gave them to Grandma. She loves them – they're quite exciting."

Teresa took the little book from her and smiled. "Thank you. For everything."

Sadie bent down to kiss her. "You're welcome," she whispered, then went to the kitchen to help Grandma.

Her mother wasn't the only one who'd enjoyed the pleasure of the afternoon and early evening. In fact, it had bordered on pure bliss for Sadie to watch Harrison joke with Doc, rave about her pies, sip his coffee, and tease Grandma. Somewhere between the praise for her baking and Doc's and Grandma's snorts of laughter, she, despite her valiant efforts not to, had fallen in love.

And she didn't feel like a dead woman anymore either. If anything, she'd never felt more alive.

Sadie couldn't sleep. She tried, for hours, but the realization of her feelings toward Harrison wouldn't leave her be.

She lay on her pallet and listened to her mother's steady breathing. The woman was getting better every day, and sounded better every night. She would be able to make the journey home soon, unless something upset her and she relapsed.

And therein lay the problem. Now Sadie didn't want to go. More specifically, she didn't want to leave Harrison – at least not without letting him have a chance to fall in love with her. Surely he felt something, but the indications were all mixed up. Did he only want her body and not her heart? Was it the other way around? Was he conflicted in some other way?

Sadie groaned and turned over, trying to get comfortable. She was willing to risk it. That look he'd given her before supper ... and how he'd always treated her with deference and respect ... and how he'd cared for her mother, a fallen woman he'd never even met ... well, it all had to add up to something, didn't it? And besides, her heart was no longer her own – the traitorous thing had gone after Harrison despite her plans not to.

Sadie had been a lot of things in her short life, but a coward was not one of them. She would just have to face facts – she was deeply in love with Harrison Cooke.

Okay, then what to do about it? Should she tell him how she felt, and if so, when and how? Or wait it out and see if he made the first move? What if he didn't give an indication of his feelings before her father showed up – press him then or cut the rope? She sighed. Nobody had ever told her that love would be so blasted *complicated* ...

Did she hear her mother wheezing? Sadie stilled her own breathing and listened intently. Nope. Not a wheeze, not a cough, nothing.

Sadie let go of the breath she'd been holding. Her mother was on her way to a full recovery. But still, they should probably stay here until she was back to complete health, just to make sure ...

*BOOM!*

Sadie sat up with a start. What was *that*?

A shout from outside suddenly drew her attention, then another.

She looked around. What could be happening? Had the outlaw escaped? She quickly tossed her blankets aside.

There was a sudden rapping on the front door. "Doc! Doc! Mulligan's is on fire!"

Sadie jumped to her feet and reached for her clothes that she'd neatly folded and placed on a chair. She pulled on her blue calico quickly and listened as Doc and Grandma came out of their room and went downstairs. Teresa groaned and opened one eye. "Go back to sleep, Mama. Nothing to worry about."

"Mm-hm," she mumbled in response, closed her eye, and snuggled deeper into the blankets. Sadie smiled and left the room.

Grandma had gone through the back door of the kitchen and was running to the small barn behind the house. Doc was already heading out the front door with Henry Fig, and Sadie followed them off the front porch and into the street. She stopped and watched the men silhouetted against a bright orange glow, and gasped as the sky itself seemed to come alive with smoke and flame. It was a really *big* fire – Mulligan's saloon was quickly being consumed!

Sadie realized that Grandma must have gone to the barn for buckets or anything else the men could use, and decided she had best help her. But when she turned to run back into the house, a man came out of nowhere and grabbed her. Her yelp of surprise was quickly cut off by a large hand clamped over her mouth. She instinctively bit it, and smiled at the muffled curse of pain, but he stuffed a handkerchief into her mouth before she could cry out.

The man was soon joined by another, who dragged her away from the house toward a couple of horses. She kicked and clawed at them until one grabbed her wrists and lashed them together. The other took the bandana from around his neck and tied it around her head to hold the handkerchief in place.

The bandana smelled atrociously bad – and familiar. *Oh, no ... not again!*

She struggled violently but futilely as a dark cloth sack was yanked over her head. She listened as one man mounted his horse, then nearly lost her breath when she was roughly grabbed and tossed up to him. An arm locked itself around her waist, pinning her against her captor as the dreaded outlaws, once again with Sadie in their clutches, kicked their horses into a gallop and rode as fast as they could out of town.

# TEN

Flames shot into the sky as the sheriff and the other men were in town tried their best to battle the raging fire. But the fight was in vain. Mulligan's was lost.

Mrs. Mulligan stood across the street in her nightclothes, a shawl wrapped about her shoulders, and bitterly wept. Mr. Mulligan slowly walked across the street to join her once it became apparent the fight was hopeless. He pulled her into his arms and watched as everything they had went up in flames. "It'll be all right, my girl," he whispered against her hair in his soft Irish brogue. "It'll be all right."

Part of the structure caved in on itself and came crashing down. Mrs. Mulligan let out a wail at the sight, and buried her face in her husband's chest.

Mrs. Dunnigan marched down the street toward them. Her husband Wilfred was with the other men, trying to rescue what they could. "Fire cleanses away all sin!" she huffed as she arrived, out of breath.

Mr. Mulligan glared at her. "Don't start, Irene. If you know what's good for you, don't start!"

Surprisingly, Mrs. Dunnigan heeded the warning. "You'll be needing a place to stay while you rebuild. Wilfred and I have plenty of room." She held a hand out to Mrs. Mulligan, who looked at it warily.

Mr. Mulligan stared, his mouth open in shock. "You've always hated our place. Called it a den of iniquity."

"Hated your place. Hated what it did to men. But I never said I didn't like you. Now let me take your wife back to the mercantile where I can fix her a cup of coffee."

Mr. Mulligan hesitated a moment, then gently steered his wife into Mrs. Dunnigan's arms. She, in turn, led her away to help in whatever way she could. And for that, he was grateful. It was easy to forget how folks could come together in a time of crisis. Even Irene Dunnigan. He shook his head in wonderment, then turned back to the fire

Just then, Harrison thundered up on his brother's beautiful black horse Romeo. He reined the steed in and jumped off. "What happened? I could see the fire from the farm! Came as fast as I could!"

"You're too late. It's gone, all gone." Mr. Mulligan sank onto the steps leading up to the sheriff's office.

Doc, the sheriff, and several other men crossed the street and joined them. Doc sat next to Mr. Mulligan. "I'd say you look like a man who could use a drink, but I think you may be out of luck."

Mr. Mulligan couldn't help but chuckle. "All the whiskey in town is gone! Now, when we all could use it the most."

There was no help for it. The rest of the men laughed as well.

"Don't worry, Paddy," the sheriff said. "We'll all help you rebuild. Mulligan's will be back up in no time."

Grandma joined them. "Where's Mrs. Mulligan?"

"Irene took her back to the mercantile. Offered to put us up until we got our place re-built."

Everyone looked shocked for a moment before Grandma spoke. "Best enjoy it while you can Mulligan. No offense, Wilfred," she added as she turned to Mr. Dunnigan.

He waved a dismissive hand in the air. "None taken. We'd love to have you stay with us. And I'm sure that, once you have a new place, Irene will be back to her old self."

Some of the men laughed at that as well.

"I've already gotten some lumber in to start work on the hotel." Mr. Van Cleet offered. "You can use what you need."

"And I still got lotsa roofin' shingles from when I put up my barn last fall," another man said.

Harrison smiled. "You've got first pick of my stock this spring!"

Another man offered nails, and several said they'd chip in for a new bar. Frequent customers that they were, they deemed it a sound investment.

Harrison watched with pride as the people of Clear Creek continued to offer materials and the strength of their backs to help Mr. Mulligan rebuild. Sadie should see this. But she must still be at the house, caring for her mother. He turned and looked at the little white house at the other end of town.

In that moment, he knew without a shadow of a doubt he wanted to build a life with Sadie Jones. He could stand it no longer – life was too precious, and too short. He smiled, swung up into the saddle and trotted down the street to tell his prairie princess he loved her, and wanted her to be his wife.

"Didja hafta set fire to Mulligan's, you idjit? What were you thinkin'? It'll take *months* to rebuild!" one of the men wailed.

"I meant to just set the shed on fire, but a dog started barkin' at me! I threw the torch at it to chase it off ... but it landed on the whiskey barrels on the back porch ..." The other man whined as he held a hand over his fresh black eye. "You didn't hafta wallop me fer it! We got what we wanted, didn't we?"

The first man calmed at the remark and glared at a bound and gagged Sadie as she lay atop a familiar pile of hay. "We shouldn't o' brought her here. Only a matter of time 'fore Harrison comes back. It's a good thing we followed that cow trail home, or he'd've spotted us sure!"

*Harrison!* Sadie was immediately alert at the sound of his name.

"Well, what were we supposed to do, leave her out on the prairie while we fetched things? Let's get what we came for and go." The second man shuffled over to a stall, pulled up a few loose floorboards and yanked something out of its hiding spot. He stood and went to join the first man, who was bent over Sadie, looking at her like a starved dog looks at a pork chop.

How had it come to this, back in the hands of the same outlaws who'd abducted her before? And how did they know Harrison? In fact, wasn't this the very same barn he'd brought her to the night of her rescue?

She thought on this for a moment. If that was the case, then these two had to be Harrison's stepbrothers! He'd talked of them, mentioned they were (his word) "dissolute," but she hadn't met them yet. Did he have any idea they were part of the outlaw gang?

"What are we going to do with her?" Black Eye asked. Was that Jack or Sam?

"Well, we know what we're gonna do with her eventually," the other said, and they both fell into hysterics. "It's what to do with her 'tween now and then that's the question."

Black Eye leered at her with his one good eye and grabbed her ankles above her bonds. "Let's undo these here ropes and see what's under that dress." He licked his lips as his hands travelled up her legs. Sadie squirmed with revulsion at the contact.

"Not here, idjit!" the Puncher interrupted, slapping Black Eye on the back of the head. "We'll take her to the hideout and have her there. If'n we're lucky, Jeb'll be there; if he ain't, then we got her all to ourselves. Either way, he'll be happy we got rid o' her."

"Can't we just keep her? Keep her up at the hideout and use her when we want?"

The other chuckled. "Not a bad idea. But first we need to have her tell us what's in that mailbag. Can't be havin' Harrison's brothers comin' home from prison anytime soon. If that letter Harrison was so fired up to get is in there, I wanna burn it. Bad enough we're stuck with him, but somebody's gotta do the work 'round here!"

They both laughed again at that. It obviously didn't take much to set them off, and it was also obvious neither of them could read. Which meant Sadie had a chance. What sort of chance, she wasn't sure, but she'd take anything she could get right now. And that meant getting her hands on that mailbag.

Harrison jumped off Romeo and stepped onto the Wallers' porch. The front door was wide open, but the inside of the house was dark. A prickly sense of warning came over him and he instinctively drew his revolver. Something wasn't right. Where was Sadie?

"Hello?" he called into the empty hall. A tiny sound caught his attention. He cautiously entered the house and spun first to the dining room on his left, then the parlor on his right.

Sadie's mother was in the parlor, sitting in the dark, weeping.

Harrison went straight to her. "Ms. Menendez! What happened? Where's Sadie?"

Teresa wiped her eyes, opened her mouth to speak, but began coughing instead.

Harrison lit a nearby oil lamp. The woman had obviously been crying for some time – her eyes were red and swollen, her face puffy. "Let me get you some water." He ran to the kitchen, where he knew a pitcher of water would be on the sideboard. He poured her a glass and hurried back to the parlor.

The woman drank greedily before speaking. "Sadie ..." she rasped. "Two men ..."

"What men?" Harrison asked as his body tensed.

"I don't know. I come downstairs to see what was going on. Saw the light coming through the upstairs window, could smell the smoke. Fire ..."

"Yes, it woke up the whole town. But where is Sadie?"

"The door was open. I saw her outside ... looking down the street." She began to cough again. Harrison patted her back until it settled. She nodded her thanks and continued. "She started to come back into the house ... and two men took her. I tried to scream, but this cough ..."

Harrison helped her take another drink before her coughing could silence her again. She couldn't cry out for help because of it, yet her hacking may have saved her life. Even if she had caught the outlaws' attention, they would likely have run rather than take a chance of being spotted. "It's all right. You witnessed what happened, and that helps. Did you see what direction they went?"

"I was coughing so hard I couldn't follow. But I think they headed south."

South? If that were the case, he should have passed them on the road when he came riding into town moments before ... unless they left the road and headed across the prairie. "Are you sure they went that way?"

"I'm sure. They didn't pass in front of the house. I don't know if they took the road or one of those cow trails. When me and the other girls first came to town, we sometimes followed them out to the prairie to pick flowers ..." Another coughing fit, another drink of water.

Harrison stood as he thought. There were two main cow trails – one led out onto the open prairie, the other back toward Harrison's farm. Could it be? He'd had his suspicions before but ... "How many men did you say? Two?"

"Yes."

"Thank you, Ms. Menendez. You sit here; I'll get Grandma to take care of you."

"Harrison?" she rasped. "Find my little girl. I just got her back. I can't stand the thought of losing her again. And ... and I know you feel the same."

He gave her a look of deep compassion, then smiled. "You are quite right, dear lardy. And fear not, I'll find her and bring her back." Especially now that he had a good idea where to look ...

He ran from the house, swung up onto Romeo, and galloped back toward the crowd of people down the street. He brought the horse to a skidding stop.

"What's the matter, Harrison? There another fire?" the sheriff shouted up at him.

"Has anyone seen my stepbrothers?"

Everyone looked around. "Nope. Ain't seen 'em," Wilfred Dunnigan offered.

"I was afraid of that," Harrison said to himself.

"What's going on, Harrison?" Grandma asked.

"Miss Menendez needs you back at the house. She saw two men take Sadie and ride south."

The sheriff jumped to his feet. "Are you saying Sam and Jack took her?"

"Everyone else within a mile of town has been here, fighting the fire. I know they were in town earlier, but from the looks of it they never came home."

"They only left our place when we closed the saloon – a couple of hours ago," Wilfred added.

"Sam and Jack ... don't that beat all! Sorry to hear it, Harrison," the sheriff told him. "Give me and some of the boys a minute to get our horses and let's round 'em up!"

"That's exactly what I was hoping you'd say, Sheriff. We'd better hurry – I have a pretty good idea where they might be taking her!"

The men sprang into action and quickly got their horses and guns. Grandma and Doc, meanwhile, hurried back to the house to tend Teresa and prepare for any wounded that might be brought back to town. Who knew what the night's outcome would be? In the meantime, Doc and Grandma were going to do one of the things they did best – pray.

# ELEVEN

*Thank the Lord for small favors!* Sadie thought – in this case, the rank idiocy of her captors. Not only had they placed her and the mailbag on the same horse, but they had bound her hands in front of her, not behind her back!

Now she might have a chance. If she was very careful – and her abductors continued not to be – she could leave a trail of mail. Thus, when Harrison or anyone else came looking for her, they could follow it to the outlaws' hideout. Harrison knew where it was, but if her guess was right, no one else did. Anything would help, and the sooner she was found, the better chance she had of staying alive.

If her situation weren't so precarious, she might find it amusing: once again, her life was held in the balance by the U.S. Postal Service.

"Ain'tcha gonna blindfold her?" Jack (the one she'd previously called "Black Eye") asked. By now, she had learned which was which. They were indeed Harrison's stepbrothers, and from what she'd gathered from their conversation, their father hadn't a clue his sons were in over their heads with a band of outlaws. It seems Jack and Sam (the Puncher) kept him liquored up most of the time to avoid too many questions or inquiries as to their whereabouts, and Harrison was so inundated with farm work he didn't have time to be nosy.

She heard enough to figure out they rustled cattle
for Jeb while he and some others stuck to robbing
stages and wagon trains passing through to the south.
It made it look like there were two separate outlaw
gangs, where in reality there was only one.

"What for?" Sam answered. "She ain't comin' back."

They laughed. Sadie ignored them and eyed the
mailbag hanging from the saddle horn. If she leaned
forward enough while they rode, she could pull out a
letter or two at a time and drop them. The darkness
would shield her work, but hopefully one of her
potential rescuers would still see them. *Please Lord,
let it be light soon!*

"Let's go! Sooner we get up to the hideout, sooner we
can have ourselves a little fun!" Sam yanked her
against his chest. "I'm gonna take you first, missy," he
hissed, his breath hot and rancid. She turned her face
away and cringed. He laughed, kicked his horse, and
they galloped out of the barn and up the road.

After a few moments, Sadie leaned forward, but
Sam pulled her back again. She strained against him,
trying to lean down enough to reach into the mailbag,
and panic began to take hold. If she couldn't leave
something for Harrison or any others to follow, it could
take them much longer to find her. And time was not
on her side – the outlaws were sure to kill her as soon
as they were done with their "fun." She could identify
both of them, and probably Jeb, their leader, as well. A
witness wouldn't be tolerated.

The only thing that would buy her any time would
be their use of her ... but who knew how much time it
would give her? And did she really want to endure
that? Perhaps death was a preferable alternative ...
*Oh Lord, please! Please save me!*

The arm around her tightened as her captor
laughed, then licked the side of her face. She screamed
into the gag and struggled, but his grip was too strong.

Out of pure desperation Sadie did the only thing she could think of. She kicked his horse. Hard.

Harrison, the sheriff and four other able-bodied men rode out of Clear Creek as if their lives depended on it. In this case, it was Sadie's life at stake, and Harrison was determined to save it.

He'd often wondered over the last year if his stepbrothers had anything to do with the current crime wave in the area, not to mention the unsavory events that led to his two older brothers, Duncan and Colin, being arrested over a year and a half ago. Until now, he hadn't any proof of their guilt – Jack and Sam always had some sort of alibi when livestock went missing.

Still, it was obvious that Duncan and Colin had been lured into the wrong place at the wrong time and framed for cattle rustling off a wagon train. Harrison had managed to get new information from his stepfather that had set him on the trail of the real bandits. But none of that mattered at the moment – right now, rescuing Sadie was his only goal.

They reined in their horses a mile out of town at his signal. "We should split up. They may have gone back to the farm or, if my guess is right, they've gone to the cabin above the ridge. But we can't be sure which."

"Henry, you pick two of the boys and check Harrison's farm," ordered the sheriff. "The rest of us will follow Harrison up to the ridge."

"If they're at the farm, be ever so careful. Ride after us and fire off a few shots to signal you've found her. We'll come join you."

"Will do, Harrison! Butch, Andy – follow me!" Henry said as he and two others spun his horse around and took off toward Harrison's farm.

"If she's there, Henry'll know what to do," the sheriff reassured.

Harrison nodded, turned his horse, and the remaining three headed across the prairie. After about ten minutes, he signaled for a stop. They listened carefully for gunshots and, when none were forthcoming, once again sped toward the line of pines in the distance.

Harrison had guessed right – they hadn't taken her to the farm, but to their cabin hideout. Hopefully. He prayed in earnest as they rode in the pre-dawn darkness: that the outlaws had only the one hideout, and that they would reach Sadie before any of the dirty scoundrels had a chance to touch her. If any of them, even ... no, *especially* his stepbrothers, touched a single hair on her head, he'd see them hanged higher than Haman. And maybe shot for good measure. But he couldn't let such murderous thoughts cloud his thinking, he knew – he needed his wits about him.

By the time they reached the tree line, though, he'd imagined several more clever ways to exact justice on his stepbrothers.

"Which way?" huffed the sheriff as they brought their horses to a stop. The sky was just starting to lighten in the east.

The animals were breathing hard and steaming by now. Harrison knew that they would need their strength to make it up to the ridge. "Best to walk the horses for a bit. It's about two, maybe two and a half miles up through the trees. There's a stream nearby – we can leave the horses there."

The sheriff nodded and they set off, Harrison in the lead. He let Romeo pick his way along a deer trail that led through the pines and alders. But soon it faded, and the horses had to find their own way through the ever-thickening trees and brush. Occasionally, they would stop and listen for sounds of other horses crashing through the wood, but there were none. His brothers must have had enough of a head start to have already reached the cabin. Sweat popped out on Harrison's brow with the thought. He risked the noise he knew it would make, and pushed Romeo a little harder.

Soon he heard the sound of water. They headed for it and, when they reached the stream, found a suitable spot to leave the horses. The men dismounted and checked their guns. Harrison studied the trees around them. "There was a stand of alder several hundred yards from the cabin. It shouldn't be far from here. If we head upstream, we'll come to it."

The men nodded and followed. Sure enough, a minute later they reached the stand of trees Harrison remembered and began to cautiously pick their way along another deer trail that led away from the stream.

Before long, they reached their destination. Harrison dropped to his belly behind a fallen log and signaled the others to do the same. They could see the cabin through the trees, smoke rising from the chimney in lazy blue tendrils. "We've got to get them away from her somehow," he whispered

The sheriff peeked over the tree. "I don't suppose one of your animal calls is gonna work this time?"

Harrison grimaced. "Jack and Sam may not be the smartest, but they do have memories. They'll not fall for that twice." He surveyed the area around the cabin. Only two horses were in the rickety corral, and all was quiet. A good sign. He knew that if he heard Sadie begin to scream, he would likely go mad. "We could set the cabin on fire," he mused.

"Not a bad idea. It'd get them out of there quick-like."

"There's a back door. I'll make my way around to it; you and Bart go to the front and set the cabin aflame. While they're distracted, I'll run in and get Miss Jones."

"They won't hurt her, will they? Use her as a shield?

"If I know Jack and Sam, they'll rush to save their own skins. Neither of them will think quickly enough to use Miss Jones to barter with."

The sheriff and Bart nodded, and went to work making torches out of whatever they could find. Within moments, they had what they needed and each man began to get into position.

Harrison, meanwhile, was crawling on his belly as he circled around through the trees to the back of the cabin. It had been much easier the previous time, when it was dark. Now that the sun was rising, he had to be extra careful not to be seen.

As soon as he was out of sight, the sheriff and Bart slunk their way to the structure, lit their torches of dried pine branches and threw them on top of the roof. In moments, the fire had engulfed the shingles.

Harrison, gun drawn, tiptoed to the back door and listened. Nothing. Not a sound except the fire crackling and roaring overhead. Then he heard a roof beam snap and cringed. Good Lord, what if they were asleep or passed out drunk? And Sadie was undoubtedly bound and gagged ...

Knowing he had to act fast, he burst through the back door. By now the cabin was full of smoke, and the flames on the roof were making their way inside. "Sadie! Sadie?" he called through the haze. He coughed, and pulled his bandana over his nose and mouth as he frantically searched the main room, then ran into the room where he'd first seen Sadie bound to a chair. No one. He checked the smaller third room. Still nothing.

"Oh, Lord, no," he whispered as realization dawned. He ran back into the main room and opened the front door. The sheriff and Bart stood outside, their guns aimed at him. "Don't shoot! It's me, Harrison!"

They lowered their guns. "Where in tarnation are they?" the sheriff called over the roar of the fire, confused.

"Not here!" Harrison managed between coughs as he ran from the porch.

"But what about them horses?" Bart asked.

Harrison looked at the two horses panicking in the corral, and silently cursed himself for his stupidity. "Those aren't Jack and Sam's."

"Well, if no one's here, and those horses aren't Jack and Sam's, then where are they?" the sheriff lamented.

Harrison brushed past the sheriff as he began to scan the area. "I wish I knew ..."

Sadie fought back tears as Jack roughly carried her through the trees. They'd gone to the cabin as she'd expected, but only stayed long enough to get a few things.

The cabin had been stripped bare. Apparently, some of the other outlaws were still nearby, their horses in the small corral, a fire slowly dying inside the fireplace from before dawn. A note had been left telling those who were able to meet up at the "other" hideout where they would make plans for their next job. Sam had ungagged her only long enough for her to read the message to them. Then Jack and Sam had gathered some blankets that were left and a cast iron kettle, and headed off into the woods further up the ridge.

They rode for at least half an hour before they came to another makeshift corral, but there was no cabin to be seen. The men had tied up their horse and continued on foot, Sadie slung over Jack's shoulder. She occasionally grunted when Jack stumbled on a rock or root, but otherwise tried to stay silent during the rough trek to wherever it was they were going, while wondering how far it could be.

She didn't want to do anything more to provoke the men. Sam had been so mad when she'd kicked his horse — almost getting both of them thrown off — that he'd stopped, dismounted, yanked her off and put a knife to her throat. She would have been killed right there if Jack hadn't talked his brother down out of his rage. Finally Jack, probably deeming her defilement more important than his brother's temper, had thrown her over the saddle, well out of reach of the mailbag. That left no way to leave a trail. It didn't help that Jack would occasionally smack her rump and regaled her with all the dire things he'd planned for her unwilling carcass.

Finally they arrived. Jack's heavy breathing slowed as he dropped her onto the hard ground. He bent over her and tried to catch his breath as Sam, mail bag on one shoulder, blankets rolled up and slung with a rope over the other, set the kettle down next to her.

Sadie looked at it, then glared at Sam. Maybe if she acted bravely, she'd feel the same way.

Sam leered at her. "Yer mine, missy. And I'm gonna enjoy every inch o' you." He wiped his mouth with the back of his hand.

"Hey, what about me? I carried her all the way up here. I should get her first!" Jack argued.

"You're too tired. Besides, ya don't want her first. I'll get her all warmed up for ya. She'll be sweeter when she's broke in a little."

Jack pulled her to her feet. "I said, I want her first!"

Sam shoved him and she fell to the ground. They had retied her ankles, apparently not wanting to chance her escaping on foot. Perhaps they weren't the best runners. She kept that bit of information in mind as Sam yanked her back up and hefted her onto his shoulder. "Let's go."

Jack grumbled, picked up the rest of their effects and followed along like an obedient dog. After a few moments, they went around a small stand of trees and came upon what looked like the entrance to a mine shaft. Sadie caught a glimpse of it as Sam turned to look around before they entered the darkness.

Inside, the air suddenly became still and cold. She didn't like the way the darkness swallowed them up so quickly, and began to struggle.

"Stop that! Mind yerself!" Sam scolded as he slapped her hard on the rump. His large hand stung, and she stilled her movements. Unable to help herself, the tears finally broke free. At least in the pitch blackness, they wouldn't be able to see her fear. Maybe she'd get lucky and there would be no light when they performed their heinous deeds on her body and then murdered her. Perhaps it would all be easier to stomach in the dark ...

No. She knew better. It would be horrible regardless.

*Lord, help me!*

# TWELVE

Sadie fell to the ground in a heap. She listened as the two men rustled about in the darkness before she heard the distinct sound of a match being lit. She had to squint against the light as Sam took a lantern from a large rock and lit it. He adjusted it and hung it from a nail protruding from a beam as she squinted at their surroundings.

They were indeed inside some sort of mine shaft – a dead end, from the looks of it. The space was maybe twelve feet square, reinforced with some posts and beams. She didn't notice any fresh marks in the rock that would indicate it was in active use. Several barrels sat against one wall, with a couple bales of hay, a sack of grain and some crates and boxes against the others.

Sam went to one of the barrels, took off the lid and brought out a whiskey bottle. He pulled the cork out with his teeth, took a long swallow, wiped his mouth with the back of his hand and leered.

The dark chill returned to Sadie's spine.

"Go take a look around," Sam ordered Jack. "See if anyone else has come up yet."

Jack dumped his load to the ground. The kettle hit a rock and the noise echoed off the walls. "Why do I gotta take a look around? We was just outside!"

Sam spun on him. "Git out! Go outside while I ..."
He turned back to Sadie, eyes glazed with lust. "...
while I get her ready for ya."

"Ain't no reason I can't have her first!" Jack
growled. "You take everythin' first!"

Sam punched him square in the gut, doubling Jack
over in pain. "I said, git! Take a look and make sure no
one followed us!"

Jack straightened, eyes full of rage. "Better hurry it
up, 'cause I aim to take my time with her!" He turned
and stomped back to the mine's entrance. Sadie
watched as he disappeared into the darkness. It looked
like *her* time was running out.

Sam grabbed her by the wrists and dragged her to
the center of the cave, then reached for the blankets
they'd brought and began to untie them. He looked
around, deciding where to spread them, then threw
them down behind the barrels. Apparently even a
hardened criminal liked his privacy while committing
the unthinkable. Returning to her, he pulled her to her
feet. "Now, missy," he drawled, his breath reeking of
whisky, "let's you and me have ourselves a time."

He picked her up, carried her behind the barrels
and threw her down, then straddled her hips to hold
her in place. He pierced her with such an inhuman
look of lust that it made her go cold. Her whole body
went numb with fear as he tried to kiss her through
the gag, then twisted around to cut the bonds on her
ankles. Grinning as he turned back, he grabbed her
bound wrists and held them above her head, then
undid his gun belt with his other hand, pulled it off
and threw it aside. The belt holding up his pants soon
followed it.

He grunted in frustration as he fumbled with her
clothing in an attempt to rip the bodice of her dress
open. He cursed when it didn't yield, then pulled a
knife and held it to her throat. "This is all gonna have
to come off, missy." He smiled as he poked the point

through the collar of her dress with the knife and began to slice it away.

Sadie braced herself. If she was going to die anyway, she'd rather fight him and have him slit her throat than meekly endure what Sam was planning ...

*Click.*

Sadie and Sam both froze at the sound. *Could it be ...?*

"Take your filthy hands off her, Sam. Or I shall no recourse but to paint the walls with your brains."

Harrison stood behind Sam, a gun to the back of his stepbrother's head. His face was locked in determined rage. Sadie smiled in relief, not feeling one bit sorry for the outlaw.

Sam dropped the knife and put his hands in the air. Harrison snatched it up, threw it into the darkness, then yanked Sam off Sadie and pinned him against the wall, the gun in his face. "Give me one good reason – why shouldn't I shoot you right now?"

Sadie lay frozen in place. She'd never seen a man so fiercely angry.

"What's the matter, Harrison?" Sam had the nerve to drawl. "Afraid I'd ruin her 'fore you got the chance?"

Sadie instinctively closed her eyes.

Harrison slammed the butt of his revolver into Sam's face. "Any other witty *bon mots,* brother?" He let go, and watched Sam slump bonelessly to the ground. "I thought not. Cur." He holstered his gun, bent down and shoved Sam up against the rock wall, as far away from Sadie as he could get him.

Then and only then did he turn to Sadie. "Are you all right, princess?"

"I will be," she said weakly, willing herself not to faint.

Gently, Harrison picked her up, carried her to the middle of the cave and set her on her feet. He wrapped her in his arms and held her tight, mumbling something unintelligible into her hair.

Sadie tried to say "thank you" – and only then did both of them realize she was still gagged. "Oh. Terribly sorry," Harrison said in embarrassment, and quickly removed the bandana and handkerchief from her mouth. Sadie gulped air, perhaps a little too quickly as her knees went weak. Harrison, thankfully, caught her before she could drop.

And now she began to weep in earnest, from the trauma of the night and morning, the realization that she'd be dead if not for Harrison, and the relief that hopefully it was now over.

He held her to him, stroking her hair. "There now, princess." he whispered. "You're safe now. They can't hurt you anymore. I'm here." He kissed her forehead, her ear, her cheek. His lips were soft and warm against her skin. She couldn't think or speak, and didn't want to. Having him hold her, as her body began to shake uncontrollably, was enough.

It was a couple of minutes before Sadie could stop spasming and sobbing. But when she did, she suddenly realized that her hands, still bound in front of her, were accidentally pressed against a particular – and highly inappropriate! – portion of Harrison Cooke's anatomy. "Oh dear!" she exclaimed, pulling away suddenly. "I didn't mean … I just … sorry, I …"

"Sh," Harrison said sharply. He unsheathed his own knife, cut the rope around her wrists, and began rubbing her hands to bring back the circulation. "It's quite all right, under the circumstances."

"W-what do you mean?" she asked, confused.

He looked into her eyes, and she could see the love alight in his face. "Sadie Jones, I know this is hardly the romantic setting one would hope for. But I love you madly, and I want you to be my wife, for ever and anon. And if you say yes, rest assured that not only will I never let any harm come to you, ever again, but that I will never object to any place you choose to put your hands."

Sadie had been through too much over the past several days to hesitate at such an offer. "Yes, yes!" she cried, throwing her arms around his neck.

He kissed her then, not the soft and tentative kiss of the fearful suitor, but a kiss of resolution, of promises, of protection. Of possession. She was his and his alone, and he was just as equally hers. No arguments, no complaints, no hesitation. It was a kiss that spoke of lifetimes, and of eternity.

And Sadie reveled in the knowledge that with a single kiss he had claimed her so completely, and banished her fear so thoroughly. She could live on a kiss like this. A moment before, she had been resigning herself to death; now she was ready to stand against the armies of the world, so long as it was under this man's banner.

Harrison finally broke the kiss and held her tightly to him. "I love you, Sadie Jones. I've loved you from the first moment I saw you." He looked into her eyes and captured her again. "I've nothing to offer – no lands, no title, no money, a dozen or so pigs that I don't even own. But you'll have my heart as long as I live, and beyond into the hereafter. I'll love you with all my strength and being."

Before Sadie could answer, a low moan echoed from a corner of the cave.

*Nope, not this time*, she thought. Without batting an eye she let go of Harrison, stomped over to where Sam was beginning to rouse, and kicked him in the back of the head. Sam went limp and silent again. Satisfied with the result, she returned, locked her arms around Harrison's neck and pulled him down for another kiss.

How long it lasted, neither one knew. But neither was inclined to stop ... at least until the sheriff came upon them. "Um ... sorry to interrupt ..."

Harrison reluctantly lifted his face from hers. "I love you, my princess," he whispered and kissed her forehead again. "My brave and beautiful prairie princess. And now I'm going to make you my queen." He held out his arm, she took it, and they followed the sheriff outside.

Sadie sat up in bed and let Doc examine her. The ride back to town had been slow. They had come out of the cave to find Jack on his knees, hands over his head and several guns pointed at him. Both Jack and Sam were handcuffed, tethered by a length of rope to the saddle horns of their horses – which were led by Andy and Bart from the posse and forced to walk all the way back to town. It was especially rough on Sam, who had a splitting headache.

Sadie rode with Harrison astride Romeo, her dress wrapped about her legs, her body leaning against Harrison's broad chest. She slept part of the way once they reached the prairie, and awoke with a start as she realized something. "How did you find me?" They were the first words she'd spoken since leaving the mine shaft.

He sat up straighter and wrapped his other arm around her. "I followed your trail, dear heart."

"My trail? What trail?"

Harrison chuckled. "The mail, of course! Once we found it, it led us right to you. Very clever, princess."

"Wait ... the *mail*? I wanted to use the mail, but I never got the chance!"

"Well ... there was a trail of it all the same. In fact, if it hadn't been there, we may not have found you for hours."

Then she remembered. When Sam threatened to kill her, his knife caught on something as he pulled it from his boot. It must have been the mailbag – he'd accidentally torn it. The mail must've been falling out through the tear one letter at a time, and none of them had even realized it.

Now Sadie started laughing, with joy. The good Lord *had* been watching over her! And she didn't stop laughing for the remainder of the journey back to town.

"Nothing broken, just a few bumps and bruises." Doc announced.

Harrison stood at the end of the bed. "Thank the Lord for that!"

"You go on down to the kitchen and let her rest. Grandma's got something on the stove." Doc waved Harrison toward the door.

Suddenly there was a commotion downstairs. "Here now!" they heard Grandma exclaim. "You can't just barge in here! Who do you think you are?"

Someone came stomping up the stairs. Sadie's eyes immediately grew wide. She knew only one person who would storm into a house like that ...

Horatio Jones burst into the bedroom in a huff. "Sadie! There you are! What's going on? Why are you in bed? Get your things together, pronto!"

Doc stood in open-mouthed shock. Harrison, on the other hand, crossed his arms, his eyes narrowed to slits.

Sadie looked at all three men, and swallowed hard. "Hello, Papa."

"Don't you 'hello, Papa' me, young lady! You've got a lot of explaining to do!"

"And I'm sure she shall be quite willing to explain everything, Mr. Jones." Harrison replied, his shoulders squared and his jaw set. "After she's rested."

Her father noted the stance, and bristled. "And who are you?"

"Harrison Cooke, at your service. Miss Jones' betrothed."

"Her ... *what?*" Horatio asked, his jaw dropping.

"Her betrothed." Harrison repeated and glanced quickly in her direction. She nodded at her father. "Sadie has been through something of an ordeal, and is under physician's order to rest until fully recovered. She would appreciate your cooperation in this, and I would be happy to continue this discussion downstairs in the parlor."

Harrison's flowery verbiage seemed to slow Horatio Jones down a bit. He looked Harrison up and down in confusion. "Where in blazes are you from, son? No one around here talks like that! He turned to Sadie. "You don't *have* to be marrying him, dear?"

Sadie smiled. "Perhaps not, Papa! But I plan to, nonetheless."

Horatio Jones looked Harrison over a second time, suddenly seeming a bit outgunned. "Who ... where did ... consarn it, what in Sam Hill is going on here?!"

"I understand this may all be rather unnerving," Harrison said calmly, motioning Horatio to a chair next to Sadie's bed. "But I believe that after you have been acquainted with the events of the last several days, it will all be clear."

Horatio dropped into the chair like a steer being hit in the head with a sledgehammer. "If you say so, son." He shook his head and turned to Sadie. "Him?" he asked, jerking his thumb over his shoulder at Harrison.

Sadie laughed, despite her exhaustion. "Papa. I love him, and I'm going to marry him. If it hadn't been for Harrison, I'd be dead now."

That got his attention. His face drained of color. "That dandy saved your life?" he said, incredulous.

"Twice," Sadie affirmed. "And I doubt the outlaws he tracked several miles into the wilderness thought he was a dandy."

"Really?" Now Horatio looked up at Harrison with a new respect. "But still, Sadie, that don't mean you have to get hitched ..."

"She loves him, *Horacio*," a voice spoke from the doorway. "That should be reason enough.

All heads turned toward Sadie's mother. She entered the room slowly, never taking her eyes off of Horatio.

It took a second, but a spark of recognition lit in Horatio's eyes. "Oh my ..."

"Papa," Sadie began. "This is ..."

"I know who this is," Horatio interrupted. "Teresa ..."

"And here I thought you'd forgotten about me," Teresa said, one eyebrow raised.

Horatio's eyes took on a faraway look. "I'd never forget you," he whispered, then rubbed his hand over his face. "I don't know about anyone else, but I think I need a drink."

"I'm afraid you're a victim of bad timing, sir," Harrison calmly informed him. "Before we could catch the outlaws, they burned the saloon down. Accidentally, so I'm told, but burned down nonetheless."

"Figures," Horatio groaned, then looked over at Sadie again. "What kind of a crazy town is this?"

"A town where I could spend the rest of my life with the man I love," Sadie spoke softly.

Teresa smiled, tears in her eyes. Harrison reached her in a few quick strides and put his arm around her. "I was going to ask you for your blessing, Ms. Menendez."

Teresa nodded, unable to speak.

"But with both her parents here, so much the better!" he concluded.

Horatio seemed to be trying desperately not to slip into shock. "I, I don't feel right about this at all. Sadie, go get your things – we're leaving!"

Teresa suddenly straightened. "She's not going anywhere, *Horacio*! She's been abducted, nearly killed, and threatened with the worst things a woman can be threatened with! You leave her be!"

Horatio turned white. He closed his eyes and swallowed hard. "Sadie ... I was so afraid I'd lost you. When we couldn't find you ..." He shuddered. "I was about to go out of my mind, girl!"

Sadie leaned toward him and placed her hand on his. "I'm sorry if I scared you, Papa. But I'm fine now – Harrison saw to that. I love him with all my heart. And," she added, pointing to Teresa, "I found Mama. She was dying, but the Lord made her well again."

Horatio took in the sight of Teresa standing next to Harrison, and his face softened. "I suppose I owe you an apology, young man. You saved my daughter's life. And Teresa ... I *know* I owe you an apology. Can you forgive me?"

Teresa frowned in thought. "I may need a little time ... but yes."

"And I accept your apology as well," Harrison said heartily. "Now, Mr. Jones, perhaps we should repair to the parlor – we have much to talk about. And I'm sure Dr. Waller has some ... medicinal spirits around here somewhere ..."

# EPILOGUE

*Four months later ...*

"Yeeeee-haw! Here they come!" Henry Fig yelled as he galloped through town. A thunderous roar could be heard behind him. Everyone ran out into the street to watch.

"No, no! Get off the street! You people want to get killed?" the sheriff yelled. The townsfolk quickly got out of the way as they felt the ground shake.

Within moments, hundreds of cattle came into view, driven by the men of the Big J – almost a thousand head of some of the finest beasts anyone in Clear Creek had ever seen. But to Horatio Jones, it was simply a little wedding present to Mr. and Mrs. Harrison Cooke, whose ranch (formerly a pig farm) was located south of town.

Sadie and Harrison watched their new stock – or at least part of it, a few hundred – lumber through town. The rest had been driven by another route, to a corral Harrison had built at the other end of Clear Creek. He'd wanted to give some to the sheriff and his men for helping him rescue Sadie and bring his stepbrothers to justice. He also planned on selling each person in town a steer, at well below market price, to help them out for the following winter. It was the gentlemanly thing to do.

"Do you think you'll like cattle ranching?" Sadie yelled over the sound of hundreds of hooves trotting along the street below them. They were on the balcony of the second floor of Mulligan's new saloon.

"I'll enjoy it, I'm sure! Your father is a very generous man!" Harrison replied in dramatic understatement. Horatio Jones, for all his bluster and bewilderment, had finally consented to letting Sadie marry Harrison, but had insisted on helping the young couple start out properly. Harrison thought that meant a bit of livestock and perhaps helping him spruce up his family's farm. But Horatio never thought that small. Instead, he'd built them a new ranch house, a new barn, a little cabin for Harrison's stepfather ... and now nine hundred head of cattle, give or take a few. It was unheard of, but here they were.

"Always did prefer a good steak to ham." Colin Cooke said as he joined them.

"I still like ham." Duncan, the eldest Cooke, added. "But I shan't be picky."

Harrison put his arms around his two older brothers. "Looks like we're in the cattle trade now, chaps."

"Anything's better than rotting in gaol, Harrison – give me a branding iron over leg irons any day!" Colin sighed. "You're the best brother, Harry. Mother would be proud."

"You can thank Sadie's father for speaking with the warden himself. Not to mention writing the governor."

"We can't thank him enough for all he's done on our behalf – and yours," Duncan said. "And certainly Clear Creek will never be the same because of him. I have a feeling this little town is going to start growing now."

"It already has," Colin added, waving an arm at the torrent of cattle below them. He turned to his new sister-in-law. "Will your mother be visiting again soon?"

Sadie smiled. "She and my father will be getting married next month. I asked them to have the wedding here, in the new church."

"But ... we don't have a clergyman yet." Duncan said.

"There's one coming from the Nebraska Territory. He's the son of one of my father's friends, and also knows Mr. Van Cleet. He'll be here in time for the wedding."

"Colin was right. Our little town is indeed already growing." Harrison said with a smile.

They continued to watch until the last steer thundered past on the street below. Harrison removed his arms from around his brothers' shoulders, put them around his wife and kissed her. "Well, princess, let's go have a look at our wedding present."

They left. Duncan and Colin continued to watch as the dust settled and the townsfolk followed the cattle to the corral. "I suppose we should go help out," Duncan suggested.

"I suppose so," Colin replied.

Duncan turned and headed downstairs. Colin was about to follow when the stage came rolling in, pulling up in front of Dunnigan's Mercantile. Colin watched as Wilfred and Irene came rushing out. Irene Dunnigan looked exceedingly happy, which raised Colin's suspicions. He decided to stay put and see what all the excitement was about – from a safe distance.

A young woman got out of the stage.

Even from such a remove, he could see she was incredibly beautiful – a Greek marble come to life. His mouth suddenly went dry and his breathing stopped. If there was ever such a thing as love at first sight, then this was it.

But then he saw the heavenly creature hugging Irene and kissing her on the cheek. "Oh dear," he mumbled. This beauty must be a relative of the

Dunnigans'. Which meant that Irene Dunnigan would be in charge of her.

Colin's heart almost sank. Almost. Because if there was one thing he enjoyed, it was a challenge – he liked to brag that as an Englishman, he was descended from a long line of empire-builders and dragon-slayers. And no one in Clear Creek could dispute the fact that Irene Dunnigan was more than the usual challenge.

To win that young lady's heart, Colin Cooke mused with a smile, he would have to live up to the reputation of his dragon-slaying forebears ...

**The End**

# Her Prairie Knight

# ONE

*Clear Creek, Oregon, June 1858*

Colin Bartholomew Cooke had just seen an angel!

Well, not really an angel, but a lady who was, in his eyes, everything an angel ought to be. Beautiful, of exquisite form, with honey gold curls that bounced beneath her hat as she walked. He swallowed hard and wondered how those golden tresses would look if unpinned and allowed to cascade down her back. Would they descend to her tiny waist? Or travel further on to her shapely hips? His heart skipped a beat at the thought.

He couldn't tell from his vantage point what color her eyes were, but what did eye color matter on an angel? Maybe they changed color depending on her mood. Was that a trait of angels? Just so long as they didn't turn a fierce red ...

... like Mrs. Dunnigan's.

Colin sighed, his shoulders slumping as he watched his new-found angel hug Wilfred Dunnigan first, then move on to greet the devil's own. Irene Dunnigan: moralizer and harridan. The bane of Clear Creek.

Though Colin and his older brother Duncan were newly released from prison – and would be forever grateful to be out of the dreadful place – it did have one redeeming quality. It didn't have Mrs. Irene Dunnigan in residence.

Everyone in Clear Creek avoided the self-righteous, cantankerous creature as best they could – which was not very well, as she and her husband owned the town mercantile. Worse still, Wilfred Dunnigan was usually busy in the back, while Mrs. Dunnigan handled the counter and the cash. Of which there was little; out here on the frontier, most folks relied on store credit. Maybe that's what made the woman so cranky ...

He watched as the stagecoach driver hauled down a few satchels and a trunk. Wilfred picked up the trunk while Mrs. Dunnigan and the angel gathered up the satchels. The Dunnigans talked and laughed as they led her inside. His angel must be planning to stay awhile.

Colin quickly closed the window and headed downstairs. He, Duncan and his other brother Harrison had watched some of Harrison's new stock being driven through town from a second-story balcony of Mulligan's saloon. It was a big day for his little brother. He, and his new wife, Sadie, had just received a thousand head of some of the finest cattle in three territories. The stock was a gift from Sadie's father, the richest rancher in the Far Northwest.

This meant that the brothers now found themselves plunged into the cattle business. It would be a far cry from pig farming, something they'd done since settling in Clear Creek eight years ago. But it would bring greater prosperity to their family, not to mention the town, and for that they were immensely grateful. It had been the dream of their birth father to travel to the American West from England, settle, and then raise cattle. Now it was a reality. If only their father had lived to see it.

"Everyone's gone to the corral, Colin. Best get down there or your brothers will tan your hide!" Mr. Mulligan began. "And don't forget to tell the folks to come back here when they're done! This is a fine day for our town – we need to celebrate!"

"Happy to oblige, Mr. Mulligan!" Colin said, and ran out the swinging double doors of the saloon, quickly crossing the street to the stagecoach. Willie, the driver, was just about to enter the mercantile with the mailbag. "Good afternoon, Willie! Can I be of assistance?"

Willie looked at him, then cast a wary eye at the mercantile. "If'n you want to take this in, I'd be much obliged."

Colin watched as Willie's eye began to twitch. It often did when the poor man was nervous or agitated – a logical reaction when an encounter with Mrs. Dunnigan was in the offing. "I'd be happy to help. Hand it to me."

Willie smiled. Several of his front teeth were missing; the unfortunate result of a stage robbery four months ago. On the sunny side, that robbery had brought Harrison and Sadie together. "I can't tell you what a help that'd be. I don't have much time, and would really like to go set a spell with Mulligan."

Colin grinned in understanding. What Willie really meant was that he'd like to "set a spell" with a glass or two of Mulligan's *uisgebaugh* – and without Mrs. Dunnigan. "Glad to do it. Best go see Mulligan, then – I'll take care of this." He reached for the mailbag. Willie gratefully surrendered it, then skedaddled across the street to the saloon.

Colin laughed as he watched him go, then turned toward the mercantile. He took a deep breath to brace himself, walked up the front steps and opened the door.

A tiny bell rang over his head to announce his arrival. He looked this way and that but didn't see anyone. He went to the counter and tried to peek through the half-opened curtain that separated the front and back of the building. The Dunnigans' living quarters were upstairs, the mercantile and storerooms on the first floor. They must be upstairs and hadn't heard him come in.

The floorboards overhead creaked slightly in confirmation, followed by the sound of bright laughter. *His angel!* He felt his face warm at the sound, and had to swallow. She was above him, probably right over his head, sitting in the small parlor. He closed his eyes and sighed when the sound came again.

"What are you doing standing there like that?" a voice snapped.

Colin opened his eyes to find Mrs. Dunnigan standing in front of the curtained doorway, a ladle in her hand. Her face was scrunched up as she glared at him with her dark, beady eyes. He lifted the mailbag in front of him like a shield. "My apologies, ma'am. I brought in the mail for you ..."

"Well, don't just stand there, put it on the counter!"

"Yes, ma'am," Colin complied. It was all he could do not to look at the ceiling when the delightful laughter once again filtered down to tickle his heart and senses.

"Where's Willie? Why didn't he bring it in?"

Mrs. Dunnigan's voice pulled him out of his dream-like state. "He said he wished to speak with Mr. Mulligan."

"You mean he went to go drink!" she huffed. "Drink, and then drive the stage out of here?! I'll see he's fired!"

"I believe this is his last stop, ma'am. He'll likely take a room for the night, then depart in the morning."

"What does it matter? No decent man drinks and then handles horses!"

Colin sighed. She did have a point ... or would have, if the livery stable hadn't been less than fifty yards from both Mulligan's and the mercantile. Clear Creek wasn't exactly London. "I'll see to the stage if it makes you feel better, Mrs. Dunnigan."

"See that you do! Now get out of here, unless you want to buy something!"

Colin listened. No laughter from above. He had to get the information he wanted quickly. He had to know who his angel was! "I would like to purchase some of your delicious cinnamon candies."

She waddled behind the counter and opened a jar. "How many?"

"Give me a dozen."

The floorboards creaked again, and the delightful laughter rained down. The sound touched him like a sweet caress, and he leaned against the counter to steady himself.

"I hope you have money! You know you Cookes don't have store credit anymore!"

"Quite." Colin nodded and reached into his pocket. "I saw someone get off the stage. Do you and Mr. Dunnigan have a guest?"

She stopped putting candy into a small bag and spun to face him. "It's no business of yours if we have a guest or not!" She threw the last piece of candy in the bag and tossed it onto the counter in front of him. "That'll be three cents!"

He handed her the money just as he heard footsteps coming down the stairs. Mrs. Dunnigan moved with a speed he'd never seen before. She came around the counter and began to shove him toward the door. She had him out on the porch of the mercantile before he could object, and was back inside before he fully turned around, which was just in time to have the door slammed in his face.

Colin stood there for a minute and stared at the door like a lovesick dolt. What was happening to him? This was ridiculous – he had to get a hold of himself. Angel or no, prison term or no, no woman should be having such an effect on him!

The door suddenly opened, and he was lost. The beautiful young woman, the angel, the mythic goddess, was standing right in front of him! And she was even more lovely than he could have possibly imagined.

"I believe you paid for this, sir?" Her voice was just as heavenly.

An odd tingling sensation made its way up his spine and he shook as if chilled. She stood there, his bag of candy in her hand, and held it out to him. He took it without saying a word.

She smiled. "Good day, sir."

He nodded, too dumbstruck to speak. He wanted to, but his brain was incapable of forming anything resembling words. Before he knew it, the door had closed and she was gone.

He slowly looked at the bag of candy in his hand. He didn't know who she was, where she came from, how long she was staying, if she was a relative of the Dunnigans, or what she was doing there. But now, at least, he did know one thing.

This angel had blue eyes.

Isabelle Dunnigan, known to her intimates as Belle, turned to find a sour look on her aunt's face. She was beginning to understand that this was not unusual.

The older woman went behind the counter and slammed the lid back on the candy jar before putting it on a shelf. Uncle Wilfred stood nearby and hid a smile. He'd been the one to hand Belle the bag of candy, and whispered to her to give it to the gentleman just outside the door who'd forgotten it. She did so without question, but now wondered if it had been a good idea. Aunt Irene looked about to bust a gut, her face was so red.

"I'll not have any of those Cooke boys sniffing around here, Wilfred!"

Uncle Wilfred calmly turned to face his wife. "Now, Irene, there's no way to keep them away from her. And besides, of all the men in town, they are the closest in age to Belle."

"I don't care – they're no good! I wish the whole lot of them would pack up and leave!"

Uncle Wilfred sighed and turned to Belle. "That there was one of the Cooke boys. Polite fellows, born and raised mostly in England. Came out west and settled here a little after we did."

"Englishmen, here? Fascinating," Belle commented. "Auntie, why don't you like them?"

"Why? I'll tell you why!" She waddled out from behind the counter. "Their pa drinks himself into a dead drunk every night! Two of the brothers just got out of prison and two more just went in! Thieves is what they are, common thieves! The only decent one of the lot was their mother – at least she had some manners! But Jefferson Cooke drank too much, and paid no mind when she got sick. Worked the woman to the bone, he did! He killed her just as sure as I'm standing in front of you. I don't want you anywhere near them, you hear me, girl?"

Belle stood and gaped at her. Her first day with Aunt Irene and Uncle Wilfred, and she already felt like her life was being taken over. Again. Hadn't she just left the same situation behind in Boston? Her father had kept her under such tight control, she couldn't even pick out what she wanted to wear on her own. Any dress she chose, he didn't like. If she chose a hat, he didn't like it. Nothing she did was good enough. Her hair was too light, her eyes should have been brown, her walk was too sprightly ... if it wasn't one thing, it was two – or more – others.

James T. Dunnigan hadn't always been so controlling and strict. He didn't fall into it until after her mother died. But since then ... she sighed inwardly. It was almost as if he was trying to turn Belle into a copy of Mother.

Her mother had loved to wear green. Belle preferred blue, but her father insisted she wear green all the time. He made her wear her mother's hats, her mother's gloves. Yes, she was sentimental about her mother's things and loved wearing them ... at first. But it soon became apparent something was very wrong with her father. His constant trips to the gambling houses should have been her first clue. But it was his insistence she do and be everything her mother was that told her his sanity was slipping.

Belle let go a shaky breath. She was *not* her mother. She was her own person and wasn't about to let anyone, including her Aunt Irene, turn her into something she wasn't. She'd been through that with her father, may he rest in peace. And though his last few years were almost unbearable for her, she still missed the man he used to be ...

"Well? Don't just stand there, girl – I want you to promise me you'll have nothing to do with any of those Cooke boys!"

"Now, Irene," Uncle Wilfred interjected. "Be reasonable. They gotta come get things from the mercantile now and then, not to mention fetch their mail. You can't expect them to stay away."

Aunt Irene picked up her ladle and waved it at him. "This is my store and I'll serve whomever I wish. And that means I'll also *not* serve whomever I wish!"

Belle looked helplessly to Uncle Wilfred. "I don't understand."

"Your aunt's had a hard time the last few months. We've been sharing our place with the Mulligans while they rebuilt their saloon after the old one burned down. They just left a few weeks ago. Things have been a bit cramped, and now you're here."

Belle looked at the wood-planked floor. "Oh. I see."

"No, don't take it wrong – you're my niece, and I wouldn't want you anywhere but with us now that your pa has gone on to glory. You'll live with us and work here in the mercantile. And when it comes time to be thinking 'bout marrying, well ... you can do that here, too. There'll be plenty of gentlemen to choose from."

"Gentlemen?" Aunt Irene snapped. "*What* gentlemen?"

Uncle Wilfred took a calming breath. "Let's worry about that when the time comes, dear. Now, back upstairs, both of you. It's time to eat and I'm hungry."

Belle paused before following, and glanced back at the front door. She wouldn't mind a chance to get to know the gentleman who'd so recently stood on the other side of it. Had he been one of the men her aunt said got out of prison? She found it hard to believe. His countenance was one of awe and wonder. He'd looked at her as if she was the most beautiful star in the universe. He hadn't tried to flatter her or looked her up and down as if she was his next meal. She'd gone through enough of that on the journey here to last two lifetimes.

Luckily for her, she had been able to travel with friends of her father's, who were heading west to settle in Oregon City. She'd enjoyed the family's company during the three-month trek and had learned a lot from them. She'd also discovered what it was like to have freedom, real freedom, something she'd not enjoyed in a very long time. Freedom of choice was a precious thing, and she wasn't about to give it up to her aunt. Not in a million years.

Belle decided she'd just have to find a way to get to know the gentleman on the other side of the door. It was, after all, her choice. Especially if anything having to do with marriage was involved.

"Where have you been all this time?" Duncan asked Colin as he joined him on the fence of the corral. "Harrison needs our help."

Colin watched as Harrison had some of the drivers separate several dozen steers from the rest of the herd brought to town. The sheriff and a few other men laughed and smiled as the drivers set to work. The steer were a gift from Harrison to the men who'd helped him rescue Sadie when she was kidnapped by outlaws. Kidnapped the second time, actually; the first time he'd been on his own.

Colin smiled. Their little brother always had been a generous sort.

Duncan slapped him on the back, jumped off the corral fence, and made his way toward Harrison and the rest. Colin followed, eager to watch as more townsfolk gathered. It would be their first business transactions as the new owners of the Triple-C Ranch. Harrison, in another act of generosity, was selling off some of their new stock at incredibly low prices to help the townsfolk make it through the long winter. One steer would see a family through quite nicely, including the several new ones that had settled in town over the last couple of months.

And more were expected to join in the months ahead – Mr. Van Cleet was planning to build a hotel, and craftsmen would be coming from all over to help. At this rate, Clear Creek would need a bank, a land office, a new schoolhouse – maybe even a second mercantile. Colin smiled at that thought; either Irene Dunnigan would have to become a lot nicer, or risk going out of business.

But the first priority was the new church – an even more welcome sight than a pleasant Irene Dunnigan. And, also thanks to Horatio Jones's generosity, it was almost complete.

"Ok, gather 'round!" Harrison called to the crowd. "We'll separate out a few at a time, and put them in the adjoining corral! Then you can take your pick from there!"

The people cheered and headed for one of two smaller corrals to wait for the cattle to enter. The air was full of lively laughter, happy conversation and the lowing of hundreds of cattle. It was the most excitement the young town had ever seen. And though the upcoming transactions would bring in much less than market value for the animals, Colin knew the sales would still start them off well.

He took up his post at one end of the corral to handle the money and receipts, and forced himself to concentrate. Would Wilfred come claim a steer? Did they need the animal to make it through the winter, or were they set well enough? The real question, of course, was did they have three mouths to feed this coming winter, or just two?

By the end of the day, Colin hoped to find out. Even if it meant giving the Dunnigans a steer for free.

# TWO

Sadie Cooke gathered what she needed and set the table for supper. The men would be home soon, and would no doubt be plenty hungry. She knew that selling cattle could work up a mighty big appetite. After closing a business deal, her father – one of the biggest if not *the* biggest cattleman in three territories – could put away quite a feast. And he was just one man – there were three Cooke brothers.

She hummed a hymn as she checked on the fried chicken she'd prepared, one of her new husband's favorites. Tonight was special, and she wanted everything to be perfect. In fact, she'd left the sale early to do just that.

Life for Sadie the last four months had been like a fairy tale, and she thanked the Lord everyday for the blessing of her new family. Her birth mother and father, reunited after nearly twenty years, were now getting married. She had a wonderful husband and two delightful new brothers-in-law. Nothing could make Sadie any happier than she was.

*Except* ...

She sighed. Men were wonderful creatures, really they were. But what Sadie wouldn't give for some female companionship. She was barely nineteen, so much younger than most of the farmers' wives in the area or the few women in town. The ones who were close to her age were so busy with their husbands and children, they hadn't much time for socializing. Of course, she adored Grandma Waller, the doctor's wife – but she was just that, a grandma, to everyone in town.

No, it just wasn't the same as having someone her own age to talk to. Especially about ... certain things. Things between a man and a woman, for example; things she was still trying to learn and didn't want to discuss with Grandma. For some things, there was just no substitute for being able to talk to another girl.

"What's for supper, princess?"

Sadie looked up as Harrison walked into the kitchen. She smiled and winked at him. "Something special."

He went to her and took her in his arms. "I have something special right here." He kissed her then, gently. Slowly. The serving spoon in her hand slipped from her fingers and fell to the floor with a clatter.

"I hope this doesn't mean supper will be late again," Colin commented as he entered the kitchen.

Harrison broke the kiss and glared at him. "No, but you can fetch your own dessert."

"Tsk, tsk. Break the kiss and look how you ... hmmm. Can't quite think of a rhyme for that."

Sadie laughed. "Do you always try to make up a rhyme for everything?"

"No," Colin began. "Not everything. Only when it amuses me or irritates my brothers."

"He used to do it all the time as a child," Harrison added. "It drove Duncan positively mad."

"Oh, I wouldn't say that. He rather enjoyed them while we were unjustly incarcerated. They did, after all, help to pass the time."

Duncan entered the kitchen and grimaced at Colin's calm recollection. "The gaolers felt otherwise. They had you flogged."

Sadie gasped.

Duncan waved a dismissive hand in the air. "Just a few strokes. One for each rhyme. Seemed several of the guards didn't care for Colin's poetic renditions of *their* lives. Especially when he recited his poesy to our fellow prisoners."

Colin held up his hands in defense. "I merely sought to entertain!"

Duncan put a hand on his shoulder. "Let us hope, dear brother, that henceforth you save your recitations for more appreciative – and less well-armed – audiences."

"As I was not asked to return, I think it safe to say it was a limited engagement."

"Like a bad opera in London?" Harrison tossed in.

Duncan and Colin exchanged a quick look. "Something of that sort, yes," Colin said.

The two brothers didn't speak much of their time in prison. Falsely accused of cattle rustling, they'd been locked away for almost two years. They had only been released a little over a month ago. But in that time they had endeared themselves to Sadie and her father. Horatio Jones was a good judge of character, and had taken all three brothers under his wing.

"Supper is ready, if you would help get these things to the table." Sadie removed the biscuits from the oven. The three men went to work and carried food into the dining room.

The new ranch house had a dining room, sitting room, parlor and kitchen, plus a small office off the sitting room, on the first floor. Upstairs were the four bedrooms. It was the biggest house in the area, and the townsfolk had helped immensely with its construction. The raising of the new barn last month was the talk of the town, and Sadie felt Clear Creek had truly become her new home after the event. She now knew almost everyone in the area by name.

"The Dunnigans have a house guest," Colin calmly informed them after the blessing.

Duncan dished himself up some mashed potatoes. "Someone is visiting the Dunnigans? On purpose?"

"Stop," Sadie scolded. "Even Mrs. Dunnigan must have some relatives and friends."

"It's a young lady," Colin began. "I'd say about your age, Sadie."

Sadie's head snapped up.

The action caught all three men's attention. She looked at each one, and shrugged in an attempt at nonchalance. "How nice. Is she staying long?"

"I really couldn't say. I didn't have a chance to ask, as I needed to get to the corral and help with the sale. Perhaps you should call on the Dunnigans tomorrow and introduce yourself."

Sadie did her best to suppress her excitement at the mention of a woman her own age in town. "Maybe I'll do that. If I have the time, of course."

Colin took two pieces of fried chicken, then passed the platter to Duncan. "Oh, but you must go pay the woman a visit. She might feel rather out of place with no other young ladies to talk to."

Sadie noted the hopeful gleam in his eye. It seemed Colin had some ulterior motive ... "Perhaps. In fact, it would be nice if you drove me into town, Colin. I need to pick up a few things, and I'm still not quite used to driving the wagon by myself."

"Why, I can't think of anything I'd like to do more."

"I could drive you," Harrison offered.

Colin almost dropped his chicken leg. Sadie watched as his neck began to turn pink. Aha! He already had an eye for the girl. "Oh, I think Colin should drive me. I'm sure he'd love to help get what I need from the mercantile"

Colin took a generous bite of chicken and gave a casual nod.

"She must be pretty," Duncan stated.

Colin stopped his chewing and eyed his brother.

"I thought so. Otherwise you'd not be so eager to put yourself in harm's way. Or at least in Dunnigan's way."

Sadie looked from Colin to Duncan. "What is that supposed to mean?"

Duncan smiled. "Even more than most sane and rational men, Colin usually avoids any threat of doing battle with Mrs. Dunnigan, Dragon of the Mercantile. But of a sudden, he doesn't seem to mind accompanying you on your errand to the dragon's lair – in fact, he seems quite eager. And what better motive has a man ever had for facing a dragon than the possible treasure of a fair young maiden?"

Colin swallowed hard. "I've simply come to the conclusion that Mrs. Dunnigan and I should try to start over again, as they say, on the right foot. Let bygones be bygones."

"Bygones? What bygones?" Sadie raised a curious eyebrow. "Do I want to hear this?"

"Oh, yes! You must hear this!" Harrison laughed. He saw the pink creep up Colin's neck to his face. Even his ears had turned a glaring shade of red. "Well, brother? Will you tell her or shall I?"

Colin tossed his chicken onto his plate. He wiped his mouth with his napkin, sighed and looked Sadie in the eye. "You might as well know. I am the most disreputable scoundrel you could ever meet."

"What?" she asked, then looked at his brothers. "Did someone let in one of the steers? Because I'm smelling a lot of manure right now."

"I speak only the unvarnished truth, dear sister. Shall I list my crimes and vices? Robbery ... abduction ... forgery ... ah, let me think ..." He paused, his face contorted slightly as he feigned concentration.

"Liar of the worst possible sort," Duncan added between mouthfuls.

"Ah, yes, we mustn't forget that," Colin agreed. "Oh, and a vandal. There, I think that about covers it, don't you?"

Harrison and Duncan nodded enthusiastically.

Sadie could only stare. "And who, may I ask, were your victims?"

"Only one. Mrs. Dunnigan."

A smile curved Sadie's mouth. "So am I to understand you robbed, abducted, forged, lied to and vandalized Mrs. Dunnigan?"

"Absolutely, though not in that particular order." Colin reached for his chicken again.

Sadie sat back in her chair. "Oh, do tell. I can't wait to hear it."

Duncan and Harrison began to laugh. Colin ignored them and waved his drumstick about as he talked. "Let me see ... this all took place shortly after we settled here. There were just a few families here at the time – the Wallers, the Dunnigans, Mulligans, Whites, Figs, Browns, and Turners. I think after our arrival it brought the population up to twenty!"

"Oh, get on with it," Duncan chided.

Colin chuckled. "I broke the same window in the back of the mercantile at least three times. Duncan and I used to raise Cain and toss stones behind the building when we came to town with our parents. But that pales in comparison to the kidnapping."

Sadie listened and laughed as they each took turns and gave their own rendition of Colin's antics. The horrid abduction was nothing more than Colin borrowing Mrs. Dunnigan's cat to help Mrs. Mulligan catch a rat in the saloon. His "robbery" consisted of knocking over a container of candy in the mercantile after which Mrs. Dunnigan accused Colin of stealing several pieces, while in reality she miscounted the candy while cleaning up the mess. (She never did own up to that one). Then there was the time he wrote Mrs. Dunnigan's name on a receipt he found on the counter. It was nothing short of forgery in her eyes, when in reality he was terribly bored waiting for his mother to pick out cloth for a new dress. But after the previous incidents, Mrs. Dunnigan saw fit to blame Colin for anything that went wrong, even if he wasn't even in the vicinity.

"So, as you can see, Mrs. Dunnigan and I go way back, and have a long history of ... *encounters*."

"Well, that certainly explains a lot. I wonder how happy she'd be to know you'd like to meet her guest."

"Whoever said I wanted to meet her guest? I'm far too busy."

Duncan burst into laughter.

"Clearly not so busy you can't volunteer to take Sadie to town tomorrow!" Harrison said with a grin.

Colin maintained his veneer of hauteur. "You take her, then. I've got plenty of work to do around here."

"And deprive Mrs. Dunnigan of yet another *encounter* with you? Oh, I think not."

"Well, it doesn't matter to me. But do inform me of your plans before I retire so I know when to make myself available."

"Make yourself presentable, you mean," Duncan mumbled between mouthfuls.

Sadie laughed at the three men. She had indeed married into a happy family. One would never know that Duncan and Colin had just come home from prison, that they had two half-brothers who were outlaws and currently under lock and key themselves, or that Harrison had handled the farm and the death of their mother after Jefferson Cooke took to drinking. Speaking of which ... "Should I take a plate up to your step-father?"

The three men sobered. Duncan set down his fork. "I'll do it. He needs to learn to come eat with us, not stay hidden away in that cabin all day and night."

"I'll fix him a dinner plate along with some dessert."

"Dessert?" Duncan's eyes lit up at the word. He had the biggest sweet tooth of the three. "What's for dessert?"

"Chocolate cake – I made it early this morning."

The brothers glanced at one another. Harrison turned to his wife in shock. "How did you manage to bake a chocolate cake and none of us discover it? You know it's our favorite!"

"I have my secrets, gentlemen. Besides, you've been busy all day – herding cattle, giving out steers ... ogling Mrs. Dunnigan's guest ..."

They all laughed at that, even Colin. The meal over, the men got up from the table and glanced at the front door with the same thought in mind. And it had nothing to do with chocolate cake.

They stepped out onto the front porch, as was their new habit after dinner, while Sadie prepared the dinner plate. Each man eventually looked at the small cabin that now housed Jefferson Cooke. The old ranch house was hardly fit to be lived in anymore, so they'd torn it down. But Jefferson refused to live in the main ranch house with the rest of them. This left the Cooke brothers wondering - what secrets did their stepfather have that would make him hide out in his new little cabin for weeks on end?

Pretty soon, they would have to find out.

Jefferson Cooke poured himself another drink. He held the bottle of cheap whiskey over the glass until the last of the precious elixir trickled down and plopped into it. He stared at the empty bottle in his hand, still upside down, and pondered how he was going to obtain another. This was his last.

"Just my luck," he grumbled. Actually, he mused, he could use a bit of luck – he hadn't had any in quite a while. He wondered which would be easier to get his hands on, more booze or more luck. In his case, probably the former. His luck, thin at the best of times, had run out the day Honoria died. He'd been drunk ever since.

He threw the bottle into the stone fireplace, where it shattered.

No luck, no whiskey, and no way to get any of either; at least not until morning. And that meant he'd have to go into town. It had been a long time since he'd been to Clear Creek. November, he thought. But he wasn't sure.

He fell into his chair by the fireplace and stared at the shards of glass amidst the ashes from the morning fire. He liked the early morning, even when he had a splitting headache from the night before. Honoria had liked the early morning, too. There were a lot of things she liked, like afternoon tea. He could never get into that habit – he'd usually been out working. But she liked to stop her work for a few moments and have a cup – when she could get it, that is. It didn't take long to run out, and out in the boondocks it took plenty long to get more. Wilfred would have to order it from Oregon City, and it could take months to get it to Clear Creek. But when it did, She was in heaven, and some of the other ladies in town picked up on it. Soon Mrs. Dunnigan started regularly stocking it.

Jefferson closed his eyes a moment and snarled at the drink in his hand. Seeing as how it was his last, he wasn't ready to see it go quite yet. It was his answer to tea, only he didn't stop at having it at just one point in the afternoon. Lately it had been day and night ... except now it was gone. Unlike Honoria, he wouldn't have to wait months to get more. But come morning he'd have to ask Sadie or one of the boys if they were going to town and if they could get him a bottle...

The boys. His lower lip quivered. Those three weren't really his boys, they were Honoria's. His boys, Jack and Sam, were locked up . He'd been so drunk since the trial, he didn't even know where they'd gone to serve out their sentence. But he'd find out. Oh, you can bet he would. And he'd find a way to make those other boys pay for sending Jack and Sam away.

At least Jack and Sam had looked after him. They'd made sure he had plenty of whiskey to help him cope with Honoria's death. They'd worked the farm for him while that worthless whelp Harrison ran wild. They'd kept him well informed of his stepson's misdeeds. Harrison should have been sent to rot in prison with the other two, but had somehow managed to escape any blame.

And now he'd gone and got himself married to an heiress. An incredibly *wealthy* heiress. How was Jefferson going to compete with that? Everything he was, everything he had, his stepsons had stolen from him: his wife, his farm, and now his own flesh and blood.

But he'd make them pay. He'd make them pay with everything they had. Including their lives.

Jefferson smiled at the thought, and slugged back his drink.

# THREE

Four days.

It had been four days since Colin had seen his angel. Cattle ranching was taking up more time than he and his brothers had anticipated. Sadie had warned them of the work involved, but knowing it was one thing – living it was quite another. Stubborn as they were, Colin, Duncan and Harrison had to find out for themselves.

They found out rather quickly.

"Do you think your father can spare a few of his cowhands until we hire some help?" Colin asked Sadie as they drove to town.

"I can write him and ask, but it might be faster to send someone if you think you need the help immediately."

"Sending someone would be quicker ... but we have no one to send."

"I don't suppose I could volunteer for the job?"

"Absolutely not! How can you even consider such a thing? The very suggestion alone would be enough to send Harrison into ... what's the word ... 'conniptions'?"

Sadie smiled. She knew how protective her husband was. In fact, all three Cooke brothers were incredibly protective of her. The thought of riding across the prairie by herself was ludicrous. But her offer was genuine nonetheless. Besides, it wouldn't even be the craziest journey she'd made that year. "It could take a couple of weeks to get in touch with Papa, and possibly another week before he sends someone. Can you hold out until then?"

"We'll certainly try. It means a lot of hard work, but we'll manage. If any of us had actual brains – present company excluded, of course – we would have asked some of the drivers to stay on until we found other help."

Sadie hid a smile. "I'll ask Papa to send Logan. He's one of the Big J's foremen, and a good teacher. He can help out until you hire on more hands, not to mention show you how to do a few things."

"I hate to admit defeat in this endeavor, but we do need help. And a good teacher would be most welcome in my book."

"Logan Kincaid is one of the best in the business. You'll like him, I'm sure."

"I look forward to making his acquaint–" Colin stopped in-mid sentence and took in the sight before them.

Men. Lots of men. In fact, it looked like every unmarried man within ten miles of Clear Creek was lined up outside Dunnigan's to get supplies. Colin gripped the reins so hard his knuckles turned white.

"Oh, my! What are all these people doing here?" Sadie gasped.

"Isn't it obvious?" Colin asked through gritted teeth.

Sadie looked at the men lined up, then at Colin's tight-lipped expression – and suddenly remembered what it was like when she'd stayed with Doc and Grandma Waller. Men had come to be tended by Doc Waller for the smallest scrape or scratch. Grandma had sent more than a few off with a hard swat of her broom.

"Oh, my," Sadie repeated flatly.

"Indeed."

Colin guided the horses and wagon to the other side of the street. He set the brake, jumped off and helped Sadie down. She grabbed her basket out of the wagon and they crossed to the mercantile. Or at least to the middle of the street, where the line ended.

"Is Mrs. Dunnigan giving something away?" Sadie asked innocently.

"No, ma'am!" Tommy Turner, the eldest son of Mabel and Frank Turner, exclaimed with excitement.

"Then why is everyone in town?" Colin asked, noting the gangly youth's eager expression.

Tommy took off his hat and turned it in his hands. "Ah ... er ... well, it's on account of Miss Dunnigan."

"*Miss* Dunnigan?" Colin repeated, feigning ignorance.

Tommy glanced quickly toward the mercantile. Harvey Brown, a middle-aged farmer, came strutting out of the building and into the street like a preening peacock. The line moved up a space or two.

"What the devil is going on?" Colin whispered under his breath. "Harvey!" he called out. "Who's in there, President Buchanan?"

Harvey hurried over, his short little legs moving faster than Colin thought possible. "Might as well be the Queen of England!" He quickly glanced back toward the mercantile, his cheeks red and flushed.

With what, Colin didn't want to know. "Seems everyone is making a terrible fuss over the Dunnigans' house guest. She is a house guest, isn't she?"

Harvey looked at him. "Oh, yes, yes! Come to stay, in fact! Gonna be working with Wilfred and Irene! This sure changes things!"

"What things?" Colin snapped. Of course, he knew. Business was obviously going to pick up for Dunnigan Mercantile. If his guess was right, the men would try to pay off their bills to stay in good standing with *Mrs.* Dunnigan so they could call on the newly arrived *Miss* Dunnigan.

"I'd best get back to my farm!" Harvey exclaimed as he wiped his sweaty face and balding head with a handkerchief. "I need to make a list of things I need to pick up tomorrow!" And with, that he was off.

Colin and Sadie watched him trot to his wagon, parked in front of the Triple-C's. They glanced at each other, mouths agape, then to the long line of men waiting to get into the mercantile. One would think they really were in line to gain an audience with Queen Victoria.

"Oh, yoo-hoo!" Colin and Sadie turned at the sound. Mrs. Mulligan was quickly making her way down the street. Right behind her was Mrs. Fig. "Sadie! Have you heard the news?"

"What news?" Sadie asked. For Heaven's sake, no one made this much of a fuss when *she* first came to Clear Creek ...

Mrs. Fig stopped in front of her, nearly out of breath "We have another woman in town! And that means we can start a sewing circle!"

"Oh yes," Mrs. Mulligan chimed in. "And when the new preacher gets here and church services start, we can form a choir."

Colin looked from one excited face to the other, including Sadie's. It amazed him how one woman added to their ranks could make such a difference. "A sewing circle?" he quipped. "What's so exciting about that?"

"Don't you have sewing circles where you come from?" Mrs. Mulligan asked.

"None that I belonged to," he drawled.

Mrs. Fig giggled like a schoolgirl. "Oh, you silly dear! You must know a sewing circle is where women get together and visit."

"Ohhhh," he began. "Rather like afternoon tea?"

"Have you invited Miss Dunnigan to join yet?" Sadie asked.

"Didn't have to. It was Belle's idea. She asked us!" Mrs. Fig exclaimed. "You must come meet her – she's delightful. She's come all the way from Boston!"

"Boston?" Colin remarked, eyebrows up. "What the devil is she doing way out here?"

"Oh, it's a sad story," Mrs. Mulligan bowed and shook her head as she spoke. "Her mother passed some years ago and she just recently lost her father. The poor dear has nowhere else to go."

"Wilfred and Irene are her only living relatives," Mrs. Fig added with a nod of her head.

"Poor girl," Colin commented as he took in the line of eager men. He quickly turned to Sadie. "Best make introductions, then. If we wait to go through this line, I'll never get back in time to help Harrison and Duncan move some of the stock."

"But we really shouldn't cut in front of all these people." Sadie told him.

"I'm sure Mrs. Dunnigan won't mind. In fact, I'm positive she'll be happy to wait on us."

"Why is that?"

"Because we have something the others don't."

"What's that?" Mrs. Mulligan asked skeptically.

Colin gave her a wide grin. "Cash." He held out his arm.

Sadie glanced at Mrs. Mulligan just long enough to see the woman's eyes widen. She stifled a chuckle and took his arm. With Mrs. Mulligan and Mrs. Fig leading the way, the four of them crossed the street and went straight to the mercantile door.

The men at the head of the line grumbled at them. Wilfred sat in a chair near the door and whittled a piece of wood. "Morning, Mrs. Cooke, Colin. You might have to wait awhile," he said without looking up from his whittling. "My niece and wife are awful busy in there, and can't handle more than two or three customers at a time."

"Oh, we're not here to shop." Colin began. "Mrs. Mulligan and Mrs. Fig wanted to introduce Sadie to your niece, and inform her of Sadie's intentions to join her sewing circle."

Wilfred looked up. "I can pass that along."

Sadie noticed Colin's jaw tighten. "Actually, I do need a few things and we must get back to the ranch. If I give you my money and scribbled down a list, would you mind filling my order?"

"Can't. I'm out here to make sure these fellas ..." He waved his knife at the line of men. "... don't get any ideas about all going in at the same time. Too much work for the women to try to keep up."

"I understand." Sadie answered and turned to leave.

Wilfred lowered his voice to a whisper. "But if'n you want to go in real quick-like, Irene can get you what you need and introduce you to Belle. I'm sure she'd love to know there's another gal her age in these parts."

Sadie beamed. "Why, thank you, Mr. Dunnigan. That's very kind of you." She detached herself from Colin and headed for the door.

Colin couldn't believe his luck! He stayed on her heels and was about to follow her in when Wilfred grabbed him by the belt of his trousers. "Not you, Colin."

"But I need to ... to ..."

"Your sister-in-law can get whatever it is you need." Wilfred said as he pulled him away from the door.

Several men in the crowd laughed. "That's showin' 'im, Wilfred!" one man yelled from the middle of the line.

"Yeah, no fair! Wait yer turn like everyone else!" another cried.

"What about us?" Mrs. Mulligan practically huffed.

"You ladies can go in." Wilfred waved them inside. They smiled their thanks as they passed, while the men in line watched them with envy. Colin, on the other hand, closed his eyes and stifled a groan.

"Best get to the back of the line, Colin!" someone called. More laughter followed.

Colin fought to keep his anger at bay. The sight of all of them, waiting to see *his* angel, almost drove him mad. After all, he'd been the first one to set eyes on her – didn't that give him first rights, so to speak? And he didn't like the idea of every unmarried man within ten miles panting after her like a pack of dogs.

He knew he was being irrational, but it was hard to keep his emotions bottled. In prison, if you wanted something, you had to take it fast or it was gone. Often, he'd had to fight for it, and to the victor went the spoils. For the guards, it was sport to watch the prisoners fight over a scrap of food or dirty piece of candy, so they made no effort to break it up. Sometimes he witnessed men almost kill each other.

Colin had to sternly remind himself that he was no longer in prison, nor was Belle Dunnigan a prize to go to the winner of a bare-knuckled brawl. She was a person, and he was a gentleman ... albeit a gentleman quite willing to fight for her favor or honor if it came to that. Should he desire to court her – and he did – he was going to have to give the matter some thought. "I'll just wait here for Sadie," he said, doing his best to be nonchalant as he leaned against the doorframe.

Wilfred took up his whittling again. "Suit yourself."

Colin sighed. Between Wilfred guarding the door and Mrs. Dunnigan guarding his angel from the inside, she might as well be in an impenetrable fortress, locked in the highest tower. How was he going to get past them to reach her, let alone be introduced or spend any time with her?

Suddenly, he was struck with an idea.

The men in the street were lined up to meet Miss Dunnigan under the guise of needing something from the mercantile – knights hoping to win her hand. He was sure they'd try all the usual ploys – flowers, candy, trinkets – all rather ironic, as they'd likely have to purchase them from the mercantile, perhaps from Miss Dunnigan herself.

But he knew something they didn't. He, after all, was an Englishman. And any Englishman worth his salt knew that the best way to win the hand of a fair maiden was not to give mere tokens of affection and lay them at her feet. No, it was to slay a dragon.

Colin smiled at the thought.

# FOUR

"And this is Mrs. Sadie Cooke. She hasn't been here long either – she came here in the winter – and has the most beautiful new house south of town. Why, she would just love to join the sewing circle!" Mrs. Fig beamed as she talked.

Between Mrs. Fig and Mrs. Mulligan, neither Belle nor Sadie had been able to get a word in edgewise. Belle listened and nodded at the two women as she waited for an opening. Finally, they took a breath at the same time. "It's a pleasure to meet you. How do you like living in Clear Creek?"

Sadie smiled, probably as relieved as Belle was. "The town grows on you. And I do like the people." She looked directly at Aunt Irene as she spoke her last words, a warm smile on her face.

That got Aunt Irene's attention. She stared at Sadie Cooke a moment, her usual iron-fisted demeanor relaxing slightly. Belle could see it in her eyes. Auntie, she'd quickly discovered, had a reputation for being a tough old battle-ax. Uncle Wilfred had told her several stories since her arrival about the woman's battles with the good (but not, it seemed, good enough) people of Clear Creek. Maybe she wasn't expecting anyone to smile at her.

It did, however, confirm Belle's suspicions about her aunt. The poor dear needed ... an *outlet*.

Thus, a sewing circle, which it had taken her a couple of days to talk her aunt into. But she had to do something – the alternative was to live with her aunt's constant sour expression, and she didn't think she could stand it for more than a few weeks before she cracked. Some other form of social interaction was a matter of survival.

"Where should we have our first gathering?" Mrs. Fig blurted.

Belle pulled away from her aunt's softened expression. "I'm not sure."

"Oh, might we have it at your home, Mrs. Cooke?" Mrs. Mulligan pleaded. "Unless it's too early for you to entertain. But I admit, I'd love to see what you've done with the place since the barn raising!"

"Oh, it's a lovely home," Mrs. Fig told Belle. "Biggest house in these parts. And so elegant!"

"I'll have to check with my husband, but I don't see why not," Sadie said. "In fact, I think it's a wonderful idea."

Mrs. Dunnigan, back to her usual self, shoved a bag of nails at a starry-eyed Willie, the stagecoach driver. "That'll be twenty-five cents!" She turned to Belle. "Make sure you pick a time when Wilfred can mind the store on his own."

"Yes, Auntie. Late afternoon would work best, I think. Perhaps after lunch, for those ladies who are married? Their men will have returned to their work by then."

"Yes, you're right." Sadie said. "And I would love to bake something for us. We could have a real afternoon tea! Harrison just received a batch, special-ordered from Oregon City."

Mrs. Fig clapped her hands together. "Oh, this is going to be lovely! Our first sewing circle!"

The women continued to make plans as Willie and the other men looked on. Mrs. Dunnigan watched as they slowly circled around barrels, tables of merchandise, and various other items to worm their way closer to Belle.

Well, she knew how to deal with that! She turned, grabbed a hatchet that hung from two nails pounded into the wall, and banged the butt end on the counter.

Everyone jumped at the sound, Belle yelping in surprise.

"You men have been here long enough! Time to pay and leave!" Aunt Irene bellowed.

The men stood frozen in place. It took another whack on the counter to get them scrambling to the over to it to have their purchases added to their tabs.

"And you'll have to pay before I sell you anything else! Don't come back here until you're ready to pony up honest money!"

Belle closed her eyes and sighed to herself.

Her aunt quickly finished her work, stuffed the receipts into a cigar box and escorted the men to the door with a few waves of her hatchet. They quickly high-tailed it out of range, and out of the building.

Belle was still lamenting her aunt's behavior when she saw him. He stood in the doorway, his mouth curved up in a tiny smile. His hazel eyes were bright, almost mischievous. He slowly crossed the threshold, walked right up to the group of women, and tipped his hat. "Ladies," he began, then turned to Sadie. "Is there anything I may assist you with?"

Belle found it hard to tear her gaze away. At least, until Aunt Irene raised her hatchet and began to swing it around in the air. "Colin Cooke, get out of this store!" she screeched, slamming the blade into a table.

The display made several men who were just entering the store turn tail and run right back out again.

Belle put her face in her hands as her aunt tried to pull the hatchet free. She huffed and puffed as she yanked at it, but it wouldn't budge.

"Allow me, dear lady," Colin Cooke said. The sound of his voice brought Belle's face out of her hands. He approached her aunt, giving the woman a wide berth, swept his hat off his head and bowed. He then reached over, wrenched the hatchet from the display table one-handed, and offered it to Aunt Irene as if it were a bouquet of flowers.

Aunt Irene's face turned red as a glowing poker. She sucked air through her nose, her lips pressed so tightly together they turned white, and she glared at him.

"I'll just put this up where it belongs, shall I?" he added, then took the hatchet behind the counter and hung it back on the wall.

"I'm so glad you're here, Colin," Sadie quickly interjected. "I need to get a few things, not to mention have you help me carry them to the wagon."

"Happy to be of assistance," he replied with a smile as he approached. His eyes locked with Belle's ... and he froze.

She gasped, unable to help herself. By Heaven, he was handsome! She hadn't had time to study him much during their brief encounter the day of her arrival, she'd been too flustered from her travels. But now, rested and alert, she noted that he stood in stark contrast to the other men who had lined up outside the mercantile over the last two days.

He was tall and clean-shaven. He emitted an exotic scent, perhaps some sort of soap imported from England – masculine, clean, with a hint of spice she could not identify. Unlike the other men she'd met in town, this smell made her want to get closer to him. She blushed at the thought and involuntarily took a step back.

He raised a single eyebrow at the action. "I don't believe we've been properly introduced."

Sadie had been watching the two, a knowing smile on her face. She took her cue to jump in. "Oh, I'm terribly sorry. Colin, this is Miss Isabelle Dunnigan. She's Mr. and Mrs. Dunnigan's niece from Boston."

"Do tell." His words poured out like honey. Then he did something that no doubt would be told by the next four generations of townsfolk. He bent at the waist, took one of her hands in his and said, "I am Colin Bartholomew Cooke. And I am at your service."

Belle was finding it hard to breathe and wished she could loosen her corset. She guessed she was the only woman in town, or perhaps within a hundred miles, who wore one. She managed a smile but nothing close to intelligent speech. She wanted to speak his name, anything. It was such a handsome, strong name – Colin ...

He bent even further, raised her hand to his lips, and ever so gently kissed it.

Belle thought she might faint. First from his kiss, but then from the most blood-curdling yell anyone had ever heard.

Aunt Irene roared up to them like the U.S. Marines storming Chapultepec Castle – only louder. "What's the meaning of this? Get! Out!" she screamed.

Belle's eyes went wide as saucers. She'd been so mesmerized by Colin Cooke she'd forgotten all about her erstwhile guardian – and bodyguard, apparently.

Uncle Wilfred came running through the door. "What in tarnation is going on in here?"

Aunt Irene pointed an accusing finger at Colin, who was still slightly bent over, holding Belle's hand. "Get out, you no-good, dirty Cooke! You boys ought to all be shot!"

"Mrs. Dunnigan!" Sadie exclaimed. "He has done nothing wrong!"

"Done nothing wrong?! He *kissed* her!"

"Her hand!" Sadie protested.

"Oh dear, oh dear!" Mrs. Fig moaned. "What a disaster!"

"Kissing a woman's hand – a disaster?" Colin asked innocently. "Where I come from, it is how one treats a lady."

"I don't care if it's how you treat the Queen! You'll not be touching my niece!" Aunt Irene spat.

Belle finally found her ability to talk. "Auntie, really – you ought to be ashamed! He's the only man to walk through that door and treat me like a lady, and you tongue lash him for it?"

"He kissed her hand?" Uncle Wilfred commented, still catching up to events.

"It's no laughing matter! Get this trash out of my store!"

"Auntie!" Belle couldn't believe the woman's behavior. She'd heard stories from her father, laughed at the ones Uncle Wilfred had shared over the past few days, but nothing had prepared her for this. "I've made a terrible mistake coming here," she whispered to herself.

Colin must have heard her. Her hand still in his, he straightened up and tenderly looked into her eyes. "Will you be all right?" he asked gently.

She stared at him, words escaping her again. The nearness of him was overwhelming. She could feel the heat of his body wrap itself around her, bringing with it an unexplainable sense of peace that covered her like a blanket. She knew, knew as well as she knew the earth went around the sun or that two and two made four, that she would always be safe with this man.

From Aunt Irene, not so much. "I said get out!" the older woman screeched, grabbing Belle by the arm and yanking her hand out of Colin's. "Young lady, you get upstairs this instant and stay there!" She shoved her toward the curtained doorway leading to the back of the store.

Uncle Wilfred sighed heavily. "Irene, you're overreacting."

"I'll not have any man, especially a *Cooke*, slobbering all over my niece!"

"He kissed her hand!" Sadie argued. "It's customary for gentlemen to do that!"

"Especially those of the aristocracy. In fact, it's expected." Colin contributed.

"A‑ris‑*toc*‑ra‑cy?" Aunt Irene spat as she gave Belle another healthy shove toward the curtain. "Your family is about as far from the aristocracy as anyone can get! How dare you touch her!"

Mrs. Mulligan's eyes narrowed. She'd spent a few months living with Irene Dunnigan, and had experienced enough of her rants to last for awhile. "Come along, Colin. You and Sadie come over to our place. Lunch is on us!"

"Yes, lunch is on Mrs. Mulligan!" Mrs. Fig added enthusiastically, hearing in the invitation a chance to escape the war zone.

Belle turned back and glanced from one face to the next. Aunt Irene's was beet‑red with fury. Uncle Wilfred was doing his best to not laugh or give his wife a good tongue‑lashing, she wasn't sure which. Sadie's eyes were narrowed, her jaw tight. And Colin Cooke ...

Colin Cooke stood, his eyes fixed on Aunt Irene as if they were steel bayonets. Gone was the bright, mischievous twinkle, banished the second the woman had laid a hand on Belle. Was he afraid her aunt would inadvertently hurt her? Or ...

Sadie reached into her reticule, pulling out a list and a handful of cash. "I'd like to make a few purchases before I leave," she said sharply, slapping the money onto the nearest surface.

Aunt Irene's eyes riveted on the cash and she froze. Her upper lip twitched once, twice. Everyone stood and waited to see what she would do next. Even Colin's hardened expression turned to curiosity as they all watched her battle with indecision.

"Here is the list of things I need." Sadie added, holding a piece of paper out to no one in particular.

Belle saw the opportunity and took it. She picked the list from Sadie's hand and, squaring her shoulders, marched behind the counter to fill it. Sadie followed, along with Mrs. Mulligan and Mrs. Fig.

Belle watched Colin, hat still in hand, smiling at her. She smiled shyly back and felt herself blush, then quickly turned her attention to the list. "Thread ... what color?"

"Two spools of red, two of blue." Sadie quickly answered.

Belle turned and went to a cabinet behind the counter. She opened it, pulled out a flat wooden box full of thread, and brought it to Sadie so she could make her selections.

She kept stealing quick glances at Colin as she worked. He stood as before, smiling at her, his eyes again bright with mischief. Aunt Irene also stood, scowling at Colin. Uncle Wilfred watched with amusement, but did not abandon his post. She instinctively knew that if Aunt Irene started in again, he was ready to quell any outbursts. She could tell he'd had enough. Supper was going to be a very interesting time, she thought with a frown as she put away the thread.

Belle spent the next ten minutes putting together Sadie's order while Mrs. Mulligan and Mrs. Fig looked on. Aunt Irene never once took her eyes off Colin, and Belle began to dread the moment when he and the rest of the women would leave. His presence was so ... *strong*. Solid. A strange sensation, especially from a man she'd just met, but there it was. She wasn't sure she could stand to be parted from it. She also sensed his concern for her, and it was comforting.

On the other hand, she imagined that Colin Cooke would be a force to be reckoned with if truly riled — there was that sort of firmness to him. Not something that would lead to meanness – more like a survival tactic.

Then she suddenly remembered something Aunt Irene had said. *Two of the Cooke boys just got out of prison, and two more just went in ...*

Belle choked back a gasp. Colin Cooke must have been in prison! How horrible! But why had he been there? She spun to face him, not caring if her action brought attention to herself, and stared.

His face softened into a pleasant smile as his eyes fixed on her with a look meant to connect them, fuse them together. How he was able to do it, she couldn't begin to understand, but he succeeded. Her eyes were glued to his, and she stood frozen to the spot behind the counter. The warm-blanket sensation came over her again, and something deep inside her melted and ran like so much candle wax. Her breathing slowed, as if he controlled it, and her body relaxed.

The man was utterly, and completely intoxicating ...

"Miss Dunnigan, did you hear me?"

"Oh!" Belle had to blink a few times to break the spell Colin Cooke had so easily conjured. She wasn't even sure who had spoken. "What did you say?"

Sadie smiled, glanced at Colin, then back to Belle. "Can you come to the ranch at one o'clock on Thursday? We'll have our sewing circle then."

Belle tried to read the expression on her aunt's face, but it was still aimed at Colin. If Uncle Wilfred hadn't been standing there, she was sure Aunt Irene would have launched into another tirade. But thankfully, she seethed in silence. Perhaps he knew she'd crossed the line with her husband. She certainly had with Mrs. Mulligan, and everyone else in the store ... perhaps even with the men outside, too frightened at this point to enter. "Oh, yes. Of course. I would love to join you."

"You can drive out with Mrs. Fig and me." Mrs. Mulligan offered.

"Why, thank you," Belle replied, trying without success to keep her gaze from drifting back to Colin. "Thank you very much. I'm looking forward to it."

"As am I," Aunt Irene added, though she certainly didn't sound excited. More like she'd had her jaw wired shut. "Pick us up at noon. We'll all drive out together."

Belle thought she saw Colin stiffen at the remark, but wasn't sure. His smile hadn't diminished in the slightest. But his eyes had changed. They now held a look of warm affection, and it appeared he didn't care a whit who noticed.

Aunt Irene took a step forward. "And you," she hissed as she looked up at Colin. "You had better not—"

"Irene." Uncle Wilfred didn't raise his voice, didn't make a threat, didn't move an inch. But his tone was such that it chopped off Irene's conversation sharper than her hatchet could've. "I think you need to see about something in the back."

Without another word, Aunt Irene headed toward the back room. But just before she left, she looked over her shoulder and glared at Colin Cooke. The message was clear: *this is NOT over!*

Sadie paid for her items, and the quartet left, Colin giving Belle one last smile as he departed. Once the door closed behind them, Belle's shoulders slumped. Yes, supper was going to be difficult indeed ...

# FIVE

As luck would have it, on the day of the sewing circle, Mrs. Dunnigan came down with a sudden and terrible case of indigestion. Later, the townsfolk of Clear Creek would argue as to whether it was divine intervention, or that Mr. Dunnigan had made breakfast that morning and slipped his wife a good dose of Professor Pomodori's miracle elixir. As evidence for the latter theory, the good Professor had been run out of town back in March for peddling the nasty stuff.

Either way, Colin couldn't believe it when he saw the Mulligans' wagon pull up to the front of the house with only Mrs. Mulligan, Mrs. Fig, and his angel aboard.

From his position in the hayloft of the barn, he was able to hear Belle's laughter as Sadie came out of the house to greet them. Mrs. Mulligan and Mrs. Fig dominated what conversation there was (their mouths were in constant motion) while his angel climbed down from the wagon. He itched to be there to help her, to feel her small hands in his, her small waist as he lifted her from the wagon and gently placed her on the ground ...

He smiled. Why settle for simply letting her feet touch the ground when one could just as easily carry her to the porch? Or better still, into the house!

"See something interesting, dear brother?"

Colin nearly jumped out of his skin. Had Duncan not been born in England, he would swear his brother was part Red Indian – he could sneak up on anyone without making a sound. "Do you *have* to do that? It's fortunate I didn't turn and strike you!"

"Or more likely, fall from the loft." Duncan said casually and smiled. He watched the chattering women make their way into the house. "My, she is pretty. At least from what I can see at this distance. Perhaps I should find an excuse to go have a closer look?"

"Don't you dare! Mrs. Dunnigan already wants to burn me at the stake. I certainly don't need your help to hasten the deed."

Duncan grinned and continued to watch as the front door closed. He turned to Colin. "Surely you can think of a reason to have to go into the house? You do live there, after all."

"As do you, but I don't see you concocting a way in."

"*I* don't have a reason to."

Colin relaxed. The thought of Duncan and himself coming to blows over Belle had crossed his mind, but now he knew his brother wouldn't challenge him. And of the three, Duncan was the one blessed with the most striking looks. He could have any woman he wanted in the blink of an eye, and his brothers knew it. Thankfully, it didn't seem as if Duncan did.

"What are you two doing up here?" Harrison asked as he climbed the ladder to the hayloft. "I thought we were going to check on the stock near the creek."

"Colin needs to go into the house for a while."

"Whatever for?" Harrison asked. "We've already had lunch. Let's go."

"Your wife has guests." Duncan stated.

"Yes, I know. Sadie's very excited to be able to entertain. You'd think she was hosting her first cotillion."

"Only one of the Dunnigan women could make it," Colin said as he gazed longingly at the house.

Harrison raised a curious brow, and looked to Duncan. "Ah, I see. And I suppose it's *Miss* Dunnigan my wife is entertaining today?"

"You suppose correctly," Duncan replied.

The sound of a wagon approaching drew their attention to the newcomers. With so few women in the area, it wasn't hard to figure out who was coming. Sure enough, Grandma Waller guided her wagon alongside Mrs. Mulligan's. She had Mabel Turner and Lucy White with her. That meant they were hosting every grown woman in the immediate area except Mrs. Dunnigan and Mrs. Van Cleet. And perhaps either or both of them would be along later.

To Harrison and Duncan, this meant a call to action. As if reading each other's thoughts, they looked at one another and smiled conspiratorially. "I daresay, Colin, but I do believe you need to go into the house," Harrison stated rather matter-of-factly.

Colin eyed him suspiciously. "Just as I told Duncan earlier, I haven't a good reason to go in. And should I do so, I've no doubt that dear Mrs. Fig wouldn't hesitate to tell Mrs. Dunnigan. There's always one gossip in the bunch." In this one, he thought to himself, there might be several.

"I agree with Harrison," Duncan said, taking a step or two back and cracking his knuckles. "You really should go into the house and have yourself tended to." He grinned devilishly at Harrison.

Colin stiffened. *Uh-oh ...*

"I completely agree," Harrison deadpanned. "You *must* have Sadie take care of that."

Colin knew he shouldn't ask but ... "Take care of ... what?"

Duncan pulled back his arm and let him have it.

Colin was right. He shouldn't have asked.

"Oh, how exciting! And everything is so pretty!" Mrs. Fig exclaimed with a little clap of her hands.

The women were seated around the dining room table. Sadie had made gingerbread cookies along with a pot of tea. "The tea set belonged to Harrison's mother. She brought it all the way from England, and he wanted me use it," she said as she served.

"It's all so lovely," Belle agreed and admired the pretty chintz design. She almost felt like she was back in Boston, as if this corner of the Oregon Territory had been transformed into a society matron's parlor near Coolidge Corner or Harvard Square.

"Isn't it? I've never seen anything like it," Sadie said as she poured herself a cup and sat down.

Mrs. Mulligan took that as her cue to begin. "As this is our first time together, let's introduce ourselves," she stated in her Irish brogue.

"Introduce ourselves? We all know each other," Grandma chided.

"Not everyone is acquainted with Miss Dunnigan," Mrs. Mulligan reminded her.

Grandma subsided, and turned to Lucy White. "Tell the woman 'howdy' so we can start."

Belle watched Lucy. She seemed a bit shy, looking more at her hands folded in her lap than the ladies seated around the table. Sadie had mentioned before the others arrived that Lucy didn't leave her farm very often.

Finally she looked at Belle and smiled. "Howdy. I ... I like your dress."

Belle unconsciously touched the lace trim of her flowered dress and returned her smile. "Why, thank you. It's nice to meet you."

Lucy bowed her head, took her hands out of her lap and placed them on the table. Her own dress was her only one, and was patched in several places. Sadie had also shared with Belle that she wanted to have the sewing circle make a new dress for Lucy. Belle agreed whole-heartedly, especially now. She saw the look of longing in Lucy's eyes when she first spied her own outfit. The problem was that, according to Sadie, Mr. White was proud and refused all charity. The ladies would have to think of a way to give the dress to Lucy without making it look like pity.

"Sadie, I simply adore what you've done here!" Mrs. Fig said. She took a quick sip of her tea. "Ooh, that's hot!"

"I think you should let it cool a bit," Sadie suggested.

Grandma studied her teacup. "Sure is fancy. Almost afraid to drink out of it. Makes me feel like a queen. Do we dip our cookies in it?"

Sadie laughed. "You can do whatever you like. This isn't a formal tea. I wouldn't know the first thing about one of those. Go ahead, everyone, enjoy. Mrs. Mulligan, I have a suggestion for something to make."

Mrs. Mulligan had taken up her teacup and was blowing on it. "Oh? What did you have in mind?"

Sadie made sure not to glance in Lucy's direction. "I'd like to make a dress. But I'm not a very good seamstress."

"I can help you," Belle volunteered. "I've made several dresses."

Lucy looked up. "Did you make that one?"

Belle again fingered the delicate lace trim. "No. A dressmaker made this for me. But I've sewn others myself."

Lucy sat up suddenly. "It was made *for* you?"

Belle took in the ladies seated around the table. Their eyes were wide as they studied her clothes with interest. In their world, only rich women enjoyed the luxury of a dressmaker. Sadie, as the daughter of a wealthy cattle baron, probably had experience with dressmakers while growing up. Out here in the Oregon territory, however, they were few and far between.

"So our first suggestion is for a dress," Mrs. Mulligan announced. "Belle, why don't you and Sadie work on that? The rest of us can start something for the new preacher – we have a month before he arrives. What do you think?"

"I think these cookies are the best I've ever had!" Grandma said as she happily dipped one into her cup.

"Grandma!" Mrs. Fig said, aghast.

Mabel Turner, who'd been quiet all this time, finally spoke. "Sadie said we could do whatever we wanted. None of us knows about this sort of thing. What does it matter, anyhow?"

"It don't seem proper to dip," Mrs. Fig protested.

"Tarnation, Fanny Fig, it's just a cookie! Who cares if I dip, or not?" Grandma retorted.

Sadie shook with silent laughter and glanced at Belle.

Belle also just managed to stifle her giggles. The ladies of Clear Creek were a far cry from those of Boston, and she found their antics and country ways refreshing. The constraints of Boston's "Brahmin" society could be stifling at times, and she was glad to be away from the snobbery of the women there.

Granted, not all of Boston society women were snobbish – but most of her mother's friends were. After she died, they deemed it their duty to see Belle "married well," and took it upon themselves to get the job done. But she would have none of it and was soon seen as an ungrateful girl who, without their help, would wind up a spinster. Between such motherly matrons and her father's slipping sanity, she'd began to turn down more and more invitations, and was in danger of becoming a recluse.

"I vote we make a quilt for the new preacher to welcome him," Mrs. Mulligan said. She looked to Mrs.

Fig, dipped her half-eaten cookie into her teacup, and took a generous bite.

Mrs. Fig frowned.

Belle could stand it no longer. She began to giggle.

"Land sakes, child, what's so funny?" Grandma asked.

"I'm sorry. I hope I'm not being rude. It's just that ... this is the most fun I've had since my arrival. I'm so glad you invited me."

Sadie again smiled. "You're welcome. There are so few women nearby. In fact, the only two not here are your aunt and Mrs. Van Cleet. She and her husband have gone to Oregon City."

"Gonna start work on the new hotel soon." Grandma said and reached for another cookie. "Gone to get supplies and hire some workers. Be a grand sight once it's built!"

"I think we should hold a dance when it's done," Mrs. Fig suggested, now seemingly over her consternation in regard to cookie-dipping.

Several of the ladies were about to comment when they heard a ruckus in the foyer – the sound of boot-clad feet and an odd scraping noise coming through the front door. Sadie sat up to see what was amiss.

Duncan and Harrison entered, Colin supported between them. Colin had one of the worst black eyes any of them had ever seen. Much of his face was red and puffy. Bits of straw hung from his hair and clothes, and blood oozed from a gash on the right side of his forehead.

Belle stood without thinking. She froze, realizing what she'd done, but couldn't help it. The sight of an injured Colin Cooke had cut her to the quick.

Naturally, everyone looked at Colin, then Belle, and back again.

"What happened?" Sadie asked as she got up and went to the men, causing everyone's attention to refocus.

Duncan and Harrison exchanged a quick look. Finally Duncan said, "Colin had a ... bit of an ... accident."

"Accident?" Sadie exclaimed. "What sort of accident? Good Lord, is he conscious?"

Colin raised his head. The action looked like it pained him greatly.

Belle cringed, gasped, and rushed to Sadie's side. The rest of the ladies just gawked at the sight.

Finally Grandma sprung into action. "Bring him into the kitchen, quick-like." She turned to Belle and Sadie. "You two, come with me. The rest of you, decide on what sort of quilt you want to make for the new preacher. We'll take care of Colin!"

Belle could almost swear she saw the other two Cooke brothers smile as they dragged their load into the kitchen where they deposited him at the kitchen table. "Well," Harrison said, "we have work to do. If you would be so kind as to patch him up and send him out to the lower pastures by the creek, we'd be forever grateful."

Colin snarled at him.

"Unless, of course, you think he's unfit, and needs to rest here in the house awhile," Duncan added.

Colin reached up to his forehead and winced when he touched the gash. "Ow-w-w ..."

"What happened?" Sadie demanded.

Duncan and Harrison again exchanged glances. "He fell out of the hayloft," Harrison stated. "Not the first time. But on previous occasions, he didn't try to break his fall with his face ..."

"What?" Grandma said as she pulled a dishrag from a peg. "Sadie, put some water on this and deal with that cut. Harrison – Doc keeps a bag under the seat. Get it." Harrison hurried from the room, and she turned to Duncan. "You go fetch my husband."

Duncan quickly glanced at Colin. "That hardly seems necessary. He should be fine."

"Fine?!" Belle hated the sound of panic in her voice. "He fell out of a hayloft and you think he'll be fine?"

"Of course," Duncan stated calmly. "After all, the wagon broke his fall. Left a terrible dent in the bed, though – we'll have to brace it up, I should think."

Belle, appalled, quickly went to Colin and sat in the chair next to him. She took in the sight of one of his hands and noticed how red his knuckles were. "Oh, you poor thing! What a horrible fall it must have been! Maybe we ought to take him to see the doctor anyway?"

A lopsided, if painful, grin had formed on Colin's face as Belle continued to examine his wounds.

"Poppycock," Duncan retorted. "He's had a half-dozen tumbles worse than this."

Grandma's eyes narrowed. "Fell out, or was pushed out?" she whispered to him.

Duncan immediately took on an air of affront. "Are you suggesting that one of us would push our own brother out of the hayloft?" he whispered back.

Grandma continued to glare.

"He fell of his own accord. We had nothing to do with it. If only he hadn't landed ... face first, thus the black eye. And the um ... gash." Duncan shook his head in pity.

Grandma grimaced as she pictured Colin hitting the wagon bed with his face. She leaned toward Duncan. "You might want to take care of your hand, or the bruises on your knuckles are gonna show. Just what were you boys doing up there, pretending you were Old Smoke Morrissey?"

The reference to the reigning bare-knuckle boxing champion made Duncan smile. He glanced at his own reddened knuckles and looked sheepishly at Grandma.

"The lengths you boys go to ...," she hissed, rolling her eyes.

Duncan gave her a smile and a wink, then nodded toward the table. Belle was holding Colin's completely uninjured hand. The two gazed at each other with curious wonder. One might get the impression Colin was feeling no pain whatsoever – his facial expression was euphoric.

Grandma sighed in resignation as Sadie came back into the kitchen with the wet cloth. Grandma took it from her and went to Colin.

Belle let go of his hand. "Will he be all right?"

"Oh, he'll live, I can guarantee that," Grandma said flatly and placed the cloth on his hand.

Harrison returned and set Doc's bag on the table. Grandma opened it and began to dig through the contents. She pulled out a few bottles, set them on the table, followed them with some small pieces of white cloth, then opened one of the bottles.

Colin finally tore his gaze from Belle and noticed what she was doing. He looked up to Grandma, his eyes harboring a hint of worry. "What, may I ask, is that?"

Grandma smiled. "Something that'll fix you right up." She poured out some of the contents onto a piece of cloth. "Miss Dunnigan, would you hold this to the cut on his forehead for me, please?"

Belle nodded and took the cloth from her, then gently reached out toward Colin, who once again had a contented smile on his face.

Grandma turned back to the bag. "It might ...

"OWWW!"

Grandma smiled in satisfaction. "... sting a little."

"Oh, I'm so sorry!" Belle exclaimed.

"Now, child, just keep holding that cloth against that nasty gash. It'll clean it. Then use it to clean the rest of his face."

Colin's eyes began to water as he sat stiffly and did his best not to cry out again.

"Alcohol works best on a wound like that," Grandma said triumphantly.

Harrison and Duncan both hid their mouths behind their hands. Belle was so wrapped up in tending Colin she didn't notice. Colin noticed, though, and sent them a venomous look.

Sadie, finally wising up to what was going on, placed her hands on her hips and glared at her husband. She crossed to the other side of the kitchen and grabbed a broom from the corner. "I thought you two had work to do?"

Harrison straightened, his face full of mirth. "I dare say, wife, what are you planning to do with that broom?"

Sadie raised up the broom as if it was her turn in a cricket match. "Get out, you scoundrels, or you'll find out!"

Duncan immediately ducked out, but Harrison wasn't quick enough. Sadie caught him a good one in the backside as she chased him out the back door.

Belle sat in horror, watching the whole scene but not quite comprehending it. She was more concerned with the patient – a patient who looked very angry, but was trying not to make a fool of himself in front of her. "I'm sorry if it hurts."

His gaze suddenly softened. "No need to worry. I'm sure it looks much worse than it is."

Grandma poured some clear liquid out of another bottle onto a cloth and handed it to him. "Hold this over your eye. It will help it a little."

"What is it?"

"Witch hazel. Now do as I say."

He obeyed and cautiously held the dampened cloth against his eye. It did feel good, though not as nice as Belle's ministrations as she continued to clean him up. He sighed in contentment.

Belle smiled at the sound.

Grandma turned to Sadie. "Best you go back and see to your guests. I'll stay here with these two."

Sadie tried not to laugh as she glanced quickly at Belle and Colin, then back to Grandma. "I'll do that." She then left to allow Colin a chance to court Miss Dunnigan, albeit at the cost of a black eye and a head gash. The Cooke men would do anything to help one of their own win the heart of a woman ... but she wished that in this instance, they'd done a bit less.

# SIX

Belle sat, her eyes locked with Colin's – both his healthy one and the one almost swollen shut. She found it next to impossible to look away. She was conscious that Grandma Waller had turned her back to them on purpose and only pretended to fuss near the enormous cook stove on the other side of the kitchen, but her real intention was to let the two of them be.

Belle decided to take advantage and returned her thoughts to Colin.

As if sensing her full attention again, he adjusted the damp cloth over his blackened eye and smiled.

Belle's insides fluttered. She knew he had to be in horrible pain, but he hid it well. Suddenly feeling shy, she took the cloth she held and dabbed at his cut again.

He stopped her by taking her hand in his.

She sucked in a breath, swallowed. None of the young men in Boston had ever affected her like this, not even the well-bred, high-achieving young gentlemen from Harvard and the other colleges.

"Thank you for you kind attention," he whispered.

Belle stopped breathing altogether, and nodded as a chill went up her spine. All she could do was sit and stare at him. Even in his current unfortunate condition, he was still handsome in a rugged, black-and-blue sort of way.

"Well, Colin, you feeling up to getting back to work?" Grandma asked as she came to the table.

He let go of Belle's hand, clearly disappointed, and turned stiffly in his chair. "Give me a moment more – I'll be right as rain."

"Mmmm-hm." Grandma's voice was suspicious. "I bet a few gingerbread cookies and a cup of tea will speed things along."

Belle swore the man's smile could melt not only butter, but also Grandma Waller. He looked at the woman, tilted his head slightly to the side, and grinned his thanks.

"Just the tea and cookies, Colin. Then out you go," Grandma admonished as she left the room.

Colin turned back to Belle. "I thought she'd never leave."

Belle's eyes widened.

"Oh, don't worry. I'm not going to take the opportunity to ravish you while she's gone. I am first and foremost a gentleman."

Belle let loose a giggle.

"You don't think so?" he asked. The brow over his one good eye rose in question.

"I'm sorry. It's just that you look so ridiculously horrid, yet sound as though nothing has happened. You must hurt everywhere."

"I daresay I don't feel my usual self. But as my brother assured you, it's not the worst spill I've taken. I shall mend." He smiled at her.

Belle's mouth went dry, but the same blanket of contentment and peace that had covered her the day he came into the mercantile did so again.

"You have astoundingly beautiful eyes," he stated matter-of-factly.

"Oh ..."

"Am I being forward? I'm afraid I haven't exercised my manners very well. It's been some time since I've used them in the presence of a lady. Other than my sister-in-law, naturally ..."

She wondered if he was referring to his time spent in prison or his time spent in the Oregon Territory, or both. "I assure you, your manners are the best of any gentleman I've had the pleasure of meeting since my arrival, with the possible exception of your brothers."

"Ah, my brothers," he chuckled and gingerly dabbed the cloth over his black eye a few times. "Yes, they've been out in polite society a time or two. Especially Duncan, as he's the oldest.

"How old is he?"

"Thirty, believe it or not, as of the end of next month. July 31st, on the dot."

"And when is yours?" she asked shyly, suddenly feeling very much alone with him. The mere fact that she was *indeed alone* with him, made her feel almost scandalous.

"October 7th. Harrison's is in December, the 25th. A Christmas present from our mother."

"I don't think I would want my birthday on ... on Christmas," she stammered. He had taken her hand again, and heat radiated from it.

"Truly?" he questioned. "I believe he does receive twice the amount of gifts. But there may be drawbacks as well – I'd have to ask him ..." His thumb slowly made its way across the back of her hand.

She was shocked that his touch was affecting her so dramatically. She closed her eyes a moment. "I ... I would think it better to receive birthday wishes ... and gifts apart from ... the Christmas holiday." Egads, was she starting to pant? She felt a furious blush creep into her cheeks.

He smiled and squeezed her hand. Then he sat back in his chair, broke the contact and glanced at the door leading from the kitchen to the rest of the house. "What do you suppose is keeping Grandma?"

She followed his gaze. "I ... I really don't know what's keeping her," she said nervously.

He took his other hand from his face and dropped the cloth on the table.

His eye looked awful, and she cringed. "Oh my ..."

"Is it so horrible?"

"I'm afraid so."

He pursed his lips. "Perhaps I should wear an eye patch. Do you think I'd look dashing, or more like a villainous pirate?"

His joke broke the tension. She smiled despite herself. "A pirate, for sure."

He laughed. The sound was wonderfully deep and masculine. "But I've no ship. How can I ever hope to pillage and plunder without a ship?"

She smiled. "I'm quite sure you'd find a way." And if she didn't get out of the kitchen fast, Belle feared he would surely plunder her heart. If he hadn't already ...

On Saturday, two days since the first meeting of the ladies' sewing circle, Sadie planned to visit the mercantile in the afternoon so she and Belle could choose the fabric for the dress they were to make. The other ladies had already begun working on the squares for the new preacher's welcoming gift.

To have a full time preacher in town was a milestone for the little community, and the ladies wanted to make the gift special. Up until now, all they had was a Methodist "circuit rider" who came to town once every two months. Mrs. Mulligan had told Belle how Harrison and Sadie had to wait for his visit in order to get married. But it had given Harrison time to take care of getting pardons for his brothers (with substantial help from Horatio Jones, Sadie's father) and see that the outlaws responsible for Sadie's abductions – yes, plural! – were put behind bars. Too bad said outlaws had turned out to be Harrison's own stepbrothers.

Belle found Sadie's adventures wonderfully exciting and romantic. Fought for and rescued by Harrison, who then asked Sadie's father for her hand in marriage. And then to be wed out on the prairie, just as the first spring wildflowers began to poke through ... Belle sighed. It was like a Thomas Hardy novel. If only such things would happen to her ...

The bell above the door tinkled and Sadie entered. "Hello! Have you picked out any fabric yet?"

Belle stepped from behind the counter and went to one of the display tables. "I found three I think Lucy might like. This pink would look beautiful on her."

Sadie looked at the pink calico fabric and frowned. "It is very pretty ... but it wouldn't hold up to the type of work Lucy does on her farm."

"Oh ... that didn't occur to me. I guess I'm not used to thinking of the women here as farmers' and ranchers' wives. Clear Creek is certainly not Boston."

"That's all right. You'll get used to it. I hope you don't miss Boston too much, though. I know I sometimes miss El Paso."

Belle nodded and smiled. "What if we make her two dresses? She'll need one for church and the other can be a work dress."

"That's a great idea! I'll gladly cover the cost of the extra dress."

"Why don't you take care of one, and I the other?"

"Are you sure?"

"I do have a little money. Though not as much as people think."

"What do you mean?"

Belle sighed. "Aunt Irene seems to be under the impression that I have a small fortune at my disposal. But my father ..." She shook her head

Sadie held up a hand to stop her. "I'm sorry. I shouldn't have asked. You don't have to tell me."

"It's all right. Unfortunately, my father gambled away most of it a couple of years before he died. I had to sell most everything to pay off his debts before I could even come west."

Sadie's face fell. "I'm so terribly sorry. Are you sure your aunt doesn't know?"

"I'm positive – and neither does Uncle Wilfred. Without a proper dowry, how am I to find a husband?"

Sadie laughed. "I wouldn't worry about that around here. I'd be more worried about your aunt finding out about the money. But I'm sure you mean more to her than your father's bank accounts."

Belle wondered. After watching Aunt Irene interact with the townsfolk and seeing her attitude toward legal tender, or the lack thereof, she would almost bet which was more important. But she supposed she would have to tell her – and better sooner than later. "I also think this blue would be nice on Lucy."

Sadie examined the fabric. "I agree – I like it better than the pink. Now, let's find something more suitable for every day. I don't suppose you have any denim in stock?"

They did, and after going through every bolt of cloth agreed on some denim for a skirt, and sturdy brown wool for a work dress. Before they knew it, they had enough material for a Sunday dress, a work dress, a work skirt and two linen blouses. It felt good to be doing something for the shy woman.

Belle wanted to get started immediately. "But how are we ever going to give these things to Lucy without her – or her husband – looking on it as charity?"

"I don't see anything wrong with a little charity, and I'm a horrible seamstress. I'm sure Lucy would be happy to be part of my training. Perhaps I can tell her I'm *her* charity, because I need the practice!"

Belle laughed. "I'm not sure how I'll be as your teacher, but I'll do my best. We can make the dresses first. That way we'll have the Sunday dress done in time for the first church service."

Sadie sighed. "That's a good idea."

"What's wrong?"

Sadie bit her lip before she spoke. "Ask me."

"Ask you what?"

"How Colin is."

Belle felt herself blush head-to-toe. She'd tried hard the last two days *not* to think about him, and failed miserably. The mere mention of him sent her insides into a tailspin. All she could do was smile and shrug.

"He's fine, except for his eye." Then Sadie grinned puckishly. "Also, he's right outside."

Unable to stop herself, Belle's hands flew to her mouth as she gasped and looked to the door.

Sadie stifled a laugh. "Where is your aunt, by the way?" she whispered.

Belle pointed to the ceiling. "Preparing lunch."

Sadie smiled, put a finger to her own lips, and stealthily went to open the door. Belle quickly smoothed the skirt of her dress, pinched her cheeks a few times, and then fled behind the front counter.

She'd just come to a skidding stop when Colin entered. "Miss Dunnigan. How lovely you look."

Her hands flew to her mouth again. *He* looked positively awful! Half his face was green and purple, his black eye was still half-swollen shut, and the gash on his forehead had scabbed over. The other half, though, was back to normal, the skin healthy and already tanned from the early summer sun. But in her shock, she blurted the first thing to come to mind. "Where's your eye patch?"

He burst out laughing.

Sadie, who had just returned to the bolts of cloth they'd chosen, waved at him to be quiet, lest he alert Mrs. Dunnigan upstairs. Belle did her best not to join his laughter, but it was an effort. It was their private joke, something only the two of them shared. That in itself made her feel like she carried a bit of buried treasure.

Colin quickly suppressed his laughter, but not his smile. "I'm afraid if I sported an eye patch I'd be run out of town. Pirates, even the most dashing ones, are not tolerated in Clear Creek. So I must instead don this disguise to hide my true identity. Tell me, is it working?"

Sadie watched Belle's face turn purple with the effort to not start guffawing. She shook her head as she carried the bolt of linen to the counter and began to measure how much she'd need.

"I daresay, but the sea is unusually calm this afternoon." Colin glanced around the mercantile, then pointedly looked up at the ceiling.

"Well, storms can come up out of nowhere," Belle said, her restraint audible. "I suggest you be ready to batten down the hatches should the need arise."

Colin sauntered up to the counter and stood next to Sadie. He tipped his hat. "I wholeheartedly agree. A squall can blow in at any time." He again glanced at the ceiling.

"But not until after lunch," Belle assured him. If there was one thing Aunt Irene loved more than money, it was food.

"Ah. Glad to hear it."

"May I get something for you?"

Colin glanced behind her as Sadie went to get the other bolts of cloth. He leaned over the counter and suddenly looked into her eyes. "I think I should like some candy," he said in a whisper. "Cinnamon, if you please."

How did he *do* that? She'd been captured again by his gaze – and with only one eye, no less! She nodded, breathless, and turned to get what he wanted.

Or ... was *she* what he really wanted? But if he found out about her current state of near-destitution, would he consider her as a serious prospect for marriage? He was an Englishman, after all – didn't Englishmen expect wives to come with dowries?

It was easy for Sadie to discount it – she'd had a rather large one. Belle had been an heiress, yes, but most of what she'd inherited were debts. Gone were the days of trips to the dressmaker, the jeweler, and weeks spent in New York and Philadelphia. Gone were the parties and balls, the operas and soirees. And likely, she feared, gone was the marriage to a suitable husband of means.

Belle turned back to Colin – and was held by his eyes once more! She swallowed hard. This certainly wasn't Boston – but no man in Boston had ever given her anything like the look this man did. It was astoundingly comforting, seductive, *decisive*.

Perhaps she needn't worry so much about the lack of a proper dowry ...

However, there was something else she needed to worry about. "Colin Cooke! What are you doing in my store?" Aunt Irene bellowed as she charged through the curtained doorway.

He smiled and winked at her with his one good eye. "Buying my favorite candy, of course."

"Great jumpin' Jehoshaphat, what happened to you? Have you been brawling like that no-good stepfather of yours?"

Colin immediately straightened. "Jefferson's been brawling?"

"Two nights ago. Don't you know what your stepfather does nowadays? Despicable, it is! He's nothing but a drunkard! I've no doubt you'll follow in his footsteps, and it looks like I'm right!"

"How do you know this?" Sadie asked as she joined Colin.

"Know it? I saw it with my own eyes! The ruckus he was making woke me up!"

"So that's why we haven't seen much of him lately," Sadie whispered to Colin. "He didn't want to see any of us, wanted his meals left on his porch ... I thought he might be sick, but ..."

"He did the same to me some days ago," Colin quietly replied. He began to absently rub his chin with one hand. "Mrs. Dunnigan, has my stepfather come to town before this?"

"Yes. Five days ago. I saw him go into Mulligan's. Mark my words, you'll find him dead in a ditch one of these days – and good riddance, too!"

"Aunt Irene!" Belle objected. She didn't know Colin's stepfather, but wishing someone a drunkard's death hardly struck her as a proper attitude, regardless of the person's shortcomings.

"Your uncharitable opinions are duly noted, Mrs. Dunnigan," Colin calmly, if coldly, told her. "But in the future, you would be wise to keep them to yourself. Belle, I would like one dozen pieces of cinnamon candy. Sadie, make your purchases – we should be getting back to the ranch."

"I'm sorry, Belle," Sadie began as she unfolded a bolt of cloth. "It looks like we'll have to start on this later."

"Quite all right. Go home and see to your father-in-law."

Surprisingly, Aunt Irene did keep her mouth shut for the moment. But Belle was just as surprised that she hadn't a clue about Colin's injuries. Mrs. Fig must not have come to town since their meeting at Sadie's house. That would also explain why Belle hadn't been subject to one of Aunt Irene's tirades. She unconsciously sighed in relief.

"Mrs. Dunnigan," Sadie asked. "I was wondering if Belle could come to the ranch in a day or two. We want to get started on some dresses, and there's more room to work at my home."

Mrs. Dunnigan glared at Colin. "Will *he* be there?" Her face was set like a battering ram.

Sadie took a breath and looked as if she was counting to ten before speaking. "I don't see that it matters – but as we'll be sewing, I somehow doubt it. Colin is a worse seamstress than I am." She reached into her reticule, pulled out some money and handed it to Belle.

Belle quickly took it, counted out the amount needed, handed Sadie the change and looked expectantly back toward Aunt Irene.

"Well, I suppose it's all right ... so long as Belle doesn't have to suffer the company of the likes of him!"

Now Belle *knew* Sadie was counting, if only because she was doing the same! Her aunt was infuriating! It was time to have a talk with her.

Colin, silent all this time, took his bag of candy, tucked it into his shirt pocket and gathered up the folded pieces of fabric.

"Do you want me to wrap that?" Belle asked softly.

He gave her a warm smile. "No need – I have something in the wagon I can put it in. But thank you." He winked with his one good eye, gave a single nod, and turned to leave.

"Come to the house in the morning if you can," Sadie told Belle. "Or do you need me to come fetch you?"

Aunt Irene sniffed. "If she's going out to your ranch, Wilfred won't have time to run her out. Come get her if you want her."

Sadie's jaw tightened. "I'll do that. Expect me tomorrow at ten." She forced a smile and left.

As soon as the door closed, Aunt Irene spun on Belle. "Mark my words, young lady, those Cookes will all come to a bad end! I'll tolerate this foolishness of yours for only so long before I've had enough!"

Belle's mouth fell open in shock. "Auntie! Why do you hate them so? What have they ever done to you?"

Aunt Irene's whole body began to shake, and her face turned so red that Belle feared the woman might be having a heart attack. Yet she did not answer, only stomped from the room and all the way up the stairs.

Belle was left standing behind the counter, still in shock. What could possibly have happened to turn Aunt Irene into such a venomous, hateful creature? She was almost afraid to find out.

# SEVEN

Sadie walked into the mercantile precisely at ten the next day, and Belle had never been so happy to see another human being. Or more specifically, another human being who didn't complain all night about everything under the sun.

Aunt Irene had been exceptionally cranky after Colin and Sadie left the day before. Even Uncle Wilfred had been forced to escape for a while, deciding to visit the sheriff at his office and do his whittling there. Belle couldn't blame him for his reaction, but the downside was that it had left her all alone to face the brunt of Aunt Irene's ire. With prayer, she was sure she'd manage over time to forgive him. Lots of prayer.

"I'm so glad you're here!" she told Sadie as she grabbed her shawl and bonnet.

"Why, what's wrong?"

"Belle!" a voice snapped from behind the curtain. "Are you leaving? Make sure you don't talk with any of those Cooke boys!"

Sadie grimaced and nodded. "I see."

Belle closed her eyes and absently rubbed her temple. "Yes, Auntie!" she shouted back, then whispered to Sadie, "please, let's get out of here."

"Yes, let's." Sadie took Belle by the elbow and steered her to the door.

Once outside, Belle relaxed in the relative silence. At least outside the mercantile, no one was shouting at her. "Thank you for inviting me over to work on Lucy's dresses. I don't think I could have spent another day with Aunt Irene."

Sadie led her down the steps of the mercantile to the street. "I understand. And I commend you – I don't think I would have lasted this long living in close quarters with her. I beg your pardon if that's wrong of me to say, but everyone here knows how difficult it is to be around her."

"No need to apologize – it's the truth," Belle said as they walked down the opposite side of the street. "I just wish I knew what to do about it. Where's your wagon?"

"It's at the livery stable. Duncan wanted to have Mr. Berg, the new blacksmith, check on something."

"There's a new blacksmith? What happened to the old one?"

"He left shortly before you arrived. He figured he'd make more money smithing in Oregon City. The new one came yesterday – *from* Oregon City, oddly enough. He's a friend of Mr. Van Cleet."

"Are the Van Cleets back already?"

Sadie shook her head. "Mr. Berg apparently came on ahead. The Van Cleets should be back next week. Mr. Berg says they have a surprise for everyone."

"A surprise? For the whole town?"

"Yes. I wonder what it is." She shrugged. "Probably to do with the hotel they plan to build." They reached the livery stable and stood to one side while Duncan spoke with the newly-arrived Mr. Berg.

Mr. Berg was a bear of a man – taller than Duncan, and Duncan was the largest of the Cooke brothers, a little over six feet. He had long blonde hair tied back with a leather thong, his jaw was covered in golden stubble and his blue eyes were piercing. He looked to be carved out of marble, solidly built and probably frightfully strong. A strange combination of handsome and scary - the last man anyone would want to pick a fight with.

He also spoke with an accent – Scandinavian or maybe Prussian, Belle thought. The Boston streets were a cacophony of accents these days, as wave after wave of immigrants arrived in the harbor from all over Europe, Ireland especially. She remembered the society matrons and their husbands bemoaning the "riffraff" coming into the area, but she'd loved listening to the musical voices of the newcomers. Besides, her ancestors had been immigrants to these shores too, once upon a time ...

"Ah, I see you ladies have finally laid eyes on the astounding Mr. Berg," Colin quipped as he walked up behind them.

Belle turned as her heart fluttered. "Astounding?"

"Yes. As in, it's astounding that Mr. Van Cleet convinced him to leave Oregon City and come set up shop here in Clear Creek."

"Did you find him?" Sadie asked, obviously not speaking of Mr. Berg.

"No. But I haven't checked the saloon yet," Colin said flatly as he went to join the other men.

Belle looked at Sadie. "Are you looking for someone?"

"Jefferson, their stepfather. Your aunt was right – he's been coming to town late at night and drinking. We're not sure if he came home last night and left again before any of us noticed, or just didn't come home at all."

"Oh, I'm sorry to hear that," Belle said. "It seems we both have family troubles."

Sadie put an arm through hers. "Yes, but at least we have family. There are so many who don't."

Belle sighed in agreement as Colin and Duncan spoke in low tones to Mr. Berg. Colin slowly approached the ladies, but Duncan tipped his hat to them, spun on his heel, and strode deeper into the stable.

"Are we ready to head back?" Colin asked.

"Yes. Where is Duncan going?" Sadie asked.

"To hopefully find out what our dear stepfather has been up to this last week – and bring him home." He didn't sound confident.

Sadie nodded sadly, and the three of them walked over to the wagon.

Colin helped them both up, and Sadie quickly scooted to the opposite end so Colin and Belle could sit next to each other. Belle saw it and blushed – Sadie was definitely playing matchmaker. She certainly hoped Colin didn't mind. She stole a glance in his direction as he clambered up, and saw his smile. No, he didn't seem to mind a bit.

He settled himself and looked at her ...

... and it happened again. Belle's eyes seemed to meld with Colin's, horrid black eye and all!

It was a tight fit for the three of them on the seat, so there was hardly any part of his right side that wasn't touching her left. She supposed Sadie had room to scoot over a little further on her end, yet she didn't. The heat radiating from his body seeped through her dress and into her bones. With the contact of such exquisite sweetness came the thought she might faint. She hoped neither of them noticed her blushing from being so close to him – and the impropriety of it. Part of her thought Sadie should be seated against him, not her ... but the rest of her never wanted this to end.

Maybe Colin was thinking the same thing. He turned the wagon and began to head home, but by way of the prairie rather than through town. It was a roundabout way to go, which meant it would avoid any chance of gossip should anyone see them seated as they were – but would also mean more time spent together side by side.

Within minutes, Clear Creek was behind them, and Colin steered the team onto the main road. With him so close, Belle found it difficult to breathe for the first mile. But she settled down the further from town they got, and she was able to relax and enjoy the ride.

"There's someplace I'd like to show Belle, if we have the time," Sadie said.

"Depends on what it is. We have a few spare moments, but not enough for a major detour. What did you wish to show her?"

"The big oak tree by the creek."

"Ah, yes – His Majesty."

Belle looked in confusion from one smiling face to the other. "His Majesty?"

"We found the tree shortly after settling here." Colin explained. "Our mother named it, God rest her soul."

"It must be a very large tree."

"An understatement," Colin chuckled.

After another mile they again left the road, and Colin steered the buckboard west. The gentle prairie roughened up, with trees dotting the landscape. They continued another half-mile before he brought the team to a stop, set the brake and jumped down.

Belle scooted to the end of the seat and stopped short. Colin's arms were outstretched to her, his eyes (even the black-and-blue one) full of anticipation. He smiled and motioned her to climb down. She did so, and when his hands came around her waist she thought she might swoon. Warm ... strong ... safe ... they encircled her and held her as if she was made of the most precious china, yet with the power of a giant.

*Oh, Lord, help me,* she thought to herself, *but I don't want him to ever let go!*

Alas, he did let go, if only to help Sadie down. But even though his hands were absent, she still felt them, in her soul if not on her skin. How, she didn't know, but there it was. Her knees were weak, and it took an effort of will not to faint. Instead, she moved to the horses and absently patted one on the neck, figuring if her legs gave way, she'd have something to lean on that wouldn't make her face flush. Again.

How could a man affect her this way? Was this normal, how it was *supposed* to be? She'd never had a chance to speak to her mother of such things before she died. Nor had she felt comfortable asking any of her mother's friends about it; it seemed too private a matter to discuss with them ...

"I can't wait for you to see this!" Sadie exclaimed.

She looked at Sadie – her own age, and newly married besides! Surely she could ask her! But she'd have to wait for a private moment – away from the sewing circle, the Cooke brothers, and especially Aunt Irene!

Colin smiled at Belle, and held out his arm. "It's a bit of a rough trail. Might I assist you?" he asked softly.

Belle watched Sadie head happily down the faint trail. The shoes she wore were more practical for such treks than the ones Belle wore. She'd have to take his arm if she didn't want to fall flat on her face. But could she stand to let go of him when the time came? She swallowed hard and slowly hooked her arm through his. He smiled warmly, settled her arm more securely and led her off.

The trail gently wound its way into a small canyon. Unless one knew the area, one would never know it was there. Trees became more abundant the further down they went, until finally Belle could hear water. *That must be the 'Clear Creek' the town is named after*, she mused. She also understood why they'd left the wagon up above – there was no way it could have made it so far down on so narrow a trail. It could be widened, she supposed, but it would take a lot of work – and the Oregon Territory wasn't exactly overrun with engineers.

They reached the bottom and the canyon floor flattened out into a pretty green meadow. Clear Creek ran to one side of it and near the water, where it pooled and became almost like glass, was the biggest oak Belle could have possibly imagined. "Oh ... it's beautiful!"

Colin sighed appreciatively. "It certainly is." He turned them around to look at the rest of the meadow. The grasses here were greener, probably due to the creek. Purple irises dotted the plain, foxglove sprouted along the creek bed, and wild daffodils grew around the base of the majestic oak.

"No wonder your mother dubbed it 'His Majesty'."

"He's a grand thing, isn't he?" Colin stated.

Sadie had already reached the tree and stood looking out over the creek. "Belle! Come look!"

Belle sensed Colin's reluctance to let go of her, and shared it. She waited for him to start toward Sadie, which he did – eventually.

"Heavens, look at that!" Belle exclaimed as they drew close. The natural pool formed beneath the tree's branches was gorgeous and deep. The water moved so slowly there, it looked almost still. A small beach had formed on their side of the pool. On the other side, Belle could see natural rock ledges just below the water's surface. "What an incredible place!"

"Best swimming hole around," Colin stated proudly. "When it's not too cold to use it. Another few weeks and the water will be perfect. For now, it's limited to wading."

"I can't wait to try it!" Sadie began. "We had a large pond near my father's house, but this is so much nicer."

"Can you swim?" Colin asked.

Belle felt disappointment sink into her stomach. "I'm afraid not. I never learned."

"Well, we can remedy that as soon as the water is a bit warmer."

Belle gasped. "Truly?"

"Truly. Nearly everyone knows how to swim out here in the wilderness. One never knows when it will come in handy."

Belle supposed he was right. It would be just one of many survival tools here in the West. And she was going to have to learn how to use those tools – the sooner the better.

"I have a wonderful idea," Sadie said. "Let's plan a picnic! We could come down and spend an afternoon. You'll come, won't you, Belle?"

"Of course – I think it's a wonderful idea! What a beautiful place!" The thought of a picnic with Colin and his family was exhilarating. The thought of what Aunt Irene would say about it ... wasn't. Her face once again fell. "Oh, dear ..."

Colin leaned down and whispered, "I know what you're thinking."

She looked at him, confused.

"And you needn't worry so. I'll take care of your aunt. She'll let you come."

Sadie heard that and turned, looking very dubious about his assertion. But Belle sighed against him before she could stop herself. Sadie shrugged, turned back toward the pool and smiled to herself as she picked up some stones and tried skipping them across the pool's surface.

Colin pulled Belle's arm out of his and turned her to face him, his hands now on her shoulders. He leaned down, looked into her eyes, and swallowed hard. "Were it not for the chaperonage of my dear sister-in-law, I should very much like to kiss you."

Belle sucked in her breath. She didn't know what to say, to think, to feel!

Colin gave her the warmest of smiles. "But considering her hands are full of rocks at the moment, I'd say it was better for both of us if I abstained."

His eyes positively sparkled when he talked. Belle smiled shyly as her own eyes darted to Sadie. She kept thinking she should be utterly scandalized by his forward behavior, but she wasn't in the slightest. And clearly neither was Sadie, who kept skipping stones, glancing their way each time she bent to pick another up from the ground. Surely she would have stopped them by now had they been acting inappropriately! But she hadn't.

Sadie trusted Colin. That spoke volumes to Belle – it meant she could trust him too. And Belle was sure Sadie would stop Colin cold if he crossed the line of propriety.

When she looked back at him his face had calmed, but his eyes roamed her features as if he were trying to memorize every last inch. They stood there for who knows how long – simply gazing at one another, taking each other in – before Sadie produced a loud whistle using a blade of grass between her fingers.

Colin smiled ruefully. "I believe our time is up."

Belle simply nodded, unable to speak. The heat from his hands felt as if it would burn right through her shawl and the sleeves of her dress, straight down to her shoulder bones.

"We have to go now," he whispered as he leaned a little closer.

Speech still eluded her as her eyes darted to his mouth.

One of his hands found her chin and he tilted her face up to his. "I dare say, but I do believe Sadie has run out of rocks," he said, barely audibly.

Belle's heart thundered in her chest so hard she thought it was going to explode. Every fiber of her being felt alive in his presence. She could feel him tilt her head back, his own lowering to hers to eliminate the distance between them. Oh, yes – Colin was going to kiss her! Her eyes naturally closed. What would it feel like? How long would it last? What would happen afterwards? *Dear Lord, please don't let me faint!*

*Thump!*

"OW! Egads!"

Belle's eyes sprang open. Colin still held her chin in one hand. His other was rubbing his right hip as he scowled in Sadie's direction.

Apparently their chaperone hadn't run out of rocks after all.

Duncan entered Mulligan's and waited for his eyes to adjust to the dim light. He'd been speaking with Mr. Berg about working at the Triple-C now and then until he and his brothers could hire on more help. Mr. Berg had readily agreed. Duncan paid him for adjusting a few things on the Triple-C's buckboard, took his horse, and went to Mulligan's, the one place he and Colin hadn't checked yet.

It probably should have been the first place they'd looked, given Jefferson Cooke's proclivities. But they'd hoped to find him at the mercantile getting reacquainted with Wilfred, or down at the sheriff's office playing checkers with either Sheriff Hughes or Henry Fig. Even a visit with Mrs. Dunnigan would have been preferable to what Duncan found him doing. Or, in this case, not doing. After all, it was pretty hard for a man to accomplish much of anything when he was passed out drunk in a corner.

Duncan sighed and shook his head. That's what he got for not assuming the worst, he thought as he went over to the slumped form propped in a chair; his body wedged upright by a table.

Mr. Mulligan stood behind the counter and watched him as Duncan crossed to the other side of the empty saloon. "He's been like that since the wee hours of the mornin','" he said in his Irish brogue. "I thought it best to leave him 'til one of ye boys came to fetch him home. Figured by now you'd realize he'd gone missin'."

"You figured correctly," Duncan sighed as he stared down at his slumbering stepfather. "How long has he been coming into town on his own?"

"Since last week. Been here most every night."

Duncan finally gave Mr. Mulligan his full attention. "Doing anything aside from drinking?"

"Been playin' a lot of cards with some men the past few nights. Strangers. I've not seen 'em in here before."

"Strangers? Did they say where they were from?"

"There's a wagon train holed up on the south trail. They likely belong to it. Should be pulling out this morning – they don't camp for more'n a few days." Wagon trains often crossed the prairie a mile or two southeast of town. They often stopped nearby to repair their wagons and rest before making the last leg of their journey to Oregon City.

"I don't suspect he'll be coming in to play cards tonight," Duncan said. "Where's his horse?"

"Tied out back. I fed him this mornin'."

"I appreciate it." Duncan reached into his pocket and tossed a coin to Mr. Mulligan. "For your time, and the feed." He bent down, pulled Jefferson out of the chair and slung him over one shoulder like a sack of grain.

Mr. Mulligan hurried from behind the counter and led Duncan down a wide hall to the back of the saloon. Sure enough, Jefferson's horse was tethered near the rear porch. "Be so kind as to fetch Romeo to me, will you?" Duncan asked.

"Right away," Mr. Mulligan said, and quickly complied.

Duncan loaded his stepfather onto his horse and waited for Mr. Mulligan. Once the other man arrived with Romeo, he took a rope he'd tied to Romeo's saddle and used it to secure Jefferson Cooke to his own, then gave Mr. Mulligan a curt nod of thanks and mounted.

"Duncan, it's none of me business ... but you know how me and the missus feel about ye boys." Mr. Mulligan unwound the reins of Jefferson's horse from a hitching post and handed them to Duncan.

Duncan simply nodded.

"What's happened to the man? This isn't the Jefferson Cooke I know."

"Nor the one I know, either. Some people ... just aren't able to cope with loss, I suppose. At least he was here for us when our mother died. Colin and I ..." Duncan looked away for a moment. "... we didn't even get to say goodbye."

Mr. Mulligan nodded. "Well, I hope ye boys can bring the old Jefferson back."

"As do I. As do I." He kicked Romeo and, pulling Jefferson's horse behind him, headed home.

# EIGHT

Duncan and Colin stared at the elaborate headstone on their mother's grave. Harrison had buried her beneath her favorite reading tree, an oak at the top of a small rise several hundred yards from the old barn.

The new barn, much bigger than the old one, obstructed the view of the tree – they used to be able to see it from the front porch of the original ranch house. Of course, not being able to see the tree since coming home from prison made it easier to avoid dealing with her loss. But it was high time they did. Jefferson, Harrison had argued, still hadn't dealt with it, and look what happened to him. But they'd deal with Jefferson later. If he ever got around to sobering up, that is.

"Do you think she likes it? Her headstone, I mean," Colin asked.

Duncan reached out and touched the smooth marble. "It's beautiful. Elegant. Of course she'd like it. She'd be impressed knowing it came all the way from Oregon City."

"I wonder if Harrison buried her with any 'penny dreadfuls.' You know how she loved to read them up here."

Duncan closed his eyes a moment. "I'm sure he did. Of course, this isn't as grand as 'His Majesty' down by the swimming hole, but I suppose 'the Earl' will do."

Colin chuckled. "I wonder how many other trees she named and didn't tell us."

"Probably more than we'd like to know." Duncan took a deep breath before continuing. "Have you asked Harrison about the details of her death?"

"No."

"Neither have I. Other than if she had a decent burial. I didn't bother with particulars."

"I know," Colin sighed.

"It was nice of Sadie's father to get Mother this headstone."

"Quite so. Had to have cost a fortune. Generous chap, Horatio is."

Duncan smiled as he admired the grave marker. Daffodils, their mother's favorite flower after settling in Clear Creek, had been intricately carved into it. "Do you ever wonder what our lives would've been like had we never left England?"

Colin chuckled. "Ah, yes. You'd have gone to Eton, no doubt. I'd have been close on your heels, Harrison not far behind. Then Oxford. After that, a commission in Her Majesty's army or the life of a country gentleman, I suppose." He paused before adding, "a life of sheer boredom. Provided we didn't get shot in the Crimea or some place."

"Not to mention Harrison would never have met Sadie. Think of the horrid end she would have come to, had he not rescued her."

Colin smiled. "The Lord works in mysterious ways. He seems to always make sure we're in the right place at the right time."

"And had we not left England, you'd never have set eyes on Miss Dunnigan."

Colin smiled but said nothing.

"Do you want to marry her?"

Colin's eyes brightened, his grin now wide. But still he said nothing.

"You realize of course, that marrying her means you'll have Mrs. Dunnigan as your ... er, aunt-in-law. I hope you're up to that."

Colin's smile suddenly vanished.

"I wonder if I would have preferred London," Duncan said, changing the subject. "Hyde Park, cards at White's, perhaps a ball or two with our cousin."

"Which cousin?" Colin quickly asked, happy to retreat from considering the possibility of Mrs. Dunnigan as a future relative.

"The Earl, of course."

Colin laughed. "Oh yes, him. Good heavens, we had to have been in our nappies the last time we saw him. Do you think he's still alive?"

"I don't know. In fact, I'm not sure who would stand to inherit if he wasn't able to produce an heir. As I recall, most of our cousins are female."

"What is he, a fourth cousin? And isn't he the one Mother said was involved with a crocodile?"

Duncan smiled. "Yes, on both counts. I'd forgotten about the crocodile. What was that about?"

"I haven't the slightest." Colin had to swallow and closed his eyes. "Mother would have known," he whispered

They stared at the grave in silence for a moment before Duncan asked, "Do you feel as guilty as I do for not being here?"

Colin suddenly looked at him. "Of course. But even if we had known, there still would have been nothing we could do. We have to trust that the good Lord knew what was going on. I try to draw comfort from that."

"You always were the eternal optimist, Colin."

"In case you haven't noticed, dear brother, this isn't civilized London, or even Sussex for that matter. This country is still wild, and terribly wicked in some places. Harrison can attest to that as well as you and I."

Duncan nodded. "Harrison did us proud, the way he handled things while we were gone. He had his share of trouble – but thank the Lord, he pulled through."

"As did we," Colin said. "As best as could be expected, all things considered."

Duncan and Colin looked at each other, both with the same pain harbored in their eyes. Prison had been a living hell – brutal, savage, unyielding. Being there on false charges made it worse; being English, doubly so. But to come home to find their mother dead because Harrison was forced to work the farm rather than take care of her had cut deeper than anything else. Now after being home a month, the two brothers at long last had this moment to take it all in.

And together, Duncan and Colin finally wept.

Belle pushed the lace curtains aside, opened the window of her small room and breathed in the fresh morning air. The sun shone brightly and there wasn't a cloud in the sky. It was going to be an absolutely beautiful day.

The smell of coffee and fresh-baked cinnamon bread wafted into her room and mingled with the fresh air. If there was one redeeming quality Aunt Irene had, it was her incredible cooking. She and Uncle Wilfred should be running a restaurant, not a mercantile. But then, there was no need for a restaurant in Clear Creek – at least not yet.

The Van Cleets were to return any day now, perhaps even today, and the whole town was talking about it. Mr. Berg had relayed the message about the 'surprise' to almost everyone in Clear Creek. People were so excited, they could hardly stand it.

Belle poked her head out the window, crossed her arms on the sill and looked across the prairie. Her room was in the back of the upstairs living quarters above the mercantile. There was a small barn behind the building that housed her aunt and uncle's wagon. She tried to imagine what the view from her window would look like if Clear Creek were a much larger town. More than likely she'd be looking at the back of some building, an alley between them. She loved the view of the countryside, but she missed the bustle of Boston, and longed for a bigger town.

Well, there was no going back, only forward. Which wasn't so bad, since "forward" meant possibly getting to see Colin that morning. Sadie was coming to town.

Belle smiled and carefully ducked back inside – she'd hit her head a few times leaning out her window in the morning and had learned not to move too quickly. Once back inside, she smoothed down her blue calico dress, checked her hair, then went to join her aunt and uncle for breakfast.

"The stage is coming early today," Uncle Wilfred announced. "Should get here right before the Van Cleets do."

"What makes you think they'll return today?" Aunt Irene asked.

"Willie told me he'd get here early, on account of the Van Cleets coming in right behind him. They're bringing folks from Oregon City with them."

Aunt Irene snorted. "They'll be drinking and gambling in Mulligan's, no doubt!"

Belle gritted her teeth. Aunt Irene always seemed to find the most negative aspect of any situation. "Auntie, they're probably the workers Mr. Van Cleet hired to build the hotel. I'm sure he hired respectable help."

"Don't care who they are – they'll be trouble, mark my words!"

"And they'll be needing to buy supplies," Uncle Wilfred said, giving Belle a wink. "Best make sure the shelves are stocked this morning."

Aunt Irene's eyes narrowed in disapproval. "In that case, Belle, you'll work behind the counter today. I'll handle the rest. And be sure to wear your apron – the beastly things will be salivating enough as it is with you in that dress!"

Belle fought the urge to roll her eyes. If Aunt Irene had her way, she'd dress Belle in sackcloth and ashes to keep the men away. But the almighty dollar had done that more effectively – deprived of credit, the local men had run out of money quickly, and Aunt Irene refused to sell them anything else until they paid their tabs. Other than Doc and Grandma Waller, the only ones with cash, it seemed, were the Cookes. Belle smiled at the thought.

"Here now, what's this about?" Uncle Wilfred asked as he took in her beaming face.

"What?" Belle asked innocently.

"That look."

"Oh, I was wondering what the Van Cleets' big surprise is." *And if Colin will be with Sadie this morning.* She hadn't seen him in a few days, and missed him terribly. For days she'd imagined, dreamed, wondered what it would have been like to be kissed by Colin Cooke.

She sighed to herself. If only Sadie hadn't hit him with that rock ...

"Well, I'd best get downstairs and get to work," Uncle Wilfred said as he got up from the table.

Belle took a few sips of her coffee and helped herself to a slice of cinnamon bread. "Auntie?"

Aunt Irene's head whipped up. She'd been staring at the table, her coffee untouched. "What do you want?" she snapped.

Belle started. Aunt Irene was more on edge than ever today. "Can you teach me how to make your cinnamon bread? It's so wonderful!"

Aunt Irene blinked a few times, almost as if she was forcing back tears. "Of course. But you have to mind how much cinnamon you use," she said as she wagged a finger at her. "Not too much, and not too little. Or you might as well throw the whole thing out!"

Belle smiled. "I understand. I'm looking forward to learning how you make it."

Her aunt sat a little straighter in her chair, smiled, and finally picked up her coffee and took a sip. Her whole manner had transformed.

A shout from outside drew their attention, then another. Belle and her aunt looked at each other as they both stood.

"The stage is here!" Uncle Wilfred yelled up the stairs.

No sooner had he said it than Belle could hear the sound of the stage pulling up in front of the mercantile. She took another sip of her coffee, wrapped her cinnamon bread in a napkin and headed downstairs, knowing that her first priority was sorting the mail.

Willie entered the mercantile, took a quick peek around and, seeing that Aunt Irene was still upstairs, moseyed up to the counter with the mailbag. He offered Belle a wide, toothless grin. "Mornin', Miss Dunnigan," he drawled, tipping his hat. He set the mailbag on the counter and added, "might fine day, ain't it?"

Belle smiled. Willie was a sweet man, a little shy but starting to come out of his shell. "Yes, it is. Have you brought us anything else?"

"Yes, ma'am. Yer uncle's getting' it," he said and looked bovinely into her eyes.

She stepped back from the counter and sighed. She was getting used to that sort of look from the unmarried men in the area. Clearly, Clear Creek needed to import some more women – of good repute, mind.

She took a deep breath as she thought of the looks Colin had given her ... no, those weren't the same as the other men's. Not the same at all ...

"Van Cleet's wagons oughta be rollin' in soon," Willie surmised as he leaned against the counter. "Gonna be a mighty ruckus when they get here."

Belle turned to face him. "Wagons? How many are there?"

Willie pushed his hat back. "Shucks, Miss Dunnigan. I'd have to say at least fifteen."

"*Fifteen*? That many?"

"Well, 'at's 'bout as many as I could count," Willie said shyly. "Might be more'n that."

Belle smiled. She had to remind herself the man could barely read or write. "You're probably correct. How many men?"

"Ah, a good twenty or more. I ran across 'em just yesterday, makin' their way here. But it's slow going on account of the surprise."

"You saw the surprise?"

"No, ma'am." Willie looked this way and that, as if to make sure they were alone, and winked conspiratorially. "But I heard it."

Belle was about to comment when Uncle Wilfred came through the door carrying a few boxes. "Best help me fetch the rest, Willie. I think they're coming!"

Willie hurried out the door to help bring in the new bolts of fabric Aunt Irene had ordered. Since the sewing circle had started, the ladies had been quite busy and needed more than the mercantile carried.

Aunt Irene hurried down the stairs. "I just saw Doc and Grandma heading up the street toward the other end of town. And Henry and Fanny Fig just drove by in their wagon! No one's going to be coming in today with those Van Cleets getting back!"

"No one's been coming in anyway, since you cut everyone's credit off," Uncle Wilfred grumbled to himself.

Sadie walked in. "Did you hear? The Van Cleets are back!"

Aunt Irene spun on her. "Back to ruin us! I'll have nothing to do with any of them!"

Sadie exchanged a quick look with Belle, who shrugged helplessly. She didn't know what was wrong with Aunt Irene, and wished she could be more like Uncle Wilfred, who let his wife's odd behavior roll off his shoulders and go about his business. It wasn't so easy for the rest of Clear Creek to do so.

"Mrs. Dunnigan, would you mind if Belle went with me to greet the Van Cleets?" Sadie asked.

"Yes, I would mind! She has work to do and can't possibly leave!"

Belle's face fell, and she sighed. Here we go ...

But this time, Uncle Wilfred put his foot down. "Now, dear, there's no reason why Belle can't go watch along with everybody else. In fact, why don't you go, too? I'll mind things here."

"Why on earth would I want to? Who knows what sort of filth that Cyrus Van Cleet is bringing into this town?"

*Cyrus* Van Cleet ... Belle was sure she knew that name from somewhere. But where?

The sound of booted feet outside the door pulled her from her thoughts. Colin! She straightened and fought the urge to smooth her dress. Sadie glanced toward the door and winked, confirming his presence on the other side.

Belle's heart raced in her chest, and it was all she could do not to squeal in delight. Good heavens, one would think she was a silly young schoolgirl! But the elation she felt just knowing he was one door away couldn't be denied. She closed her eyes a moment. Was she falling in love?

*Oh, dear.* Or to borrow a phrase from Uncle Wilfred, "great jumping horny toads!"

"Belle, you go on with Sadie. Your aunt and I can handle things here for a spell."

"Uncle Wilfred – do you mean it?"

"'Course I do." He waved his hand toward the door. "Go find out what the big surprise is. In fact, me and your aunt will lock up in a few minutes and join you."

"We'll do no such thing!" Aunt Irene spat.

Wilfred was looking very close to having had enough of this. "Suit yourself, Irene. You stay here and sulk – I'm gonna see what the big hoohah is about. C'mon, girls." Without another word, he walked past everyone and out the door.

As Sadie and Belle turned to follow, Belle saw Aunt Irene's eyes narrow to dark slits. Her jaw became tight, her face red. Belle quickened her step, and didn't relax or slow down until she was at street level. Whatever her aunt planned to do next, she didn't want to be around for it.

What folks were in town that morning had already gathered by the livery stable to peer down the road leading into Clear Creek. Wagons could be seen approaching in the distance and the people oohed and ahhed at the sight.

Belle looked around for Colin but didn't see him. Where had he gone? Had she'd been mistaken in thinking he'd been on the other side of the mercantile's door earlier? Her heart sank. "Didn't Colin drive you into town?"

Sadie smiled. "He went to speak to Doc about something. Don't worry, he'll be along."

Belle inwardly sighed in relief.

The women reached the stable and listened to the rest of the townsfolk speculating. "What do you suppose it is?" Henry Fig asked.

"Could be most anything!" Mr. Mulligan exclaimed. "Gotta be huge, though – look at all those wagons! How did Cyrus pull this off?"

"Yeah," said Sheriff Hughes. "For one thing, where'd he get the money to pay for all the building supplies and the men?"

"A lucky hand in a poker game?" Frank Turner suggested.

The men continued to guess, but Belle began quizzing Sadie. It turned out Cyrus Van Cleet had come to Clear Creek not long after the Cookes. He and his wife Polly lived simply in a one-bedroom yellow house just outside of town, owned a wagon, one horse, one cow, a few chickens. So where *had* Cyrus gotten the money to fund the building of his hotel?

Belle racked her brain. She'd heard the Van Cleet name mentioned numerous times since her arrival a little over two weeks ago, but its significance was just out of reach. The fact that it was familiar puzzled her even more. How would she have heard of Cyrus Van Cleet? She'd certainly never met the man – he hadn't been in town since she'd shown up ...

The first wagon rolled up to the waiting crowd. A wiry gentleman was seated next to a petite woman, both of advanced age but spry. They had to be the Van Cleets.

The man took off his hat and waved at the waiting townsfolk. "Hellooooo, Clear Creek!" he hollered. He sounded like an Easterner, but his clothing was pure Western.

Several men took off their hats and waved back. "Hellooooo, Cyrus!" Mr. Mulligan shouted.

"Look, Polly! A reception committee!" Mr. Van Cleet exclaimed to his wife.

Mrs. Van Cleet smiled at the townspeople, her blue eyes sparkling, then turned to her husband. "We'd best get to work, Cy."

Mr. Van Cleet laughed. "Follow us, folks, and see what we've brought! After we're through with all we have planned, this town will be shipshape!"

*Shipshape* ... Belle's jaw dropped in sudden recognition.

The people cheered and followed Mr. Van Cleet's wagon as it made its way toward the new church. Sadie took a step, then realized her friend hadn't moved. "Belle, aren't you coming?"

Belle nodded numbly. She took a moment to collect herself, still shocked at the surfacing of the memory she'd been searching for.

No wonder the Van Cleets were able to bring so many supplies and men into the middle of nowhere to build their hotel – and more than just a hotel, if her guess was right. After all, Cyrus Van Cleet was one of two brothers who owned the Van Cleet Shipping Company, which made him one of the richest men in Boston. Or he would be, if he were still in Boston.

That was the new mystery – what was Cyrus Van Cleet, a Brahmin's Brahmin who could trace his family's arrival in Boston almost back to the Pilgrims, doing in Clear Creek, several days' dusty travel from civilization? And did the people of Clear Creek know who he was, and why he was here?

Belle caught up to Sadie, intent on finding out.

# NINE

The Van Cleets' lead wagon pulled up in front of the new church. The structure was almost finished, but the interior was still lacking – no paint yet, no pews, no pulpit. At this point it was little more than a misplaced and ungainly-looking barn, but it would serve well enough if it had to.

Cyrus Van Cleet, however, was not satisfied with that. "Good citizens of Clear Creek!" he shouted from the wagon. "I've brought a few gifts from Oregon City!"

The people cheered as several hats flew through the air. Belle giggled at the townsfolk's obvious excitement. If only the society matrons back in Boston could see this. Out here, people truly appreciated generosity.

Mr. Van Cleet waved to a gentleman astride a beautiful Appaloosa. That man and another positioned themselves on either side of the wagon bed, and each grabbed one end of a rope hanging from a sheet that covered the bed.

Belle and Sadie looked at each other, then at the canvas of the covered wagon – which wasn't actually canvas, but a much lighter material.

Cyrus pulled his wife Polly up to stand beside him. "May this gift ring true for all of us and all the generations to come!"

The two men spurred their horses into action, pulling the cover off as they did to reveal the gift underneath – a huge bell for the church's steeple!

"Shall I have your name carved upon it?" a deep male voice whispered in Belle's ear.

Immediately, she sighed and smiled. Colin had finally turned up.

"A beautiful bell." He drew a little closer, his whisper lowered. "Like you, Miss Dunnigan. Beautiful Belle."

A shiver went up and down Belle's spine. She fought the urge to face him, instead turning to Sadie. Or at least where Sadie had been – she had gone to the wagon with the rest of the crowd. Belle could hear her words of admiration mingled with the others as they studied the Van Cleets' gift.

"I've brought craftsmen who will build the pews and pulpit, as well as workers to construct the hotel!" Mr. Van Cleet announced over the din.

The townsfolk cheered – Belle, Colin and Sadie along with them. This was an exciting day in Clear Creek, one that even Irene Dunnigan wasn't likely to object to!

Unable to stand it any longer, Belle turned around. "Mr. Cooke," she said and curtsied.

Colin grinned. "Miss Dunnigan," he replied with a tip of his hat.

And then it happened. The noise of the crowd fell away. The movement of the people around them seemed to still, and Belle and Colin became the only two people in existence. Belle vaguely recalled reading about such a phenomenon, probably in some novel, but still marveled at the fact that it was actually happening – to her.

Her mouth went dry, her eyes wide. Colin's body drew closer, his face lowering toward hers as one arm came up and wrapped around her. Time itself slowed. His eyes locked with hers.

The bell suddenly sounded as men pushed it to the edge of the wagon. The people cheered at the beautiful noise. Everyone had to be focused on unloading it, because no one seemed to be paying Belle and Colin any attention. Certainly, no one was saying or doing anything to stop them, despite them being out in public. Was it really going to happen this time?

Belle quickly prayed that Sadie wasn't holding a rock.

And before she knew it, his lips ever so gently brushed against hers. *Ohhhh ...*

"Welcome to Clear Creek, Miss Dunnigan," he whispered.

Belle's knees went weak, and her head swam. Good heavens, it was better than she'd imagined – and over the last several days she'd imagined it often! Actually, what she'd imagined was far more intense, but she was perfectly happy with his gentleness and restraint. She could feel the muscles in his arm flex with the effort it took to hold himself back from the sort of kiss he really wanted to give her.

Forget Aunt Irene's words of approbation – Colin Cooke was a gentleman!

He released her, except for one hand that slid down the length of her arm to take her hand. He squeezed it, smiled, then turned his attention to the new church bell, pealing periodically as more than a dozen men worked to get it off the wagon.

Belle stood next to him, the warmth and feel of his lips still fresh and alive. She fought the urge to reach up and touch her mouth, but reveled in the contentment of her hand in his. It was a large hand, and it fit him: capable, strong and, for Belle, larger than life. She'd not met any man of his ilk in Boston.

And speaking of Boston, Mr. Van Cleet was heading straight for them.

Colin held out his hand as the older man approached. Mr. Van Cleet smiled and took it. "Well,

Colin, how are you?" he exclaimed as he shook it vigorously. "Haven't had a chance to catch up with you or Duncan since you returned! Been busy as a bee, I tell you!"

"Harrison's been keeping Duncan and me almost as busy. I don't suppose you've heard about the cattle?"

"Of course I have – it made the papers in Oregon City!"

Colin's eyebrows shot heavenward. "Really? I didn't know our affairs were such big news."

"Over a thousand head of cattle is big news anywhere, son," Mr. Van Cleet said before he turned his attention to Belle. "And who do we have here?"

Colin beamed. "Mr. Van Cleet, may I introduce Miss Belle Dunnigan. She's newly arrived from Boston not two weeks ago."

"A relation of Wilfred and Irene's?" Mr. Van Cleet asked with a smile. But Belle could see his jaw tighten at the mention of Boston. Did the man not want anyone to know his origins? Had something happened among the Cabots and Lowells that drove him here?

"Yes," Belle answered. "Uncle Wilfred invited me to come here after my father's death."

"I see. So sorry about your father. Were you raised in Boston then?" he asked, the rictus smile still in place.

"Yes."

"I was a Boston man myself once. But adventure called me away – and here I am!" He took her free hand. "Mind if I steal her away from you, Colin? I'd like to introduce her to Polly. And I'm sure the boys would love another hand to help with the bell."

Colin let go, tipped his hat and smiled. "It would be my pleasure, Mr. Van Cleet."

Belle watched Colin make his way to the wagon where the rest of the men labored. Even Sadie had gotten in the middle of it and was helping to guide the bell off the wagon. Mr. Van Cleet stayed where he was, his smile firmly in place, and turned to her. "I wonder if I know your family, Miss Dunnigan. Tell me, who was your father?"

Belle smiled in return. "James Dunnigan."

Mr. Van Cleet's smile broadened. "Of Dunnigan Mills?"

"Indeed."

"Why, I had no idea he'd passed on. My condolences. Whatever are you doing out here, then? Dunnigan Mills was booming when I left to come out west."

Belle spied Colin, now totally occupied alongside the other men. The sight of him comforted her. "Things change, I'm afraid, sir. And what of your business? Are you not Cyrus Van Cleet of Van Cleet Shipping?"

Mr. Van Cleet glanced about before he spoke in a low tone. "Miss Dunnigan, you are quite correct. But you see, the people of Clear Creek don't know that. This may seem an odd request, but I would much appreciate it if they didn't find out."

So she was right. "I certainly won't tell ... but I must confess, I don't understand why you would keep your origins a secret."

"Because, Miss Dunnigan, I longed for a simpler life. I could feel my soul shriveling back there, if you'll pardon an old man's purple prose. So I sold my half of the company to my brother Reginald and came out west to seek ... well, not fame and fortune, obviously – I'd had that, and enough of that, in Boston. No, I came out here looking for adventure!"

"Adventure?"

"I'm not a numbers man like Reggie. I like building things. Our father built the shipping company, my brother excels at running it. I came out here to start my own empire."

Belle smiled. "And you don't want people to know because ...?"

"Because I want them to be able to be a part of it, and not think I'm just giving them charity. This little town means a lot to me, Miss Dunnigan, and I want to see it prosper. Everyone here has stories – stories they think might keep them from settling someplace like Oregon City or Portland."

Now he had Belle's attention. "Stories? What kinds of stories?"

Mr. Van Cleet demurred, shaking his head. "It's not my place to say. But stay here long enough and you'll find out. You obviously already know about the Cooke boys, or at least I assume you do. You and Colin were holding hands."

Belle blushed. "Um … yes, we were."

He shook his head again. "Terrible thing to be framed by your own kin, then left to rot in prison."

Belle gasped. "Framed?" Up until now, she hadn't thought much about the time Colin had spent in prison. The only one in town who seemed to fret over it was Aunt Irene, who fretted over everything; no one else ever mentioned it. The town was incredibly happy to have the Cooke brothers back safe and sound, from what she'd seen and heard – that alone told her some sort of false accusations were probably involved. But while she wanted Colin to tell her in his own time, Mr. Van Cleet's statement had both given her a sense of relief and piqued her curiosity.

"Framed by their own stepbrothers, Jack and Sam. Horrible business, but at least it's over now." He patted her hand. "Miss Dunnigan, thank you for telling me you'll keep my secret safe."

Belle looked at the people gathered around the bell. The men had finally removed it from the wagon and folks were touching it here and there as they admired their new town treasure. "Of course, sir. As you've said, it's not my place to say."

"Good. Now, come see what else I've brought!"

He led her to the crowd circled around the bell. Colin immediately went to her, and she looked at him shyly, his interest quite apparent as his eyes once again locked on hers. She saw Tommy Turner hurrying their way – and stop short when he noticed Colin's focus. Disheartened, Tommy kicked at the dusty ground in defeat before walking away.

"You seem to have frightened off one of my suitors," she said, smiling.

Colin followed her gaze, saw Tommy sulking, and chuckled. "He's got a few years to go before he's ready to take on a knight of my caliber."

"A knight? As in saving the damsel in distress and slaying dragons?"

"But of course. I come from a long tradition of them."

"I don't think there are any dragons around for you to battle."

"Oh, you'd be surprised," he mused, thinking of her aunt.

"Really? And what about damsels in distress? Are there any here to rescue?"

"Perhaps. But let us hope she doesn't need the kind of rescuing Sadie did. She and Harrison were lucky to come out of that particular adventure alive."

"Mrs. Mulligan told me the story. Dangerous though it may have been, it all seems very romantic now."

He smiled. "Do you like romance, Miss Dunnigan?"

"Yes, Mr. Cooke. Yes, I do."

He flashed her his warmest smile, like she'd just given him a challenge. And Colin seemed like the kind of man who loved a good challenge. "I shall remember that."

"Belle!" a voice screeched.

"And speaking of dragons ...," Colin said flatly and took a step back.

"Belle, you get yourself back to the mercantile this instant!" Aunt Irene snapped. "You've dallied here long enough! And as for you, Colin Cooke, don't you have cattle to take care of? It's a wonder any work gets done around your place!"

"Good morning, Mrs. Dunnigan," Colin said as he tipped his hat. "Come to see what Mr. Van Cleet has brought?"

She looked up at him and scrunched up her face. "I don't care what Mr. Van Cleet has brought. Get out of my sight!"

Belle was starting to understand how Uncle Wilfred felt. "Auntie! How can you be so rude?"

She spun on Belle. "I said get back to the mercantile!"

Belle kept her anger in check, but only just. It was one thing to be a little cranky or out of sorts, but Aunt Irene had no excuse for treating people so poorly. "Where is Uncle Wilfred?"

"He's at the mercantile waiting for you! We have work to do!"

"I'll be along in a moment. I must tell Sadie I'm going."

"Let this riffraff tell her!" her aunt barked as she shoved Colin out of the way, grabbed Belle's arm and began to drag her off.

Belle looked back to see Colin begin to stride angrily after them. She waved him off. While she appreciated his willingness to join the fray, she felt that she should be the one to deal with this dragon. It was high time someone did.

Jefferson Cooke rode into town slowly on account of the splitting headache he had from the night before. He tried to sit up a little straighter to hide the fact that he felt worse than cow dung on a ... well, suffice it to say he felt poorly.

But he wasn't about to let on, in case Sadie or one of his stepsons saw him. The wagon was gone, so he knew she must be in town with one of the boys.

Probably Colin – he seemed to be the appointed escort of late while Harrison and Duncan worked the new cattle. Still, Jefferson knew Colin would have his fair share of work waiting for him when he got back. He always did. Escorting Sadie to town meant he came in later than the others for supper. Maybe prison had taught his worthless stepsons a thing or two after all.

But Jefferson had to wonder – why didn't Harrison drive her? He was married to her, after all. Why did Colin always do it? Did Colin have his own reasons for coming to Clear Creek, and if so, what were they?

He pushed the thoughts aside. The ride to Mulligan's was excruciating, and it was all he could do to stay on his horse, let alone sit up straighter and tip his hat when Mrs. Dunnigan passed him dragging a young woman behind her toward the mercantile. Must be Wilfred's niece – Mr. Mulligan had mentioned that she'd come to live with the Dunnigans.

He briefly pondered what the girl might have done to deserve being saddled with the likes of Irene Dunnigan for an aunt. But then, what had he ever done to deserve being stuck with three worthless stepsons?

Duncan, Colin and Harrison would be the death of him. They'd bombarded his cabin, taken his whiskey away, and put him to bed – nightly, right after supper – all in the name of Christian charity and love. Yeah, sure it was. The fools were determined to sober him up, and he wanted no part of it. At least they hadn't found his hidden stash yet.

But he'd been able to find solace in playing poker over the last week or two, and had agreed to meet with several men he'd played a few games with. They said they were wagon scouts, looking at giving up life on the trail and finding a place to settle, and they wanted to have a morning game before they left for Oregon City. But despite his usual inebriated state, he sensed they were something more.

Jefferson rode up to the hitching post in front of Mulligan's. A few horses were already tethered, and he recognized one as belonging to one of his new poker partners. He smiled. With any luck, they'd be playing for whiskey.

He eased himself out of the saddle and briefly looked down the street to a crowd gathered near the livery stable. Colin stood away from the crowd facing him. But he wasn't looking at Jefferson. He was watching Mrs. Dunnigan drag her niece back to the mercantile.

Jefferson glanced between his stepson and the mercantile just as Mrs. Dunnigan slammed the door. Hmmm ... so that was what brought Colin to town so often! He started to chuckle, but it made his head hurt. Still, the amusement of knowing that the self-righteous Irene Dunnigan would die before letting the likes of Colin near her pretty little niece was worth the pain. He enjoyed anything that made his stepsons suffer – and suffering a loss was the best kind. He ought to know; he'd lived with loss long enough. Let those boys have a turn and know what it was like.

He glanced at the mercantile one last time, smiled, and went into the saloon.

# TEN

Aunt Irene shoved Belle behind the counter. Belle turned to retort, only to have a white apron flung in her face before she could so much as open her mouth. What was wrong with the woman? Had she lost her mind?

"Start tallying everything in the jars first! Then move on to the canisters! I want it all counted today! I already did the displays while you were off gallivanting with those no-account Cookes!"

Belle held the apron in her hand and counted to ten. *Lord, help me to remember she's my aunt and my elder, because right now, I'd like to kill her.*

"And when you're done with that, you can scrub the back storerooms, and clean out the stove upstairs. The barn could use a good scrubbing, too."

Belle's jaw dropped. Aunt Irene wanted her to *scrub the barn*? Wasn't slavery illegal in the Oregon Territory? "Auntie, it would take at least three days to do all you ask."

"Stop complaining and get to work!"

"But ..."

"No arguments! If I'm going to feed and shelter you, then you're going to do as I ask with no complaints!" Belle watched her aunt pace back and forth like a caged animal for a moment before she suddenly stopped, looked around, then headed for the curtained doorway behind the counter. "I'm going upstairs to tend to a few things. Don't you dare leave!" She could only stand and stare as the woman waddled past and tackled the stairs to their living quarters, huffing and puffing the entire way.

As soon as Aunt Irene was gone, Belle let go of the breath she'd been holding. "Good Lord ..." She glanced upward. *Help my aunt with whatever is bothering her. Because I don't think I can stay here if this keeps up much longer.* She sighed and put on the apron.

She had just finished counting the last jar of candy when the bell above the door rang. She turned and sucked in her breath. A man and a boy entered, a ferocious and wild- looking pair dressed in buckskins trimmed with fur. Each sported what looked like a hat made from some sort of animal – not raccoon or beaver, but something larger. But it wasn't their attire that caught her attention, but the number of weapons they wore. Each sported pistols and knives. The boy also had a bow and quiver of arrows to boot, while the man used some sort of walking stick.

Belle had heard about fur trappers wandering the streams and rivers of the West – but she'd never expected to come face to face with any. She shuddered and forced herself to greet them. "May I help you?"

The man took a few steps forward as the boy continued to look around. "*Oui,*" he began.

Belle's eyes widened. A Frenchman? Or perhaps Canadian – that was more likely here.

"We need supplies," he said in a thick accent as he glanced at the different goods on sale. "I give you my list." He reached into his buckskin shirt and pulled out a piece of parchment. "You give me what on list."

Belle nodded as he handed her the list. It was written in a neat hand and, thankfully, in English. She had learned some French in school – every well-brought-up Boston girl did – but she was rusty, and thanked Heaven she wouldn't have to translate anything. "Right away, sir." She looked at the list more closely and then spoke slowly so he could understand. "Some of the things on this list you can find at the livery stable. We don't carry them here."

He came to the counter. "Which?"

Belle pointed to several items at the bottom. "Mr. Berg, the blacksmith, can help you with the harness, and other things for your horses and wagon."

The man nodded and continued to stare at the list.

Belle watched him as he pondered what she said. He was a big man, as tall as Mr. Berg, with his face half-covered by a long beard and mustache, and half the rest by the furred hat made from ... well, who knows what.

"I come back. I leave boy here."

Belle nodded and turned to the boy who now stood next to the bolts of cloth stacked on a table. He was touching the pink calico Belle had suggested for Lucy over two weeks ago.

"*Non! Ne touchez pas cela!*" the man yelled.

Even if Belle hadn't understood the French words – *No! Don't touch that!* – she could've guessed the meaning from the tone. The boy drew back his hand as if the calico was on fire. The man reached him in a few steps, grabbed his wrist and pulled him to the counter. "You stay here. She get our things. I be back."

The boy shook his head in protest but the man made some sort of sign with his hand, quelling any complaints, then strode out of the mercantile. Belle and the boy both watched him go, then turned and looked at each other.

He was young, probably twelve or thirteen years old, and dirty. His face, his hands, his clothes hadn't been washed in ages, and he smelled as bad as he looked. She hadn't noticed the state he was in when he and, she assumed, his father first entered. But up close, it was impossible to miss. She also wondered how he and his father were able to wear the furred trim and accessories at this time of year. It was the beginning of summer, after all.

"I'll just get your father's list together," Belle said as she picked up the parchment. "He is your father? Um ... *votre père?*"

The boy nodded, and she notice how green his eyes were. He took a step back, and she watched his eyes widen as they landed on the jars of candy behind her. She smiled. "Would you like a piece?"

The boy took a step back, eyes wide. Could the boy understand English? He'd understood his father, but ... she furrowed her brow in concentration. "*Vous aiment un ... morceau de sucrerie?*" She hoped she'd said it correctly.

The boy took a cautious step forward to stand where he'd been before, still looking longingly at the candy.

Belle walked over to the jars. "Which one?" she gestured to the candy as she spoke. After a moment of silence, she shrugged and said, "I'll give you a few pieces for free."

The boy just looked at her, then the candy.

She opened a few jars, took a piece from each and set them on the counter. "Let me see ... *sucrerie gratuite?* Free candy."

A tiny smile lifted one corner of the boy's mouth as his green eyes brightened.

Belle smiled again and pushed the candy across the counter to him. He reached for it slowly, never taking his eyes off her ... and then snatched it up so fast it made Belle jump. He shoved a piece into his mouth and sucked a moment, ignoring her completely, then closed his eyes and popped in another piece. She could tell he was rolling both pieces around, savoring them. How long had it been since the child had a piece of candy – or food, for that matter?

She turned, put some candy into a small bag and held it out to him. She'd pay for it herself rather than see anyone go hungry. And if Aunt Irene objected ...

well, then maybe Aunt Irene could find herself a new slave.

Just as the boy gingerly reached for the bag, the door to the mercantile opened, and Sadie and Mr. Van Cleet entered. The boy spun to face them, but relaxed at the sight of the older man.

"Well, I see you've met young M. Duprie," Mr. Van Cleet said as he stepped up to the boy and patted him on the top of his furred hat. It seemed odd, as the boy was almost as tall as Sadie. Perhaps he was older than Belle had first thought.

"Where's your aunt?" Sadie asked cautiously.

Belle rolled her eyes and pointed to the ceiling.

Sadie nodded. "Colin was upset when you left."

Belle sighed. "I didn't have much choice at the time. She's getting worse every day. I just don't know what's ailing her."

"I believe your aunt is a good woman, Miss Dunnigan," Mr. Van Cleet said. "I know she means well. But she does go about things rather ... aggressively." He smiled sardonically.

"I'm sorry, Mr. Van Cleet. I hope my aunt's behavior didn't upset your arrival."

"I don't think anyone took notice, other than Colin. We were all too busy unloading the wagons."

Belle let go a heavy sigh. "Is he terribly angry?"

"No," Sadie said. "Frustrated, though. He wanted to come in and ask you himself, but thought it better if we did."

"Ask me what?"

"Remember my suggestion of a picnic down by the creek and 'His Majesty'?"

Belle giggled at the mention of the giant oak. "Yes."

"Well, Colin, Mr. Van Cleet and I thought it would be nice to make it a bigger affair. And, now the whole town is coming."

Belle smiled. "That's wonderful! When are you going to have it?"

"Saturday – and I'm going to need help with it. Mrs. Turner, Mrs. Fig and Mrs. Mulligan are already organizing the other women to take care of the food, while I thought the two of us and your aunt and uncle could organize some games and prizes. The men will handle the rest."

"After food and games, what else is there?" Belle asked.

"Oh, you'll see, Miss Dunnigan, you'll see!" Mr. Van Cleet laughed and slapped the young M. Duprie on the back. The boy choked on his candy, his face suddenly red, and gasped for air. The older man, realizing the boy was choking, quickly slapped his back again. *Hard.* The candy flew out of the boy's mouth ...

... and landed squarely on Aunt Irene's chest with a little *plop* as she entered.

Everyone froze.

Aunt Irene's eyes narrowed in on the sticky piece of candy a moment before she reached up and yanked it off her dress. "Who did this?" she huffed. She then looked about the room, her glare landing on the Duprie boy. He stood, eyes wide, muscles tensed and ready to flee. She wrinkled her nose. "What is that *smell?* Get this disgusting creature out of my store!"

The boy needed no further urging, and turned to run for the door, but was stopped by Mr. Van Cleet's hand on his shoulder. "He's harmless, Mrs. Dunnigan. And he's with me."

"With you?" Irene asked, seemingly affronted that Cyrus Van Cleet would associate with such as him.

"Yes, with me. I brought the Dupries back with me from Oregon City. Anton Duprie is one of the best trackers in the west. Came down from the great northern woods of British Canada to settle in Oregon Territory. I convinced him Clear Creek would make a fine home for them."

"You seem to be able to convince a lot of folks to come settle here," Sadie commented.

Belle nodded. "Such as Mr. Berg."

"And I'd say about half the men you brought to build the hotel," Sadie added with a smile.

Aunt Irene tossed the sticky piece of candy at Belle. "Well ... well, I don't care who they are or who brought them. They can't come in my store looking and smelling like animals!"

Belle took the candy and dropped it in a small box they used for trash. "Auntie, M. Duprie placed quite a large order. I'm filling it now. He'll be back soon to pick it up."

Her aunt looked from one face to the other. "He can't have any of it unless he pays cash!"

Mr. Van Cleet laughed. "Oh, there'll be no problem there! Now, I must be on my way. Come with me, Cosime," he said to the boy. "And I'll see all of you fine ladies at the picnic!" Mr. Van Cleet and Cosime left.

Having been turned back on one front, Aunt Irene decided to attack on another. "Picnic? What picnic?" she huffed.

"The men Mr. Van Cleet brought with him are finishing the church this week," Sadie told her. "We're celebrating with a picnic down at the creek on our ranch."

"Riffraff! The whole lot of them!"

"I was hoping you'd help me plan some entertainment."

"Entertainment? Young lady, the only entertainment any of those men are interested in is the kind that comes from a bottle."

Sadie was making an effort to stay calm, even as she had to force aside the mental image of roping Irene Dunnigan and dragging her behind the Cookes' wagon. "They were quite excited when Mr. Van Cleet told them. And it's the least we can do to welcome them to town and thank them for finishing the church."

"That's the Van Cleets' business, not ours!"

"Auntie, it's the new church. And some of these men might want to settle here after their work on the hotel is done—"

"I don't care! I'll have nothing to do with any picnic – and neither will you!"

Belle stiffened. "I want to help," she replied, her voice dropping.

Her aunt spun on her. "The only help you'll give will be right here in my store! Do you hear me?"

"Mrs. Dunnigan," Sadie interjected. "Belle should be allowed to—"

"She'll do as I say! Mind your own business and get out of here!"

Sadie stood straight, her jaw set. "No."

Aunt Irene looked at her, stunned. As if she'd never heard the word "no" before. Which, Belle thought, maybe she hadn't. It would explain some things. "What ... did you say?" she finally choked out.

"I said no. I've come in here on business, and I intend to finish it." She turned to Belle. "I think we should start right away."

Belle looked from one face to the other. It was now or never. She took a deep breath. "I agree. Saturday is only a few days away. I can help you after my work here is finished."

"I'll have Harrison or Colin bring me back into town. We can meet with Mrs. Mulligan and go over the details."

"What details?" Aunt Irene snapped. "What are you talking about?"

"We need to plan for the picnic. If you do not wish to participate, that is your choice," Sadie stated calmly.

"Well, I *don't* wish it! I won't, and neither will Belle!"

"Auntie," Belle spoke quietly. "I am going to help with the planning. There is no work to be done after we close the mercantile. It's not going to hurt to go down the street and meet with Sadie and Mrs. Mulligan for an hour."

Aunt Irene's face turned red as her eyes narrowed. "You step outside that door tonight and I won't let you back in."

"What?" Belle knew it might just come to this. She'd be taking a gamble – and she knew from watching her father what happened when gambles were lost. She had to consider her next move carefully.

Sadie stood next to her, in enough shock for all three of them. Her mouth opened and closed but nothing came out.

"You heard me. You step outside that door tonight and you'll never set foot back inside this house again."

"Auntie, you are being ridiculous." Belle kept her voice low and calm, as if dealing with a child throwing a tantrum – not far off from this situation, actually.

"Am I? You think I don't have eyes? You two have probably concocted this whole thing just so you can see that disgusting man!"

"*What?*" Sadie blurted out. Belle simply rolled her eyes.

"I saw you down the street! Thought at first my eyes were playing tricks on me, but no, I saw it plain as day!"

"Saw what?" Belle asked flatly. She was pretty sure she knew what, but she wanted to see what her aunt actually said.

Aunt Irene didn't disappoint. "I saw you throw yourself at that Cooke boy! In public, no less! Why, you're nothing more than a ..."

"Than a what?!" Belle interrupted sharply. Sure enough, Aunt Irene had seen the kiss. But – and this came to her like a revelation – so what if she had? No one else seemed to mind – not Sadie, not the other townspeople, certainly not Mr. Van Cleet, who could likely buy and sell Aunt Irene out of pocket change. Even in Boston, a well-bred, single Englishman and landowner delicately smooching the heir of a New England manufacturer wouldn't have done much more than raise eyebrows and start a little gossip. And this wasn't Boston – this was Clear Creek, in the middle of the Wild West! Enough was enough. "What am I nothing more than, *dear auntie?*"

Sadie took Belle's hand and pulled her away from her aunt a foot or two. Belle let her. At this point, she wondered if Aunt Irene might try to slap her – or vice-versa.

"Than a shameless whore," Aunt Irene replied, teeth gritted.

Belle had known what her aunt was going to say, which helped her to not react. But it stung all the same. She took another deep breath, her nostrils flaring, and turned to Sadie. "You'd better go – I'll see you tonight. And if you see my uncle, please tell him to come back to the mercantile, will you?"

Sadie bit her lower lip. She knew now that Aunt Irene was completely past the point of reason, and that Belle was not going to tolerate it further. Perhaps Uncle Wilfred would be able to talk some sense into his wife – and keep his niece from doing something rash if well-deserved. "I'll do that. And I'll see you tonight." She left.

After the door closed, the room was silent except for the rasp of Aunt Irene's breathing. Belle fought to get her emotions under control. Never had she been so angry. Her aunt's words were not only hurtful but untrue, and she would not let her life be controlled by someone who would say such a thing. But at the same time, she loved her aunt, and had to figure out what was wrong. Was Aunt Irene losing her mental faculties? Or did she really hate the world and everyone in it that much?

Tears fought for release, but she managed to hold them back. She watched as her aunt turned from her without a word and went back upstairs. *Lord, please ...*

*show me what to do. Before I do something You won't like ...*

"It's not your fault," Sadie assured Colin as he drove them back to the ranch. "Mrs. Dunnigan would complain if she saw you so much as look at Belle, let alone kiss her. You know how she is."

"I should never have taken the liberty. It was wrong of me."

Sadie sighed in frustration. Colin had been angry ever since he watched Mrs. Dunnigan drag Belle back to the mercantile. After Sadie explained what happened while she was there, he'd gone deathly silent. Until now.

"Belle obviously didn't mind."

"Had you seen us, would you have stopped it with another rock?"

Sadie had to laugh at that. "Colin, I don't think throwing a boulder would have kept you from kissing her this time. I've seen the two of you together and, I can honestly say, I believe Belle joined in without any reservation."

A slight smile curved his mouth. "Really? Well, she didn't slap me, so I suppose that's a good sign."

"Trust me, it's a very good sign. You're going to court her now, of course."

Colin smiled. "Of course. Though I suppose driving you to town can't be used as an excuse anymore to see her."

"You'll have the excuse again. Belle and I need to meet with Mrs. Mulligan tonight."

"You mean after all that was said, Belle is still going to meet with you and the other women?"

"So she said. It'll just be me, Mrs. Mulligan and maybe Grandma. But Mrs. Dunnigan should be better.

Mr. Dunnigan will have had a chance to calm her down."

Colin shook his head. "I'll definitely drive you, right after supper. The mercantile will be closed by then." He paused, then added, "I do hope Wilfred can pour oil upon the troubled waters. Poor Mrs. Dunnigan is getting worse every day."

"I know. We'd best step up our prayers for her."

"It's going to be quite busy at the new church with all those prayers for that woman!"

Sadie laughed. "I would think you'd be praying harder than anyone else. If my guess is right, you're going to be related."

"Why does courting a girl have to lead to marriage?" he said in exasperation. "Belle may well refuse me."

"I doubt that. I've seen the way she looks at you."

Colin's jaw tightened as he tried not to smile too much. The thought of marrying Belle settled into the pit of his stomach and warmed him head to toe. Good Lord, had he already fallen in love?

Well, of course he had, he realized. He'd fallen in love the first time he'd seen her alighting from the stage, him standing up on that balcony like a besotted Juliet. It had just taken a couple of weeks for his brain to catch up with his heart.

Sadie caught his look and pressed her lips together to hold back the giggles threatening to erupt. It didn't work. And once she got started, Colin began laughing so hard he nearly fell out of his seat.

Sadie calmed down first. "Why don't you woo her with some of your poetry?"

"My poetry? Hmmm, that's not a bad idea."

They looked at each other and, unable to help themselves, started laughing again. But they both knew wooing and winning Belle would be easy. Wooing Mrs. Dunnigan into giving them her blessing would be another matter.

There was, indeed, going to be a lot of prayer going on. And, Colin thought, he'd better sharpen up his sword for some dragon-slaying.

# ELEVEN

That evening, Belle left the mercantile feeling tense and relieved at the same time. Uncle Wilfred had managed to not only talk her aunt into letting her attend the planning meeting for the town picnic, but had also vetoed any suggestion of throwing Belle out on the street, now or ever. However, it turned out that before discovering the tempest at home, he'd invited the new preacher who arrived with the Van Cleets' wagon train to supper.

Having the Rev. Josiah King meet Aunt Irene after she'd been so riled up was a risk, but it worked out well nonetheless. After all, how much "sin" could the new preacher harbor for Aunt Irene to complain about? At long last, it seemed, there was someone in town she approved of.

He was a pleasant enough fellow, Belle thought, but didn't really seem the preacher sort. He was tall and muscular like Colin, built as if he'd known hard work. His hair was cut shorter than she thought a preacher's ought to be, close to the skull like a Roman centurion. His grey eyes, though gentle, held a steeliness to them that spoke of a difficult life. Naturally, she and her uncle wanted to know what sort of life he'd had before coming to the Oregon Territory, but his answers were vague. "A bit of this and a little of that," did not constitute a real answer to the question "what did you do before becoming a preacher. So that was the tension.

"May I escort you to the meeting, m'lady?"

"Oh!" Belle exclaimed. Colin had come out of nowhere, and was smiling and offering her his arm. She took a deep breath. "You scared me half to death."

"I do apologize. You did seem to be doing some rather heavy wool-gathering when I walked up behind you."

"I suppose so – I didn't at all hear you coming," she said as she took his arm.

"As you are here rather than in your parlor, I assume your uncle worked his magic on your dear Aunt Irene?"

"Yes, he did. And they are currently entertaining a guest."

"Do tell?"

"Yes, he's the new preacher – recently arrived from the Nebraska Territory."

Colin's brow furrowed. "The preacher is here already? Huh – I thought he wasn't expected for some time. But plans change – as I'm glad your aunt's did. Shall we?"

Belle nodded, and Colin escorted her down the street to Mulligans'. They went around the back instead of through the front doors. Customers would be coming into the saloon at this point in the evening and Colin didn't want to parade Belle (or Sadie, whom he'd delivered earlier) past them to the Mulligans' private quarters.

They entered the building and headed up a set of back stairs. There was a small landing at the top and a single door. Colin knocked and, after a moment, Grandma Waller answered. "Land sakes, Colin, it took you long enough! Did you get lost along the way?" Grandma took Belle's arm from him and pulled her inside. "Now mind yourself while we ladies take care of this picnic business!" And with that, she shut the door in Colin's face.

He sighed in contentment as the lingering warmth of Belle's arm so recently held in his sent a tingle up his spine. As he made his way down the stairs, he began to whistle. It was going to be incredibly fun courting the damsel – especially when there were respites from the distress.

The day of the picnic dawned clear and bright. So, oddly, did Aunt Irene, who actually hummed as she helped Belle prepare and bake several pies. She not only gave Belle permission to go, but was planning on going herself with Uncle Wilfred. Belle didn't understand the sudden change in her aunt but, like Colin a few nights before, she wasn't going to object. Maybe the good Lord had heard all the prayers said for her, and seen fit to answer them right away. *Thank you, Father! Continue to heal her heart – it's working! But all things in Your time. I know this is only the beginning. Please give me the patience I need to see this through.*

Belle took another pie from her aunt. "I'll set these by the window. They should be nice and cool by the time we leave."

"Yes, and your uncle and I have the prizes all ready."

"Prizes, Auntie?"

"Why, yes, we're donating a few things for your games. You didn't think a few pies would be enough to give away, did you?"

Belle tried to keep her mouth from flopping open in shock. *Lord, You work fast!* "I had no idea. That was very kind of you, Auntie."

Aunt Irene smiled, the first time Belle had seen her do that. "It's the least we can do. Now you and I have some chores to finish before it's time to go. And you'll need to change, of course. I think you should wear your blue dress."

Belle watched her aunt's face. The grin looked as if someone had painted it on. In fact, it was so foreign she blinked to clear her vision. Was she seeing things? Why on Earth was Aunt Irene *this* happy? Something wasn't right. "I'm sure we'll have time to change. The men won't be finished with the church for another few hours at least."

"Your uncle and I will head to the picnic area with Mrs. Turner and Mrs. Mulligan to set up. You can get yourself ready and come out later."

"But, Auntie, it's several miles to the Cooke's property. You don't expect me to walk, do you?"

"Of course not. Mr. King will escort you."

"The new preacher?"

"Of course."

*Oh dear.* Belle suddenly felt uncomfortable. The new preacher had acted strangely, and now so was Aunt Irene … *No, it's probably nothing …*

"And I'm sure the two of you will have plenty of time to get acquainted on the drive out."

Good Lord, no – was Aunt Irene trying to play matchmaker with her and the new preacher! Did *he* know about this? She stared at her aunt, dumbfounded. Several days ago she'd called her a whore for letting Colin Cooke kiss her. Today she was having the new preacher drive her to the picnic without a chaperone! What next – nuptials under "His Majesty" that afternoon?

She turned away from her aunt. Of course, the thought of getting married to the new preacher that same day was ridiculous, but this was a pickle all the same. Colin would be at the picnic, and she didn't want to have to handle two men! Knowing Aunt Irene, though, the Rev. King probably had no idea what was going on. Yet. *Oh, that poor man...*

Belle closed her eyes and sighed. If her guess was right, this was going to be some picnic.

Several hours later, Belle found herself sitting on a buckboard next to the Rev. Josiah King. He seemed rather surprised to find that neither her aunt nor uncle were with her, and was obviously under the impression they'd all be going to the picnic together. Belle almost apologized to him when he told her that, but decided to hold her tongue and see how things developed.

To see Colin, Duncan, and Henry Fig speaking with Sheriff Hughes as they neared the sheriff's office set her teeth on edge. Almost the whole town was going to the picnic, so the sheriff had asked some of the men to stay behind to keep an eye on things while everyone else celebrated at the Cookes' place. She had no idea Colin had volunteered, or perhaps had *been* volunteered. She wondered who'd done the volunteering – she could make an educated guess ...

"Fine day for a picnic," Mr. King called out to the sheriff and gave him a friendly wave.

"Wonderful day! You folks have a good time, and welcome to Clear Creek! Be nice to finally have our own preacher!" the sheriff called back.

Mr. King smiled and re-settled himself on the seat which brought him a few inches closer to Belle. She didn't think he did it on purpose, but the shocked look on Colin's face told her *he* figured he had. Mr. King must have also caught his look – he raised his eyebrows in confusion.

Belle turned on the seat as they passed and waved to Colin, her eyes pleading as if she was being abducted. After all, what else could she do? She had to admit – Aunt Irene couldn't have planned this any better. She managed to work it so the new preacher drove her out to the picnic while the two single Cooke men had to stand guard duty. But at least Colin and his brother would be relieved at some point – they couldn't patrol the town the entire time. The picnic was being held on their ranch. And besides, no one would expect Harrison and Sadie to take care of everything! When Colin arrived, she could explain to him about Aunt Irene's little plot.

She shook her head and sighed. She knew her aunt's earlier behavior was too good to be true. Everyone kept saying that the woman meant well, but she was beginning to have her doubts ...

"Such beautiful country. I should have thought to come out here sooner." The Rev. King's voice pulled Belle out of her lamenting. She should stop feeling sorry for herself and focus on being cordial to the new preacher. Not too cordial, however ... "Yes, it is. I didn't think I would like it at first – it's so different from living in a big city. But I think I'm beginning to like it."

He smiled. "Yes, I can see that." He cleared his throat, then asked, "weren't two of the men speaking with the sheriff our hosts?"

"Apparently."

"Are they taking the first watch?"

Belle grimaced. "I'm afraid so."

He chuckled – a deep, rolling sound. Under other circumstances, Belle might have found it soothing. "Seems odd for the hosts of the picnic to stay behind in town to perform guard duty, don't you think?"

"Very odd, Reverend."

"Your aunt is an ... interesting woman, Miss Dunnigan."

"Oh, you don't have to tell me," Belle replied with some asperity.

Rev. King was silent for a minute, before finally saying, "you know, I think I've been hoodwinked."

"I believe we both have."

He stopped the wagon, looked at her, and smiled sardonically. "Your aunt asked me some very interesting questions the other night after you left. And she went out of her way to inform me that you'd make a fine wife."

Belle groaned and began to massage her temples. "Oh, Auntie ...," she sighed in frustration.

Rev. King nodded sympathetically. "It just occurred to me that I left something undone at the church. You don't mind if we turn around and go back, do you?"

Belle was still fuming at Aunt Irene's folly. "No, of course not," she grumbled.

"In fact, I think it would be best if I finish up a few things that still need attention. Would you mind terribly if one of the Cooke men drove you to the picnic? I could come out later."

It took her a second to realize what he was driving at. "But ... the picnic is for you and the men who worked on the church," she replied lamely.

"Yes, *after* the work is done. It's not all done yet, though. Afterward, I'll come out, I promise. Besides, there should be another one of our hosts in attendance, don't you think?"

Belle blushed. "I suppose you're right."

Rev. King smiled. "And I'm sure he'd love to escort you, Miss Dunnigan. While I, in turn, avoid a black eye.

"I beg your pardon?"

"Miss Dunnigan, you may have guessed from my ... obfuscations at supper that I haven't always been a Reverend. I did spend some time, as the saying goes, 'out in the world.' And one thing I learned there was that when a gentleman looks at me the way Mr. Cooke was doing as we drove past, a black eye could well be in the making."

She couldn't help it – she laughed. "Oh, Rev. King, if anyone can tell you about black eyes, it would be Colin Cooke!"

"So I've heard," he said with a grin as he turned the wagon around.

Colin sat in a chair outside the sheriff's office and fumed. He couldn't believe it – Belle going to the picnic with the new preacher? How did it come to this? He had the day all planned out: what he would do, what he would say, even how many kisses he might steal. As long as it didn't get too painful, via Sadie's rock-throwing skills or some other assault, physical or verbal. A man had his limits, and he was starting to think he'd suffered enough bruises and rants for one courtship, thank you *very* much.

But Belle had let him kiss her a few days ago – and in public, no less. She must feel something for him. What girl lets a man kiss her like that and not hold some affection? And he knew she wouldn't let just anyone take the liberty he had. She was too much a lady.

He was still upset with Mrs. Dunnigan and her cruel treatment of Belle. There would certainly be no more of that once he married her! Not on your life!

Wait a minute ... *once he married her?* He *had* thought that – it had popped into his head alongside Belle's name, just as natural together as tea and milk. He quickly scanned the street as if someone close by might have heard his thoughts. Henry Fig had strolled down near the Wallers' house while Duncan had planted himself in front of the mercantile.

He leaned back in the chair and pushed his hat back. Marriage. Well, why not? He couldn't deny his attraction to her, and he was pretty sure of hers toward him – or at least, Sadie was sure. He had land and income and a certain amount of breeding. She was not only well-raised but beautiful, with the face of an angel. His angel. Marrying her would simply make permanent what they both already knew.

But Colin knew he wasn't going to get far sitting here babysitting the town. He got up and looked down the street to see if Duncan was still sitting in front of the mercantile. He wasn't. He sighed and went to go find his brother.

But he'd only taken a few steps into the street when he heard a wagon roll into town. It approached from his end and he turned to see who it was. His heart set to racing. *Belle ...*

The preacher – what was his name, King? – stopped the wagon next to him. "Excuse me, Mr. Cooke?"

Colin glanced up at him and tipped his hat, trying to be nonchalant.

"I was wondering if you'd mind escorting Miss Dunnigan to the picnic. I need to tend to some things at the church."

Colin slowly looked at Belle. *The Lord be praised!* "I, er ... think I can manage that. But the sheriff did want three men on duty at a time ..."

"It shouldn't take me long to get my business done. And then I'd be happy to take up your post until the next man comes."

"Why, that's very kind of you," Colin said, and meant it.

Belle leaned forward to look past Mr. King. "Harrison and Sadie must need the help. You should be there. Why are you standing guard?"

"Names were drawn from a hat, as I understand ..."

"Hmmm, I see. And my aunt did the drawing, I suppose?"

Realization dawned on his face. "You suppose correctly."

Belle and Mr. King glanced at each other, shook their heads and laughed.

Colin got the distinct impression they knew something he didn't. But he stopped pondering what it might be when the preacher jumped from the wagon and, instead of helping Belle down, motioned for him to do so. He smiled. By rights, the Rev. King should be helping her, but he obviously knew of their mutual affection, and would not come between them. Cripes – for all he knew, the preacher saw the two of them kissing earlier in the week.

He reached up, his eyes glued to her tiny waist, when he heard a commotion down the street. All three turned to see Duncan launch himself off the porch of the mercantile in hot pursuit of Cosime Duprie. The lad raced across the street and began to run in their direction, Duncan hot on his heels. "Stop him!"

Colin froze. He had to – Belle had already begun to fall into his waiting hands, and if he moved now she'd fall flat on her face. Rev. King, however, was not so encumbered, and rushed to intercept. Cosime dodged him well enough, but not the hitching post in front of Mulligan's saloon. He hit that hard enough to bounce off it and land himself square on the seat of his buckskin trousers.

Duncan grabbed said pants and the attached belt and pulled him to his feet, then dragged him, kicking and punching, to the saloon steps. "Stealing, are we? Hasn't your father taught you any manners?" he said none too kindly, seating himself on the steps and pulling Cosime across his lap. "Stealing's not allowed around here," he added, and swatted the boy's backside. Cosime's entire body stiffened, but he didn't cry out. "Breaking into the mercantile could land you in jail!" Another swat.

Colin knew what he was doing. The pain and embarrassment of a good spanking might keep Cosime from suffering the horrors they themselves had for nearly two years. He would probably be doing the same thing as Duncan if he'd caught the boy breaking into the mercantile and stealing.

Belle, however, didn't see things that way. "Mr. Cooke!" she shouted as Colin finally set her on her feet. He'd managed to hold her up between himself and the wagon while the entire scene unfolded. "Stop it! Stop it this instant!"

Duncan froze in shock, his hand in mid-air.

"What are you doing, spanking him? He's a little old for that, don't you think?"

Duncan scowled at the lad squirming in his lap. "You're right. A sturdy switch would be better!"

Belle put her hands on her hips. "Let him up!"

"Miss Dunnigan, I might inform you that he broke into the mercantile – how, I have no idea – and stole from you." He pried a small white bag out of Cosime's hand. "See? I know it's only candy, but the fact is he broke in while no one was there ..."

"Oh, for crying out loud," Belle sighed, shaking her head. "Let me see that." She held her hand out, and Duncan gave her the bag.

She took it and examined the contents. "I knew it. Mr. Cooke, I gave him this candy the other day. He accidentally left it on the counter after being frightened by my aunt. He just came back for it, that's all. Yes, maybe he should have waited. But I don't think his English is very good and I've noticed he's extremely skittish around strangers. He was probably afraid to ask you to get it for him."

Duncan continued to hold the struggling youth in place. "Still, it's no excuse to break into a business."

Colin laughed. "Duncan, I don't think a few pieces of candy will mark the lad a criminal. Especially when the proprietress insists they're his."

Duncan wasn't ready to give up yet. "What will happen when Mrs. Dunnigan finds out?"

"I paid for the sweets myself," Belle told him. "There is nothing for my aunt to find out. Let him go, please."

Duncan shrugged and released his hold. Cosime rolled off his lap and sprang to his feet.

Belle took Cosime by the shoulders. "Are you all right? Ah ... *êtes-vous tout droit?*"

The boy rubbed his sore behind and glared at Duncan. Duncan grumbled an apology.

"He didn't mean to strike you," Belle began gently. "He thought you were stealing."

The boy looked back to her, fighting back tears. Duncan must have really walloped him. They all watched as the lad pulled his furred hat, now slightly askew, back into place, then sniffled and stomped off.

Rev. King stepped forward. "I'm afraid you haven't made a friend out of him, Mr. Cooke. He'll certainly avoid you from now on."

Duncan got up. "He's a bit of a wild animal. His father ought to keep a closer eye on him."

"The Dupries lived too long in the northern forests among the Indians. Trust me, it'll take more than a spanking to tame Cosime. But he's got a good heart."

"Well, he could have simply asked me to go into the mercantile and get his candy, even if his English isn't very good, I'd have understood him well enough."

Rev. King shook his head sorrowfully. "No, Mr. Cooke. He wouldn't have been able to."

"Why not?" asked Belle.

"Because Cosime cannot speak."

# TWELVE

"Can you imagine having lived among the Indians and growing up a savage?" Belle asked Colin as he drove them to the picnic. "What do you suppose happened to that boy to cause him to lose the ability to speak?"

"To begin with, I don't think 'savage' is the word I'd use. You yourself spent a little time with him in the mercantile the other day. Would a savage have stayed after his father left? No, he'd scurry away and avoid people. Trust me when I say, I've seen *savage* ... and Cosime isn't. However, I can understand how he could become mute. I've seen it happen to grown men, though – never a boy."

Belle knew he was referring to his time in prison. She turned to him as the wagon bumped along. "Jail must have been horrible."

He sighed, and she noted how his shoulders slumped. "It's certainly not an experience I wish to repeat. If Duncan hadn't been there with me, I would never have survived. We fought to keep each other sane, and as safe as we could ..." He trailed off, and closed his eyes a moment. She watched his face as he visibly wrestled with the memories. "Sometimes I wonder if I'm a better man for it. But I suspect it's the opposite."

"What did it teach you?"

Colin looked at her with a tenderness she had never seen in any eyes except her father's. "Mercy."

Their eyes locked and Belle froze, captured in his gaze. She knew she needed to speak before she did something foolish. "What of Duncan?" she whispered despite herself. "How has it affected him?"

Colin pulled back on the reins and brought the team to a stop. They were somewhere between Clear Creek and the picnic, but too far away from either for anyone to see ...

Belle swallowed, her mouth dry. That odd warm blanket of peace that so often accompanied Colin whenever she was with him surrounded her. He turned to her and put one arm over the back of the wagon seat. He could easily put it around her and draw her to him if he so chose, and Belle quickly pondered if she should let him. They would surely kiss. But it wouldn't be the chaste brush on the lips he'd given her in town a few days ago. No, if he kissed her now, she sensed it might consume them both.

Something inside her stomach fluttered, which she expected. What she didn't expect was the thing in her soul opening like a door. It was the oddest sensation, as if her very being was about to welcome this man into the deepest part of her heart. She felt the heat of his body as he scooted closer and studied her face. Their eyes remained locked.

"Duncan," he replied, his voice soft. "It hardened him. He trusts no one, not even enough to admit he doesn't. He protected me the entire time, even more than I protected him. And sometimes, he had to become rather ... well, *savage* to do so."

His arm slid further across the back of the wagon bench and brushed her back. Her entire body shivered at the contact. She looked at his face, now so close to hers and still healing up. He smelled of soap, leather, and pure, raw masculinity. The heat from his body felt warmer than the sun overhead, the air about them charged as if they were in the eye of a hurricane. She'd never felt or heard of anything like it before, had never even read about it in a novel.

Oh, how she wanted to kiss him!

Colin leaned closer, pushing his hat off his forehead with the hand that still held the reins, his eyes still focused on hers.

"Duncan..." Belle gulped. "... seems quite sane, considering everything the two of you endured." She could barely hear her own voice now.

Colin reached up and brushed her cheek with the backs of his fingers. "You are the most beautiful thing I have ever seen."

She found herself gasping for breath. "I ... I..."

"Shhhh ...," he said softly. "Miss Dunnigan ... Belle ... once again I ... I find that I should very much like to kiss you."

Her face lit up. Every fiber of her body, every nerve ending was screaming *yes!!!* She now understood why a lady should never be alone with a gentleman – it was too overwhelming. There were obviously some things a lady could attempt to fight but not win. And her attraction to Colin Cooke was definitely one of them. Emotionally as well as physically, she was defenseless against him ... and she adored the feeling. Her eyes closed, her head tilted back ...

"But ... I'll not demean you."

Belle suddenly opened one eye in confusion. Colin's face was now farther away, a few inches perhaps, but with a look of compassion. She had been so prepared for a good, thorough kiss that she thought she might faint from the sudden change. "What?" came out in a squeak.

His jaw was set, his body wound tighter than a piano wire. It was obviously taking an effort to keep himself under control. "I care for you, Belle Dunnigan – deeply, madly. And I'll not let anyone imply that I took advantage of you out here on the prairie. You're to be cherished, as if you were the most precious jewel in the world."

And Belle had thought Colin's *kiss* would be her undoing! But his words ... not only did he want her as men had wanted women since time immemorial, but he was binding himself to protect her – from attack, from the slanders of gossips, even from himself if need be. He was sacrificing his own desires to preserve her reputation.

She closed her eyes and choked back a sob. He would not demean her or bring her to ruin – not even when she, in her own passion, was almost begging him to. She knew, deep within her heart, that had he kissed her, she would have been utterly lost – and knowing that, had drawn back. He was truly a gentleman, far above the standard of Boston society, let alone that of the Oregon wilderness. And he was willing to wait for her.

And as she realized that, in a wagon on the prairie between Clear Creek and the town picnic, with the sun shining overhead and the early summer flowers dotting the earth around them, she also knew that she was utterly lost anyway – not in the throes of passion, but in fathomless, endless, hopeless *true* love with Colin Cooke.

Harrison helped Mr. Dunnigan arrange prizes on a small table he'd hauled out to the picnic site from the ranch house. The Dunnigans had donated bags of candy and of nails, a hammer, kitchen utensils, squares of cloth for quilting (which Mrs. Dunnigan had folded and tied with ribbon) and various other small trinkets from the mercantile. It was at least twelve dollars' worth of merchandise for the participants in the games. "There, I think that does it. Unless you have more?"

"Nope, this is all we brought," Mr. Dunnigan said brightly. "Should be enough for everyone. Are you going to play?"

"Of course. I brought the pig, after all."

"Kinda doesn't seem fair if you're in the pig-catching. Maybe we ought to let loose a steer and see how you do."

"I'm afraid I'm not as adept at that yet."

"Your help coming soon?"

"We certainly hope so. Sadie sent word to her father to loan us one of his foremen. He'll probably travel with Sadie's parents when they come for their wedding. We'll simply have to hold out until then."

"It must be pretty hard to keep up with all the work. Especially when it's just the two of you."

*Two?* "I beg your pardon?"

"You and Duncan. Colin seems to be spending most of his time in town these days," Mr. Dunnigan said with a wink.

Harrison smiled. "You don't say. I shall have to inquire of my brother what's caught his interest of late. Even so, he is still doing his share of work around the ranch – when not falling out of haylofts and the like." They both laughed at that.

"He's a fine young man," Mr. Dunnigan added. "All three of you are, Harrison. I'm proud to know you boys."

"Thank you, Wilfred. My brothers and I appreciate your friendship."

Mr. Dunnigan sighed. "Gonna be hard convincing Irene we have to part with Belle one of these days."

Harrison sighed and nodded. "Yes, I'm afraid I have to agree with you there. And Duncan tells me that Colin can't hold out much longer. He fully intends to court the young lady."

"'Intends'? Ain't that what he's been doing the last few weeks?"

"Well, I believe he wishes to make it official. And without risk of injury."

"Ah. Well, I can understand that ..."

Just then, Sadie approached and went directly to Harrison. He pushed back his hat, took her in his arms and gave her a quick kiss.

Mr. Dunnigan smiled and turned away. "I think I'll just mosey on over and see what trouble Irene's causing."

Harrison laughed. "We'll see you later!"

"What did I miss?" Sadie asked as she watched Mr. Dunnigan chuckle to himself and leave.

"Nothing of importance, except he knows Colin is courting Belle. And seems to approve."

"Oh. But is he going to talk Mrs. Dunnigan into it? Otherwise, she might make things even harder than she already has, especially for Belle."

"He'll do his best, I'm sure. Speaking of Belle, where is she?"

"I don't know. I thought she would come with the Dunnigans, but I haven't seen her ..." They automatically looked to the trail that led to the meadow. Lucy White was coming down the hill, along with her husband Theodore and their two small children. A few other families followed, and Harvey Brown was up at the top of the hill. But of Belle, no sign. "I've been so busy helping the Mulligans with the planks and crates they brought to set the food on, I hadn't noticed who else was here," Sadie concluded.

Harrison suddenly raised his head and laughed. "Well, would you look at that!"

Sadie again turned toward the trail. Just coming down the hill, not far behind the stumbling Harvey Brown, were Colin and Belle, arm in arm. They heard Colin say something to Harvey and the tinkle of Belle's laughter as the couple made their way along the trail.

"I don't believe it," Harrison exclaimed. "How did he manage to get out of guard duty and escort Belle to the picnic?"

Sadie also stared, but more in concern. "And without a chaperone."

"You don't suppose they came with Harvey, do you?"

Sadie looked at her husband skeptically. "Mrs. Dunnigan ... allowing Belle to travel with *two* unmarried gentlemen?"

"You're quite right, dear wife," he said as he tilted his hat back into place. "I hadn't thought it through ..." He trailed off, then asked, "Do you suppose Mrs. Dunnigan even knows?"

"She will the minute she turns around."

They watched Mrs. Dunnigan, her back to the trail, as she spoke with Fanny Fig under the shade of "His Majesty." The townsfolk had placed their blankets, baskets and other items around the massive tree trunk until the picnic got fully underway.

Now Belle's laughter caught everyone's attention, as she and Colin were over halfway down the trail. Some turned and waved at the newcomers, others headed over to greet them.

Mrs. Dunnigan also turned to look, with a huge smile on her face. Then the smile vanished. Her eyes widened, closed tight, opened and widened again. She snorted like an about-to-charge bull, threw down the serving spoon she held in her hand and took a few steps forward, glowering at the couple as they reached the bottom of the trail.

Belle and Colin didn't notice. But they were walking toward Harrison and Sadie, who most certainly did.

Mrs. Dunnigan took one last look at Belle with Colin, glanced around herself and let fly with a noise somewhere between a wail and a locomotive whistle. Belle turned just in time to see her aunt drop to the ground in a faint that had it been on the stage, would have brought applause and some gasps from the audience. As it was, it did elicit a gasp from Fanny Fig, who threw up her arms in shock before making her way to her fallen friend.

Harrison would have been running to her as well if he hadn't noticed Mrs. Dunnigan looking for the best possible place to land beforehand. He turned to Sadie, who stood with her mouth open in shock. "Oh, dear."

"Auntie!" Belle exclaimed as she pulled away from Colin and dashed toward her aunt, who now lay in the grass on her back. Fanny Fig knelt beside her, fanning the unconscious form with her reticule, its long thin strings of beads hitting Mrs. Dunnigan in the face.

Harrison rolled his eyes at the scene. "Do you think they rehearsed it?" he asked his wife dryly.

Sadie was about to object to his cynicism, then stopped and thought about it. "Most likely," she replied before making her way to the gathering crowd.

Colin, meanwhile, watched in exasperation as he joined his brother. He grinned despite himself. "Did you see that? I didn't know Mrs. Dunnigan had it in her."

"And I didn't know our little picnic would come with a show." Harrison laughed and put his arm around Colin. "Come along, dear brother. Let's go see what she does for an encore."

Colin's face took on a more serious look. "Frankly, I'm afraid to find out."

Aunt Irene's eyes fluttered open as Fanny Fig continued her furious fanning/beating. Belle reached out and grabbed Fanny's wrist to stop her. At this point, she was convinced her aunt hadn't really fainted. Who could possibly stay insensate when one's face was being whipped by beaded fringe?

"Doc Waller!" Fanny cried.

Belle looked at the faces of the townsfolk who'd gathered. Doc Waller wasn't among them, but Grandma was. The old woman pushed her way through and bent to look at the patient. "You all right, Irene?"

Belle watched Aunt Irene moan and her eyes roll back.

"Someone fetch me a cup of water!" Grandma yelled.

"I don't think she's in any shape to drink anything," Harvey Brown commented.

"I'm not going to have her drink it! Nothing brings a person around quicker than a cupful of cold creek water thrown in their face."

Aunt Irene's eyes fluttered once more. Belle closed her own eyes and sighed. How far was her aunt going to take this?

"Here ya go, Grandma," Mr. Dunnigan said, handing her a cup.

"Land sakes, Wilfred! How'd you get this so fast?"

"Went to the creek the minute I seen her go down."

Belle looked at her uncle, who didn't seem overly concerned. *It seems I'm not the only "doubting Thomas." Oh, Auntie, really?*

"Belle ...," Aunt Irene moaned. She sounded like she was auditioning for the part of the ghost in *Hamlet*.

"You want this?" Grandma asked Belle, shoving the cup at her. Belle took it. "If she closes her eyes again, toss it at her. She'll come around." Obviously, she suspected Aunt Irene's faint was nothing more than theatrics as well.

Not all of the other townsfolk were so astute. "I'll help you take her back to town, Miss Belle," Harvey Brown offered.

"That's mighty neighborly of you, Harvey, but I'll take Irene back to town," Uncle Wilfred replied. "No sense you missing out on any of the festivities."

"Oh, well ... if Miss Belle is going to be staying, I'd be happy to keep an eye on her, Wilfred."

Belle stood as Harvey looked her up and down and smiled. Maybe she ought to toss the cup of water in *his* face ...

"No need, Harvey – the Cookes will look after her," Uncle Wilfred told him.

Aunt Irene moaned again.

Doc Waller finally showed up, a fishing pole in one hand, a lovely trout in the other. "What's all the commotion?"

"Irene's done 'fainted'." Wilfred drawled. "We'd best get her back to town."

"Belllllle ...." Aunt Irene wailed. "I need Belle!"

Doc Waller handed his pole and fish to Harvey. "Let's have a look." He knelt next to Aunt Irene and began to examine her. "Any headaches lately, Irene?"

She looked at Belle. "Yes," she moaned. "I think Belle should take me home and take care of me."

Grandma snorted. "A young gal from Boston taking care of a sick woman? What does she know about doctoring? I'll take you home myself and give you a good dose of castor oil! Trust me; it'll fix you right up!"

Aunt Irene moaned again. "Belle! Belle, where are you?"

Belle was now having trouble keeping a straight face. She felt sorry for her aunt, stooping to such childish antics – but not so sorry that she wasn't willing to have just as much fun with it as her uncle and the Wallers. "I trust your judgment, Mrs. Waller. If castor oil is what she really needs, then you'd best get her home and give her some."

Her aunt perked up at that. "Oh, Belle, just take me home, will you? I'll feel much better after I lie down."

"You're already lying down," Grandma quipped. "Seems to me you should be feeling better already."

Aunt Irene scowled. "Don't tell me how I should feel! You're not the doctor!"

"I agree with Grandma on this one," Uncle Wilfred said with a chuckle. "Now let's get you up and I'll take you home."

"But ... but what about Belle?" Aunt Irene screeched.

"What about her?"

"She's going home with us!"

"Why should she? She isn't feeling poorly. Harvey, give me a hand, will you?" Harvey helped Uncle Wilfred pull her aunt up from the grassy ground. She stood unsteadily and tried to grab Belle for support, but Uncle Wilfred, God bless him, was quicker and grabbed her instead. "Belle will be in good hands with the Cookes and the Figs. And Colin can bring her home," he added.

Belle couldn't believe her uncle had said it. She *could* believe how quickly Aunt Irene's face reddened in fury. The townsfolk backed up en masse.

"She will NOT stay with any of the Cookes! *Especially* Colin!" She turned to Belle in a rage. "You're coming home with me, young lady! NOW!"

Everyone stood in shock – except for the Wallers and Wilfred. "Mercy! She's done gone delusional!" Grandma cried.

"I think your diagnosis is correct, dear," Doc Waller chimed in. "Quick – you men carry her to Wilfred's wagon! And keep a tight hold on her – if she's beside herself, there's no telling what she might do!"

Harvey Brown, Theodore White, and Mr. Turner all got a hold of the raving Mrs. Dunnigan and began to haul her away. "Unhand me, you scoundrels! I'm not leaving without Belle! You either come home with me this instant, young lady, or don't come home at all!"

Wilfred proved he wasn't the only Dunnigan who could put on an act. "My poor dear! Don't do yourself a mischief, Irene – we'll take care of you!" he sobbed.

Harrison and Colin, standing off to one side, both held fists to their mouths to keep from laughing. The battle of wills being played out would be something to tell their children. And their grandchildren, and their great-grandchildren ...

The Van Cleets, just arrived, watched as Mrs. Dunnigan was hauled across the meadow to the trail, struggling and breathing threats and murder all the way. "Great Scott, what's happened?" Mr. Van Cleet exclaimed.

Doubt suddenly assailed Belle – what if her aunt's mental faculties truly had failed? Should she go home with her to make sure? Or would doing so simply play into her aunt's twisted game? Might she try something even more drastic to get what she wanted? "She was fine, I think, sir ... and then she fainted. Or ... maybe she fainted. I'm not sure ..."

Mrs. Van Cleet laughed and put an arm around Belle's shoulder. "Don't you worry none about your aunt. We've watched her do the same sort of thing before. Trust me; once your uncle gets her home he'll have a talk with her. He just won't shame her by doing it here out in front of everyone."

"It seems to me that perhaps a public shaming might do her some good," Mr. Van Cleet remarked.

"Cyrus!" Mrs. Van Cleet retorted, scandalized.

"Just a thought."

Colin came up behind them and put a hand on Belle's shoulder. "Your aunt will be all right."

She turned to him and put her arms around him, not caring what anyone else thought. "Oh, Colin ... I don't know how Uncle Wilfred puts up with it."

Colin sighed heavily. "Neither do I." He smiled at her, then turned – gently, so as not to dislodge her arms – to the rest of the crowd. "Now ... what say we have a picnic?"

# THIRTEEN

The afternoon grew warm. After a lunch of fried chicken, ham, fresh bread, biscuits, potatoes, vegetables and fruit pies, folks had to rest a bit before the real fun began.

And what fun it was! Many of the townsfolk waded in the shallow parts of Clear Creek to cool off after some of the more strenuous games. Tommy Turner caught the young pig Harrison had brought – and greased – much to his parents' delight, since whomever caught the animal got to keep it. Grandma Waller won Blind Man's Bluff and got the quilting squares and a new ladle. Lucy White won the feather dance, able to keep it afloat the longest, and picked the hammer and a tablecloth as her prizes. And just as the game of tug o' war was to begin, Duncan and Henry Fig showed up.

"About time!" Harrison called. "Come, you two – join our team!"

Duncan approached slowly, turning to look up the trail, then back to his brothers. "I was hoping Jefferson would be here by now."

"I'm not sure he'll come," Colin told him. "I asked him about it last night, but ... well, he wasn't exactly in a talking mood."

"He's been going to town quite a bit to play cards. Could be he's looking for a game."

"He won't find one today," Henry said. "Mulligan's is closed. And I think the wagon train camped outside of town moved on."

"You're right, Henry. Which makes me wonder all the more." Duncan surveyed the scene. Some of the women were near the creek with the children old enough to go wading. Others lounged on blankets under "His Majesty's" shade. Belle and Sadie were chatting with Lucy White while keeping an eye on the White and Turner children playing nearby. The remaining food had been consolidated onto a table made from a couple of crates and a wide plank, but Tommy Turner and several men were still chowing down. Everyone looked happy and content.

"Harvey!" Colin called as he noted Harvey Brown working his way toward Belle and Sadie. "Come choose your team! We're about to start."

Duncan smiled and looked to Colin. "He's still trying, is he?"

"Of course. Just with the wrong lady."

"She's the only lady," Harrison added. "But I think it's safe to say, dear brother that, after today the whole town knows she's yours."

"Yes ... well, someone needs to inform Harvey," Colin said flatly. "He's been buzzing around Belle all afternoon."

"Speaking of Belle, what happened to Mrs. Dunnigan?" Duncan asked. "She and Wilfred came back to town early. We could tell she was in a state, but no one would tell us why. Wilfred even offered to stand guard with Rev. King, once he unhitched his wagon and put his horses up at the livery."

Harrison and Colin glanced at one another. "We'll tell you later," they both said at once.

Duncan and Henry noted their pained looks and decided to let it lie. Besides, it was time for the tug-of-war.

Much to the Cookes' dismay, Doc took what men wanted to play and split them into two teams himself, and did it carefully to keep them balanced. Mr. Berg, who'd come not an hour before Duncan and Henry, had brought the rope with him from the livery stable. One team – Colin, Harvey Brown, Henry Fig, Theodore White and Sheriff Hughes – crossed the creek where it was shallow and headed up to the chosen spot. Doc called for the women, children and the older men to follow him and the other team – Harrison, Duncan, Tommy Turner, and Mr. Berg – up the creek to where it narrowed.

The place they'd picked had a steep bank on both sides, and the water was fairly deep. Oregon creek water in June was fine for wading, but decidedly chilly for swimming. Neither side relished a loss and subsequent drenching.

Mr. Mulligan tossed one half of the long rope across the water to the opposing team. When ready, the men positioned themselves. Doc stood to one side, raised a gun Harrison had given him, and fired. Screams and shouts rent the air as the women cheered the men's efforts. Even the children let loose a screech or two as the men fought for control of the rope. The older men, including Mr. Mulligan and Mr. Van Cleet, laughed and heckled both teams as they began to strain with the effort it took to keep their ground.

The men grunted as they tugged and pulled, each team in turn looking as if they had the win only to lose ground and come perilously close to falling in. Finally, as if tired of the whole affair, Mr. Berg gave one powerful tug, putting all his weight into it, and Colin was instantly yanked into the creek. Everyone burst out laughing as Colin yelped in surprise and hit the water headfirst. Three of the men behind him, seeing Colin's feet leave the ground, wisely let go of the rope before they too were dragged in, but Harvey Brown, not as quick as the others, followed in Colin's wake.

Unfortunately, upon surfacing Harvey began to panic. He grabbed at Colin's neck and shoulders as he fought to stay afloat, repeatedly pulling him underwater.

"Harvey!" Colin sputtered. "What are you doing? Good Lord, man, get a hold of yourself before you drown me!"

"What for? He's got a hold of *you,* hasn't he?" Mr. Mulligan laughed.

"I can't swim!" Harvey cried.

Thankfully, the water was only chest-high, and finally Colin was able to pry Harvey's loose and stand him up. Harvey blinked a few times in shock when he realized the water was only four feet deep, then sheepishly made his way to the nearest bank as the townsfolk laughed even harder. Harrison and Duncan had fallen to their knees in hysterics. Belle and Sadie were laughing so hard they had to hang onto each other for support.

It was a perfect ending to the event. Between the food, the camaraderie, the games and Irene Dunnigan's impromptu performance, everyone agreed it was the most fun the townsfolk of Clear Creek had ever had together.

Everyone but one.

Jefferson Cooke stood near the picnic baskets and munched on a piece of chicken as he listened to the laughter coming from up the creek. He ate a piece of pie next before turning his back on the whole affair and mounting his horse. From the saddle he could better see through the trees to where everyone else was. No one had noticed him when he rode down the trail. No one noticed him now. And no one would notice him leave.

He turned his horse and cantered across the meadow to the trail leading up out of the canyon. Nobody cared if he came or went, he grumbled to himself. Nobody would say a thing. His name was tarred black by those worthless boys of Honoria's.

Jack and Sam should be the ones being cheered on by the townsfolk, the ones hosting the picnic. But they'd been tricked, robbed of their birthright and locked away. It should be Jack and Sam that had the women, too. For all Jefferson knew, one of his boys had had Sadie sparking for them before that whelp Harrison came along and stole her for himself. And the Dunnigan girl? One of his boys could have had her sweet on him in less than a day, maybe even marry her. If he hadn't been rotting in jail, that is.

But no, Colin had staked claim – he'd heard Harrison and Duncan talking about it only yesterday. Jefferson had figured Mrs. Dunnigan would take care of Colin by now. He wanted to watch him suffer as she cut him to pieces with her sharp tongue. But even she was no match for the luck those boys seemed to have.

He reached the top of the trail and looked over the teams, wagons, and the few horses left there, including Romeo, Duncan's magnificent black stallion which he'd hobbled a short distance away from the others. Sam had wanted the horse when he was a colt, but Duncan earned the money doing extra work in town and bought him before Sam could. Just one more slight among all the others.

Jefferson snarled and reached up to gingerly rub his throbbing temple. He took one last look behind him, then rode his horse past the waiting wagons. He didn't care if Mulligan's was closed or not. He needed a drink.

Belle had her arm hooked through Colin's as he drove them back to town. Most of the townsfolk had already left. He'd offered to take her back at the same time, but she'd wanted to stay behind to help Sadie and the Cookes clean up. Colin didn't mind, as it gave him a chance to change into some dry clothes.

It was dusk before they were done, the setting sun casting a golden light on the trail as they made the climb out of the canyon to the wagons. It was a beautiful sight, and Belle stopped at one point to take it all in. Colin smiled as he waited for her, took her hand when she'd had her fill, and continued the climb.

At the top, they'd helped Harrison and Duncan load the table Harrison had brought into his and Sadie's wagon. Belle sighed as she watched Harrison kiss Sadie before helping her up onto the buckboard, realizing how much she wanted what her new friend had. But soon, she thought, she just might. She was going back to town with a man she'd fallen in love, and who showed every sign of feeling the same way about her.

She looked at Colin, who sat with a smile on his face. Dare she rest her head on his shoulder? The rocking back and forth of the wagon was making her sleepy, and the thought of resting against him warmed her. But Duncan was following along behind on his horse Romeo. What would he think?

As if sensing her thoughts, Colin pulled his arm from her own and put it around her shoulders. He looked at her then, letting her know it was all right to get closer.

Which she did. All the way back to town.

"Irene, be reasonable!" Wilfred said while ducking. The vase barely missed him as it flew over his head and crashed against the parlor wall.

"Reasonable? REASONABLE?! You left her there with those Cookes! What have you done? She'll come back ruined, I tell you! No decent man will want her then!"

Wilfred looked at the shattered pieces of china scattered on the floor. He obviously was getting nowhere with her. Maybe Grandma Waller was "joking on the square" when she said Irene was delusional. She was beyond even his control at this point. Even prayer didn't seem to work anymore. "Irene, you can't go on like this. Neither can I, or Belle for that matter. Now calm down and let's have some tea—"

"Tea! How can you think of drinking tea at a time like this?" A hurled spatula missed him, wide to his left.

He sighed sadly. This had happened several years before, too – it was why they had come out west from Kansas. He'd hoped a different environment would calm his dear wife's soul. And it had worked ... for a while. But clearly she was going crazy again – and he was out of ideas.

"I won't see our niece ruined because you didn't – wait! Where do you think you're going?!"

Wilfred's shoulders were slumped in defeat as he headed for the door. "Out. I need to make sense of all this. Because, at this point, you sure ain't making any."

His wife immediately blocked his path. "You're not going anywhere! You'll stay right here!"

Something in Wilfred snapped. "Woman, I ain't your dog, and I ain't your slave!" he yelled at the top of his lungs. "I'll do what I please! Now *move* it, or I'll move it for ya!"

Her mouth dropped open in shock. He'd never spoken to her in such a fashion. Her body seemed to deflate as she stepped aside. "Wilfred," she said, her voice shaky. "If you set foot outside that door ... you'll regret it."

"If I don't," he replied threateningly, "we'll both regret it." He left, not even bothering to close the door behind him.

She stood there a moment, shaking like a leaf, before pulling together enough of her rage to stomp over to the broken vase. She began to pick up the pieces, mumbling to herself the entire time before she suddenly stopped. She turned, her face flaming, and threw the shards on the floor before storming out the door herself.

She tore downstairs, through the mercantile, across the porch and into the street ... just in time to see her husband go into Mulligan's saloon.

Colin guided the team past the livery stable and would've headed down the street to the mercantile, but Duncan rode up and waved him to a stop in front of Mulligan's. "What's wrong, brother?"

Duncan pointed to horses tethered outside the saloon. Jefferson's was one of them. "Jefferson must've come to town to wait for Mr. Mulligan to open up."

"Oh, dear," Belle sighed. She wasn't the only one with family problems, she saw.

"But who else is in there?" Colin asked. "Everyone from the picnic has gone home, as far as I knew."

Duncan frowned. "Maybe some of the wagon train stayed behind. Maybe he managed to find a game after all." He snorted in frustration. "Miss Dunnigan, I do apologize, but I may need Colin's help talking him into coming home with us. He may not want to go without a fight." He felt bad about it – the whole way back to town, he'd ridden behind Colin and Belle at a distance to give them a little privacy. The last thing he wanted to do was force them to part.

"It's all right, I understand. I can ... I can walk home from here." Belle sounded like she was trying to convince herself.

"But your aunt ...," Colin began.

"Has probably gotten a thorough talking-to from my uncle. I think it'll be safe for me. For you ..." She left the thought unfinished.

Colin had to admit that she did have a point. "All right. But if there's any trouble, run back here. We shan't be inside long, I promise." He kissed the top of her head, jumped down, then helped her down as well. He wanted to hold onto her, for her own safety as well as his sake, but resisted.

"Thank you, Colin. I had a lovely day." She kissed his on the cheek and turned for home.

Colin would've melted on the spot had other responsibilities not been calling. With a sigh, he went to assist a now-smirking Duncan with getting Jefferson home. But in that moment, he also made up his mind about another important matter.

As soon as circumstances would permit, regardless of what his family or hers had to say, he was going to ask Belle Dunnigan to marry him.

Belle entered the parlor quietly. A lamp was lit, but there was no sign of her aunt and uncle. Perhaps they were already asleep in their room. Or after the theatrics that afternoon, maybe Aunt Irene was too embarrassed to face her. She went into the kitchen, knowing that Uncle Wilfred liked a snack before he went to bed, but that room too was empty.

Curious, she went to their room and knocked on the door. "Uncle Wilfred? Auntie? I'm home."

"All right, dear," came her aunt's voice from inside.

"Are you both in bed? I can put out the parlor lamp if you are."

"No, leave it on. I'll get it later."

Belle thought it odd her aunt sounded so subdued. But possibly her uncle had indeed managed to calm her. The poor woman was probably sitting in there with her tail between her legs after downing the huge piece of humble pie he'd served up. She could just picture Uncle Wilfred sitting in his chair by the window, eyeing her disapprovingly. Perhaps now things would be more bearable, and they could all look forward to peaceful days. One had to hope. "I'm going to turn in, then. I stayed behind with Sadie to clean up. All that work has tired me out."

"You do that, dear."

"Good night, Auntie." Belle smiled, then went to her room to get ready for bed.

Once there, she put on her nightclothes, brushed and braided her hair, then closed the window, crawled under her quilt and snuggled into the mattress. She was exhausted, but not so exhausted that she couldn't stop thinking about Colin's gentle kisses or his worry for her as they parted. If she thought she was in love before, now she *knew*. She could happily spend the rest of her life with Colin Cooke – all he had to do was ask. She envisioned him going down on one knee several times before sleep blissfully carried her away.

But sleep didn't come so easily for everyone in the Dunnigan house. For down the hall in her room, Aunt Irene sat, her hatchet and a bag of nails in her hands. And waited.

# FOURTEEN

Wilfred studied the board again. His checker rivalry with Sheriff Harlan Hughes was sort of legendary in Clear Creek. Furthermore, this was their last game of the week, and they'd gone into it tied, so whoever won this one had bragging rights for the next week. Men were gathered around the small table where they played – this match was garnishing more attention than any poker game had in months.

If Wilfred was honest with himself, just being able to this well lately was a mercy. He hadn't won a week of checkers against Harlan in a month. He'd been too distracted trying to keep the men away from Belle since she arrived ... not to mention keeping Irene and her hatchet away from the men.

Speaking of which ... Colin Cooke, Belle's beau (and Irene's chief antagonist), was leaning over his right shoulder studying the board. His brother Duncan stood behind the sheriff, doing the same. Even their stepfather had pulled up a chair, abandoning his cards to come watch with the other men. Wilfred was beginning to feel a bit crowded.

"Go on, Wilfred, make your move. I haven't got all night," the sheriff urged, annoyed.

"Yeah, we wanna get back to playing poker, but we can't until you beat Sheriff Hughes!" someone called from across the saloon. Men laughed and slapped each other on the back.

"Don't rush me! Let me figure this out!" Wilfred grumbled. He raised a hand above the board, his fingers poised over a piece. The sheriff pulled out his handkerchief and wiped the sweat from his brow. The closeness of the crowd was causing the air to heat up something awful.

Wilfred suddenly picked up his piece and in one brilliant move took out four of Sheriff Hughes'. "Ha!" he exclaimed. "See if you can top that!"

The sheriff shook his head. How had he not seen it? The picnic must have really worn him out. "Unbelievable. Just unbelievable." He held out his hand across the table to shake Wilfred's. "Congratulations."

Wilfred shook, then let out a whoop of triumph. "I believe I've outplayed you this week, Harlan, so that makes me the winner!"

Sheriff Hughes sat back in his chair. "Yep, it sure does," he replied, still shaking his head in wonder. "Tarnation."

The men gathered around laughed again, and a few slapped Wilfred on the back to congratulate him before they dispersed to their tables. Even Jefferson snickered, then returned to the game he'd left.

Or tried to. Duncan grabbed his arm and stopped him. "We're heading back to the ranch. You'll come with us, won't you?"

Jefferson wrenched his arm from him. "I'm not a child you can order about, boy. Get on home and leave me alone."

Colin came around the table where Wilfred and the sheriff were setting up another game – this one just for fun. "You've had enough whiskey and poker for one night. Now come home before these chaps take you for everything you've got."

Jefferson looked to the men sitting at the corner table where he usually played. They were the same wagon train scouts he'd played with before. They'd left for a few days, but were already back. "I'm fine, and I prefer their company to yours. Now leave me be – I can make it home on my own."

Duncan rubbed his face with his hand before he spoke. "We know you've been out of sorts these last months, but it's time to stop all this. Come home and let's talk about things."

Jefferson spun on him. "Things? What things? Like how you boys cheated Jack and Sam out of everything they had?"

Everything went silent. Several men at the table froze and watched to see what Jefferson would do next.

"Get out of my sight and leave me alone!" Jefferson looked his stepsons in the eyes, spat on the floor, then went to the table and sat down.

Colin and Duncan looked at each other, then at their stepfather. Colin pulled at Duncan's sleeve. "This is getting us nowhere. Let's go." They turned and left.

But once they were outside, Duncan stopped Colin. "We can wait at the edge of town. He'll have to come home eventually, but with how much he's been drinking, someone needs to make sure he gets home in one piece. Once we're home, we can sober him up and talk with him."

"Hopefully," Colin added.

Duncan shrugged, conceding the point.

Colin's brow furrowed in thought. "Do you mind getting the horses ready? I just remembered one other thing I need to do." Without waiting for an answer, he walked back into Mulligan's. He went to the table where Wilfred and Sheriff Hughes had started their next game. "I'm sorry to interrupt, Mr. Dunnigan, but I need to speak with you tomorrow. There's something I'd like to ask you."

Wilfred looked up at him. "This wouldn't happen to have anything to do with Belle, would it?"

Colin smiled. "Yes, sir, it would."

Wilfred began to chuckle. "Come by the mercantile in the morning then, son."

"I'll do that."

Colin left again. Jefferson watched him go, and seethed. He'd overheard what Colin said – that sorry excuse for a stepson was going to ask Wilfred for his niece's hand, no doubt. Jefferson slugged back another drink. The worthless whelp certainly didn't waste time! If Jack or Sam were there, they'd show her what a real man was. She wouldn't give either of Honoria's brats a second thought if his sons were there to court her.

He poured himself another drink, his jaw tight, hands shaking. Jack would show her what for. He wouldn't ask her to marry him, he'd tell her! And Sam – he'd just take her, the way a man ought to, and make her like it! Yep, that's what his boys would do!

"Are you gonna play poker or sit there and stare at the wall? What's the matter with you, anyway?"

He snarled at the man who spoke. He didn't even know his name and didn't care. He downed his drink, grabbed the whiskey bottle and stood. "I'm leaving. Play without me."

"But we just dealt you in!"

"Well then, you can just deal me out!" His hands shaking, Jefferson turned and left the saloon.

In the middle of the night, Belle awoke to an odd banging sound.

She thought at first she was hearing things, but no, there it was again. She slowly sat up. Was someone ... hammering something?

She sat still, waited, and in a moment, heard it a third time. It sounded like it was coming from the parlor ... "What in the world?" she said to herself as she got out of bed, went to her closed door and listened once more. Silence.

Belle put on her robe and stepped out into the hall. She took several steps forward before she stopped. "Uncle Wilfred?" She took a few more steps. "Auntie?"

She finally stepped into the parlor and couldn't believe her eyes. Aunt Irene stood near the door leading from the parlor to the outside landing and staircase. She had her dreaded hatchet in her hand and was holding a few nails in her teeth as she looked at the board she'd nailed across the door.

"What are you doing?" Belle gasped.

Her aunt spit the nails out, put one hand on her hip and waved the hatchet around with the other. "Your no-good uncle has gone to the saloon! I'll not sleep with a man who takes to gambling and drinking, and I won't allow him in my house! He can sleep in the livery stable for all I care!"

Belle's eyes widened. Aunt Irene had made sure Uncle Wilfred wouldn't be able to get through the door, all right – the board had enough nails in it to hold off Santa Anna's army! "Auntie, you ought to be ashamed!"

"*I'm* not the one who ought to be ashamed! You're the one coming home after dark, after traipsing around with that Colin Cooke! Get out of my sight, you ... you ..."

"Don't say it. Don't you dare," Belle warned.

Her aunt's eyes narrowed. "... you little whore!"

Belle took a deep breath. Only the hatchet was keeping her from walking over to her aunt and slapping her across the face, elder or no elder. Right now, spending the night in the livery stable with Uncle Wilfred sounded mighty good compared to spending the rest of the night with her aunt. She turned on her heel without a word and marched back to her room to pack.

She could hear Aunt Irene huff and puff her way down the hall after her. Reaching her room, she slammed the door behind her. At this point she didn't care if she slammed it in Aunt Irene's face – in fact, she rather hoped she had! She doffed her robe and took her dress from where she'd hung it, all the while waiting for her aunt's verbal explosion from the other side of the door.

But there was no outburst, no screaming, no insults. Just the sound of a key turning in the lock.

Belle froze. Aunt Irene had just locked her in her room.

The more she thought about it, though, the angrier she got. So, that's the game you wish to play, eh? Well, it was about time Aunt Irene learned that she wasn't a little child to be pushed around. And – here Belle looked at the window – there was more than one way to escape a madhouse. Fueled by her fury, she hauled out her satchel and started filling it.

Jefferson mounted his horse and sat a moment to get his bearings. Dizziness hit, and he gripped the saddle horn with one hand to keep his seat. Those spells were coming more frequently, even when he wasn't drinking. They'd started when Jack and Sam were sent up the river.

He shook his head a few times to clear it, then turned his horse around to head home.

Behind him, he heard the saloon's double doors swing open as someone stepped outside. The creak of leather followed – whoever it was had just mounted a horse.

He didn't even reach the sheriff's office before the man rode up beside him. "None o' my business, mister.

But I couldn't help overhear what those younguns and you was talkin' about."

"What's it to you?" Jefferson slurred.

The man shrugged. "Well, my guess is your sons are Jack and Sam Cooke."

Jefferson stopped his horse in front of the mercantile. "What do you know about Jack and Sam?" he snarled.

"Not much. Just what folks say along the trail."

Jefferson squinted at him in the moonlight. "Do I know you? Have we played cards?"

"We've played a few times, 'member?"

Jefferson took another look, then sat up straight in his saddle and took a swig from the whiskey bottle in his hand. "You do look familiar ..."

"I should. Mind if I have some of that?" the man asked, pointing to the bottle.

Jefferson held it to his chest protectively "I don't recall your name."

The man flashed a brilliant smile. "Name's Jeb. Now do you 'member me?"

"Not right now, I don't." But he handed him the bottle.

Jeb took a long swallow, grimaced and spat most of it out. "You call this whiskey? This is terrible!"

Jefferson eyed the bottle. "Does me fine."

"Then shoot – you oughta try some *good* whiskey, friend! I gotta bottle back at my camp, straight from Kentucky. Why not come with me and share it?"

Jefferson squinted at him again. He still couldn't remember the man very well, but did recollect playing cards with him last week. And a good bottle of Kentucky whiskey was tempting ...

"Come with me an' you can tell me what really happened to Jack an' Sam. I hear yer stepsons done swindled 'em good."

"Worthless, the lot of them! Jack and Sam should have it all by now – the new house, the stock ..." He glanced at the upper story of the mercantile and saw the lamp burning in the window. "... the women. Those stepsons of mine took it all!"

Jeb leaned toward him. "Bet you'd like to get back at 'em, wouldn'tcha?"

Jefferson snarled. "That's a mighty stupid question, ain't it?"

Jeb laughed. "When a man takes sumpin' from ya, you take sumpin' from him."

Jefferson looked at him a moment, then glanced at the lighted window of the mercantile. His face contorted with his rising anger. He reached over for the bottle.

Jeb handed it back. "Yeah ... you'd like to pay them boys back for what they did to Jack an' Sam. And like I said, take sumpin' from them to make things even, right? I can help ya do that."

"Can you now?"

Jeb smiled again. "You have no idea. For instance, I can get them steers those boys were given, turn around an' give 'em to you. Come with me, an' I'll tell ya how."

Jefferson slowly grinned before he took another swig from the bottle. "That does sound mighty fine. But I also want to get even my own way." With a look born from months of jealousy and rage, he turned his horse toward the mercantile and threw the whiskey bottle as hard as he could at the lighted window. It crashed through the glass, hit the lamp, and knocked it over. "Lead the way. I could use some good whiskey," he added.

Jeb laughed as the first flames shot up from the parlor floor and caught the curtains on fire. He kicked his horse, and the two of them galloped out of town.

"How long do you suppose he'll stay?" Colin asked as he absently picked at the reins in his hand.

Romeo shifted restlessly, and Duncan patted his neck to calm him. "Not sure, but we can at least assure he gets home safely."

They waited behind the last building on the street, directly across from Doc Waller's house. They would easily be able to watch Jefferson leave town, as the road went right past them, yet from their position they would go unnoticed. They could follow him home at a distance.

"I'm going to talk to Wilfred tomorrow," Colin said casually.

Duncan gave a low chuckle. "Harrison and I were wondering how long you'd be able to hold out. But Wilfred won't be a problem. It's Mrs. Dunnigan you have to worry about. Have you thought ..."

A sound caught their attention. "What was that?" Colin asked. "It sounded like glass breaking."

Suddenly they heard horses approaching at a good gallop. Two riders rode out of town but didn't stay on the main road, instead veering to the left and heading across the prairie.

"Who is that leaving in such a hurry?" Duncan asked.

"I'm not sure, but I think one of them was Jefferson."

"What? Heavens, man, it's amazing he can stay on his horse with as much whiskey as he's had! He must be gripping his saddle for dear life!" Duncan kicked Romeo and cantered to the middle of the road leading into town.

Something wasn't right. He turned as an odd light caught his attention. "Colin!" He spun Romeo around and rode up to the wagon. "Get on, *now!*"

Colin had no idea what was going on, but he didn't hesitate. He jumped onto Romeo's back behind

Duncan, and they raced down the street to the mercantile. The upper story was in flames.

"Good God!" Colin yelled and jumped off. "Belle!" He ran up the steps and tried to open the door, but it was locked. He kicked it open, entered, and immediately tore across the room and up the stairs to the second story. Smoke was already filling the stairwell, forcing him to cover his nose and mouth with the bandana he wore around his neck.

"Belle!" He reached the top of the stairs and tried the door. Locked again. *Oh, Lord, please!* He backed up a step and tried to kick it in as well. It gave, but not enough – something was blocking it from the inside. He tried again, but it still wouldn't open. "Belle! Mrs. Dunnigan! Can anyone hear me?"

Duncan was suddenly behind him. "What's wrong?" he yelled over the increasing roar of the fire.

"Something's blocking it!"

"Together then!" With that, the two brothers stepped back, then rammed into the door with their shoulders as best they could. Whatever was blocking gave a little more.

"Again!" Colin cried. They rammed it a second time, and the door cracked, the barrier holding it loosening enough to allow the door to open.

"Mrs. Dunnigan!" Colin cried as he saw her flattened against the wall of the kitchen. One side of the parlor was completely engulfed in flames. They didn't have much time. They grabbed her and pulled her from the wall, through the parlor and toward the stairwell.

"Noooo!" she cried and flailed at them. Colin couldn't believe it! Didn't the woman realize she could get them all killed if she kept this up?

"No time to argue!" Duncan yelled. He got behind her and pushed as Colin pulled. Finally they got her through the door to the landing.

Colin turned to Duncan. "Can you take care of her? I've got to find Belle!"

"No, no!" Mrs. Dunnigan cried. "You can't!"

"I'll manage," Duncan replied. "Go!"

Colin took off. She had to be in one of the bedrooms – there was nothing else up here. He struggled to breathe as he ran down the smoke-filled hall and tried the first door. It opened. "Belle! Where are you?" He could hardly see because of the smoke, but there was no answer.

He ran back out into the hall and went to the second door. Locked. What was it with locked doors tonight? "Belle?" he yelled as he pounded on it.

Nothing.

He tried to kick it in. Nothing.

He rammed it with his shoulder. It didn't budge.

"Belle!" He began to choke. The smoke and flames were becoming too much, and his strength was failing. If he didn't get out now, he wouldn't get out at all. But he had to find Belle! He again rammed his body against the door. "No! NO! Belle!"

Someone grabbed him from behind and began to pull him away. "No! Belle!" He began to cough and couldn't stop. His vision blurred, his knees went weak. Someone picked him up, and he suddenly realized he'd been slung over a very broad shoulder.

"No-o-o ..." And then, only blackness – and the thought that Belle, his precious angel, was surely no more.

# FIFTEEN

Belle was all packed – now she just had to figure out how to leave. She loved her Aunt Irene, but the woman had clearly gone "round the bend," and it wasn't safe to stay under the same roof as her right now. She checked the door as she rubbed her eyes, which had suddenly become dry and irritated. No, still locked – and since it swung into the room, trying to ram it open from her side wouldn't help. Even if she had been big and strong enough to do it, which she wasn't.

That left only one other reasonable option: the window.

Belle pulled the curtains aside and lifted the window up. She stuck her head out to see if there was a way to climb down or slide down or somehow escape her captivity short of dropping twenty feet straight to the ground. Directly below ... nothing. To the left ... nothing. To the right ... only a bright light and a lot of smoke ...

*Smoke?!* She took another look. "Oh, no!" she gasped as she realized that the light and smoke were coming from the parlor at the front of the house! "Fire!" she screamed out the window, hoping someone, anyone was still awake to hear her. "Fiiiiiire!"

The room was heating up, and smoke was filling it. She began to cough and become disoriented. She made for the door, stumbled and fell, but in doing so pulled a quilt off of her bed. Hurriedly, she stuffed it in the crack under the door, hoping it would buy her some time.

She began crawling back to the window, dragging her satchel and coughing horribly. She tried to cover her nose and mouth, but couldn't manage to do it and crawl at the same time. Finally she just held her breath until she reached the windowed wall. But when she touched the sill, she found the wood was hot. *Very* hot, and the flames were nearing that opening as well. She was trapped!

"Oh, Lord! Help! HEEEEEEELP!" she cried, though she didn't know if she could even be heard above the roaring flames. But what other choice did she have?

Another coughing fit struck her, and she toppled away from the window, only to land on a pair of booted feet. She yelped in alarm at the contact.

Hands grabbed onto her, and whoever it was tried to pull her to her feet.

"Auntie! My aunt is ... is out there!" she protested, pointing to the door. But her rescuer said nothing, instead carrying her back to the window. She gave in, unable to stand and barely able to breathe.

She heard his boot hit something on the floor near the window. Of course, her satchel. He grabbed it by the handle, tossed it out the window, then pulled Belle to her feet and began to send her after it.

"No! I can't!" Belle cried. She couldn't see the ground below – they were too high, and there was too much smoke. If the fire didn't kill them, the fall surely would. But her rescuer was determined. And at least out there, the air was cooler and cleaner. She was able to get in a few deep breaths, and it lent her some strength.

She looked down again, and saw a wagon was under the window with something in the back of it. Before she knew it, she was falling, and she prayed urgently for a soft landing.

*Whumpppf!* She hit what felt like a pile of folded blankets, hard enough to knock the wind out of her but, as far as she could tell, not hard enough to break anything. She rolled onto her side just before she heard another impact behind her, and felt the wagon shake. And did she hear a horse nickering? Perhaps ... she wasn't sure of anything right now. Including how the wagon had gotten there - it certainly hadn't been there a minute earlier ...

The body behind Belle rose up and crawled past her onto the driver's seat. Horses neighed, and the wagon quickly moved away from the burning building, past her uncle's small barn and away from the danger. She looked up and saw her room now engulfed in flames. Had her rescuer not gotten her out when he did, she'd be dead right now.

But who *was* her rescuer?

After a minute, the wagon stopped. They were now over a hundred yards from the mercantile, which thankfully stood alone. The buildings on either side, one of which was the sheriff's office, had at least ten yards between themselves and the now-raging inferno. At least they wouldn't go up in flames also.

Belle coughed, swallowed, and slowly sat up. This wagon was familiar, as were the blankets she was seated on. She suddenly realized she was in the wagon Colin had used to drive her out to the picnic and back to town. It belonged to the Rev. King! And she and Sadie had loaded the quilts and blankets into it themselves – Aunt Irene and Uncle Wilfred had brought them out in case some folks didn't have one. But when Colin and Duncan had gone to find their stepfather and she'd headed for home on her own, she hadn't been able to carry them with her ...

"Auntie!" she cried. *Oh, Lord! My aunt! Where is she? I'm so sorry I was angry with her!* She began to sob uncontrollably.

She felt arms curl around her, and she held onto her rescuer with everything she had. A hand stroked her hair, patted her back to comfort her, but it didn't stop the tears from coming. She'd lost her aunt and uncle, the only relatives she had ...

Or had she? Where was Uncle Wilfred? Was he home when the fire broke out? And had someone rescued Aunt Irene before getting to her? She didn't actually know, did she?

She tried to calm herself, took a deep breath, coughed and almost retched. The hands of her rescuer still stroked, patted and drew her close. A small pair of arms. Not Colin's, certainly, or Duncan's, or her uncle's, or ... She gulped down several breaths, then pulled away to see who had saved her life.

"Oh!" she said, almost laughing. "It's you!"

Cosime Duprie gave her a hint of a smile, his eyes round with concern.

And suddenly Belle realized that he wasn't a boy – that in fact, he wasn't a *he*. Without the animal-skin hat covering the facial features and long hair, anyone could see the "boy" was, in reality, a young woman! And a pretty one, from what could be seen in the moonlight. Her femininity was obscured behind several layers of dirt, buckskins, and furred accessories – possibly on purpose.

She scooted away from Belle and glanced quickly around. Her movements reminded Belle of a nervous animal, on the lookout for predators.

"I think I ... *cough* ... I need water."

The girl pointed to the town.

Belle did her best not to cry again. "My Uncle Wilfred – I don't know if he was there! I–"

Once again, Cosime – or was it Cosette, or something similar? – pointed to the town, but in earnest.

"My uncle, is he alive?"

The girl nodded vigorously.

"Oh, thank God!" Belle cried and grabbed the girl in a fierce hug. "We have to go back! I have to be with Uncle Wilfred! I have to know what happened to my aunt!"

The girl looked at the flames that still raged, then to Belle. She nodded again, and quickly got out of the wagon.

"What? Where are you going?" Belle asked, confused.

The girl grabbed one of the horses' bridles and began to lead it. She walked a wide half-circle to turn the wagon toward town and stopped. She climbed back on, took the reins and held them out to Belle.

Belle stared blankly at them. This really wasn't a good time for her first driving lesson. "Aren't you coming with me?"

The girl shook her head.

"But why not?"

The girl pointed to her head, touched her hair, then her face.

"Oh. No one knows you're really a girl, do they? Only your father."

She nodded, and offered her the reins again.

Belle crawled over the wagon bench and sat next to her. She took the reins, then hugged the young woman who had saved her life. "Thank you. If there's anything I can do for you ..."

The girl again pointed to her head, touched her long hair and her face, then held a finger to her lips and made a *shhhh* sound.

"I understand. Your secret is safe with me."

Cosime – or whatever her name was - smiled and hopped down from the wagon. She went to the back and took something from it, then let part of it fall to the ground as she coiled the attached rope. Belle gasped – it was a three-pronged grappling hook, like the ones used by mountaineers! So that was how she'd gotten into her room to save her – and maybe how she'd gotten into the mercantile to retrieve her bag of candy earlier.

But what kind of woman performed such feats? Belle thought about it, then saw the answer was obvious: a woman who lived out in the wilderness, alone except for her father. A woman who'd had to live her whole life by her wits and her brawn.

The rope coiled, she picked up the hook and began to head northeast, probably toward the camp Mr. Van Cleet's men and workers had set up outside of town. Her father was likely waiting for her there.

Belle sat and watched her depart, fascinated despite herself. Colin had referred to Belle as "his angel," and now, it seemed, she had one of her own – of the guardian variety!

*Colin!*

The thought snapped Belle back to reality, to finding her aunt and uncle, and making sure everyone else in her life was safe. She gave the horses a slap with the reins and quickly headed back to town. "Fire! Help! Fire at the mercantile!"

Colin had fought like a savage – Duncan couldn't hold him on his own. It finally took Anton Duprie, the French trapper who'd carried him from the burning building, punching him in the jaw to stop his struggling. He fell into his brother's arms, unconscious.

The men were by the steps to the sheriff's office, a safe distance from the tempest that had once been Dunnigan's Mercantile. Nearby, Mrs. Dunnigan was in hysterics, Mr. Dunnigan trying to calm her the best he could amidst his own grief. "No, my Belle, my Belle! What have I done? Ohhhh, what have I done?" she wailed.

Duncan dragged Colin farther away from her. The last thing his brother needed was to come to and hear *that*. He still had no idea why Mrs. Dunnigan had barred the door, or why Colin was unable to get into Belle's room. All he knew was that his brother was safe.

And that was in large part thanks to Anton Duprie. He'd come out of nowhere, racing in just as Duncan was dragging a kicking and screaming Mrs. Dunnigan out. Like Colin, she'd tried mightily to run back into the burning mercantile and find Belle, and it had been all Duncan could do to stop her. All the other men were busy trying to fight the fire.

And now the trapper was nowhere in sight. Go figure.

Colin came back to reality, and immediately began to cry. Duncan held him as the tears fell. There were no words to give comfort, nothing he could say. All he could do for his brother was what he was doing.

Men ran hither and yon, both locals and Van Cleet's men, trying in vain to put out the fire. But it was no use – the mercantile was lost before they'd even known it was on fire. Too little, too late, the saying went. And now they would mourn, for it was not only the mercantile they'd lost.

As Colin's sobs subsided, Duncan noticed that some of the men had stopped, looking with shock at something behind Duncan and Colin – in the opposite direction from the fire! Duncan turned his head as best he could while keeping a hold of his brother.

And then his jaw dropped.

Mr. King's wagon, the one he and Colin had left at the end of town, was coming down the street. And Belle was driving it – or at least trying to.

"Colin?" Duncan said and shook him. "You'd better look at this ..."

"No. I don't wish to look at anything! Don't you understand? *She's gone!*"

But just then, he heard her voice: "How do I stop this thing?!"

Belle, lacking a better idea, pulled back on the reins with all her remaining might. It worked – the horses stopped, albeit with no small protest. She shook herself and barely managed to climb down, almost falling on her face in the process. Her nightdress was torn and dirty, as if she'd been dragged through the streets rather than riding. Blood seeped from a wound on her head, her braid was coming loose and she was covered in enough soot and grime to pass for one of the Dupries.

Doc Waller ran to her, but she pushed him aside and kept stumbling toward the Cooke brothers in front of the sheriff's office. "Colin?" she croaked as she fell to her hands and knees a few feet away.

Colin's head slowly rose. He looked first up at Duncan, then at the crumpled, bloodied form to his right. He whimpered in shock, and pulled himself out of his brother's grasp, lunging toward her. "Belle!" He pulled her into his arms, and they sat and held onto each other and wept. But it was quite apparent that their tears were ones of joy.

"I thought you were lost!" Belle sobbed.

"I thought *you* were!"

"I'm not."

"I know ..."

Mrs. Dunnigan had stopped caterwauling just long enough to hear the commotion. She turned to look, then pushed Wilfred away and began to hurry over. The Mulligans blocked her, grabbing her arms to keep her from causing trouble. She struggled to wrench free of their grasp. "Let go of me! I'll not be kept from my niece!"

Then she stopped and stared.

Colin and Belle were locked in a deep, passionate kiss – the kind that could bind hearts and overturn kingdoms. Mrs. Dunnigan's face began to contort with rage, but then it faded as she saw something, something she hadn't seen in a very long time.

Love. Her niece and the Cooke boy were deeply, undeniably, *rightly* in love.

Wilfred arrived at her side now. "Don't you dare take one more step, Irene. Leave them be. He was almost killed trying to save her. And the only reason he didn't was because he saved you first."

"He ... he did?"

"Yep."

"But ... but who saved Belle?"

"Don't rightly know. But here she is, and I ain't gonna argue with the Lord about it. Are you?"

"No," she whimpered. "I ... I thought I'd lost you when you went into the saloon ..."

"Aw, woman, you ain't getting rid of me that easily! I just went in there to see if Harlan had set up a game. The light's better in there – our eyes ain't what they used to be."

She dropped her head sadly. "This, it's all my fault. I ... I..."

"How can it be your fault? Did you start the fire?"

"No, but..."

"Stop, Irene. You're safe, so is Belle, and I can't ask the good Lord for more. The mercantile ... we'll rebuild it. Better than new."

Irene turned to look at Belle and Colin, who still sat and held each other. Colin had Belle's head tucked under his chin and was murmuring softly to her. "I am a fool, Wilfred."

"No. The fool says in his heart that there's no God."

"Well, I was sure acting a fool. And all the time, I was standing in God's way. Look at them, Wilfred. It doesn't get any righter than that."

"I'd be inclined to agree. So what we need to do now is help instead of hinder. Sound right by you?"

Irene nodded in agreement, and fell into her husband's open arms.

Colin's world had narrowed to the woman in his arms. "My Belle ... I was beside myself, thinking you'd died ..."

"And I was so worried about you," she said in a voice barely recognizable.

He pulled back and looked at her. "Egads. You look positively awful, my angel."

Belle smirked. "You don't exactly look shipshape yourself, dear."

He smiled. "But how did you escape? I couldn't get to you!"

"I'll explain later. Too ... hard to talk." She coughed twice, and wished she could spit, but that would definitely *not* be ladylike. She settled for swallowing hard instead.

"Hush, then. We'll get you some water. and have Doc take a look at you." He once more tucked her head beneath his chin. "I love you, Belle. I love you so much."

Belle smiled, and let him hold her for as long as he wanted.

Unfortunately, others had different ideas – most notably Doc Waller. At his behest, several men, including Duncan, helped Colin and Belle to their feet. Doc and Grandma immediately began to guide the couple toward their house.

Colin, with one arm around Belle, followed without question. He wanted her tended to as soon as possible. He might feel like death, but she looked it. He could only imagine what had happened to her, and couldn't imagine how she'd escaped the fire. She had to have jumped, it was the only explanation, but how had she done so from a second floor window without being even more seriously injured? She shouldn't even be able to walk! And how did she get the wagon? What was she doing driving it? She looked like she hadn't the strength to climb onto it, let alone guide it through town.

"Leave them alone, leave them alone!" Grandma ordered as the crowd tried to follow them into the Wallers' home. "Doc'll take it from here. You men get that fire under control so the wind don't cause problems if'n it kicks up. Last thing this town needs is to lose another building." Grandma took a quick look around. "Brigit?"

Mrs. Mulligan came through the crowd. "You take care of Irene and Wilfred. Doc and I'll see to Belle."

She nodded her quick agreement, turned and went back to help the Dunnigans. They'd not only lost everything they had, but the town had lost many of the goods they needed to survive. There would be a lot of work to do in the next few weeks to make sure no one suffered even worse.

Once inside the Wallers' home, Belle collapsed. Colin and Duncan immediately bent to help her, but then Colin coughed and collapsed himself.

"Oh, dear," Doc said, shaking his head. "Duncan, get Colin settled in the parlor. Then help us take Belle upstairs."

Duncan did as he instructed and soon had both where the doctor wanted them. Doc then tended to Belle, while Grandma took care of Colin. "It's amazing you and that girl are alive," Grandma scolded Colin as she doctored the burns on his hands and arms. "Now, you let Belle alone for tonight so she can rest. You'll see her tomorrow. Can you make it home?"

"He can if Mr. King doesn't mind me using his wagon to get him there," Duncan said.

"Mmmm, I don't think he'll mind — we've got ourselves a real generous preacher. Take your brother home — he needs his rest, too, for all the sweet talkin' he'll be doing tomorrow."

Colin grimaced as he got up from the settee. "Sweet talking? You mean Belle?"

"I mean Mrs. Dunnigan. That fire did more than burn down the mercantile – I think it burned down some walls in her cranky ol' heart! If'n there was ever a good time for you to ask for Belle's hand, this is it."

"Why does everyone assume I'm going to ask for her hand? Am I so transparent?"

"Yes," Duncan replied, leaning over his shoulder.

Colin pondered this. "Well, then. Tomorrow it is."

# EPILOGUE

*Three weeks later ...*

Horatio and Teresa were the first to emerge from the church. The townsfolk cheered and tossed flower petals at the couple. The new bride and groom hurried to a wagon festooned with flowers and ribbons to wait for the others.

Specifically, Colin and Belle, who came out next. They were followed by the Rev. King, who'd just performed Clear Creek's first double wedding. Blossoms again flew in abundance, as they ducked and ran through it as best they could. Colin laughed in triumph as they reached the wagon and kissed his new bride.

Harrison, Sadie and the Dunnigans filed out as Horatio helped Teresa climb up to the wagon seat, then climbed up himself. They watched as Colin took Belle by the hand and faced the crowd.

"Well, big brother, you're now part of the club!" Harrison teased.

"Club? What club is that?"

"The matrimony club! And trust me when I say, you'll love it!"

Colin turned to Belle and kissed her again. "I dare say I shall," he whispered in her ear. She didn't blush this time, only smiled.

"Wait 'til ya git her home!" someone yelled from the crowd. Everyone laughed.

"Oh, I may never leave home again," Colin quipped. This time, Belle blushed.

"You stop speaking of such things here! It's indecent!" Mrs. Dunnigan admonished.

"Irene," Wilfred chided her. "Don't you remember what it was like when we were first wed?"

"Well, I ... um ..." she stammered, turning pink.

Duncan joined them just as the remaining flowers were thrown. It was one of the happiest days in Clear Creek – and it wasn't over. The whole town was coming to the ranch for the wedding supper. Well, almost the whole town – Jefferson Cooke wasn't expected. He'd kept himself locked away in his cabin since the night of the fire.

Horatio stood. "OK, folks, time to head out! Follow us, and be sure to bring your appetites!"

Cheers went up. Horatio Jones never did anything small. He'd brought part of his household staff to cook and serve. He wanted today, his wedding day along with Colin's and Belle's, to be a day they all would remember for a very long time.

And they certainly did. One person in particular.

Before the Triple-C's "wedding wagon" could pull away, the stage rolled into town on an unscheduled visit. All heads turned as it came to a stop right behind the Cookes' vehicle. But no one got off the stage. Whomever was inside simply waited.

All eyes were fixed on it by the time Willie climbed down and opened the door. A very well-dressed man emerged, pulled a handkerchief from the pocket of his waistcoat and held it over his nose as he took in the curious stares of the onlookers. If no one in Clear Creek had ever seen a dandy before, they surely had now. His suit was impeccable, his hat flawless, and he smelled like Paris looked. Clearly, he wasn't from around Clear Creek.

Another man got off the stage, this one not quite so well-dressed and much shorter than the first. He fidgeted and looked nervously about before taking in the wedding party surrounding the other wagon. Pulling a pince-nez from his breast pocket, he perched it on his nose and told the crowd, "Excuse me, gentlemen, ladies, but I am looking for a D. M. Sayer." His British accent was so crisp, it made the Cooke brothers sound like day laborers from Louisiana by comparison.

*Sayer?* The townsfolk looked at each other before glancing around ...

"I'm Mr. Sayer."

All heads turned toward the voice.

The fidgety little man made his way through the crowd to stand before the man who'd just spoken. "Are you Duncan Mackenzie Sayer? The son of Benedict Sayer?"

Duncan looked him up and down. Like his traveling companion, he certainly didn't dress – or sound – like he belonged out West. "Who wishes to know?"

The taller man approached and now looked Duncan up and down. "My, you're not exactly what I expected."

Another Englishman. "And you are?" Duncan demanded.

He raised the handkerchief to his face and inhaled, as if the entire wedding party had been doused in cow manure. "That depends upon whom *you* are."

"Are you Duncan Mackenzie Sayer?" the little man repeated.

"Yes. Yes, I am."

"Sayer?" Horatio asked, befuddled. "Wait, I thought your last name was Cooke!"

"Legally, it is still Sayer," Duncan explained. "We took on the Cooke name when our mother married Jefferson. She felt it would make us more of a family if we did." He shrugged as if to say, *well, it was a nice theory.* "We've continued living under that name out of respect to her.

"Then, you do claim to be Duncan Mackenzie Sayer, the son of Benedict Sayer?"

"He just told you he was," Colin quipped.

"What's this all about?" Harrison demanded. "Who are you?"

"I'm Mr. Ashford, Anthony Sayer's solicitor."

"Anthony Sayer," Duncan repeated, puzzling over the name. "What does he have to do with me?"

"I'm here to confirm that you exist. Of course, I'll need to see your papers to give proper verification. You do have them, don't you?"

"Have what?" Colin asked, as confused now as everyone else.

"He's talking about birth papers, documents to identify his mother and father," the taller man said in a condescending tone

"Of course I have them," Duncan said, still confused.

"Bugger, I was afraid you'd say that," the taller man said flatly.

"Then let me be the first to congratulate you," Mr. Ashford continued.

"Congratulate me? For what?"

The little man reached into his coat, pulled out a folded leather case and opened it to reveal some very ancient-looking documents. He handed them to Duncan. "Congratulations. You are the new Duke of Stantham."

The three brothers' were distracted by a high-pitched wail from Mrs. Dunnigan. They turned just in time to see her faint. It looked real this time, and several people in the crowd darted over to help her.

It also gave Mr. Ashford's words enough time to sink in. "Duke of Stantham?" Colin and Harrison exclaimed at the same time.

"Unfortunately," the taller man spat.

"Good Lord!" Harrison muttered to himself. "Anthony Sayer ... isn't that the cousin who had something to do with a ... a ..." He waved a hand in the air, looking for the word.

"Crocodile," Duncan finished for him.

The taller man groaned and buried his face in his handkerchief.

"Right," Colin agreed. "But I thought that particular cousin was only an earl."

"He was next in line to inherit, and became the Duke of Stantham some ten years ago," Mr. Ashford told them.

"Surely there were others in line to inherit before Duncan," Colin said.

"Certainly. But they've all met with rather untimely deaths. That left Mr. D.M. Sayer. If something were to happen to him, then his brother Colin Bartholomew Sayer would inherit. I don't suppose he's around?"

"Right ... here, sir." Colin numbly raised his hand as Belle gave a *yip* of surprise. Duncan, meanwhile, was engrossed in the documents he'd been handed. He studied the papers carefully, his lips moving as he read.

"And if something were to happen to Colin ...," Harrison began.

"Then one Harrison Nathaniel Sayer would inherit," Mr. Ashford finished for him. "Would that, perchance, be you, sir?"

"Quite," Harrison replied, blinking rapidly.

"But what if something happened to Harrison as well?" Sadie asked as she hooked her arm through one of her husband's.

"Then the title and estate would fall to the Duke's fifth cousin, Thackary Cuthbert Holmes."

"Thackeray Cuth ... who the devil is that?" Colin asked.

"That would be me." The taller man said calmly as he produced a snuffbox from his pocket, took a pinch, and sniffed. Some of the townsfolk nearby stared open-mouthed at the man.

"Married?" All heads turned back to Duncan, who was furiously going over the documents in his hands. "This says I have to get *married?!*"

"Yes." Mr. Ashford replied sharply. "In fact, in order to inherit, you have to get married by the date specified, or the title and estate go to the next in line."

"But this can't be right; this says I would have to be married no later than the ninth of August, 1858! That's ... that's only five weeks from now!"

"So it is," Mr. Holmes cooed.

"Your cousin, the Duke, wanted to ensure that his successor was ready and able to produce an heir. He himself had only daughters and, as you are probably aware, there were very few males among the cousins. Until we found you three."

Duncan looked to Colin, who could only shrug. "Sorry, old boy, but I'm afraid you'll be saddled with it."

"Me? What am I going to do with a duchy?"

Another, shorter wail from the middle of the crowd. Apparently Mrs. Dunnigan had gone down again.

Harrison pulled Duncan and Colin aside. "Father would have wanted you to have this, Duncan. If he hadn't been killed, he'd have inherited. It's something our parents only dreamed of happening to any of us."

Duncan closed his eyes. "I realize that, and it's an honor to be sure, but who knows what shape the estate is in?"

"As opposed to ours here, six months ago?" Harrison pointed out.

"I'd say it must be good enough for old *Thackary* standing over there to travel halfway around the world to see if we're still alive and able to inherit," Colin added. The three brothers eyed the tall dandy, who stood looking down his nose at Willie as he took another pinch from his snuffbox.

Belle and Sadie, standing with their husbands, watched Duncan battle with the decision. He finally looked at them all helplessly. "You're right. It must be quite the estate. And I know it's what Father and Mother would have wanted. But it's impossible – I don't see how I could make it work."

"Colin and I can handle the ranch while you take care of this whole affair. Horatio will help, I'm sure," Harrison said.

"But you're forgetting one thing," Duncan began. "I have but five weeks to get married. And at last check, the only unmarried female to be found within a hundred miles just wed my younger brother." He inclined his head toward Belle

Colin sighed. "Sorry, old boy, but I really don't belong in the House of Lords. You're much better suited. Just the other week, you said you'd like to go back to London."

"I did, didn't I? But the terms ..." Duncan shook his head. "If I can't take it on, and neither of you will, then I suppose *Thackary* gets it all."

They again looked at Mr. Holmes, who was staring at the townsfolk with a disdain that rivaled Mrs. Dunnigan's. "Hmmm. Can't have that," Harrison remarked.

"What did Mr. Ashford say earlier, about your other cousins?" Sadie asked. "They all met with untimely deaths?"

"Oh, dear." Harrison looked at his brothers. "You don't suppose he ..."

"He rather looks the type," Colin mused.

Duncan turned and stared at their distant cousin. Colin had a point – Thackary Holmes looked to be everything his father had hated when he was alive, everything they'd left England and sailed to America to escape: greed, haughtiness, jealousy, envy and cruelty, wrapped up in expensive finery. A huge estate had tenants, lots of them – what sort of taskmaster would Mr. Holmes be if he were to become the new Duke of Stantham?

More importantly, could Duncan live with the regret that would surely come if he threw such a legacy away? And his brothers were right – of the three of them, he was the one most suited for the post.

But ... five weeks?!

"What say you, brother?" Harrison asked with a smile. "Are you up to the task ... Your Grace?" He added a slight bow.

Duncan took a deep breath. Then another. "Except for this one small detail. This doesn't allow me the time to travel all the way to Oregon City or Salt Lake and back, and I know there's not a single eligible female to be found nearby ..."

"That's not entirely true," Belle interrupted. Then she caught herself, clapping her hand over her mouth.

That got everyone's attention. All three brothers, Sadie and even Mr. Ashford spun to face her.

"But, angel," Colin replied. "There are no available women in town or, as Duncan just said, anywhere near."

Belle sighed. Blast it, she'd given her word. And yet ... well, the horse was already out of the barn, and she owed her new family the truth. She looked Duncan right in the eye. "I wasn't supposed to tell, but ... there is one ..."

**The End**

# His Prairie Duchess

# DAY 1

*Clear Creek, Oregon, 1858.*

### *Thirty-eight days until the Duke's stipulated deadline:*

Cozette Duprie was up a tree.

She'd always liked the sound of that phrase, how her name so easily rhymed with what came naturally to her. She was forever climbing something – a tree, a ladder, a lattice, and most recently the backside of a building (albeit with the help of her father's grappling hook). Getting down, of course, might prove to be more difficult, but she was usually up to the challenge.

In the escapade with the building, she'd suffered fewer injuries than the girl she rescued, so all in all, no complaints. She just hoped doing so wouldn't draw too much attention to herself. Attention was the last thing she needed – she and her father.

She settled in amongst the branches and watched a wagon train slowly wind its way across the prairie in the distance. It would set up camp nearby, most likely. She'd heard Mr. Van Cleet tell her father that they often camped a mile or so south of town to rest and re-stock supplies before continuing on to Oregon City. Unfortunately for this wagon train, getting supplies might prove difficult, what with the mercantile in Clear Creek burning down three weeks ago.

Cozette glanced at her bandaged hand. Her father had tended the burns she'd incurred while rescuing Belle Dunnigan from her room above the mercantile, and they were healing nicely. In fact, today she'd been told she could take the bandage off. But she'd decided to wait until she returned to camp outside of town. Watching the wagon train was more interesting.

Especially since this one seemed a bit odd. It wasn't very big, only six wagons, but that wasn't the only difference. These wagons were being pulled by draft horses instead of oxen, and horses weren't as suitable for long journeys. Perhaps they'd come from some other place in the Oregon Territory, or had lost their oxen and could only get horses to replace them.

Whatever the reason, Cozette enjoyed watching as they stopped and set up camp. She often wondered what it would be like to travel with a wagon train for months and spend time with other families around a nightly campfire.

But then, she often wondered what it would be like to do a lot of things. Like wear a dress with a pretty hat, one with lots of flowers and feathers. Or shop in a mercantile for a bonnet covered in ribbons. Or have her very own house, with wallpaper covered in delicate flower petal designs and furniture with colors to match. And lace, lots of lace – she loved to study the intricacy of it. She was attracted to the delicate patterns of china and fine cloth. She wanted to cook something on a stove instead of over a campfire, and to bake something in a real oven.

But what she wanted most of all was to sleep in a bed, a *real* bed. She often imagined a huge four-poster canopied one, fit for a queen, with lots of pillows and a mattress she could sink into and lose herself night after night in dream-filled slumber.

Cozette sighed heavily. She knew that a dream was all it was, and probably always would be.

Her current life wasn't horrible, mind you. She was free, incredibly so. She didn't suffer the conventional constraints other women did. She could hunt, fish, trap, and prepare and eat what she killed. She could start a fire and shoot a gun. She'd even helped her father take down a buffalo once.

But none of it seemed to matter when the dreams began gnawing at her again, until all she could do was lie upon her bedroll at night and weep in silence. Total silence - her voice hadn't produced any sound, not even a decent sob, in years. It had died, along with the rest of her hopes and dreams, the night her mother did.

Cozette wished she could forget that night. Who knows, maybe if she did, she'd get her voice back ...

Her father didn't know about what she called her "spells" – and because he never heard her suffering in the middle of the night, he most likely wouldn't. Still, they were more frequent of late and getting worse, the longing increasing with each passing day. But longing for what?

She wished she knew what caused them. It wasn't *just* that she missed her mother, she was pretty sure of that. But thinking of her mother did bring great sadness. She feared the memories that came to haunt her in the night. She didn't want to remember, didn't want to see in her mind's eye the horrible things that had happened to her mother, or hear the sounds of her screaming ...

Cozette closed her eyes and forced the memories down. She concentrated on watching the wagon train set up camp instead and wondered how long they would stay before moving on. No doubt, her father would have her remain hidden for as long as it took them to do so. But at this point in her life, she'd grown used to it.

Duncan sat and let his head hit the wooden surface of the desk. Again.

He'd retreated to the ranch house's study not long after the wedding party began, and had been there ever since. So far, his brothers had left him alone – they were too busy with the wedding guests and carrying out Horatio Jones' constant barrage of orders. The man ran things like a seasoned colonel, and soon had everyone settled in and armed with a glass of lemonade in one hand and a fork in the other. In moments, Duncan was sure he'd hear Horatio shout, "Charge!" followed by the sound of clinking plates and glasses as the wedding supper got underway.

But Duncan Cooke – correction, *Duncan Mackenzie Sayer* – had no appetite. He wondered if he ever would again. The enormity of the news delivered to him not an hour ago, had begun to sink in.

What recollections he had of his cousin – Lord Anthony Sayer, Earl of Stantham – were so scattered he didn't think he'd be able to make sense of any of them. He knew that Anthony had received a commission in the British Army, and then the East India Company. *His* father, the old Earl, had died while Anthony and his two younger brothers, Leonard and John, were in India. Of the three, only Anthony had come home after his death ...

... or was it before? And why did he go back to India? Did he meet and marry his wife there or in England? Blast it all! And he couldn't remember how a crocodile fit into any of it, although one did, he was sure of it. His mother had always laughed and laughed when she told that part of the story. But Duncan couldn't think straight, and couldn't remember what exactly the story was, nor why he needed to ...

"I thought I'd find you here."

Duncan looked up to see his brother, Colin, standing in the doorway. He sighed, no words at the ready, and

stared at his newly-married sibling. Colin and Belle
Dunnigan, along with Horatio Jones and his new bride
Teresa, had been united that very afternoon in Clear
Creek's first double wedding.

*Good for them*, Duncan thought morosely. But it
didn't solve his problem. He needed to get married too,
and quickly. According to the pile of documents
scattered on the desk, if Duncan didn't get married in
the next thirty-eight days, the title and estate of their
illustrious fourth cousin Anthony Sayer would have to
go to Colin. And Colin didn't want it. Neither did their
younger brother, Harrison.

Who knew having their father's dreams come true
could become so complicated? Their father had wanted
a thriving cattle ranch in the American West. That
had just become a reality, thanks to Harrison saving –
and then marrying – the daughter of Horatio Jones,
one of the wealthiest cattle barons in the country.
Father had also dreamed that one day Duncan, by
some slim chance (as in a downright bloody miracle),
would inherit the title and estate from their fourth
cousin, the Earl of Stantham.

Only the Earl had become a Duke. And now the
Duke was dead, along with the rest of Duncan's uncles
and cousins in line to inherit – all dead before their
time, most of them tragically so. He supposed part of
what bothered him was exactly *how* they came to such
untimely ends ...

"Belle and I understand if you don't want to join the
feast," Colin said quietly. "It's all so very hard to take
in. Especially to have it delivered the way it was. Not
to mention the stipulations involved."

Duncan began to drum his fingers on the desk.
"Stipulations, indeed. One of which I still don't find
possible. But your wife seems to think differently."

"Do you want me to bring her to you?"

"No, no. Enjoy your wedding day. I'll not have this business spoil it. I apologize for my absence – it is, as you say, a lot to take in. I'll join you in a moment."

Colin smiled. "Take all the time you need. Horatio has everything well in hand. Even Jefferson crawled out of his cabin and is watching from his porch."

Duncan let loose a small chuckle. "I was beginning to wonder if he'd ever come out."

Indeed, they all had wondered. Their stepfather had locked himself away in his cabin the night the mercantile burned down. To this day, Duncan and Colin still wondered if Jefferson was one of the two riders they saw gallop out of town just as the fire broke out. But by the time they returned to the ranch, Jefferson was already there and asleep.

Colin had been so relieved that Belle was safe, he didn't pay much mind to Jefferson. Duncan was in the same state about Colin. Both he and Belle had almost lost their lives that night. By a sheer miracle, they were both rescued – and by the least likely pair of heroes, the French trapper Anton Duprie and his mute son. When Belle finally told them what had happened, no one could believe it.

Unfortunately, the Dupries had gone up into the hills to hunt the very next day, so no one got the chance to thank them. Mr. Van Cleet assured everyone they'd be back soon, that they likely would be gone for a few weeks but would return. Belle especially seemed anxious as to their whereabouts, but let the matter rest along with everyone else. They'd be back eventually, just as Mr. Van Cleet said.

Colin departed to go back to his bride and their wedding guests. Duncan sat for a few more minutes, then got up and left the study.

Tables were set up outside the ranch house for the wedding supper, and everyone had formed a line where several of Horatio's household servants from the Big J were busy dishing up plates of food. Among them was Logan Kincaid, the ranch foreman who'd come to help the three brothers with their new stock.

Of all the times for this bloody Duke business to happen, Duke thought. Now he'd have to saddle Mr. Kincaid with more work than he'd anticipated. That is, if he could find any "business" to take care of at all.

He searched the faces in the crowd until his eyes fell on the one not so familiar – Thackary Holmes, the Duke's fifth cousin. The man who would get it all, should Duncan be unable to adhere to the last wishes of the Duke – namely, that the heir to the title be married in order to inherit. Duncan wasn't, and had no immediate prospects.

But then, the same could be said for Mr. Holmes, as far as he knew. Or had he a wife, who simply hadn't accompanied him to the Oregon Territory? It would, after all, be a rather hard journey for an English lady to endure. But if not, that meant old Thackary would have to be looking for a wife as well.

Good luck with that around here. Duncan smiled at the thought and went to get something to eat.

Soon he had a plate in one hand and a glass of lemonade in the other, and was winding his way through the mingling townsfolk to the head table. Colin and Belle were seated there, with Harrison and Sadie on one side, and chairs set aside next to them for Duncan and Jefferson (though Jefferson was still choosing to sit on his porch and watch the affair from a distance). On the other side of Harrison and Sadie sat Horatio and Teresa, along with Wilfred and Irene Dunnigan.

Mrs. Dunnigan, usually unafraid to speak her mind, had been remarkably quiet since Anthony Sayer's solicitor had announced that Duncan was next in line to be Duke of Stantham. She might still be in a state of shock. But then, she wasn't the only one.

The solicitor, Mr. Ashford, had found a couple of seats at a nearby table and was whispering back and forth with Thackary Holmes. The way the two were acting made Duncan wonder if they weren't in cahoots, plotting how to get their hands on the title.

The thought annoyed Duncan, and he seethed just looking at them. He didn't trust either one. If Thackary didn't come across as such a foppish cad, he'd gladly hand the whole deal over, lock, stock, and barrel. But it was obvious that that's *exactly* what the perfumed dandy wanted, and that was irksome. He not only wanted it, he was also obviously prepared to go to great lengths to get it. His presence in isolated, distant Clear Creek was proof enough of that.

Duncan tried to force thoughts of the two men from his mind and concentrate on the food in front of him. But his appetite was still nowhere to be found, and he picked at his supper and barely touched his lemonade.

"Duncan, are you saving room for cake?" Belle asked.

Of course, he might be able to handle cake ...

"I hear it's going to be incredible," she added.

"Incredible" hopefully meant *chocolate* ...

"And I'm sure it will soothe your nerves."

Well, he could certainly use that!

Then Belle leaned closer to whisper in his ear. "I have a solution to your problem. But we can't talk about it here. I wanted to tell you at the church, but thought it best to speak in private."

"You thought right. But I already know there is no ready solution to my problem." Namely, that there were no unmarried females anywhere near Clear Creek."

"But there is."

He turned to her. Colin sat on the other side of Belle, a mouth full of food, eyeing Mr. Ashford and Mr. Holmes. Harrison was doing the same. "I have only one question, Belle," Duncan replied as he reached for his lemonade. "You know what it is I wish to ask."

"Indeed I do." She leaned toward him again as he began to take a sip, and disclosed the answer to his unspoken question.

Duncan spewed lemonade everywhere and began to cough. Belle and Colin quickly came to his aid, getting him up and steering him toward the house. Harrison and Sadie also stepped over to help. "He'll be fine!" Harrison called out. "Enjoy your supper, everyone – the cake is next!"

A cheer went up from the townsfolk at the announcement, and they happily went back to eating. All but Mr. Ashford and Thackary Holmes, who watched the Cookes hurry to the ranch house.

"The Duprie boy?!" Duncan croaked between coughs. "Are you out of your bloody mind?"

Harrison and Colin stood by in shock, their mouths half-open, and stared at Belle. Sadie froze in mid-stride, a glass of water in her hand for Duncan, and waited for her to explain.

"Well, there's no need to swear," Belle replied. She was already feeling uncomfortable about betraying a confidence – Duncan's angry reaction didn't help.

Duncan took a moment to try and clear his throat. "My apologies, dear sister. But ... but you can't be serious!"

"I can, and I am. Cosime Duprie is in fact a girl, and she rescued me that night. She didn't want me to tell, but ... but given your situation, I felt I had no choice. Face it, Duncan – she's the only chance you have at present of inheriting your cousin's title and estate."

Duncan received the glass of water from Sadie and took a long swallow. "But ... but she's like a wild animal! And ... she *smells!*"

"Not to mention, she can't even talk," Colin added.

"I dare say, one would never know she's a girl," Harrison said softly, his shock still quite evident as he stared straight ahead. "How did none of us see it before?"

"Enough dirt and buckskins to cover her up and how would anyone know?" Belle stated with a shrug.

"But why would her father dress her as a boy?" Sadie asked.

"Maybe he did it to protect her," suggested Colin. "Mr. Van Cleet told me they spent a lot of time out in the wilderness with the Indians."

"And remember the reactions when I first came to town," Belle added. There had been a crowd of men from all over the area visiting the mercantile, just to get a glimpse of the newcomer."

Colin nodded in understanding. "If she were my daughter, I might well keep her disguised. Men too long without a woman can do foolish things. Like kill a father just so they can get their hands on the daughter."

"Or the mother," Harrison added.

The three brothers looked at one another. They remembered what it was like after their father had died. Their mother had refused to give up his dream of coming out west to raise cattle, and was determined to find a way. They also remembered the many men who offered "assistance," but whose idea of assistance was to bed her, then leave her. Wise to their ways, she steered clear of such men until she found relative safety with Jefferson Cooke, a recent widower who needed a wife to help settle in the west himself. It wasn't exactly a love match, but without Jefferson's protection on the Oregon Trail, who knew what would have become of her, or her three sons?

Yet in the end, Jefferson couldn't protect her from everything ...

"So in the morning, Duncan and I should find M. Duprie and speak to him about his daughter," Harrison suggested.

Duncan shook his head. "Now hold on – I haven't even seen the woman! As a woman, that is."

"No, but you've certainly had an *encounter* with her!" Colin quickly pointed out.

Duncan groaned and glared at his brother. Yes, he remembered chasing the Duprie boy ... girl ... that buckskinned guttersnipe down the street after he'd caught him sneaking out of the mercantile with a bag of candy. He'd all but tackled the child, then thrown him across his lap and given him a few good swats with his hand. Only then did he find out that the child wasn't stealing – the candy had been a gift from Belle, which had been forgotten in the midst of one of Irene Dunnigan's tirades. And now, to discover that the alleged thief hadn't even been a boy ... "Ohhhh," Duncan moaned and put his face in his hands.

"It's an encounter she'll not soon forget," Colin told Harrison and Sadie with a grin.

Belle's face paled as she too remembered what happened. "Well, we'll just ... have to work around that. If you're seriously considering inheriting this title, then this is a possible solution. I'm sure M. Duprie could be persuaded to cooperate."

"Cooperate?" Duncan sputtered. "With what? Simply handing her over to me, just like that?"

"Why not?" Belle asked. "Isn't that what they do where you come from?"

Harrison's eyes widened. "Of course! Why, you clever girl! Why didn't one of us think of it?"

Now Colin caught on. "One would think you were English, my dear." He impulsively kissed her on the temple.

"What are you talking about?" Sadie finally asked.

Duncan sighed. "They are talking about an arranged marriage between myself and M. Duprie's daughter."

"Wouldn't she be something to take to a ball and introduce to the *ton*?" Colin quipped.

"Indeed," Duncan replied, "which makes this all the more ludicrous." He turned to his brothers and gave a mock bow. "Allow me to introduce my wife, the Duchess of Stantham. A woman who runs around in dirty buckskins, cannot speak, and probably kills things with her bare hands just before she eats them for dinner."

"And who risked her life to save your new sister-in-law," Belle added pointedly. "Which tells me that beneath the rough exterior, she has some very good qualities."

The three brothers looked at each other as Belle's words hit their mark. "Very well," Duncan said. "Though I consider myself completely addled in the brain for doing this, on the morrow I shall speak with M. Duprie." He took a deep breath. "And see about making his daughter the new Duchess of Stantham. God save the Queen."

Anton Duprie watched Cozette turn his dinner on a spit. The girl could make anything taste good, even out in the wilderness with only an open fire to cook with. He could only imagine what she could do in an actual kitchen. Maybe it was time to see.

But they had roamed the wilderness for so long. Could she adjust to living in a house? Or would she long for the green forests and the freedom of the wild?

He had to admit, he was worried – worried about the way she kept more and more to herself, worried about how she looked at the other women in town. Was she envious of what they had? Or did she despise their lack of freedom? He would have to ask her.

Her inability to speak meant nothing to him – over the years, they had found ways to communicate well enough. Besides, Cozette could read and write, something most folks never realized until they saw her do it. Most just assumed she was nothing more than a dirty little savage. But he knew better. He supposed she could become one if forced to it, but he prayed that day would never come, that she would never suffer her mother's fate …

"*Est-il presque prêt?*" he asked her. *Is it almost ready?*

She looked up from her work, smiled and nodded, her eyes bright. How she loved to cook!

"We should speak in English, to practice," he continued as she removed the meat from the spit. "The people here, most of them do not understand the French."

She raised one eyebrow at him. He was the one who needed to practice – she could read and write in both languages, better than he could. If her voice worked, she'd likely speak better, too.

He sighed in resignation. "All right," he said, smiling ruefully. "*I* will use the English so to speak better."

Cozette wrote for a moment in the dirt with her finger.

Anton looked to see what she was saying. *So. To.* Then Cozette crossed out the word *so.* He rolled his eyes, frustrated at his own mistake, and tried again. "I will use the English to speak better."

Cozette smiled in approval, then motioned to the meat and gave a small bow. Dinner was served.

He sat and waited as she prepared them both a portion, then indicated for her to sit. She did, bowing her head and clasping her hands before her. "Our

Father, who is in Heaven," he began. "Bless this food we are receive and ..."

Cozette opened one eye and glared at him.

"Ah ... hmm ... bless this food we are ... *about to* receive, and bless the hands that ..." He hesitated. "Er ... made it?"

Cozette threw her head back in almost-silent laughter. Not completely silent – a little squeak escaped.

Anton almost fell over where he sat. "Cozette?"

She sat perfectly still, her eyes wide, her hand at her throat. It was the first sound she'd made in years.

"*Ma petite!* You spoke!"

She shook her head slowly.

"Well, it was ... something!" He went and knelt in front of her. "You try again, yes?"

She smiled tentatively, her hand still at her throat as if she could use it to push out another sound.

"You maybe try again after you eat, *oui?*" He motioned for her to pick up her plate. "We eat. Then maybe I tell you a story to make you laugh."

Cozette removed her hand, smiled nervously, and slowly picked up her plate.

# DAY 2

Duncan strolled down the street to the sheriff's office, hoping Cyrus Van Cleet would be there. He hadn't had the chance to speak to him yesterday at the wedding supper. But if Sheriff Hughes wasn't playing checkers with Wilfred Dunnigan, he was usually playing with Cyrus. Besides, it was almost lunchtime, and Cyrus might be taking a break from his hotel's construction to grab a game.

Sure enough, there he and the sheriff were, outside the sheriff's office, one on either side of a small table bent over a checkerboard. Wilfred stood behind Cyrus, frowning heavily as he watched the sheriff decide his next move. "Afternoon, Duncan," Wilfred said without taking his eyes from the board. Checkers was serious business in Clear Creek.

"Wilfred," Duncan said and tipped his hat. "Sheriff Hughes, Cyrus."

The sheriff and Cyrus nodded in greeting, too intent on the game to even say hello. Duncan thought it best to wait for a moment, so he took a position behind the sheriff to watch.

The sheriff made a move, smiled triumphantly, then sat back and waited for Cyrus to make his.

Several men who were working on the hotel came down the street, stopping briefly to observe the match before heading over to Mulligan's saloon for lunch. Irene Dunnigan had taken to cooking lunch and dinner for Cyrus's workers, needing something to keep her busy while the mercantile was being rebuilt. (It also served to keep her from driving the Mulligans crazy.) Because of that, she was becoming very popular with the newcomers, and Mr. Mulligan had quickly seized the opportunity to turn the saloon into a restaurant, buying produce and meat from the local farmers, including beef from the Triple-C. It was a winning situation for everyone.

Two other men came and stood behind Duncan to watch. Duncan glanced at them and immediately knew they were strangers. One was huge, even taller than Mr. Berg the new blacksmith and just as broad. He had dark hair that reached his shirt collar and obviously hadn't shaved in a few days. His eyes were a piercing bright green, and were focused on Cyrus rather than the checkerboard. The other man was of average height, but cadaverously thin, and his eyes were looking all over the place, as if he'd never seen a town before. But his clothes were fine and well-tailored – maybe he was from some big city, and had never seen such a small town ...

Strangers always made Duncan a little wary. With some reason – it was a stranger who had lured Colin and him to a wagon train two years ago, where they were conveniently accused of cattle rustling. From the looks of these two, they were also from a wagon train – probably one just camped outside of town.

Cyrus made his move, grinned, and leaned forward. "I win, Sheriff!"

Sheriff Hughes quickly glanced at the board. "Dagnabit, Cyrus! That's three games in a row! Between you and Wilfred, my reputation's gonna be ruined!"

The tall stranger snorted in amusement as his companion smiled. That was enough to draw everyone's attention. Sheriff Hughes turned in his chair to face them. "It's no laughing matter! This means war – I've got a reputation to uphold! You two obviously aren't from around these parts or you'd know what's at stake!"

The shorter man laughed nervously, as if not sure how seriously to take the sheriff's statement. "You're right, we're not from around here. We've come into town for supplies. Is there a store ... ah ... a mercantile in town?"

The taller of the two looked at his companion in annoyance before turning his attention back to Cyrus.

"Well, I hate to be the bearer of bad news, but the mercantile done burned down a few weeks ago," Wilfred explained.

"Burned down?" the shorter man repeated. "Oh, dear. So ... how do people get supplies?"

Sheriff Hughes stood. "Well, until the new mercantile is finished, folks around here just help each other out. What did you need?"

The tall man reached into his pants pocket, pulled out a list and handed it to the sheriff without saying a word. Duncan watched as Sheriff Hughes quickly read it. "Well, now some of these things Harvey Brown probably has out at his farm. I'm sure he'd be happy to sell them to you. And Mr. Berg down at the livery stable can fix anything on your wagons or harnesses. Should be supplies coming in another week if you have to have these other things to make it to Oregon City. That's where you're heading, ain't it?"

"Yes, it is," the shorter man replied. "I suppose we can camp outside of town until the other supplies come. Actually, I don't know that we have any other choice."

Sheriff Hughes held out his hand. "Sheriff Harlan Hughes. And you are?"

The man took his hand and shook it. "Lany ... ah, Lany Moss." The taller man's jaw twitched once.

Duncan watched them carefully. They were acting strangely, almost evasively. The last thing anyone in

Clear Creek needed was a wagon train full of untrustworthy strangers hanging around for a couple of weeks.

Suddenly the sheriff, Cyrus and Wilfred came to attention. Something had obviously caught their eye. In Duncan's experience, only one thing would cause a man's eyes to become suddenly riveted the way these chaps' were now. He turned along with the rest.

And sure enough, it was a woman. Although to call her "a woman" would be rather like calling the Atlantic Ocean "a pond," Duncan mused. She was petite, with long, curly auburn hair loose and flowing down to her waist. She wore a bonnet and a dress of fine quality, though not practical for crossing the prairie.

Duncan could feel himself begin to sweat. He had prayed last night for the good Lord to get him out of his current predicament by sending him the woman he needed to make everything work out. Could this be His answer? If so, he realized with relief, he wouldn't have to track down M. Duprie after all ...

Unfortunately for Duncan and the other men, the woman went directly to the tall, dark stranger and took his hands in hers. "Where is it?" she asked. Her voice was like pure silk.

Duncan grimaced in frustration. If only the Lord would see fit to give *him* a woman who sounded like that! He briefly wondered what the Duprie girl's voice sounded like, then remembered she didn't have one. It figured.

"'Tis nowhere to be found," the tall stranger said softly. His accent caught Duncan's attention – was it Scotch? Irish? "These men tell us the *mer-can-tile* burned down. I'm afraid we're stuck here for a time, Flower."

Some of the men actually sighed at the endearment.

"Oh, no – how horrible! Was anyone hurt?" she asked.

"Thank the Lord, no. Came close for a few, but they're right as rain now," Wilfred told them. "We're rebuilding, but I'm afraid that won't do you folks much good."

"I'm sorry," the woman began. "It was your business, then?"

"Yes, ma'am. But the new mercantile will be bigger and better. Me and the missus are looking forward to it."

"I'm glad to hear it." She turned back to the tall man. "But what are we going to do in the meantime?"

"We'll ha' to stay on a wee while longer. At least until more supplies come to town."

*Scotch*, Duncan realized. No wonder they seemed a little different. His family had been on the other side of that divide when they'd come out west. Immigrants were not uncommon on the wagon trains, and often not as properly prepared as the American-born travelers. That would explain the woman's dress and the tall stranger's odd pronunciation of "mercantile." "I'm sure you'll find enough to get by on in the meantime," he volunteered. "How many wagons are there?"

Now the tall stranger looked *him* over. It was quick, no more than a second, but he took Duncan completely in. Duncan found himself hoping the Highlander wasn't the type who was still bitter about Bonnie Prince Charlie and looking for some English hide to take out his frustrations on.

But the Scot only replied, "six in all. Five families, and ... uh, Mr. Moss here." Mr. Moss politely tipped his hat.

"We'll put the word out you need supplies," Cyrus told the Scot. "Bring your list tomorrow to Mulligan's Saloon across the street there. We'll see what we can do to help you." He cleared his throat. "Tell me, have we ever met before? You look mighty familiar to me."

"I dinna think so. But easy enough to meet someone from the past, ye ken. 'Tis recalling the encounter that's hard."

Duncan tried not to flinch at the word "encounter." But his eyes were drawn to the porch steps of Mulligan's, where he'd tanned the hide of ... *oh, he hated to even think it* ... his possible future Duchess. He turned back to look at the tall stranger's woman. If only the little vagrant had been dressed like *that*. Who knew what the Duprie girl looked like under all that dirt?

"Best we be going then. Gentleman, we thank ye for yer kindness and will return tomorrow." The Scotsman bowed, took the woman's hand in his and left, heading in the direction of the livery stable. Mr. Moss nodded to the men, then hurried to catch up to the other two.

The men sighed as they watched them go. "Another game, Harlan?" Cyrus asked, a huge grin on his face.

"No, thanks. Between you and Wilfred, I can't sleep at night. I'm gonna ride out to Harvey's and tell him he best get himself ready to do business with those settlers."

"Suit yourself," Cyrus laughed.

The other men shook themselves out of their dreamlike state and dispersed. Duncan took advantage of their departure to help Cyrus put away the checkerboard and pieces. "Any word as to when Monsieur Duprie is coming back?"

Cyrus stopped and thought a moment. He looked almost as if he was counting. "They're probably back already. They disappear for no more than two to three weeks at a time, according to the Reverend King. My guess is they're camped close by ... though they're more comfortable near the trees. Why do you ask?"

"Something I'd like to discuss with him. I was hoping I'd be able to see him today."

"Well, then, why don't you take a ride out yonder and see if you can't find him?" Cyrus said, pointing toward the tree line.

"Thank you – I think I shall." Duncan turned and was just about to step off the porch when he saw him – or rather, *her*. His little guttersnipe was staring at where the mercantile had stood, its new foundation and frame barely started. He recognized the look on her face as she took in the larger layout of the new building – she wasn't seeing the new building so much as remembering the old one, and the fire that destroyed it.

He was glad it drew her attention at the moment, because that, in turn, gave him a chance to study her and wonder. What *did* she look like under all those skins and dirt?

Duncan Cooke took a deep breath. Fairly soon, he would need to find out.

Cozette froze. She'd felt this odd sensation before – that knowledge that someone was watching her. You couldn't survive in the wilderness without it. But this was different ... not so much a sense of warning as of recognition.

She turned slowly, and knew who it was before setting eyes on him. Duncan Cooke, the eldest of the Cooke brothers.

She'd listened to Mr. Van Cleet talk about the Cookes with her father and Mr. Berg one day. He'd said they were a fine family that had been through a lot over the last couple of years. But whatever they'd gone through, Cozette didn't agree they were quite so fine - not after her own encounter with Duncan, the day of the picnic. Everyone else thought about it as "the day of the fire." Not her.

She absently rubbed her backside in recollection. Yes, she remembered the fire, and what she'd done in the midst of it. But when it came to Duncan Cooke, that day brought back another, and perhaps even more unpleasant, memory. Certainly a more humbling one.

So why did she now feel compelled to look at him, when she didn't want anything to do with him?! It was as if his presence willed it – and try as she might, she couldn't pull her eyes away.

She balled her hands into fists to fight the sensation, just as the memory flooded her mind once again. To think that he'd grabbed her, thrown her across his lap and spanked her for stealing candy – candy that had been given to her by the nice girl at the mercantile. (Who was now, incidentally, his new sister-in-law.) The affront of it all! Yes, he had no idea it had been given to her, and yes, she did look rather suspicious sneaking out of the mercantile when almost everyone else was off by the creekside. And yes, yes, yes, she was, then as now, disguised as a boy – he certainly wouldn't have laid hands on her (or at least not on her *derriere*) had she been dressed in several layers of petticoats. But nonetheless, it rankled.

And yet ... the smell of him ...

Cozette frowned at herself and squeezed her fists tighter.

With all the years spent in the wilderness with her father, her sense of smell was sharper than that of most people. And Duncan Cooke had a particular scent – he smelled of mint, lye soap, cured leather, and ... something else. A dark scent, like that of a wolf or bear during mating season, but at the same time distinctly, undeniably *his*. It had assailed her when he'd grabbed and assaulted her, had caused her emotions to jumble in a way she hadn't understood and still didn't. And it was doing the same thing now, even though he was standing down by the sheriff's office, a good thirty yards away!

How on Earth could this be? What kind of strange power did that man possess, that she ...

"*Ma petite*? You come with me."

Cozette nearly jumped out of her skin. She hadn't even heard her father approach.

"What is wrong? Why do you act so?" he asked.

She turned to him and shrugged. *I don't know.* Though she did.

He looked her over carefully, then glanced toward Duncan Cooke, who still stood and watched them. "Hmmm ..." was all he said. He took her by the arm and began to lead her down the street.

Instinctively she resisted. He stopped and looked at her again. "What is wrong with you?" he demanded.

She stood still and looked at the dusty ground. Her heart beat rapidly at the thought of going anywhere near Duncan Cooke. What *was* wrong with her? No man had ever made her feel like this. She wanted to hit him on *his* backside with a sturdy switch, like he suggested doing to her during their encounter. At the same time, she wanted to just stand next to him and inhale his scent. Why?

Her father grunted in frustration when she didn't answer and began to pull her along again. Toward the man. She dreaded it, and she wanted it. And if her father hadn't been holding on to her with an iron grip, she'd have fled like a rabbit. Only she wasn't sure whether she'd flee *from*, or *to* ...

Suddenly, he was there – right in front of her, his eyes roaming over her as if to take in as much as possible before he looked at her father. "M. Duprie, I'd like to speak with you. In private."

"Hmmm ...," her father said again. "In the saloon, then?" He let go of her, and the two men walked toward Mulligan's. But not before Duncan Cooke looked her over one last time. Her insides did a little flip-flop. Both hands flew to her belly at the odd sensation as her mouth dropped open. She probably looked like she was about to be sick, and maybe she was – it wouldn't be the strangest sensation she'd had in the last few minutes. But at the moment, she didn't care.

They went into the saloon, leaving her alone to wonder what they could possibly be discussing, and fighting the ever-growing sensation to be near him.

"So you see, *Monsieur* Duprie, the situation will benefit us both. Your daughter would be well taken care of. And my family would be put in a position to ensure the well-being of those involved with the Stantham estate." Duncan finished, then waited for his answer. They stood in the back corner of the saloon. Other than Mr. Mulligan, who was wiping glasses behind the bar and ignored their conversation, they were the only two men not eating.

After a moment, Anton Duprie looked at Duncan, his face an expressionless mask. Lord help him, did the Frenchman think he was joking about the inheritance? If so, he could show him the documents. Duncan hadn't thought he'd be talking with the man so soon, or he would have brought them along.

"You would take her ... to England?" M. Duprie whispered before he glanced around.

"Yes, *Monsieur*," Duncan replied as he too looked at the men scattered here and there eating lunch. None of them were paying him or Anton the least bit of attention. "We'll need to go in order to take care of the legalities involved, and see to the care of the estate."

"Never to return?"

"No, of course we would return. My family is here. I admit I don't know when, but I promise you, sir – we shall return."

M. Duprie sank heavily into the nearest chair, and began to absently comb his beard with his fingers as he stared at the floor. "I did not hide her well enough. You should never have known."

"I didn't know. My brother's wife, Belle ... she knew. Your daughter saved her from the fire."

"*Oui.* This I know. But Cozette did not tell me the woman found out."

"Cozette ..." Duncan tried out her name for the first time. It rolled off his tongue in a deep lilt.

The sound brought M. Duprie's head up. "Yes, Cozette. My treasure, my joy."

Duncan heard the pain in his voice. "You do not have to accept my offer. It is, I admit, a bit ... sudden."

"Indeed, sudden. But perhaps, the timing is good. With the plans for the town, more men come here – it makes it more ... *comment dites-vous ... difficult* to hide her. And Cozette, she ... she is different now."

"Different?"

"She takes not to the wild as before. She looks at things a woman wears. I think maybe she is tired of pretending to be a boy."

"Forgive me for asking, but why do you keep her disguised?"

M. Duprie stood and looked down the bar at Mr. Mulligan, who whistled as he polished glasses. "My wife, Cozette's mother ... she ..." He stopped and shook his head at the memory.

Duncan felt a chill run up his spine. "If we are to agree on this arrangement, I think I should know what happened."

"*Oui.* But you will not like hearing of it."

He didn't doubt the man was right. "I'll take my chances."

The Frenchman took a deep breath. "Marcelle, she was a beautiful woman. Cozette looks much like her. We had a cabin, up north. The Indians, they do not bother us. We are friendly with them. But other men in the area, they kill fathers and take wives and daughters. These men, they come in the night to my home when I am on the hunt. They kill my Marcelle – kill her in, in an ugly way. But they do not find my Cozette. She hides under the house, in a hole."

"Good Lord, man. How did she escape?"

"She waits until the men leave. She tried to save her mother, but ... it is too late. She dies in my little Cozette's arms. Since that night, my little one ... she does not speak."

Now Duncan sat in the nearest chair, his heart heavy at the story. That poor girl ... no wonder her father kept her disguised. He was trying to keep her safe from whoever had disgraced and slain his wife.

"I want no harm to come to her. You promise me – promise me you take her to England where they cannot find her?"

Duncan suddenly looked at him. Had he heard him right? "Find her? Who is looking for her?"

Duprie's eyes narrowed to slits. "For years now, men follow us. At first I think nothing of it, but then I pay attention. I see them, see them truly. These men who took my Marcelle."

"How do you know they are the same men?"

"Because Cozette sees them, and knows them. She hides under house that night, for there is a hole in the floor, and I have not had time to fix. Cozette is small enough. And she peeks out, she sees everything. She sees what they did to her mother."

Duncan closed his eyes as his chest tightened. Anger began to build, the same sort of anger he'd felt in prison. Injustice always did set him off. Senseless violence, abuse, neglect – oh, he could go on and on down the list of all he'd seen in prison, acts done to himself, to Colin, to other men locked within those walls. He had to admit that a few of the men there deserved it, though certainly not all. But when those injustices were done outside prison walls and to an innocent woman ...

"My Cozette, she is very special. Marcelle, she knows this, and tries to tell me so many times. But I am gone too much, and do not listen as I should. I do not realize how special she is until a short time ago. You must promise me, you protect her."

"No harm shall come to her. I give you my word." His voice was so hard, he barely recognized it as his own. Then he thought for a moment. What if ... "What if you came with us?"

"*Pardon?*"

"When we go to England, come with us. I imagine you'll feel better if you and I are both there to protect her, and she'll feel more comfortable if you're around."

"It is a good idea. I think on it. You may be God's answer to my prayer, *Monsieur* Duncan. I ask Him for a way to take care of and protect my Cozette. Especially after I am gone to Heaven one day."

Duncan smiled and nodded. Under the bushy beard and buckskins, Anton Duprie was just another man trying to take care of his little girl. Only ... she wasn't so little. And she might not take to the news that she was about to be given away in marriage to someone who'd turned her over his knee a few weeks ago ... well, deal with that when the time came. "Take care of her I shall. So are we agreed?"

M. Duprie stood and held out his hand.

Duncan hesitated. To shake it would set things in full motion. He could back out. He could refuse and let Thackary Holmes have it all. But could he live with the regret? Could he live with himself?

He stood, closed his eyes, took M. Duprie's hand, and gave it a healthy shake.

The older man smiled. "You have, as you say, a work cut out for you. You speak a little of the French?"

"Only a little." But at the moment, Duncan found he had little to say in any language. He'd just committed himself to marrying a woman he hadn't seen before, in a matter of speaking. And come to think of it, when would he? "I do have one question."

"*Oui?*"

"When you tell Cozette, how do you think she'll react?"

"She will do as I say. She is a good girl, she obeys her father. She knows I know what is best for her."

Duncan sighed. "Well, that's good to know. I will, of course, court her first, as is proper. But I must marry soon."

M. Duprie smiled again. "I tell her tonight, and we see you tomorrow."

Duncan could only give him a half-smile in return. He didn't envy M. Duprie when he gave his daughter the news.

# DAY 3

Anton lost his nerve. He instead spent the day out on the prairie hunting rabbits with Cozette, and avoided going into town.

# DAY 4

A day of rest after hunting. Cozette made rabbit stew. Anton prepared the hides and tried to think about anything other than what he had to tell his daughter.

# DAY 5

Anton finally worked up the guts and gave her the news. Well, part of it anyway. The part of it he could get out before she stamped her feet at him, threw a mixing spoon in his direction and ran from their camp. She returned after dark, still sullen, and glared at him whenever he opened his mouth. Eventually he decided discretion was the better part of valor, and forbore telling her the rest.

# DAY 6

Cozette kicked, screamed – silently – and even bit him at one point. But Anton would not be budged. She didn't want to budge either, but she couldn't beat him when it came down to brute strength. And at the moment it did.

But that didn't keep her from fighting, even as he stood behind her, holding her arms in a grip so tight she thought he might leave bruises. How could he do such a thing? Why was he exposing her like this? Didn't he realize what he was asking of her?

Belle Dunnigan – no, make that Belle *Cooke* – and her loud aunt from the mercantile hauled in two more buckets of water and poured them into the metal tub. They were in the back room of the saloon, and it wasn't only Belle and her aunt in attendance. Oh, no – her father had called in reinforcements. The other Cooke woman, Sadie, was there, and Mrs. Mulligan. And they were all armed and ready for battle.

Once again, she twisted in her father's iron grip, pleading with him not to do this. Once done, it would be *done* – her secret would be out. She would no longer be Cosime, the Duprie boy, but Co*zette*. And Cozette Duprie was most definitely a girl.

"Stop this minute!" her father yelled as she dealt him a kick in the shin. "You will do this! You must! It is for your own good!"

Belle stepped forward. "Please, settle down. We won't hurt you, we promise."

"Maybe we oughta!" Mrs. Dunnigan said as she set down her bucket.

"Auntie, you're not helping," Belle said with a sigh. The older woman frowned, but subsided.

Sadie decided to try something. She set down the scrub brush she was holding, opened a box she'd brought in earlier, pulled out a beautiful dress and shook it out.

Cozette caught the flash of color out the corner of her eye and suddenly stopped her struggles. She turned and stared at it, mesmerized. It was a dark rose, with white and black ribbons on the sleeves that lent a delicate look. Was it for her? How long had she wanted to wear such a pretty thing – months? Years? She couldn't believe it, but her mouth actually started to water!

Sadie smiled and opened another box, this one round. She took out a wide-brimmed hat that matched the dress, and was adorned with pale pink flowers.

Cozette sucked in her breath, transfixed.

"Will it do, *Mademoiselle* Duprie?" Belle asked.

Cozette could only nod. *Oh yes! It's so beautiful!* But she still turned to her father as he loosened his grip, her eyes wide. *Why?*

His face was sad, but firm. "You are in hiding long enough. Too long, perhaps. It is time you grow up, and be who you are. My beautiful Cozette, these women will help you. Let them take care of you. Then, I have a special surprise."

She looked at him, then back to the women standing at the ready. Mrs. Mulligan held a scrub brush and a towel. Belle had soap and another bucket of water. And Mrs. Dunnigan ... Mrs. Dunnigan held a cast-iron ladle, and an expression that made Cozette think she might get clobbered over the head with it if she didn't get into that tub.

She gulped back her fear, then reached up and slowly pulled her animal-skin hat off in defeat. Her hair was wrapped in a bandana she'd tied about her head, one gray with dirt and age, and she took it off as well. As her dark locks fell about her shoulders and halfway down to her waist, everyone but her father and Belle gasped. She wasn't sure why – surely they'd known she was a girl before this moment ...

"Well, don't just stand there gawking at her – get her in the tub before the water gets cold!" Grandma Waller scolded as she entered the room. She was followed by a woman who must be Sadie's mother – Mrs. Van Cleet had told Cozette how much alike they looked. If only Mrs. Van Cleet were there. She would feel so much better if she were.

"That dress is so pretty! Do you think it will fit?" Sadie's mother asked.

Sadie touched the dress she'd laid across a nearby chair. "I'm sure it will – we're about the same size."

"You can thank Sadie's father for the frock, *Mademoiselle* Duprie," Belle told her.

"Yes, it was a gift to me on my last birthday, along with the hat," Sadie added. "I thought it would do well for this. But first things first." She motioned toward the tub.

Cozette forced her gaze from the dress to the tub of steaming water. How long had it been since she'd bathed in hot water? She couldn't remember. She briefly wondered if it would hurt.

Her father stepped away from her. "I leave now. Thank you for your kindness in this matter," he told the women.

Cozette spun around. He was going to leave? But ... well, of course he would. She was no longer the little girl he once bounced on his knee. She was a woman. Unfortunately, she had no idea how to be one.

She gulped again as her father left and closed the door behind him with a loud *click*, then turned back to the small army surrounding the tub. Mrs. Dunnigan casually slapped the ladle against the palm of her hand. The others slowly moved to encircle her. She wanted to allow them to help her. She knew she should. Unfortunately, she just couldn't fight her instinct for self-preservation.

"Ouch!"

"Oh, dear Lord!"

"Begone, foul spirit–"

"Auntie, not – eek – now!"

"Tarnation, girl, we ain't gonna kill ya!"

"I've got her – ow!"

It was a good thing her father had left the room.

"Gads, man, sit down! You'll wear out the floor!" Horatio Jones scolded as Duncan continued to pace.

Horatio, Harrison, and Colin had accompanied their wives to town, and were sitting in the main room of the saloon. It was still fairly early in the morning, so the saloon was empty of customers. Except for Duncan and the husbands, only those involved with "bath time" were present.

And the married men – including Mr. Mulligan – were there not just to witness the transformation of "the Duprie boy" into the woman she really was, but to keep Duncan together. He'd been up all night going over the documents, still looking for a way out of the mess he'd been plunged into. But the documents were iron-clad: he must marry by the deadline in order to inherit, or lose it all.

Harrison tried to be reassuring. "I'm sure she'll not only be beautiful, but a willing and able wife. Once she gets used to being, ah, well ... a woman."

"After she's properly disarmed, of course," Colin quipped.

Duncan stopped pacing and glared at his brother. Colin stood to one side and tried his best not to laugh.

Anton Duprie now sat at a corner table. He waved Duncan over. "Something I must tell you, *Monsieur* Cooke."

Duncan walked over, but was too nervous to sit. "Yes, *Monsieur* Duprie? Is something wrong?"

"Eh ... perhaps. You see, when I explain to Cozette our plans ... she ... was not pleased."

Duncan's brow furrowed, but he said nothing, only motioned for him to continue.

"She walks out before I could finish – and does not listen to me after this. So ... she does not know ... all of it," he concluded abruptly.

Duncan chewed on his lower lip, trying to stay calm. "So ... which part did you tell her? The part about dressing as a woman, I presume?"

"Oui. But ... not the part about the marriage." The Frenchman grimaced. "For this, I apologize."

"So she doesn't know that I ..."

"She knows you are involved in some fashion. But ..." He didn't want to tell the poor *Anglais* that it was the mention of Duncan's name that caused the already-angry Cozette to cut him off and run for the hills. "But not the, the details."

"Well." Duncan took a moment to look around at the wall fixtures. His voice was still calm, but his right hand balled into a fist so tight it made his knuckles crack. "That does complicate things–"

There was a loud crash from the back of the building, followed by a piercing scream.

"That ... sounded like Sadie," Harrison said. "You'll excuse me ..." He quickly disappeared down the hall to the back room.

The other men listened intently. Mr. Mulligan's mustache twitched.

Another scream rent the air. Colin suddenly bolted upright from his chair. "That's Belle!" He, too, hurried down the hallway.

"What the bloody ... what's going on in there?" Duncan demanded.

"If I didn't know better," Mr. Mulligan volunteered, "it sounds a bit like a fight. Only, those usually happen out here – and after a few pints ..."

Anton cringed at each new bang or yell from the back of the building. "Cozette, she never did like to take the bath." He shrugged helplessly.

Another crash, followed by the sound of shattering glass came next.

"I hope that wasn't me mother-in-law's ashes. I told Mary not to keep 'em back there," Mr. Mulligan sighed as he wiped down the counter of the bar.

"Why on earth would you keep her ashes in the back room of the saloon?" Duncan asked, primarily to distract himself from the chaos in the other room.

"On account neither me nor the wife particularly wanted her upstairs with us. Old Mum O'Brian always was a crotchety thing."

"Hopefully not covering the walls and floor of your storeroom now," Colin added as he returned.

Harrison followed right behind him. "Sorry, old boy, but the women won't let us know what's going on. Grandma said, rather pointedly, that we should wait out here."

"It sounds like they're pulling each others' hair out in there!" Horatio huffed. "Maybe a good dunking in a pond would have done just as well!"

"*Oui*, she might have liked that better," M. Duprie said as he again flinched at the sound of more screaming.

Duncan groaned before he resumed his pacing.

"I say, the hallway is full of water," Harrison stated calmly. "I think there must be more on the floor than in that tub."

"Oh, not the hall floor!" Mr. Mulligan moaned. "I figured I'd only have to clean up the storeroom!"

"If I were you, I don't think I'd want to *see* the storeroom!" Colin said.

Suddenly everything went quiet. Each man looked at the others briefly before listening intently for any further sounds of disaster. But none were forthcoming.

After about a minute of silence Horatio pulled out his pocket watch. "You don't suppose ...?"

"Indeed. I don't," Colin replied, his brow furrowed in confusion.

By Horatio's count, it was a good seven minutes before they heard the door to the storeroom finally open, and two sets of footsteps come down the hall.

Belle emerged first, or at least what was left of her. Half her hair had been pulled from its chignon. Her dress was drenched, and the right sleeve torn at the shoulder. Sadie was right behind, in no better shape. But both women had wide smiles on their faces.

The men looked at them, horrified and confused. Were the grins a good sign, or had the ordeal driven them insane?

Grandma Waller arrived next, also smiling. "Well, gentlemen, we have someone we'd like you to meet."

More footsteps. Mrs. Dunnigan entered, her trusty ladle at the ready. Then Mary Mulligan and Teresa Jones, one on either side, escorted a woman into the room.

The men stood. And one man – Duncan – gaped.

Cozette was beautiful! Her face was delicate, almost fragile-looking. Her eyes were a dark green, her skin a beautiful olive bronzed by years spent in the outdoors. Her long hair was unevenly shorn (nothing the women could do about that – it had been that way before), but glistened darkly from under the hat. She was clearly nervous – her hands kept fidgeting with the skirt of the dress, the brim of the hat, the ends of her hair, as if she wasn't quite sure how to deal with all these fripperies. And her eyes darted everywhere short of the ceiling. But she was still positively radiant, with an almost fairy-tale look about her – like she'd just stepped out of a storybook.

Anton Duprie gasped, and approached slowly, as if he was worried she might bolt like a startled doe. Which, perhaps, she was. *"Ma petite?* It is you?"

She looked at her father and nodded jerkily. Everyone stood quietly and watched as the two seemed to be seeing each other for the first time.

Then another crash suddenly brought everyone's attention to the center of the saloon. Belle and Sadie tried their best not to laugh.

Duncan, chagrined, sat on the floor next to an overturned chair. He'd gone to sit, but was so transfixed by what stood before him that he'd almost missed the chair entirely. He didn't even bother to get up, just sat there with his mouth open and stared.

Anton Duprie took his daughter's hands. "My Cozette," he whispered as he looked her over. "My beautiful little girl." Impulsively, he pulled her into his arms. "You are as beautiful as your sainted mother ..."

She nodded again, the hat now askew from being crushed against him. *I suppose, Papa. I just hope you know what you're doing. But it feels strange to be beautiful. Why must I be a woman now? Why must things change?* And yet the dress was beautiful, and she loved the way the soft velvet felt against her skin. The hat, too, was a treasure – she could hardly take her eyes off the ribbons and flowers.

But ... when they'd put it on her head, and Belle had placed a mirror in front of her ...

Cozette hadn't recognized the young woman in the mirror, staring back at her in puzzlement. She'd never seen her before. Was that really her? She wasn't sure how to reconcile this vision of beauty with the picture of herself she kept in her mind. Let alone the one she was used to seeing reflected in other eyes, other mirrors – Cosime, the trapper's scruffy son, wanderer of the wilderness, rescuer of damsels from fires, alleged stealer of sweetmeats ...

But now, the woman in the mirror wasn't the only person she didn't recognize. The man who sat on the floor and gawked at her like a stunned steer couldn't possibly be Duncan Cooke, man about town and avenger of the mercantile. She knew well that he was, of course, but like her, he didn't look his normal – grouchy – self at the moment.

The saloon doors swung open, and everyone turned.

An overdressed man glided into the saloon like a spider and went straight to Cozette. "Well, it's true, then!" he began, his accent like that of the Cooke brothers – but not quite. "There *is* a woman in town. And what a woman you are, my dear. Charming!"

*That* got Duncan to his feet. "Mr. Holmes. What are you doing here?" he demanded.

Cozette cringed. *Now* she recognized Duncan! The look he was giving the other Englishman made her wonder if he was about to toss the newcomer over his knee and give *him* a good whooping.

"Simply seeing to my interests. I have a schedule to keep, after all, and I wish to wrap this whole thing up as soon as possible."

"Does that mean you're leaving?"

"That depends on my ..." He looked Cozette up and down, "... interests."

Cozette silently snarled at him. It was worth a try – baring her teeth worked on wolves sometimes, getting them to back down from her prey. And this newcomer was certainly acting wolfishly.

"You. You are that Englishman Mr. Van Cleet tells me of," Anton declared. "You have no business here. Begone!" He waved toward the saloon doors.

"I have as much right to be here as these people. This establishment is open to the public, after all."

"Not at present it's not," Mr. Mulligan said, interposing himself between Thackary Holmes and the rest of the group. "I'm the proprietor here. This is a private party, sir, and you were not invited. I suggest you leave peaceably – and quickly."

Thackary Holmes wrinkled his nose. "As if I would be found dead taking a *suggestion* from an Irishman."

"Dead or alive, makes no difference to me," Mulligan growled. "So long as you leave."

Instead of making a departure, Holmes made a grab for Cozette's arm. But he only succeeded in getting his own wrist grabbed by Duncan, who then pulled back his other hand in a fist.

Cozette, meanwhile, found herself frozen. She hated the feeling – she much preferred being the predator. But she had seen herself in the stranger's eyes ... and he clearly thought of her as his prey.

Anton Duprie jumped between Duncan and Holmes. "Enough!" He knocked Duncan's hand away from the other man. "There will be no fighting today. This ... this is the reason I keep Cozette hidden! We are in agreement, *Monsieur* Cooke, are we not? There is no need to fight for what is already won, no?"

Duncan took a deep breath, and finally nodded. "Quite right, Monsieur Duprie." But he made sure to keep his body between Holmes and Cozette.

Cozette, meanwhile, was confused. *Won? Won what?*

Anton then spun on Holmes. "And I repeat, this is none of your affair. Depart like a gentleman, *s'il vous plait!*" His tone made it clear that he was not, in fact, making a request.

Cozette peeked around Duncan at the unfolding scene. Was Duncan trying to protect her? Considering how Mr. Holmes made her skin crawl, she didn't really mind. But what was wrong with her? She normally would have been off like a shot, or at least prepared to fight. But instead, she'd stopped dead at his advance. Just like a ... well, just like a girl! She scowled. Maybe it was the dress and the hat. She wished she'd at least brought her bow and quiver ...

Mr. Holmes looked at the group like they were the lowliest of peasants. But he did, thankfully, step away. "Rest assured, I *will* be back to see to my interests." Again, he looked at Cozette as if he'd like to eat her for lunch.

She couldn't decide whether to hide behind Duncan or bare her teeth again, and the indecision kept her frozen in place. Literally frozen – she felt like her bones had turned to ice.

"Although, dear sir," he added, returning his gaze to Anton, "perhaps you shouldn't send me away just yet. You haven't heard what I have to offer."

"Nor do I wish to. *Au revoir!*" her father replied. She knew that tone of voice – and if Mr. Holmes knew what was good for him, he'd leave at once!

But apparently Mr. Holmes didn't know what was good for him. He stepped closer and whispered something in her father's ear – something unpleasant, from the way Anton's shoulders stiffened. Then he pulled back, smiled predatorily, said "good day to all you fine people" with enough sarcasm to paint the room, and left the saloon the same way he'd come in. Like a big, hungry spider.

The women of the town sprung into action as soon as Mr. Holmes left. They went upstairs to the living quarters for a few moments, returning with tablecloths, plates, silverware and napkins. They set two tables, then brought food in from the downstairs kitchen and laid it out on the bar, buffet-style. Mrs. Dunnigan and Mrs. Mulligan took up posts behind it to serve.

"Dig in, everyone! It's on us!" Mr. Mulligan announced.

Harrison and Colin were the first to grab a plate off a table and go to the bar, while Sadie and Belle disappeared to change into dry clothing that, mercifully, they'd brought with them just in case. Mr. Mulligan also left, reluctantly, to see to the state of his storeroom, or what remained of it. He'd have much rather sat down with a big plate of beef, cabbage and potatoes, but he knew he'd regret it more if he put it off.

Duncan still hadn't moved. And neither had Cozette – she still hid behind him, despite there no longer being anyone to hide from. Only when her father picked up a plate and let out a long sigh did she relax. It was his usual signal, the one that told her everything was finished and done, and it was safe to continue.

Duncan slowly turned, as if he was afraid he'd startle her, and looked down at her face. "Are you alright?" he asked her, his voice soft and low.

She'd never been this close to him before – well, not face-to-face, that is. His eyes were dark, like his brother Harrison's, but more shadowed, as if he had seen horrors beyond description. The other Cooke brother's hazel eyes were like that, but Harrison's weren't. It made her wonder – what terrible things had this man seen and experienced?

"He didn't frighten you, did he? I assure you, I won't let him hurt you."

Cozette quickly glanced at her father, but he had his back to her. How could he so easily ignore her after all she'd just been through that morning? Unless he was doing it on purpose, trying to tell her something. But what?

She turned back to Duncan and shook her head no. *No, he didn't hurt me, but it felt as if he was going to.*

She didn't trust this Holmes. Where did he come from? Why was he in town? And what did he intend for her?

"I'm relieved ... I mean, I'm glad that he did you no harm. I ... forgive me for being so forward, but you are ... quite stunning. I had no idea, under all that dirt... er, ah... I mean, that is to say, you are ... you look lovely."

Cozette smiled. She suddenly realized that he, too, was pretty stunning. Very tall, with a strong jaw and huge hands and muscles ... well, a lot of them. And if he usually stammered like that, well, maybe that meant he wouldn't mind her not speaking at all.

"Miss Duprie, I ... I owe you an apology. In regard to our first meeting ..."

She could see the remorse in his eyes. *But is it remorse for doing wrong? Or only because you now know I'm a woman?*

"I'm afraid ... well, you're going to cause quite a stir in town. You ... you truly are lovely, and ... the men here, well, with women being as scarce as they are ... they are likely to, to want to pursue you ..."

Oh, like she needed him to tell her *that!* Why did he think her father had kept her disguised as a boy in the first place?! She glanced again at her father, who was at a table with Mr. and Mrs. Mulligan, eating quietly but still not looking her way or acknowledging her. *Just what are you up to, Papa?*

"I've ... I've already spoken with your father about ... offering my services. As your protector."

*Oh, was that what Papa was trying to tell me before?*, she thought. She took a step back and looked at him again – *really* looked at him. He was so much taller than she, and quite powerfully built. He had a sheen of sweat on his brow, and his dark eyes looked as if they wanted to encompass her, or at least keep away anything that wanted to harm her. There was a hint of hope in them for something, too – but for what, she did not know.

*Why would you make such an offer to my father in the first place?* The words were right there, but of course no sound came out. She glanced toward her father once more, then back at Duncan. She cocked her head slightly to one side and raised her brow. *Why?*

"You're curious as to my offer?"

She gave him the smallest of nods.

"Because I've seen what can happen to a woman left unprotected out here. You might have not had to worry about it before, Miss Duprie, but in your current state of dress and, shall we say, beauty, no man will be able to resist the temptation to ... to be with you. Perhaps against your will."

Her eyes widened. She swallowed hard and took another step back.

"But you needn't worry about me. I am, first and foremost, a gentleman." His voice was softer than before, and she stepped closer again, as if he'd placed an invisible rope around her waist. "Your father and I have an agreement," he practically whispered. "I will be your protector."

His eyes glistened with something she couldn't put her finger on. No man had ever looked at her the way Duncan Cooke was looking at her. But one thing she read in his eyes was clear. Duncan had most definitely just made his mind up about something. About something involving her.

The question was, what?

# DAY 7

Duncan watched for stray cattle as he wondered what had come over him. When the Duprie girl had looked into his eyes the day before, it was like getting gut-punched – his knees had actually gone weak! And afterward ... he felt as if he and she had somehow been fused together.

In that moment, Duncan swore he'd heard a voice in his head: *You need someone in your life. You're lonely. To marry would ease the pain from prison and give you something of your own to live for. To protect. To give you a woman to die for. And this one, this woman before you, is she.*

Had it been the good Lord above, or simply his own lonely heart screaming the truth? Had Harrison felt like this when he'd first laid eyes on Sadie? What about Colin – hadn't he said it was love at first sight with Belle? Was any of this normal? Perhaps he'd been so worried about taking care of this duchy business that he'd lost sight of himself, and that's how she'd so utterly overwhelmed him. It had to be – his reaction to her just wasn't natural.

Or was it?

How long had it been since a woman had affected him that way? Too long ... and only because there weren't any women around to do the affecting! Colin had staked his claim on Belle from the moment of her arrival – Duncan had seen it in his eyes the first time she came to the ranch for the sewing circle. He smiled at the memory, recalling how he and Harrison had aided Colin in his quest to court Belle, and hoped his two brothers didn't decide he needed the same kind of help to secure Cozette.

Did he want to secure her? Well, his agreement with her father had already done that. But now ... now he realized he wanted more. He wanted to truly win her, to woo her into his arms.

Easier said than done, however. Yes, they'd been able to communicate to a certain extent the day before. He'd gotten her a plate at lunch, and she hadn't rejected his doing so. They'd sat opposite one another at a table with Harrison, Colin, Sadie, and Belle. She'd seemed calm enough, with the two other women sitting on either side of her.

That was fine for yesterday, but what about the next few weeks? He had only so much time to court and marry her before the deadline.

And it didn't help that Thackary Holmes was still sniffing around. What sort of strategy was he pursuing?

"You missed one."

Duncan jumped in his saddle, startling his horse enough to have to pull on the reins to steady him.

"For once, one of us was actually able to sneak up on you!" Harrison chuckled. "I don't believe it! This is a day to go down in history!"

Duncan scowled. "Hardly. I was simply lost in thought." He sighed in frustration. "I'm afraid I've done more than my share of woolgathering lately."

Harrison kicked his horse and headed toward the stray he'd spotted. "You can still back out. But then, I'd be lying if I told you it doesn't matter to me. Father would want you to have it."

Duncan rode beside him. "As do I. But I want to do this the right way. I'll not have a wife who runs from me like a frightened filly."

"She's certainly skittish. More of a *wild* filly than a frightened one."

Duncan pulled up short. "What did you say?"

Harrison stopped his horse as well, and leaned on the saddle horn. "She's like a wild filly. I dare say, you're going to have a time breaking that one."

Duncan thought a moment. Harrison had just given him an idea. "Sometimes it's not a matter of breaking, but of simply taming."

"Do you want her to fall in love with you?" Harrison asked.

"For our family, I'll do what I have to."

"You don't have to make it sound like a sacrifice, dear brother. Colin and I married for love – why not you? Can you see yourself falling in love with her? You have to admit, she's quite pretty now that she's all cleaned up."

"Yes. A beautiful piece of property needed to seal our family's fortune," he replied dryly.

"Duncan," Harrison scolded. "Give it some time."

"Time, little brother, is not something I have the luxury of. Thirty-one days left as of today. One. Month."

"Time enough, if you spend it with her. After what I saw yesterday, it may not take much." Harrison tipped his hat, kicked his horse into a canter, rounded up the stray, and drove it back to the herd which grazed nearby.

If only it was that easy to round up Miss Duprie and lead her to the altar, Duncan mused. But perhaps, if he was gentle enough with her, she'd be more receptive to the idea. Taming a filly, indeed ...

"Now let's try this one on," Sadie said as Belle helped Cozette out of the dress she'd just managed to

get her into. Grandma Waller had driven Cozette and
her father out to the Triple-C Ranch so Sadie and
Belle could have the chance to fit her for more dresses.
Some would have to be taken in, since buxom Belle
had contributed several, while the slimmer Sadie had
pulled others from her own wardrobe – an extensive
one, by the looks of it.

But dresses were not foremost in Cozette's mind
today, not when she couldn't even express her
gratitude for them.

It made it hard to enjoy the clothing, all of which
was more wondrous than anything she'd ever worn in
her life. Not to mention the pretty tea cups and
saucers she'd seen set on the dining room table for
later, or the lovely wallpaper in Sadie's bedroom, or
the beautiful bed and its wonderful coverlet. She'd
heard Sadie's father, Horatio Jones, had money. But
she hadn't realized how much until she'd come out to
the ranch house he'd built for his daughter and new
son-in-law.

*It's all so very lovely! And you are both being so
kind to me. How can I ever repay you?* The words were
right there, but they wouldn't come out. It frustrated
her not to be able to speak to them, so much so that
she had to brush away the tears before they could fall.
Thankfully, the other women were too busy tugging
and flapping her into one outfit after another to notice.

The more dresses she tried on, the more she wanted
to keep them. It felt strange – she'd never thought she
would have the opportunity to just be, let alone look
like, a girl. She'd accepted the that acting and dressing
like one was far too impractical for the sort of life she
and her father led, especially given some of the people
with which they traded.

But now it looked like Papa had decided to settle
down – no more traversing forests or crossing prairies,
no more worrying about outlaws and vagabonds who
rarely saw an unmarried woman outside of a brothel.

And if Papa was settling down, it meant he was expecting her to do the same.

But how? She didn't know the first thing about ... *anything* related to living in a town!

*But I want to learn. Yes, I do! And you two will teach me, no? You'll show me how to sew a pretty dress, to cook a lovely meal, to have afternoon tea with other ladies. But you've seen me. You know how I have lived. Will you accept me? Or will I always be like some sort of savage in your eyes? Will part of you always think of me as "the Duprie boy" that you had to redeem from her hidden life in the wilderness?*

Sometimes Cozette was glad she couldn't speak. Then she couldn't ask questions she might not like the answers to.

"Oh, this one is beautiful on you!" Belle exclaimed. "I think we should take a break, though, go downstairs and have tea."

"I agree. This has been a busy morning. I wonder, would your father like to join us?" Sadie asked.

Cozette automatically opened her mouth to speak. She hadn't done that in years! It hung open, her eyes wide. Why did it happen now? But still, no sound, so she finally shut it, looked from one woman to the other and shrugged. *I do not know.*

"Well, let's go find out if he's still here," Sadie replied. "He said he was going to take a look around."

The three women went downstairs, and Cozette sat in the parlor while Sadie put the kettle on and Belle went to get Anton. But as he was nowhere to be found, they returned to the dining room and prepared their tea.

When it was ready, Sadie poured. "Would you like sugar?" she asked Cozette.

Cozette looked at the delicate little china bowl full of sugar. What was she supposed to do? She'd never had tea before. She looked helplessly to Sadie.

"Is this your first time to tea?"

Cozette bit her bottom lip and gave a single nod. She could feel herself begin to blush with the disclosure. It was only tea, but she felt like her cluelessness about this world of women was on display. What would they think of her now?

"Let me serve you, then. Try a sip – and then if you want to sweeten it, add a little sugar." Sadie set the cup and saucer in front of her as Belle took a seat. Cozette watched as Sadie served her as well, then poured herself a cup.

"Go on, Cozette. It's wonderful! Try it," Belle urged.

Cozette carefully picked up the tea cup. Sadie and Belle did the same. The two women took a small sip then set their cups down with a delicate clink of china.

She raised the cup to her lips, feeling the heat from the beverage. It reminded her of drinking coffee with Papa around a campfire. But the spicy-sweet scent, the feel and color of the china cup in her hands was far different. The whole experience gave her an uneasy satisfaction she could not describe, like a childhood dream she couldn't quite remember was coming true.

She took a tiny sip. Oh my, it was heavenly! A tremor raced down her spine as she savored it.

"Would you like some sugar?" Sadie asked.

Cozette again automatically opened her mouth to speak. She froze in confusion. Perhaps the words were trying to come out of their own accord. She licked her lips, swallowed, and waited to see if they would come again. But no, nothing. She closed her eyes a moment in silent defeat, and frowned. Frustrating. Finally she set down her cup as she'd seen them do, and nodded.

Just as Sadie spooned some sugar into Cozette's cup, the front door opened. Belle stood up. "*Monsieur* Duprie?"

But it was Duncan. He stopped short, Colin and Harrison right behind him, and stared in shock.

Colin, who'd almost walked right into him, tapped him on the shoulder. "I say, Duncan, are your feet nailed to the floor?"

Duncan neither moved nor replied.

Sadie looked from Duncan to Cozette and back again, and smiled. This was certainly a familiar scenario. She remembered Colin being dragged into the parlor by his brothers, and Belle freezing like a poleaxed steer. It looked like it was happening again. But this time, the chute was backing up behind Duncan, and she thought she'd better do something about it. "Your lunch is in the kitchen, boys. We ladies will continue with our tea, if you don't mind."

Harrison, peering around Colin, saw Duncan gaping and grinned. "Oh, Colin and I don't mind. More for us if Duncan can't make his feet move! Lovely to see you again, *Mademoiselle* Duprie. We had no idea our wives had a guest."

Duncan tore his gaze away from Cozette just long enough to scowl at his brothers before being pulled back around again. That thing that had fused them together the day before was back, and reinforced.

Colin finally had enough. Laughing, he gave Duncan a healthy shove in the small of the back. It wasn't enough to wake him from his daze, but it at least cleared him out of the doorway.

Sadie rolled her eyes. "Enough!" she scolded. "Go eat!"

Duncan shook himself out of his trance and forced his feet to move. "Are you ladies ... quite comfortable? Do you need anything?"

Belle hid a smile. "No, Duncan. But thank you for asking."

"After you eat, why don't you have a cookie and a cup before heading back out?" Sadie suggested.

Duncan's chest began to rise and fall as his breathing picked up. "I'll, I'll do that." He spun on his heel and fled.

Cozette released the breath she'd been holding and slumped in her chair. Sadie immediately sat, Belle took a quick sip of tea, and they both looked at her with a gleam in their eyes. *Oh, dear. Whatever are they thinking?*

"I do believe Duncan was admiring you in that dress, Cozette," Sadie stated.

"It's a lovely color on you," Belle said. "Though I think we should also try the yellow."

Cozette fingered the pretty lace-trimmed collar, smoothed the fabric of the skirt. It was a lovely pink calico with a hint of green that brought out the color in her eyes. She smiled and blushed at the thought of Duncan being pleased with how she looked. She didn't want his approval, didn't need it. But it affected her nonetheless. She found the sensation fascinating, and wondered when it might happen again.

"Try your tea with the sugar. I think you'll like it," Sadie said, then added teasingly, "Duncan loves sugar in his tea. He has a terrible sweet tooth."

Cozette fought against a smile. *He's not the only one!*

"He absolutely adores chocolate as well. You don't happen to bake, do you?"

The question caught her in mid-sip, and she just managed not to choke as she slowly set her cup down. Could she bake? Yes – potatoes in ashes, or cornbread in a cast-iron skillet over an open fire. A cake or pie, in an oven ... she looked away, ashamed.

Belle and Sadie quickly glanced at each other. Belle spoke first. "Oh, it's easy to learn – my aunt is giving me lessons, and she's the best cook around. I'm sure she'd teach you too, if I asked her."

Cozette quailed. She knew well who Belle's aunt was!

Belle missed the signs. "You can come with me next week, if you like. Aunt Irene is going to teach me how to make bread and pot roast–"

Eyes wide, Cozette shook her head in quick little jerks. *I would love to ... but not if your aunt is going to try to hit me with her ladle!*

Belle's brow furrowed, but then understanding dawned. "Oh, don't worry about Aunt Irene – she's not as fearsome as she seems. At least not lately. And I can keep her calm." She gave her a warm smile. "Please do come. It'll be fun!"

Cozette glanced at Sadie, looked down at the table, then tentatively nodded.

"It's settled then! You and I will learn how to make bread and pot roast next week!"

"And I can teach you how to bake cakes and cookies if you want me to," Sadie added.

Cozette nodded again, this time with no reluctance. *You have no idea what a gift you are giving me! It's like a dream come true – no more cooking over campfires, no leaves falling into the soup, no having to chase animals away from the plates ... and to actually be able to make a real cake, in a real stove! I'm so excited–!*

She suddenly stopped as she realized that her mouth had been moving, even though no sound had come out. She began touching her mouth with her hand, unable to figure out what was happening. Not that she minded, but it was quite a shock.

Sadie leaned toward her. "It's all right, you don't have to be embarrassed. We understand. Has it been a long time since you lost your voice?"

Cozette looked at her and nodded. *So long now, I do not even remember when I last spoke. But I know that if I ever do speak again, I will do it well. I read whenever I can – Moliere, Dumas, Shakespeare, the Bible, newspapers! I love to read ...*

"It must be hard at times," Belle added. "Don't think I'm prying, but can you write?"

Cozette smiled and nodded. She'd practiced her handwriting until it was better than her father's.

"Oh, wonderful · that makes things so much easier. But I must say, it's so easy to understand you, even without you writing anything down!"

Cozette shrugged and held up her hands. *When you have to communicate this way for most of your life, you get good at it,* she thought. But she still smiled at the compliment.

"I would love to know about the adventures you and your father have had," Belle told her. "I'm sure some of them were quite exciting!"

Cozette's smile dimmed. *Ah, but there are some "adventures" I would rather not remember ...*

"But you don't have to share them with us if you don't want to," Sadie added quickly.

"Oh, yes, of course," Belle said and reached for the teapot. "More tea, anyone?"

As Belle poured them each a second cup, Cozette wondered if any of the things she and her father had been through were fit tales to go along with tea. It was hard to tell – everything about this world of ladies and dresses and ovens was still so new. Perhaps, for now, she would keep learning ... and keep her "adventures" to herself.

Duncan sat at the kitchen table, watching his brothers as they devoured their lunch. But he'd found he had no appetite.

Why was this little slip of a woman affecting him this way? He'd dreamed of women in prison – it was one of the things that kept him sane. To be honest, he'd dreamed of things he probably shouldn't have, and as soon as he'd been let out of gaol he'd found the nearest church and repented of every last one of them. But this was different. This wasn't lustful; it was more like a fountain of life-giving water in the midst of a desert, where if he didn't drink of it, he would surely die.

"I say, old boy," Colin asked. "Are you all right? You've not touched your meal."

*No, I'm not!* It was all he could do to stay in his chair. He wanted to run into the dining room, scoop the Duprie girl into his arms, run up to his room and claim her in the most primal and beautiful of ways, to make their bodies and souls sing as one, merge into one ...

Good Lord, what was happening to him?! "I'm fine," he said tersely. "Just not hungry right now."

Harrison and Colin both stood. "Perhaps if you started with dessert, it would whet your appetite for more," Harrison said, nudging Colin in the ribs.

Colin took the cue. "Oh, yes. A spot of tea and a few sweets will set you right. Why don't you go on into the dining room and have Belle pour you a cup?"

Duncan glared at his brothers. "Are you two going to have some?" he asked, eyebrows arched.

"Oh, not us," Harrison quickly said. "Couldn't eat another bite, myself. Time to return to work." He turned toward the back door of the kitchen, slapping Duncan on the back as he left.

"It's going to be a long hard afternoon out there," Colin added. "Be sure to take the sandwiches when you leave. But ... do go in and have a spot of tea first. We know you'll catch up."

"I'll do that," Duncan said darkly as Colin too departed. Then he sat in silence, staring at the food in front of him. He was hungry, actually ... but not for food. What he was feeling now went beyond any sort of natural need. Still, wasn't it too soon for him to have fallen in love with the girl? But if it wasn't that, then what was it?

Sadie and Belle's laughter floated in from the dining room.

Well, whatever it was, he supposed he'd best go in
there and find out. He wrapped the sandwiches in a
linen napkin, took two steps in the direction of the
dining room ... then spun on his heel and hightailed it
out the back door after his brothers.

# DAY 8

He hated this, this ... *purgatory* was the only word he could come up with. Duncan knew he needed to get this courting business underway, but he just couldn't bring himself to see Cozette. The longer he stayed away, the more strangely he felt. But to see her meant he'd have to keep himself under tight control. And he wasn't sure he could ...

# DAY 9

The idea struck him over dinner ... what if he just made sure he was never alone with her? Good Lord, why hadn't he thought of *that* before? It was a proper enough way to handle things – a gentlemanly way, no less – and more to the point, it might well keep him from doing something incredibly stupid!

# DAY 10

He tried to dodge the oncoming fist, but wasn't quick enough. The blow Colin delivered caught him on the collarbone and knocked him onto the seat of his pants. Thankfully, he'd landed in some hay – they were in the barn and had just put their horses up for the night.

Colin looked down at him and studied his face. "See, I told you!" he lamented to Harrison. "Look at him – just sitting there doing nothing! Any other time, I'd be sporting two black eyes by now!"

Harrison rubbed his chin. "You're right – though I would never have believed it had I not seen it." He stepped over to Duncan and held out his hand to help him up. Duncan only glared at it. "Colin's right, old boy – you're certainly not yourself of late. Are you going to tell us what the matter is? Or do we need to batter it out of you?"

Duncan refused his help and got up without it, growling as he did. "I can't explain it. I need to start courting her – I know this, the will is clear." He turned to them, holding out his hands in frustration. "But I can't bring myself to do it!"

"Does she not appeal to you, brother?" Harrison asked.

"That's the problem. She holds far too *much* appeal!"

"Ahhhh ..." Colin said, nodding. "Well, that's a different matter. Then why don't we lend a hand?

Sadie chaperoned Belle and me – and did a fine job of it, too."

Duncan shook his head. "I'm afraid this will take more than Sadie's company to do the job properly."

Harrison and Colin exchanged a quick look. Harrison let out a low whistle. "I ... think I understand. I remember how hard it was for me, and I well know how Colin suffered ..."

"Occasionally at your hands," Colin quipped.

"We're not made of stone, you know," Harrison continued, ignoring Colin. "But is it really that bad? Or is there something else?"

Duncan let out a shaky laugh. "I wish there were. I'm afraid of myself, is what it comes down to. Afraid I'll do the wrong thing, that I'll frighten her away ... not to mention face her father's gun. And I cannot even begin to tell you why."

"He *does* have it bad," Colin remarked to Harrison.

"Quite," Harrison replied. "Hmmm ... what we need is a pretense. An event, something with lots of people present."

"A dinner?" Colin suggested. "A barn raising?"

"No, no ... something more festive, I should think ..."

"A dance?" Duncan asked sarcastically.

His brothers looked at each other and smiled. "Yes! Perfect!" Colin said, and slapped Duncan on the back.

Duncan winced, and rubbed his collarbone. "When?"

"As soon as possible, I should think," Harrison answered. "You are, after all, on a deadline. Of course, the women will want to prepare for it, but we could have them include Cozette in the preparation."

"I suppose ..." Duncan said with a heavy sigh.

"You suppose? Duncan, we're – *you're* – running out of time. Pull yourself together!" Colin told him, grabbing his brother's shoulders.

"There's a weakness in your plan, however. Cozette will be the only unmarried female there. The men will be all over her. The thought of that ..." Duncan glared into the middle distance and made a fist.

"He has it *very* bad," Harrison teasingly told Colin.

"Quite."

"But you need not worry," Harrison said, turning back to Duncan. "We could invite the settlers waiting outside of town. Belle spoke to Wilfred, and he said they have a few unmarried daughters among the families. They're stuck here until more supplies come in, and would likely welcome a diversion. That should even things out."

"So long as their daughters are older than six," Duncan grumbled.

"It will be fine," Colin assured him. "I think Clear Creek could use another little celebration. It won't be anything like a grand ball, but most folks do love a good dance! And besides, you'll have to get used to hosting these sorts of things ... *Your Grace.*"

Duncan rolled his eyes. "Don't remind me. All right, let's do it." With that, the three Cooke brothers left the barn to go tell the Cooke women they were going to host a dance.

Little did any of them know what they would be bringing into their midst.

# DAY 11

Nothing travels faster than gossip. Within a day, the dance had become the topic of conversation around town. Meanwhile, Duncan went to look for the Dupries, but couldn't find them. He certainly hoped they hadn't taken to the woods again, or were camped out on the prairie somewhere. That would be rotten luck, and he'd had altogether too much of that over the last few years ...

# DAY 12

Logan Kincaid had decided to start teaching the brothers what he thought they should be doing with their new-found cattle business. And the Cooke brothers were thankful – everything he was telling them was incredibly useful for the neophyte ranchers.

But Duncan was thoroughly distracted. Knowing everything there was to know about the care and feeding of bovines wouldn't help him in his quest for a wife. He still had no clue where the Dupries had gotten to, and thanks to Logan's impromptu seminar, he hadn't been able to get to town to ask either.

And it wasn't just the title and estate he was worried about. Thackary Holmes seemed to have disappeared as well, and the thought of that foppish devil weaving some web around the Dupries set his teeth to grinding. He'd even asked Jefferson to keep an eye out for the Dupries when he came to town, but how much could he count on Jefferson to carry out his request? Jefferson acted like he didn't care – about the request, about the Dupries, about anything.

Jefferson sipped his whiskey slowly and attempted to enjoy it. But the amber liquid hadn't had as much appeal of late, and he'd be hornswoggled if he knew why. It had always used to bring him solace, or at least convenient oblivion, but since Colin's wedding, it didn't do much to alleviate his usual foul mood.

Mrs. Dunnigan's cooking, on the other hand ...

"One roast beef and potatoes. No free meals here, Jefferson Cooke! Be sure you pony up when you leave!" She set the plate of mouth-watering food on the table.

Of course, the deliciousness of the food was moderated somewhat by the sourness of her personality. She looked at him, her face scrunched up, her dark and beady eyes narrowed in challenge. Anyone in their right mind would be tempted to take the cantankerous creature out back and shoot her ... but the woman was quickly becoming known as the finest cook in the eastern Oregon territory, and anyone who tried to plug her might well get hit with some hot lead himself.

He settled for glaring at her. "What's for dessert?" he barked.

"Cherry pie and coffee!" she barked right back. "Coffee that'll do you much better than that swill you're drinking!"

"Fine!"

"Fine!" she spat. Jefferson didn't think it possible, but she scrunched her face up even tighter – it was a wonder her skin didn't snap. "I'll bring you some when you're done with your dinner!" With that, she stomped off to serve the other men in the saloon.

Jefferson watched her go, then turned his attention to his food. He angrily stabbed a piece of beef and was about to cut it with a knife, then realized there was no need. The meat was so tender it easily parted with just his fork.

He took the first bite and closed his eyes. Heaven. Which certainly beat the alternative, didn't it? And it was that question that had been preying on his mind of late.

Could it be that he was growing a conscience?

Well, stranger things had happened, he supposed as he took a bite of potato. Crispy on the outside, soft as a cloud within ...

For years, he'd used whiskey to keep the guilt at bay - guilt at not helping his wife Honoria when she got sick. Guilt at not listening to Harrison when he'd pleaded with him to take her to Doc Waller. Guilt at not wanting to be with her when she died ... or at her funeral ... or even to visit her grave. And now, guilt about the mercantile fire. But these days, not even the rottenest of rotgut could push the thoughts away.

Instead, he sat in his cabin and stared at the cold, empty hearth. Or he came into town to drink and play cards. But neither of those helped. Besides, his fellow card players hadn't been around lately – they were off doing other things. And since the night of the fire, he hadn't been real eager to find out what ...

"Oh, Mr. Cooke?"

Jefferson looked up from his food as Mary Mulligan quickly approached. He continued to chew, saying nothing.

"Mr. Cooke, would you mind giving this to Sadie when you get back to the ranch?" She handed him a folded piece of paper.

He unceremoniously snatched it from her hand. "What is it?"

"It's a list of people to invite to the dance, of course! I want Sadie and Belle to have a copy, so we can figure out who should be in charge of what. It's going to be quite the event – everyone's invited!"

Jefferson stopped chewing. His eyes widened. "Are they, now?"

"And it's lovely that we're having it out at your ranch – so kind of you! You Cookes certainly do know how to throw a party. Why, the wedding was wonderful!"

Jefferson dropped his fork, and it landed on his plate with a loud *clank*. He was about to bark something he shouldn't when he realized what she'd said. *Your ranch. You Cookes.* Ever since Harrison and Sadie got married, and that father of hers had stormed in, he'd always viewed it as his stepson's ranch. He and his two birth sons were excluded, the ranch stolen out from under him and handed to Honoria's boys on a shiny silver platter by that loud-mouthed cattle baron Horatio Jones.

Jefferson licked some gravy from his lips and looked at her. "There's gonna be a dance at *my* ranch?"

"Why, yes! I thought you knew ..."

"*My* ranch?"

Mary Mulligan looked truly puzzled. "Yes, *your* ranch! Doesn't anybody out there tell you anything?"

Jefferson's mouth began to curve into an unaccustomed smile. "*My* ranch ..."

"Well, if you could take that list to your daughter-in-law and see to it she gets to work right away ... the dance is in less than two weeks, after all. I'll drive out tomorrow to help with the invitations."

"Invitations?" he mumbled.

"Of course. You Cookes'll have to start doing things a lot more formally now that you've got a duke in the family. They're the next closest thing to royalty, you know!" She took his empty plate and trotted off to see to her other customers.

Jefferson sat and absently licked at his lips, even though they were already clean. *His* ranch? *His* daughter-in-law? *Royalty?!* How much had he missed, trying to hide at the bottom of a bottle? And might he find the answers he was looking for if he managed to climb out?

He was still pondering all that when Mrs. Dunnigan stormed over to his table with his pie and coffee.

# DAY 13

Cozette pulled another shirt out of the laundry
basket and hung it on the line. She and Polly Van
Cleet worked in relative silence – Cozette for lack of
another option, Mrs. Van Cleet because she had a
mouth full of clothespins. The Dupries had been
invited to stay with the Van Cleets until they could
build a home of their own, and Papa had happily
accepted, figuring it would be good for Cozette. He'd
been right – her small bedroom (more of a large closet,
really) and rickety little bed were wonderful compared
to camping on the ground. Though she didn't mind
sleeping on the ground in the summer, winter came
soon enough on the prairie. Her father was content to
bunk out in the barn.

They both turned when they heard the sound of a
horse and rider gallop up and stop at the front of the
house. Mrs. Van Cleet took the clothespins from her
mouth and threw them in the basket. "Go into the
house, Cozette, while I see who it is."

Cozette's eyes widened as she looked toward the
house. *What if it's a stranger?* She quickly complied
and ran into the house through the back door, but
headed straight to the Remington revolver resting in
Mr. Van Cleet's holster. He'd slung it over the back of
a chair and hadn't taken it with him when he'd left to
go rabbit hunting with Papa. She took it and
cautiously made her way to the front door, where she

peeked through the lace curtains of a nearby window to see who'd arrived. But all she could spot was a big black horse tethered at the Van Cleets' hitching post.

"See anything interesting?" Cozette jumped and spun around, only to have Duncan Cooke immediately grab her hand, the one that held the gun, and turn it to one side. She'd never seen a man move so fast or with such incredible reflexes. Nor be so quick to scold her. "This is *not* a toy, you know. You could hurt yourself!"

Cozette's eyes narrowed and her nostrils flared. Squaring her shoulders, she pulled loose from his grip and began a pantomime – pointing the gun over toward a side window, left hand on right wrist, aiming carefully and giving a slight jerk of her hands as if firing. Then she boldly looked back at him. The message was clear: *You don't know as much as you think you know about me! I know a gun is not a toy – in fact, I can probably shoot better than you!*

"I'll make some coffee, Duncan!" Mrs. Van Cleet called from the kitchen. "And I've got cinnamon bread almost ready to come out of the oven!"

Duncan needed a second to find his voice. "Er ... much obliged, Polly. Sounds fine," he called back.

Cozette kept right on glaring at him.

"Well," Duncan said carefully, gripping his hands behind him. "It appears I owe you another apology. I ... should've known that, living in the wilderness, you could probably defend yourself. I simply ... didn't want anything bad to happen to you ..."

Cozette's face softened a little.

"Are you really that good with a revolver?"

She raised a single brow. *Is that a challenge?* she thought.

Now he smiled. "That's something I'd like to see. Care to show me?"

Finally, she smiled in return.

"But if I could ask one favor?"

Cozette cocked her head to one side. "Please don't shoot me?"

She twisted up her mouth as if thinking it over, but finally nodded.

Duncan had ridden out to the Van Cleets' after Sheriff Hughes told him he'd heard Cyrus and M. Duprie discuss rabbit hunting. He thought it worth Duncan's time to see if that wasn't where he'd find the Frenchman.

But he didn't find him. What he did find was trouble – trouble in a beautiful pink calico dress that fit his little future duchess perfectly. Trouble with dark hair that glistened in the light, cascading down her back like a miniature waterfall. Trouble with a sun-kissed face that he daydreamed about waking up to in the morning on the pillow next to his ...

It was maddening to stand beside her. She was adorable, beautiful, a lively spot of brilliant color in a gray world.

His heart was quickly filling with feeling for her, and he wondered again if he should be doing this. Maybe he should have hightailed it back to town the moment he saw her ... but he hadn't the strength to pull himself away. Thank Heaven that Polly Van Cleet was watching them as she hung laundry on a clothesline and waited for her bread to finish baking.

Of course, what she was watching wasn't exactly a typical courting ritual. "Are you *sure* you can hit that?" he asked.

Cozette turned to look at him, rolled her eyes and stuck her tongue out. Then she turned back, quickly took aim and fired. The bottle he'd set atop a fence post twenty yards away shattered.

Duncan stood in open-mouthed shock. He was still getting used to the idea that she could handle firearms at all – where he came from, ladies didn't do such things. But then, where he came from wasn't where she came from ... and where she came from, she hadn't had a choice.

Cozette blew the smoke from Mr. Van Cleet's gun and smirked at him. *Now do you believe me, Mr. I'll-Be-Your-Protector?*

Duncan shook his head in disbelief before taking his gun from the holster on his hip. He looked at the other bottles, tins and flotsam they'd found to set atop the fenceposts and rails of the corral as targets. He spun the gun rapidly in his hand, reholstered it and gave her a quick sideways glance and a wink. She flinched slightly at that – but not at all when he quickly drew his gun and began to fire, taking out several of the other targets. She obviously was used to being around guns, bullets and the men who used them. But she clearly wasn't used to men seeing her as herself. That was why he was there. Or so he kept telling himself.

Cozette sighed in frustration, set her gun on the ground and turned to him, anger written on her face. She pointed to herself, then held up one finger. *I only got one shot!* She then jabbed him in the chest and held up six fingers. *You got six!* She shook her head and gave him a scowl to rival any of his. *No fair!*

"We could set up another round. But don't think you can beat me."

Her jaw slid forward as she placed her hands on her hips. If she had a voice, he swore she'd be growling at him.

But that didn't mean he wouldn't egg her on further. "You obviously got a lucky shot, is all."

She narrowed her eyes and stomped her foot.

"Tsk, tsk. I say, having a pet isn't going to help you."

Her hands balled into fists as she soundlessly snarled at him. Spinning on her heel, she began to roam the area around the small barn, looking for other things to shoot at.

Duncan began to laugh, unable to help himself. She was utterly charming! Forced to communicate in other ways, she used facial expressions and body language to say what she wanted to say. (And, by God, could he understand her!) Forced to live by her wits in a world "red in tooth and claw," she'd sharpened her wits – and perhaps, her teeth and claws – more than most people ever dreamed of.

It made him want her all the more.

She heard his chuckling, and glared at him. *Oh, so you think this is funny, do you?* Looking around again, her eyes came to rest on an old horseshoe. She bent to pick it up, stormed over and held it out to him.

"You can't possibly be serious! You can't hit that!"

Her eyes still narrowed, she held it out again. *Take it.*

He looked at it, then at her. "And where do you propose to put it? Hang it on a fencepost perhaps?"

She smiled oddly, and pantomimed tossing the horseshoe in the air.

Duncan's eyes bulged. "You can't possibly be serious!"

She nodded, her eyes bright, her jaw set.

"You'll never be able to hit it!"

She smirked as she shoved the horseshoe into his hand. *Try me. You'll see.*

Good Lord, but she was beautiful when she was angry! "There's no possible chance you can do this. *I* can't do this. No man in this town can do this!"

She bent to pick up her gun, and motioned for him to throw the horseshoe up in the air.

"You're serious? Well, I suppose there's no hope for—" Without warning, he threw it in the air, hard.

And bugger if she didn't react with lightning speed! *Bang!* She shot, and then *clang!*, the horseshoe spun away, knocked off its trajectory by the bullet.

Duncan stared at her, his mouth hanging open like the village idiot's. How *did* she *do* that? She must have cocked the gun as she picked it up, but how did she aim and fire so quickly *and* accurately?

He had to remind himself, once again, that she was no mere woman. She'd learned to survive in the wilderness, and had witnessed horrors only he himself could relate to. Now that he thought on it, they perhaps had more in common than either of them had realized.

He straightened up, then bowed to her. "*Mademoiselle* Duprie, would you do me the honor of accompanying me to a dance?"

Cozette stared at him, confused. He was asking her to go to a *dance*? A nice afternoon of shooting targets, that was all well and good – she was in her element. But how foolish would she look at a dance? She didn't know the first thing about how to act, or what to wear, let alone the dancing part! She backed away from him, instinctively searching for an escape route as if he'd just threatened her life, not invited her to a social function.

"Cozette! Duncan! The coffee and cinnamon bread are ready!" Polly shouted from the back door of the kitchen.

Duncan's eyes never left Cozette's. "We'll be right there!" he called back. He didn't want to frighten her, so he kept looking at her tenderly.

Cozette felt herself calm. He was presenting himself as a refuge rather than a threat: his stance relaxed, his features softened, a friendly smile on his face, His eyes were on her, but not the way she'd seen other men look at her since she'd began dressing as was usual for her sex. No, Duncan Cooke wasn't lusting after her, like a predator. He was admiring her. And there was a big difference between the two.

Had she impressed him with her shooting ability? That seemed doubtful - most men got angry when bested by her as a boy. She'd occasionally had to run to avoid being struck by them. But not this man – he had respect in his eyes, and something else. Something that made her spine tingle, that caused her to look at him the same way. *Oh my, oh my!*

She forced herself to turn away, to break what was pulling her toward him. She didn't understand it, only that each time she saw him, it grew stronger. It didn't help that today she hadn't noticed how handsome he was as he teased her, not to mention how he'd towered over her when he'd turned the gun away earlier in the house, how his hand had wrapped completely around hers, how warm and rough it had felt. She was quivering all over at the memory ...

The warmth of his body engulfed her, and her head snapped up. How did he manage to reposition himself behind her so quietly? And yet ... and yet she felt no urge to flee. If anything, she was having to resist leaning back into him

"We'd best go in," he said, his voice deep and soft. "We don't want to keep Polly waiting." He placed a hand on her shoulder and turned her around to face him.

Cozette sucked in a breath.

He pushed his hat back, his other hand still on her shoulder, and took a deep breath of his own. "I dare say, *Mademoiselle* Duprie, but you are ... very beautiful. I do hope you say yes."

Her head automatically cocked to one side. *Yes? Yes to what?*

He quickly solved her confusion. "The dance, of course. You will let me escort you, won't you?" He took a step closer.

Cozette found herself looking right into his broad
chest, where his shirt lay open. She blinked,
embarrassed, and looking up at him ... and up ... and
up. Heavens! His size should intimidate her with him
being so close, but instead she felt like wrapping him
around her like a blanket. And his scent ... it was like
candy, sweet and savory at the same time. She
couldn't move.

And he wouldn't.

They stood and stared at each other, his hand still
on her shoulder. Was it the sun growing hotter, or just
them? Hard to say, though she swore that even the
light shining down on them was suddenly brighter ...

"We, em ... we need to go inside," he whispered.

Cozette's knees felt weak, and she sighed delicately.
*Oh, dear! Where did that come from?*

He shuddered as the moist warmth of her breath
brushed his chest. He balled his free hand into a fist,
looked away, and moaned.

She was immediately alarmed as she watched his
whole body tighten, as if he was under a horrible
strain. Was he all right? Was something terrible
happening to him? He had made her feel safe, secure,
approved – and yes, protected. But now he seemed to
be suffering – what could she do to help him? Slowly,
without disturbing the hand on her shoulder, she
leaned to one side and tilted her head to catch his eye.
*Are you all right?*

He still tried to avoid looking at her. "Cozette," he
rasped. "You have to go into the house. Now!"

The urgency in his voice startled her, not to mention
the use of her first name. *But ...*

"*Now*, Cozette!" he groaned, removing his hand
from her shoulder and turning away. "Please, go!" he
snapped.

But she didn't immediately comply. Yes, the scold
stung, but she was more worried about him. She

motioned toward the house with both her arms, palms upturned. *We both go, yes?*

He shook his head. "I'll be there in ... in a minute. Please, just go ahead," he pleaded.

With worry in her eyes, she nodded, lifted her dress, and quickly walked to the house. Reaching the door, she glanced back one last time before going in. His posture was tight and strained, his face to the sky, both hands now clenched into fists. Was he praying? Crying? What could possibly be wrong?

He'd been fine until he'd gotten closer to her, and then he got angry. She hadn't done anything wrong, had she? She didn't think so, but what did she know? She didn't know much about him, other than he was a good shot and had two very nice sisters-in-law. *And he makes you feel warm inside, and protected, and ...*

She felt herself shiver. She had no idea what that "and" was, but she liked it, a lot!

Reluctantly, she turned away from him, went inside, and quietly closed the door behind her. But she didn't move – instead she just stood there, letting her heart slow down and her breathing return to normal.

Mrs. Van Cleet poured three cups of coffee, then looked at her. "Where's Duncan? Is he still here?"

A horse neighed out. Cozette ran to the front of the house just in time to see Duncan mount his stallion and kick him into a gallop, riding away as if his life depended on it. The sight hurt, and she felt her entire body slump. She couldn't fight it, or the tears that followed.

Duncan pushed Romeo hard, detouring wide around Clear Creek and racing toward home.

If he hadn't left when he did, he didn't think he could have controlled himself any longer. He wanted her, with everything he had. But why? Why her? He didn't understand what he was feeling, let alone the incredible strength of it. Its power confused him. Was this normal? Had Harrison or Colin gone through this? And how would they react when they saw he was?

Egads. He knew how they would react – he'd gotten a taste of it the day of the ladies' tea! He realized he'd best get himself calmed down before he faced them back at the ranch – because they *would* tease him. And right now, he wasn't likely to react well to it.

He slowed Romeo as he came to the beginning of the trail that led away from the main road to the Triple-C. He took it and let the horse canter along at an easier pace. Slowly, he felt himself start to cool down a bit.

*Cool down ...* that gave him an idea.

A few minutes later, he reached another trail, the one that led down to Clear Creek and the natural swimming hole his family had discovered shortly after settling in the area. It was considered Cooke land now – others respected that and didn't venture out there much anyway. It also helped that it was several miles out of town and a rough trail down into the canyon itself. For that, Duncan was glad – right now he needed his privacy.

He reached the end of the trail, and the beautiful meadow spread out before him, centered by the huge oak tree his mother had dubbed "His Majesty" when she first saw it years ago. It shaded part of the swimming hole, and Duncan rode directly to it and dismounted. As Romeo began to graze, he dropped his gun belt, stripped, and dove in, quick and clean.

*Co-o-o-o-old!* The water never did seem to get decently warm, not even in the middle of summer. But today, that was another one of the attractions.

He came up out of the water like a breaching whale. He'd stayed under as long as he could before coming up for air. If possible, he could do that all day – the chill and the quiet were calming. But it only eased, not erased, the throbbing ache of his heart, the burning desire to take Cozette, carry her off and claim her for his own before it was too late.

But why? His emotions were going far beyond the stipulations of the will. It felt more like if he didn't give in to his own instinct, one or both of them would suffer. Suffer what? He didn't know. And that made it hurt even more.

Duncan dove again and swam to the bottom. He tried to stay under as long as he could, counting the seconds, letting the cold tame his wild heart, before he could stand it no longer and had to surface.

But when he did, he found he was no longer alone.

"Ye dinna seem the type o' man to leave yerself so unguarded. Nor yer horse, for that matter."

Duncan immediately scanned the area. Only one other person was there – the huge Scotsman he'd met in town a few days ago, who now sat leaning against the trunk of "His Majesty." And toying with Duncan's gun.

"What do you want?" Duncan asked threateningly, then realized that was probably not the best thing to do, since the stranger had his gun and he himself was most definitely unarmed. Among other things.

"Dinna fash yerself, lad. Just out exploring, 'tis all. Saw yer horse, but dinna see you 'til now. Water must be frightfully cold. Is it a habit of yers to bathe here?"

"Not until recently."

"Odd time to be taking a bath. Should ye no be out wi' yer brothers tending yer stock?"

Duncan swam closer, to see what the Scotsman would do. "I had other business to attend to this morning." The Scotsman had no reaction, just continued to play with the gun. "I say, would you mind putting that away? You seem to have me at a disadvantage."

The Scotsman looked at the gun in his hand. "Only a disadvantage if I were here to do ye harm, man.

Which I'm not. But I canna say the same for the water. Yer lips are turning blue, ye ken."

Duncan swam closer and stood, the water reaching his waist. "In that, you are right. This *is* bloody cold."

"There's only one thing I can think of 'twould send a man into a pool o' freezing water at this time o' day."

Duncan knew it, too. He began to wade toward him. "If you don't mind," he said and pointed to his pants. The Scotsman reached for the pants which lay nearby and tossed them to Duncan. He got out of the water, quickly put them on, then reached for his shirt.

"What's the lassie's name?"

"Cozette."

"The Frenchman's lass? Weel, now – a fetching prize, to be sure."

Duncan froze, his hand automatically at his side to draw his gun, only it was still in the hands of the Scotsman.

"Dinna worry, laddie. I've no interest in the pretty wee thing. Och, I've my hands full wi' my own wife!"

Duncan relaxed as he recalled the beautiful woman who joined the Scotsman and his companion when they first came to town. "I remember her. She is lovely. You're lucky to have such a woman."

"Aye, I'll no argue wi' that. Trust me when I say, there's none like my Shona. But tell me, what brings ye here to cool yer frustration? Can ye no marry the lass?"

"Marry her? I haven't gotten the chance to ask her. I'm still courting her ... or at least trying to."

The Scotsman cocked his head to one side. The action reminded Duncan of Cozette. "And how are ye going about it? I hear the lass canna speak."

News obviously traveled fast. How else could the Scotsman know of his brothers and their cattle ranch? "It's not easy, but I'm managing."

"Aye, by dunking yerself in a freezing cold creek."

"The fact that she cannot speak does make things different, but not difficult. In fact, I'd say she enjoyed our time together this morning as much as I did."

"Oh? But where d'ye suppose *she's* taking a bath?"

Duncan glared at him. Why was he even having this conversation with this stranger? But he had to admit, it was a relief to be able to talk about it with someone, stranger or not. "If you must know, I asked her to allow me to escort her to a dance my family is hosting at our ranch. In fact, one of us was going to ride out and invite you and the rest of your company to attend."

"Aye, and so ye did. Yer younger brother, Harrison, came out a couple o' hours ago and told me. Also told me about this bonny tree, which I agree is quite fine ..." He patted the bark respectfully.

Duncan smiled. It was just like Harrison to be the first to invite the settlers. "So, will you come?"

"Aye, we'll be there. Seems some o' the families like yer wee town. Might even decide to settle here. A dance 'twould give them the chance to get acquainted wi' more o' the folk."

"And what of you and your wife? Are you thinking of staying?"

"Nay, laddie, we've business elsewhere. But I wouldna mind coming back to visit. Perhaps by then you and the lass will ha' had a wee bairn."

"A baby? I need to marry her first! The problem is ... well ..."

"... ye dinna quite know how to go about it." It wasn't a question.

Duncan turned and looked at the water. "She's so ... so different from other women. I've never had a woman affect me so. It's as if everything my mother or father ever taught me about how to court a girl is ... I can't explain it ..."

"Wrong? It won't work? None o' it applies?"

Duncan slowly turned and stared at the Scotsman. He looked him over carefully, as if expecting him to suddenly vanish. For some strange reason, it felt like he'd had this conversation with him before. "Yes. Yes, it does feel like that. But if that's the case, what am I to do? How am I to communicate my feelings for her without frightening her away?"

The Scotsman stood. "Och, laddie, that's easy."

"Easy?"

"Aye. A long time ago, I felt the same way ye do now, and a smart man gave me some advice."

"What did he tell you?"

"He said, 'Sometimes the best thing to say to a woman is nothing. Nothing at all.'"

"Did it work?"

The Scotsman shrugged. "She's now my wife," he said with a grin and stood.

Duncan couldn't help but smile back. As odd as the conversation was, the advice made sense. Especially with Cozette – he'd be meeting her on her home ground, so to speak. "Thank you. I'll have to give that a try." He held out his hand. "I'm Duncan Cooke."

The Scotsman bowed, then took Duncan's hand and gave it a healthy shake. "'Tis a pleasure to meet you, Mr. Cooke. MacDonald's the name. But you can call me Dallan."

# DAY 14

Duncan drove Sadie and Belle out to the Van Cleets' to deliver their invitation. He was nervous as a cat and dropped the reins four times between leaving the Triple-C and arriving at their destination.

Finally Sadie said, "Duncan Cooke, what is the matter with you? And are you sweating? It's not that hot yet!"

"I'm fine," he growled unconvincingly.

"Oh, you're something all right, but fine isn't it," Belle commented. "One would think you didn't want to see Cozette today."

Duncan's eyes flashed – not in anger at Belle's comment, but at the thought of *not* seeing Cozette that day. Yesterday he'd forced himself to go back to work after his bath and his conversation with the Scotsman. Today he wanted to put to use the advice he'd been given. But he also wanted reinforcements, so he'd offered to drive Sadie and Belle out. This way, he'd have three chaperones at the ready – safety in numbers.

When they got to the Van Cleets', Polly was in front of the house weeding a small flower bed. Cozette was nowhere to be seen. "Good morning, Mrs. Van Cleet!" Belle called. "How are you?"

The older woman stood up from her work and waved at them as they approached. "Fine! What brings you out? Cyrus is in town working on the hotel, you know."

Duncan pulled back on the reins to bring the team to a stop. "We know. But we wanted to deliver this to you, and the ladies wanted to visit." He jumped off the wagon, set the brake, then helped Sadie and Belle down.

Polly smiled. "How nice. Deliver what?"

Sadie pulled an invitation out of her reticule. "This." She handed the envelope to Polly.

She looked from one face to another before she opened it, read it and smiled. "Oh, how wonderful! My, this is so formal! Of course we'd love to come. Let's go inside, have some coffee and you can tell me what sort of help you need."

"That's why we're here!" Belle said as they followed her into the house. Duncan brought up the rear.

He closed the door behind him just as Cozette appeared at the top of the stairs. She flinched when he looked at her, then froze, as if her feet had suddenly become glued to the floor. He gave her a tender look and tipped his hat. *Hello.*

She looked at him, her face blank, before she squared her shoulders, held up her chin and descended the stairs. Apparently she was angry with him for some reason – probably how abruptly he'd acted (and left) the day before. He couldn't blame her for that; it wasn't exactly a shining moment of chivalry on his part.

She reached the bottom of the stairs and made to push right past him, but he gently took her arm and held her in place a moment. He put his other hand over his heart and bowed slightly: *I apologize.*

That stopped her short. She cocked her head to one side again, and her expression softened.

So far, so good. He pushed his hat from his forehead, smiled, then made his hand like a gun, pretended to shoot something in the air, and blew on his index finger. *You really are a good shot. I was impressed.*

She smiled slightly. *Thank you.*

Now he put both hands over his chest, and bowed again. *Please forgive me?*

Cozette looked away, took a deep breath and sighed in frustration. *Men!* But finally she turned back, smiled and nodded. Then she did something surprising – she reached over, took his gun from his holster and held it between them with both hands. *Rematch?*

Duncan managed to keep from laughing – this was working out better than he'd hoped! He nodded in agreement. She smiled, and by God if she didn't actually sashay down the hall in triumph. Duncan swallowed hard and followed.

Cozette walked into the kitchen. "Coffee?" Polly asked her, but she gave a casual wave of her hand – *no, thank you* – and continued right out the back door.

Now Duncan entered. "There's coffee and pie here," Polly offered.

"Thank you, Mrs. Van Cleet, but I'm afraid I must pass." He too kept walking, his eyes glued to the woman now stepping off the back stoop and heading for the barnyard with his pistol.

Polly, Sadie, and Belle looked at one another, then at the open back door which Duncan in his haste had forgotten to close. "Oh my," Belle said. "Do you think we should follow them?"

"No, it should be fine," Polly replied, her eyes never leaving the back door. "They had a shooting match out there yesterday."

"A shooting match?" Sadie exclaimed with a smile.

Belle was less pleased. "Ohhhh dear!"

"Why, Belle, what's the matter?" Polly asked.

Belle's eyes widened. "You do realize Duncan is trying to court Cozette? Doing it with a gun isn't exactly how I pictured it!"

Polly laughed. "Well, I admit it isn't the usual way. But why do you look so worried?"

"Well, but ... a gun?!"

"Dearie, I've known them a lot longer than you have. I know the Cooke men are ... different." Polly's comment got a giggle out of Sadie. "But I don't see the harm in letting them shoot a few things off a fencepost. If anything, Cozette's probably more comfortable with a revolver than she would be with a parasol."

"I think I'd feel more comfortable, too, if I had a gun to point at him!" Sadie said with a laugh.

"So I don't think there's anything to be worried about," Polly concluded as she began to slice up the pie. "After all, between the three of us there are enough chaperones, don't you think?"

Belle and Sadie gave each other a quick look. "Mrs. Van Cleet?" Belle asked. "You wouldn't happen to know where we might find a few rocks?"

Sadie burst out laughing.

Polly stood and stared at the two girls. "Now, whatever do you need rocks for?"

"It's how one chaperones a Cooke!" Sadie giggled as she stood with Belle. They left the kitchen to go out front and search for a few – just in case.

Duncan watched as Cozette expertly handled the gun, hitting everything he'd placed before her and then some. Now it was his turn.

He reloaded, waited, and took the shot the moment she threw the bottles they'd found into the air, shattering it. But he was impressed she could throw it that high as she did. In fact, he was impressed with everything she did – shoot a gun, keep her self-control, walk, smile ... be.

He found that now *he* wanted to impress *her*.

He shot again, obliterated his target, and laughed. It felt so good to laugh after all this time. And she was laughing too, albeit silently. They looked at each other, smiled, then set out to find more targets.

But there were no more bottles or cans to be found. They'd gone through all of them. Cozette turned to him, disappointment on her pretty face and shrugged, holding up her hands. *Now what?*

The expression on her face was almost more than he could bear. There had to be something else they could use. He made a point of pretending to scratch his head: *I'm thinking ...*

Suddenly Cozette held up her hand, then mimed shooting a bow and arrow, Her eyes bright, she lifted her skirts and ran for the barn.

Duncan had never shot a bow. This should be interesting. But he was having fun, and clearly so was she. Who would have thought not saying a word would be so effective?

She emerged from the barn, a bow in her hands, a quiver of arrows over her shoulder and the biggest smile he'd ever seen on her face. She was clearly planning to enjoy this immensely ... and probably knew he'd never shot a bow. Most cowboys hadn't, after all – why would they, when guns were available and cheap?

She motioned for him to follow her.

The Van Cleets' barn wasn't very large, but it would serve their purposes. Inside were several barrels, boxes, and various tools hanging from nails pounded into the posts and walls. A cot had been placed in a stall; Duncan guessed it must belong to M. Duprie.

Cozette disappeared behind the barn door, emerging with an old wooden box. She went to the back of the building and placed it on top of one of the barrels. Then she grabbed his hand and led him out the door and away from the structure, about fifteen yards. She then pointed to herself, a huge grin on her face.

Duncan knew she was going to thrash him soundly at *this* game. But it would be worth it if she warmed up to him enough to accompany him to the dance. And from there ... well, he could always hope. He was pretty sure Anton still hadn't told her about the rest of their deal, the marriage-and-duchy part, and wasn't eager to either. Barring a sudden act of probity on her father's part, his best chance was to have her want him for him. And that likely meant having her in as good a mood as possible.

Cozette expertly notched an arrow, raised the bow and pulled back on the string. Her dress wasn't made for such a movement, and he could hear a tiny sound of alarm coming from one of the seams under her arm as the stitching strained. She ignored it completely as she took aim and released the arrow.

It hit the box square in the middle.

This confirmed his previous theory – he was doomed. The only thing to do now was accept it graciously – but not quite silently. As she looked triumphantly his way, he bowed his head slightly and applauded.

Cozette grinned again – and held the bow out to him. *Now you try!* As he took it, she reached back, pulled another arrow from the quiver and passed it to him as well.

He took it, but was then left staring at the objects as if he'd just discovered them on an archeological expedition and had no clue as to their use. *Oh, boy ...*

Shaking her head, she walked behind him and lifted his arms into the proper position, then helped him notch the arrow and raise the bow to the correct height. She studied her work for a moment, then had him lower his arms. Finally she helped him place his fingers in the proper position, and motioned him to raise his arms again and take the shot.

He had been passive and cooperative the whole time, but now the action was up to him. He looked at her, trying to mask his terror of embarrassment.

She smiled in encouragement, and mimed a little push. *Go on, take the shot! You can do it!*

She wasn't going to take advantage of his lack of skill – instead, she was teaching him, while insuring that his dignity would survive the ordeal. By God, she'd make a duchess yet!

He pulled back the bow string, took aim, and let the arrow fly. It missed by less than a foot – beginner's luck? – but nonetheless flew right over the box and into the wall beyond. He barely managed not to say "crumbs" or something similar, but kept with the plan, hanging his head and kicking the straw-dusted floor with his boot.

Cozette reached back, grabbed another arrow and handed it to him. *Try again.*

He took it and notched it. Lifting the bow into position, he smiled at her before he took a deep breath. *Wish me luck.* He let loose the arrow ... and this time it lodged in a corner of the box.

Cozette jumped up and down and clapped her hands together for him, her face lit with glee. She took another arrow and handed it to him. *Again!*

He took it, and as he did he placed his hand over hers. Suddenly they both stopped as heat radiated between them. They looked at each other in disbelief before she pulled her hand away, but they both knew something had just happened, however bizarre it was.

Duncan took a step toward her, looked down at her – and their eyes locked. His breathing picked up, as did hers. They stood there for who knows how long before her eyes began to wander over him. His went straight to her lips.

She took a step closer. The distance between them was down to a few inches. If he wanted to, he could wrap her up in his arms and hold her. But he didn't just want to hold her ... and wasn't sure that if he started, he would be able to stop.

Thankfully, he still had the bow in one hand, the arrow in the other. He flipped the arrow around so the feathered end was pointed at Cozette, then raised it and tucked a lock of her hair back behind her ear. As he did it, the feathers brushed against her cheek, and she shivered in awe. In that moment, he realized she was the most beautiful woman he had ever seen – more beautiful than his brother's wives, or the auburn-haired wife of the Scotsman. And it was, at least in part, because he knew she was his. Or would be.

There was still the small problem of having her fall in love with him before the deadline. After all, wasn't that what he was aiming at, to save his cousin's estate from the depredations of Thackary Holmes? As the new Duke of Stantham, he'd have the power to practically make her a queen with or without her love.

But Duncan knew better. There was no way he could ever marry a woman simply for convenience. He could only do it if she loved him. And he *did* want her love, wanted it far more than he realized. This strange, silent French girl with the dark hair and wilderness ways was in his head, in his blood, and he desperately needed her to give him her heart.

The question, of course, was how. There obviously weren't enough arrows to get her to fall in love with him that day. He'd have to continue to find creative ways to court her. And perhaps ... he hated the thought, but perhaps he should get a little more help from his brothers, who had already been through this with their brides.

Which meant he'd best brace himself. Any help from them had a tendency to be painful.

Thackary Holmes was a fastidious man. He didn't like to get his hands dirty – and frankly didn't want to soil most other parts of himself, either. Especially his reputation, which in this case could easily be at stake. Taking over a duchy while sporting a sullied past didn't set well with him.

So he decided to do what he'd always done in order to keep his hands clean: hire some help.

The problem was, Clear Creek was full of *decent* folks. Finding hard-working, reliable scum wasn't going to be easy in this town. He was beginning to despair, if not actually panic, at the thought that he might have to carry out the deed himself.

That is, until *they* came into the saloon. Dirty. Unshaven. Raucous and loud. And obviously there to drink and gamble. Yes, these men showed prospects!

Thackary waited until they settled at a table in the center of the room and ordered a round of the local turpentine from Mr. Mulligan. Then he rose from his corner table and strolled over. "Ah ... poker, is it? I've heard of the game – always wanted to try my hand at it. Mind if I join you?"

The four men seated around the table looked at him as if he'd just grown a horn in the center of his forehead. "Yew talk too fancy fer our blood, mister. Whyn'tcha just move along?" one of them suggested in a growl. He then spat on Thackary's shoe for emphasis.

Thackary fought the urge to wipe his boot with his crisp, clean white handkerchief. "I see. I take it you don't wish to play with someone as inexperienced as myself." He feigned disappointment as he pulled a heavy coin purse from his pocket and transferred it from hand to hand.

The cleanest of the four – damning with faint praise – narrowed his eyes. "Now, hold on there. Harry didn't mean nothin' by what he said. We could, uh, always use another player. Be glad to teach ya, in fact."

Thackary quickly took each of them in. "Well, that's very hospitable of you. Don't mind if I do." He pulled out a chair and sat.

"'Sides, our fifth player ain't here yet – if'n he comes at all. Yew can fill in for 'im."

"Oh, you gents don't all travel together?"

"Just the four of us. Our fifth player's a local. He comes into town, catches a few games with us when we're passin' through."

"Passing through, you say? Tell me, what do you esteemed gentlemen do?"

They looked at one another before the cleanest one, apparently the leader, spoke. "Scoutin'."

"Do tell! Just what do you ... scout?"

"Little o' this, little o' that. There's a wagon train just outside town – maybe we'll scout for them."

Thackary knew he was lying. This was getting better and better. He couldn't believe his luck! "Will you be around this part of the country long?" he asked as the man on his left, the spitter, began to shuffle the cards.

"Long as it takes." was all the leader offered.

*Ahhh,* thought Thackary to himself. They *were* here for a reason. Splendid! Within a few games he'd find out if they were as dirty as they looked, in more ways than one, then see how much this was going to cost him. Monetarily, of course. His reputation would, once again, stay unspotted ...

# DAY 15

Duncan stood on the east side of the house and watched the sun rise. It was something he'd done often as a young boy, but it had been years since he'd taken the time. Prison drained a man of simple pleasures and made him forget about them. But today, one managed to crawl back into his memory, and he made the most of the experience.

As the light crept onto the prairie, he thought of Cozette and his time with her the day before. Her beauty, her playfulness, her laughter. He chuckled to himself. Yes, her laughter, even silent, was a delight. And she made him laugh, too. Occasionally a tiny sound would escape her as a sigh or gasp, but she was too wrapped up in the moment to notice. Or perhaps she thought nothing of it, since it was all she was capable of doing.

Would she ever speak again? Could she? He found himself longing to hear her voice whisper in his ear, or call out to him across the prairie. To listen to it echo down the gorge or up the creek for as far as it could go.

The gorge. He'd always wanted to build a cabin down near "His Majesty," and perhaps someday he would. But whoever heard of a duke living in a log cabin? Come to think of it, who ever heard of a lowly pig-farmer-turned-cattle rancher becoming a duke? Or for that matter, a former convicted outlaw becoming one? Would his years in prison affect his chances of inheriting the title? There was nothing in the will about it, and Mr. Ashford didn't bring it up when he'd first located him at Colin's wedding. But one never knew ...

He sighed as the sun rose higher. But then, who'd ever heard of a mute duchess? Let alone a mute duchess who could shoot a gun, or a bow and arrow, with such precision, grace and beauty that it took a man's breath away? And it had certainly had yesterday.

*Lord, they say You answer prayer in mysterious ways. And if Cozette is your answer to my prayer for a wife to fulfill the old duke's will, then I'll not argue with you. She's not what I expected, but I can certainly get used to her. I still have to make her into a duchess, of course, but by Jove, I do believe I can. She's courageous, passionate and stubborn. And I'm sure I will come to love her–*

Or did he already love her? He wasn't sure; he'd never been in love before. In Clear Creek, there were rarely any women around *to* love – and when one turned up, someone swept in and married her faster than you could spit.

But it was becoming no secret that Duncan had been spending time with Cozette, and once a Cooke was involved, the other single men largely backed off. They'd done it with Sadie, and with Belle. Some were fool enough to keep trying, but they eventually got the message that it wasn't getting them anywhere.

He sighed again. What would the dance be like? Should he attempt to completely sweep her off her feet, or be patient, give it more time? Not that he could afford to give much – by his reckoning, he had only twenty-three days left to cinch the deal. And if there was any sweeping to be done, would he be able to do it without scaring her off?

He supposed he'd find out at the dance, one way or another. In the meantime, he had work to do. He took one last look at the rising sun before he mounted Romeo and headed out across the prairie.

Cozette lay on her bed, and stared at the ceiling. *Duncan,* she mouthed, wondering how it would sound if she were truly able to speak it. *Duncan Cooke.* She closed her eyes and began to imagine. *Duncan, where are you? Duncan, I have something for you. Duncan, supper's ready ...*

She rolled to her side, a tear in her eye. *Duncan, I cleaned your gun for you. See my new dress? Do you like it? Did you notice my new hat? Duncan, I made your favorite dessert for you ...* Another tear formed and found a path down her face. She blinked a few times to slow them. *Duncan, are your brothers coming to supper after church? Could you drive me to town? Yes, Duncan, I'll accompany you to the dance. Does Mrs. Dunnigan scare the pants off you? She sure does me!* She smiled and laughed silently at that.

*Duncan, do you love me?*

Cozette's smile faded.

*Do you? But how can you love me? What do you really think of me? To you I must be such a ... a ...*

She shook her head and turned onto her back, again watching the ceiling through the blur of tears. *Duncan, did you know I've never felt this way around anyone? Did you know you make me feel like what my Papa says is a beautiful woman? Not how she looks, but how she just ... is. I don't know how or why you do, but it's there. Yesterday was the best day of my life, and I want more of them like that. With you ...*

She sniffed and wiped her eyes with her sleeve. *But if I am never able to speak, how long will it be before you want someone else to spend time with? Someone*

*who can tell you she loves you? Who can speak your*
*name? Who can call out the names of your children?*

Would *she* ever be able to do these things for him?
Ever?

She looked out the tiny window above her bed as the
first rays of sunshine came up over the horizon, and
wept. But she still could not cry out.

Shortly after noon, there was a knock on the Van
Cleets' door. Sadie, Belle, Mrs. Mulligan, and
Grandma Waller had arrived to begin planning the
dance – among other things. Polly answered the door,
got everyone settled in the parlor, then went to get the
coffee and cookies she'd made. Cozette came
downstairs to help and soon they were ready to begin.

"Everyone is to turn their invitation in at our place
so we know who's coming," Mary Mulligan said
excitedly.

Grandma rolled her eyes. "I don't see why you
insisted on that. You already know who's coming!"

"No, we don't! And even if we did, it's best to keep
track of these things," Mary shot back.

"There are only so many folks around here. The
ones we need to be sure of is those settlers camped
outside of town."

"Duncan told me he spoke with one of them
yesterday, Grandma," said Belle. "He said they'll likely
be coming, so we have to figure on the amount of
people we had at the wedding supper, plus the
settlers."

"My, my!" Polly began. "That will be more people at
one shindig than this town's ever seen!"

"I don't recall Clear Creek ever having a dance that
wasn't attached to something else," Grandma mused.

"I guess this will be quite the event! Who should we put in charge of food?"

"Aunt Irene said she'd do it," Belle told them. "But you know she'll want things her way."

"I don't mind," Sadie said. "She's proven to me she's a better cook than a shopkeeper. I think she ought to start cooking for the hotel restaurant when it opens."

"Now hold on there, lass – I'm not sure I'm willing to part with her!" Mrs. Mulligan exclaimed.

Belle began to laugh. "Stop, stop! Let's just take care of the dance – then you can fight over my aunt." She looked at Cozette. "And after we work out some of the other details for the dance, let's see about another dress for you."

Cozette's eyes widened. She fingered the dress she wore and shook her head. *There's no need - this is enough for me.*

"Oh, I almost forgot!" Polly suddenly said. "Excuse me, I'll be right back." She got up and went upstairs.

"Cozette," Sadie began. "We *want* to give you another dress. It's a dance, and the few dresses you have so far aren't the kind one wears to a dance."

Cozette looked at the dress she had on and smoothed the pink calico fabric. Duncan loved it, she could tell – and she wanted to wear what she knew he liked.

"Don't worry," Belle said. "What we have in mind will make you look like a princess!"

Sadie gave Belle an odd look, almost as if warning her. But Cozette smiled, eyes wide.

Just then, Polly re-entered the parlor. She went to a small table, removed a lamp and several books from its surface, then set it in front of Cozette. "Here," she said as she set down some paper, a pen and an inkwell. "You can take notes for us, and use this separate piece in case you want to tell us something."

Cozette nodded, happy to be given a job to do. She took up the pen and dipped it in the ink.

"So, Irene will be in charge of food," Mrs. Mulligan said. "As soon as the invitations start coming back, Wilfred and Irene can organize a quick meeting to see who should bring what."

Cozette scribbled it down.

"What about decorations? Who wants to oversee that?" Belle asked.

"I will!" Sadie said. "And I know just what I want. But I'll need help. Cozette, would you like to assist me with the decorations?"

Cozette looked up from the paper. Go out to the Triple-C and help decorate? Would she see Duncan? Would he be helping too? She nodded enthusiastically, feeling herself blush.

"Perfect," Sadie said. "I'll come fetch you tomorrow and we can start planning. We could even have lunch first, how does that sound?"

It sounded wonderful. Especially if it meant seeing Duncan. But ... should she? Should she get her hopes up, let her feelings grow any more than they already had? Would it be only a matter of time before he tired of her and went to find someone else, someone he could actually talk to? The thought stabbed at her heart and she had to fight back a tear.

"Cozette?" Polly said. "Is that all right with you?"

Cozette took a shaky breath and nodded.

"I'll pick you up around ten-thirty, then," said Sadie. "Now, where should we hold the dance – outside the barn or inside? There's plenty of room inside if we clear a few things out ..."

The women continued making their plans as Cozette recorded everything. She'd always loved writing, and her handwriting was pristine. It had had to be, of course, so she'd practiced. But did a man want to always be reading a note? Would Duncan enjoy reading what she wrote, anyway? And for how long, before the silence wore on him?

She continued to write down their suggestions and names of people to help with this and that. She didn't mind listening to their voices, since she couldn't listen to her own. But it also made her feel inferior, and her doubts about what Duncan might think didn't help. Would she ever be like them? Would people be watching her all night at the dance? Would she be the brunt of jokes? She had been, after she lost her voice. And now it was a definite liability – she couldn't cry out if a man ...

"Cozette? Are you all right?" Belle asked, concerned.

She took a deep breath and nodded, trying to be nonchalant about it.

"Do you have anything you'd like to add?" Sadie asked.

Cozette froze. They were asking *her*? What did she know about planning a dance, or any social function for that matter? She suddenly longed for her buckskins, her bow and arrow, the peace and challenge of tracking a deer in the line of pine trees that bordered the prairie ...

"Cozette?" Polly urged.

She shrugged and shook her head no. But the cold panic didn't disappear. What was she doing anyway? Was she out of her mind? As far as the dance, the entire town would be there, plus the settlers. They would all see her as a girl, and she'd never be able to slip back to her old life again. People would probably stare and point at her all evening!

Ever since the day her father forced her to reveal herself in the storeroom of the saloon, she knew things would never be the same, but she thought she could handle it. And since then she'd been largely sequestered out at the Van Cleets, who had known her – and her secret – for years. She felt safe with them and her father, she knew she could trust them. But the other people in Clear Creek, and the settlers ...?

But ... Duncan said he would protect her, didn't he? Yes, he did. He said so in the saloon the day he first saw her dressed as a girl. He said he would, because other men might try to take her. So should she attend the dance at all? There would be so many men ...

"I think that takes care of everything," Sadie said in satisfaction, then looked to Cozette. "Now, let's see about finding the right dress for you to wear."

Cozette stiffened in her chair. To go to the dance meant danger! She should tell them she couldn't go – even Duncan couldn't protect her from so many men! She'd seen the looks from that Mr. Holmes. And there had also been those four men standing near the hotel building site as she and her father had started their trek to the Van Cleets' place. They looked like they wanted to eat her alive!

She shuddered, suddenly wanting to flee the room and run to the barn. For some reason, wearing a dress made her feel helpless. And she was helpless, as Papa wouldn't let her carry any weapons along with it. Maybe she should start smuggling a revolver anyway, just to be on the safe side. Heaven knows she could find room in all these folds and petticoats ...

Oblivious to her distress, the other women stood. "Come along, Cozette. This will be fun!" Belle said, taking her by the arm and pulling her out of the chair.

Cozette shuddered again. Fun for them, maybe, but she felt more like she was being dressed for a fancy dinner – as the main course!

# DAY 16

"You drive a hard bargain, gentlemen. But we are agreed." Thackary shook Jeb's hand. They had met several miles outside of town to avoid suspicion, so the only witnesses to the deal were Jeb's three companions and the occasional sagebrush.

Thackary had guessed right – the quartet he'd played cards with two days ago were exactly what he was looking for. A bit pricey for his taste, compared to the common thieves of London, but so long as they got the job done, he'd be a happy man. Not to mention a newly-titled and extremely wealthy one.

"Have to hand it to ya, Mr. Holmes," Jeb said, "you're a mite nastier'n I first figgered. Ya don't look the type."

"Yes, I know. It's been to my advantage, I assure you."

"You realize who these fellas are yer dealin' with, though? This don't go right and them Cookes find out yer behind it, yer in fer a world o' hurt."

"Well then, *you* had better make doubly sure you don't fail, hmm?"

Jeb smiled, just before he spit. "Don'tcha worry none, Mr. Holmes. Me'n the boys gonna *enjoy* this job. Ya have no idea how much." Jeb's three companions sneered, a gleam in their eyes.

Thackary silently congratulated himself on finding the absolute lowest scum in the territory. ."Just so long as the job is done – thoroughly. I don't want any slip-ups."

"No problem there. We know what we're doin'."

"See that you do. Now gentlemen, I must away. I have to see if I have anything suitable to wear to a dance."

"Dance? What dance?" Jeb asked.

Thackary looked at each man before his lips formed a thin line. "Nothing for you to concern yourselves with. Besides, it's invitation-only. Now, I leave you to your work. Run along."

Jeb looked to his companions, none of whom seemed to be ready to leave. He turned back to Thackary. "What dance, Mr. Holmes?" he asked again, his voice lowering.

"Will there be women there?" another inquired hopefully.

"*Purty* women?" added another.

Thackary sighed. "The Cookes are having a dance next week," he replied patiently, patronizingly. "But unless one has an invitation, one is out of luck. Now, if you'll excuse me ..."

Three of the four men drew closer around him, as if ready to keep him from leaving. Apparently he wasn't excused. And again, they were the only witnesses ...

"Ya mean to tell me you're gonna attend a dance at the ranch of the very folks ya plan to steal from?" Jeb asked pointedly, crossing his arms.

"Of course," Thackary said with a Cheshire cat's smile.

"Ya got guts, Mr. Holmes." There was skepticism in Jeb's voice, as if he was silently adding, *but ya sure don't got brains.*

Thackary ignored it. "There's a saying, gentlemen – 'keep your friends close, and your enemies closer.' Now, please excuse me. And do stay away from that dance – I don't wish them to suspect."

At a nod from Jeb, the others stepped back, allowing Thackary to pass. He mounted his horse and left.

Jeb rubbed his stubbled jaw and watched the dandy trot his horse over a small rise and disappear from sight.

"You think there'll be women at that dance, Jeb?" Johnny, the youngest in the gang, asked.

Jeb nodded. "Course there will. Wouldn't be a dance without 'em."

"You think we can steal some and take 'em up the ridge with us? Be nice to have some womenfolk around for a spell."

"I'll tell you one thing, Johnny," Jeb replied. "We'll find out what this dance is all about, whether High-and-Mighty King George there likes it or not. An' if'n there's a pretty gal you take a fancy to ... well, we'll just see about having ourselves a good time, ya hear?"

"I sure do!" Johnny said, nodding enthusiastically.

"So." Jeb spit to one side. "He can hire us to do a job. But he cain't tell us what to do when we're done with it. Boys ... make sure yer boots are shined. We're going to a dance!"

His gang cheered, mounted their horses, and left to go do the despicable bidding of Thackary Holmes. Plus some of their own.

Sadie arrived at the Van Cleets' right on time, her husband Harrison alongside her. Cozette watched from her tiny bedroom window as he helped her down from the wagon, then escorted her to the front door. Despite herself, she wondered what it might be like having Duncan beside her, escorting her to and fro, lifting her down from a buckboard ... lying down next to her at night ...

*Whoa, filly*, she cautioned herself.

She heard them knock, and a moment later listened as Mrs. Van Cleet opened the door. Greetings were exchanged along with the standing offer of coffee and victuals, but Harrison had to hurry back to the ranch, and would she let M. Duprie know they'd like to have Cozette stay for dinner?

Cozette immediately went to the small mirror on the wall. She would surely see a lot of Duncan if she was to spend the entire day at the Triple-C! She quickly ran a brush through her hair, wishing it was longer. But that was part of the price she'd paid for being in hiding all those years: having to hack some off at times, with whatever was the sharpest object at hand, so it would still fit under her hat and stay out of view. She envied Sadie and Belle their long tresses and elaborate braids, but knew that it would grow out eventually. At least it wasn't as short as a boy's – she did at least have the option of pinning it up in some way that would be attractive.

She sighed in resignation. If only she knew a way of nicely pinning it, as opposed to just doing so to keep it under a hat. Hopefully she could get some tips on that from Mrs. Van Cleet or Sadie or Belle by the time of the dance. Not that she was sure she was going to the dance at all …

"Cozette? Sadie's here!" Mrs. Van Cleet called up the stairs.

Cozette turned to the door, then stopped and glanced around her room. All her other dresses were hanging in the armoire in the Van Cleets' bedroom. Should she change? She was wearing the yellow calico today, but Duncan liked her in the pink …

"Cozette! Come down, dear! Don't keep the Cookes waiting!"

The yellow would have to do. She took a deep breath and headed for the stairs.

"Good morning, *Mademoiselle* Duprie!" Harrison called up as he watched her descend. "How are you on this fine morning?"

He looked at her so cheerfully – almost the way Duncan had two days before when he teased her, but not so much so. She had to remind herself that not all men were ravening beasts. The Cooke brothers, along with Mr. Van Cleet and Mr. Mulligan, were good examples of what a gentleman was supposed to be. She envied Sadie all over again as she watched Harrison bend at the waist, lift Mrs. Van Cleet's hand to his lips and kiss it in farewell.

Mrs. Van Cleet blushed something fierce and giggled like a schoolgirl. "You Cooke boys are all alike! And I'm glad. Now you three run along and have a good day."

"If it gets too late, Cozette can stay the night," Sadie said. "Would that be all right with you, Cozette? I have something you could wear to bed."

Spend the night? Sleep in the same *house* as Duncan? The thought made her feel all tingly ...

"Tarnation, Cozette, what's gotten into you this morning?" Polly exclaimed. "Are you feeling well? You look flushed ..."

Cozette bit her lip – yes, she imagined she looked *very* flushed! The mere thought of being near Duncan made her plumb senseless!

"Oh, I almost forgot!" Sadie said. "You might like this for the ride." She reached into her reticule and pulled out ... what was it, a handkerchief? No ... a scarf. It was a golden color, translucent, with a spray of pastel flowers, and looked very expensive.

As casually as could be, Sadie stepped over, wrapped it around Cozette's head, and tied it underneath her chin. "There! How's that?"

Cozette blinked in shock, then glanced at the little mirror Mrs. Van Cleet kept on the wall by the front door. *Mon Dieu*, it was perfect! The scarf matched the dress she was wearing to a T, and made her look like a properly dressed woman! No, not a woman – a *lady*. She found herself beaming in gratitude.

Sadie smiled right back. "You can thank Belle – it was her idea, and her scarf. She'd been given it as a gift, but never wore it; she claims the color makes her look washed out." She rolled her eyes. "As if Belle ever looked bad in anything. But she said you can keep it if you like it. It's real silk," she added.

Cozette felt herself tearing up. *Oh no, not again.* She quickly blinked them back, clasped her hands in front of her and gave Sadie a quick bow: *thank you so much!*

"Well, shall we go?" Harrison said, moving to the door and opening it.

Cozette walked out, followed by the Cookes. As she headed toward the wagon, the tingling sensation grew. Each time she thought about seeing Duncan, it increased another notch. And when Harrison took her hand to help her up onto the wagon, she nearly jumped out of her skin. She scooted to the other end of the seat as he helped Sadie, then climbed up himself.

As Harrison snapped the reins and the horses started off, Cozette took a couple of deep breaths, attempting to steady her nerves. *This*, she thought, *could be a very long day.* But then she touched the silk scarf on her head, and decided that whatever happened, she could face it.

Sadie chatted away as Harrison drove. He engaged Cozette in the conversation, and she sensed he kept it simple so she could easily answer with gestures and expressions. He was clearly trying to adapt to how she communicated. *How kind of him*, she thought.

She stole quick glances at the couple as the horses trotted along. Anyone could see they were deeply and madly in love. She made a mental note to herself to watch Belle and Colin, and see if she saw the same thing.

Before she knew it, they had arrived at the grand-looking two-story ranch house. At least, it was the grandest house she'd ever seen in person. The barn was also huge and, as Sadie mentioned the day before, could easily accommodate a dance. She'd heard they'd been built by Sadie's father, the cattle baron, and from the looks of them he'd spared no expense.

A man she didn't recognize was sitting on the front porch of the small log cabin beyond the barn. He got up, stepped off the porch and began to make his way toward them.

"I dare say, is Jefferson coming to say hello?" Harrison asked Sadie.

"I wonder what he wants?" Sadie replied.

Harrison brought the wagon to a halt in front of the house. "I'm sure I don't know, but I intend to find out." He set the brake, hopped down and helped the two women out of the wagon, then bid them good day and went to unhitch the horses. The man from the cabin waited by the barn door, and followed Harrison in when he arrived.

Sadie stood with Cozette on the front porch of the house and watched the barn for a moment before she took her guest by the arm and led her inside. "Shall I make us some tea?"

Cozette smiled and nodded.

She followed Sadie down the hall, into the huge kitchen, and froze. The biggest stove she'd ever seen sat enthroned against one wall like a cast-iron monarch, a kettle perched on it as a crown. Her eyes widened to saucers. *Le bon Dieu, will you look at it? It's positively beautiful!*

Sadie caught her expression and laughed. "Huge, isn't it? Everyone looks at it like that when they first see it. I guess my father thought I'd be cooking for an army when he ordered it. Either that, or he just wanted to brag about how it came all the way 'around the horn' from Philadelphia."

Cozette approached the stove cautiously, as if it were the sacred shrine of some powerful god of baked goods. The heat from it reached her halfway across the room, and she noted the radius of its warmth. The thing probably heated a good part of the house in the winter. She looked at Sadie and slowly shook her head in awe. *You are so lucky to have such a blessing! You really could cook for an army with it, and then some!*

Sadie checked the water in the kettle, moved it to a different position, then took off her bonnet. "Let's give the water a few minutes, and we can have our tea. Have a seat while I go fetch the tea set."

Cozette nodded and sat, debated whether to untie the scarf, then finally decided to keep it on. She stared at the magnificent stove some more before taking in the rest of the kitchen. It was all beautiful! For many women, she knew a kitchen meant hard work and lots of it, but to her it was like a fairy-tale world. And in a way it was – she barely remembered it from her childhood, before her mother ...

She shuddered and pushed the thought aside.

The table, too, was big and could easily seat eight people. She ran her hand over the pretty checkered tablecloth and admired the work table and other furniture in the room. All were designed to be functional as well as beautiful, a help to the lady of the house.

She recalled a conversation she'd overheard between her parents many years ago. *Ma belle Marcelle, one day you will have servants to attend to you. No more will you work until your hands are red and raw. I promise you this – a grand house I will give you! You will see!"*

But Papa hadn't gotten the chance to give Mama any more than a two-room cabin in the north country. She remembered the hearth over which Mama had cooked their meals in lieu of a stove. Oh, how she would have marveled at this room ...

"Hello."

Cozette jumped and gasped. Duncan stood in the doorway to the kitchen. How did a man that big sneak up so quietly? Papa could move that silently, but that was after decades of tracking in the wilderness ...

He smiled, leaned against the door frame, and pushed his hat up with a single finger. "What brings you to our humble abode?"

Cozette looked for Sadie, but she hadn't yet returned. She smiled shyly and made as if she was holding a cup and saucer.

"Ah, Sadie must be getting the tea set together. I thought I heard her poking about the dining room."

"You heard right," Sadie said as she pulled up behind him, carrying a tray laden with tea cups, saucers and a matching teapot. It was the same pretty set she'd used the last time Cozette was at the ranch. Duncan moved out of the way, and she brought it in, setting it on the table.

A few seconds later, Belle breezed in. "Cozette, I'm so glad you're here!" She went to her and gave her a gentle hug. "Do you like the scarf?"

Cozette nodded vigorously against Belle's shoulder.

"I'd wanted you to have a bonnet, but I couldn't find one that looked quite right. Maybe we can make one for you sometime." Belle pulled back and looked at Duncan. "Aren't you glad Cozette came to visit us today, Duncan? You *will* have a cup of tea with us, won't you?"

Sadie stole a glance at Duncan as she unloaded the tray. "Yes, you should have a cup before you go back out." She then added teasingly, "Though aren't you here a little early? Lunch won't be ready for an hour."

"I came to see what was keeping Harrison. Colin's still out with Mr. Kincaid."

"Harrison is in the barn with Jefferson."

Duncan suddenly straightened, his expression serious. "Is he?" He looked at Cozette, bowed slightly, then tipped his hat. "Ladies, if you will excuse me." And off he went.

Cozette could only sit and stare after him. Oh, how she wished he'd stayed. But this was a big ranch, which required lots of work – even she knew that much. And apparently the appearance of Jefferson, whoever he was, was important.

Belle saw her pondering, pulled out a chair and sat. "Jefferson is Duncan's stepfather, as well as Harrison's and Colin's. He doesn't speak to them very much, so to have him out in the barn talking to one of them is significant. You understand."

Cozette smiled and nodded. Of course she did. It also might explain why he didn't live in the same house with them.

"I think the water's ready," Sadie said. "Cookies or biscuits?"

Belle looked at Cozette. "Which would you like?"

*Biscuit,* she mouthed as if speaking, then realized what she'd just done and brought a hand to her lips. This was happening more often. But why? She hadn't done it that much until she started to spend time with Duncan.

"Cozette," Belle began. "I hope you don't mind my asking, but when was the last time you *tried* to talk?"

Cozette furrowed her brow as she thought about how to tell them. Finally, she held up three fingers, motioned toward the door, then mimed having a hat on her head. *Three days ago, with Duncan.*

They didn't get it. "You know what? Wait right there," Sadie said, and hurried out of the room.

Cozette turned to Belle, confused.

"I think she's getting you something to write with," Belle explained. "I saw the notes you took yesterday. You have lovely handwriting."

Cozette blushed and ducked her head.

Sadie re-entered the kitchen with paper, ink pot, and a pen, and set them on the table in front of Cozette. "There, now you can tell us. Besides, this'll help us discuss the decorations." Both women smiled at her, their eyes bright.

With the pen and paper in front of her, Cozette quailed. Nowhere to hide, no excuse not to communicate. No way to hold back. And if her guess was right, Duncan was sure to return to the house before he went back to work – and would probably read whatever she wrote.

She swallowed, hard. She had never felt more exposed in her life.

*My favorite color is blue, but I think I might change it to pink. I like the way it looks on me.*

"Well ... I like the way it looks on you, too," Duncan replied.

Cozette dipped the pen in the inkwell again. *My mother loved pink. Pink flowers, especially.* Unconsciously, she patted the scarf.

"Our mother loved daffodils. What's your favorite flower?"

*Wild roses.* She paused, then quickly scribbled, *Rosa californica. That's the scientific name.* She smirked at him.

He grinned back. "'That which we call a rose. By any other name would smell as sweet' ..."

Before he'd even finished the quote, she was already writing: *Shakespeare, yes?*

"Indeed!" he answered with delight.

Cozette grinned. She and Duncan had been at the kitchen table "talking" ever since dinner ended hours ago – her writing, him responding. She'd almost exhausted the paper and ink Sadie had given her earlier, and was resorting to writing smaller and smaller to make it stretch. The others had taken their dessert into the parlor, while the two of them had stayed in the kitchen.

The day had indeed been long, as she'd anticipated. It had been all she could do after tea not to pace while waiting for Duncan's return. As it was, he didn't come in until just before dinner. Now it was probably time for him to turn in, and she worried he'd be too tired to do his work the next day if she kept him up any later. But she didn't want him to leave – talking to him was so heavenly that she couldn't stop, not even when her right hand began to cramp from writing so much.

Which it was doing now. She stopped and tried to work the kink out of it, but Duncan touched her wrist to stop her. "Allow me," he said, and gently took her hand into his and began to carefully massage it.

Cozette thought her eyes were going to roll back in her head from pleasure, and her mouth went completely dry. She'd never felt anything so good. So intimate.

"I say, your hands are ... very soft."

She stared at him dazedly.

"I mean ... seeing you wield a bow the way you did, I thought they ... they might be a bit rough from use. But ... no, they're not at all. You have the hands of a lady ..."

She felt herself lean closer to him, hypnotized by his voice, his touch.

"Cozette ... Cozette," he whispered. "I love the sound of your name. It's so wonderfully lyrical ... feminine ..."

Cozette barely managed to raise an eyebrow. She felt like she was melting from his touch.

"Yet you're so beautifully fierce, so strong. I've never met a woman like you ... never thought one such as yourself could exist. But here you are." He leaned closer, and his knee brushed against hers.

She took a deep breath ... and let it out with a long moan!

Both of them froze, their eyes wide. "Did ... did I do that?" Duncan said with a gasp.

She swallowed, her face warming at her unbidden reaction to him. And yet her heart leapt with joy. She'd made another sound!

Duncan began to massage her hand again, but had trouble controlling his voice. "That was ... b-beautiful. Do you want ... to t-try again?" he stammered.

She looked at him, her face full of wonder. No one had ever said such a thing to her before, not even Papa. Who thought an occasional groan was beautiful? But Duncan did, and it lit a fire of hope in her soul. She swallowed, took another deep breath, opened her mouth ...

... but something stopped her. It was as if an invisible hand had grabbed her vocal cords and held them tight. She made a face in frustration.

"It's all right, it's all right. Just relax, don't force it. It happens when you're not thinking about it. I heard you do it the other day at the Van Cleets'."

She looked at him, her brow furrowing. *Really? I don't remember that.*

"Yes, you did – several times, in fact. It happened naturally – maybe you didn't even notice. I thought it, it must be normal."

She slowly shook her head, then pointed at his chest with her free hand. *No, only with you.*

Now *he* blushed! "Um ... perhaps we could ... perhaps we could find a way to, to make it happen again?" The stammer was back, but his voice was soft, low, coaxing.

She chewed on her lower lip and nodded nervously as her eyes roamed his face.

His were doing the same to her. "Call me ... call me a madman, but ... I'm sure of this," he said, leaning close enough that she could smell the after-dinner coffee on his breath. "Dear Cozette, you *will* speak again. I know it. I, I don't know how I know, but I do. And I'll help you."

Another squeak escaped her as her tears began to fall.

Duncan reached up and brushed them away with his thumb. "There now, don't cry ...," he whispered.

Cozette gave her head a little shake, and pointed to her smile with her left hand. *It's okay. These are happy tears.*

His hand moved up her arm to pull her toward him, and he looked deeply into her eyes. Her breathing quickened.

"Cozette ... you never, um ... you never answered my, my question before ..."

She blinked, confused.

"About the dance?" His face was only inches from hers. "I asked you to, to accompany me ..."

Her mouth formed a little "O" of surprise. She'd almost forgotten about the dance! Suddenly all her doubts flooded back: how she didn't know how to dance, her fear of being around so many strange men, the terror of possibly being made fun of ...

... and her eyes locked on his ...

... and all her fears swept past, like leaves caught in a rushing river. Leaving only him, her protector. Her friend. Her ... she wasn't sure what else yet, but whatever it was, she wanted it. She felt herself lean closer to him, powerless to stop it, desirous for it to continue.

"Please ... say you will."

Two inches separated them. One inch. She could see the tiny flecks of gold in his eyes. She could taste his breath, his sweat on her tongue.

"Answer me, Cozette ... will you gmmph?"

Her lips were on his, her body answering him before her mind could even form a response. She looked into his eyes, which had gone wide as platters. But then, hers had as well.

Then she felt one of his large hands tangle into her hair, and her eyes drifted shut, letting her other senses take over as he pulled her close. He was so warm, so strong, yet so gentle as he lengthened the kiss. She sensed his effort to keep control of himself, and glowed – not only that he protected her even from himself, but that she could so inspire his passion. The sudden heat from the other day burst into flames around them.

Part of her wanted to run, but it was drowned out by the rest of her wanting to devour him, to be devoured, to ... she had no words, no experience with which to translate her heart's language or her body's. Like a logjam overwhelmed by snow melt, something in her had given way, and was now flooding her with raw emotion, unblocked desire ...

Wait, what was that sound?

It took her a second to realize it was coming from Duncan. And it ... was it a cry of pain?

She opened her right eye, looked down and to the right – and her whole body jerked back in shock. In the throes of passion, she'd locked her hand around his left arm, and was squeezing it, *hard!*

Eyes wide in shock, she covered her mouth with her hands. She felt her lips moving rapidly against her palm, saying *I'm so sorry, I'm so sorry, I did not mean to–*

Somehow he understood, and held up his own hands to placate her. "It's all right, it's all right," he whispered. Slowly he placed them on her shoulders.

"It's ... well, it was more than all right, actually," he chuckled.

*He isn't angry? I haven't scared him?* In a whoosh, she left out the breath she didn't know she was holding – which made him laugh again. Smiling in embarrassment, she gingerly reached out and touched his arm with a fingertip, her eyes questioning. *Are you okay? I did not mean to hurt you.*

"I'll be fine. You only surprised me ... is all. But a, a good surprise, I ..." Duncan saw he was starting to babble, and laughed once more. "I'll ... take that as a yes, then?"

Laughing silently, she nodded so forcefully she bounced up and down in her chair.

They sat there for a minute, unable to do anything but look into each other's eyes and smile. Then his hands slowly fell away from her, and he leaned back in his chair. "My dear lady ... you are a wonder."

She motioned toward him, then let her hands flutter about like sparrows. *You are ... I don't even know how to say!*

He blushed, but his shoulders slumped "I ... I'm afraid I must bid you *adieu*."

She frowned sadly, then nodded in understanding and picked up her pen. *It is late. And you have much work tomorrow.*

"Indeed. And ... and I must, above all, remain a gentleman. But ... I look forward to seeing you in the morning." He took her hand in his and brought it to his lips for a feather-light kiss. "*Jusque-là, mon bien précieux.*" Standing, he took one last long look at her as if to make sure he had enough to get him through the night, then left through the back door and went outside.

Cozette absently touched her lips as she replayed his last words: until then, my precious one. My precious one. *Yes, I will go to the dance with you,* she thought, happiness rising in her like a geyser. *I will go anywhere with you that you ask ... oh, Duncan Cooke, I love you!!!*

Harrison and Sadie had long since retired, but Colin and Belle were still in the parlor, keeping an ear on events beyond the kitchen door. "I do believe he just went outside," Colin whispered to his wife.

Belle's eyebrows were already at full mast in surprise "I do believe he just spoke *French!*" she whispered back. "Do you speak French?"

"*Un peu, mon amour, un peu,*" he quipped, holding up a thumb and forefinger. *A little, my love, a little.*

Belle pondered this – and then pondered the effect Duncan might have had on Cozette if he did. "I'd better go check on her," she said urgently, jumping out of her chair.

Colin looked at his wife and did a double take. "Good Lord, what are you doing with *that?*"

Belle looked down at the ladle she was holding, as if she had no idea who'd put it there. "Oh. I guess I take after my Aunt Irene more than I thought," she replied, clearly not pleased by the idea.

Colin tried his best not to laugh. "Give it here," he said, and when she offered it he took the opportunity to catch her arm and draw her close. She leaned over him and they kissed, sweet and slow.

Eventually she pulled away and stood up straight. "If I didn't need to check on Cozette ..."

He nodded. "And I on Duncan. But my brother is probably in need of an understanding ear – or a bucket of cold water over his head."

"Either of which you'll be happy to supply, no doubt," Belle quietly riposted.

Colin stared at her, open-mouthed, for a moment before replying. "Clearly, m'dear, I've been an untoward influence on your sense of humor.

"Clearly," she repeated dryly, her eyes twinkling.

He chuckled. "Let us to work then. I'll see to Duncan, while you get Cozette to bed."

Belle nodded, kissed him on the nose, then headed to the kitchen.

Colin sighed and looked at the ladle in his hand. Rather than set it down somewhere, he threaded the handle through his belt, just in case. He went out the front door but didn't find Duncan on the porch, so he went to the barn next.

Sure enough, his brother was standing next to a water trough, his head already dripping wet. "That bad, eh, old boy?" Colin asked.

Duncan hesitated, then said "Any worse and I might be looking down the barrel of Anton Duprie's Winchester."

"Oh my."

"To say the least." Duncan dunked his face again. "Though I had ample help."

"Ohhhh my!" Colin's smile was wide and toothy.

"Please stop," Duncan groaned.

"Well, I do gather it all went quite well – I would wager she's at least agreed to accompany you to the dance. And, after that, who knows? We'd best start planning your wedding."

Duncan shook his head slowly in disbelief. "This is so different from what I ever thought I'd be doing with a woman."

"You never thought you'd be asking a woman to a dance?" Colin teased.

Duncan glared at him in the moonlight. "No, I didn't think I'd be falling in love. Or should I say ..." He paused, looked down for a moment. "No. That's exactly what I should say."

"Well, then I should be saying 'congratulations'!" Colin came up, took Duncan's hand and shook it.

Duncan, however, didn't exactly look elated – more like stunned. "To be honest, I'm finding it so ... overwhelming. Every time I'm with her, I can't take my eyes off her, I want to take her and ... make her mine, if you understand my meaning. But there's so much more to it. I just can't explain it. And I swear if anyone were to ever harm her, I'd kill him on the spot."

Colin nodded and placed an arm around his shoulders. "Oh, I understand all too well, old sport – I felt the same way with Belle. She isn't just a woman to you. She means something more. It took me a while to grasp it ... but I found that to me, Belle represented everything I've tried so hard to protect, everything I hoped for."

Duncan stared at him a moment. "You mean Mother."

Colin hesitated before answering. "Yes ... I guess wanting to protect Belle, to comfort her was in part because of Mother. Neither of us was here to protect *her*, after all. But it wasn't just that. It was also ..." He frowned in thought. "It wasn't only about the past, it was about the future. It was knowing that I'd have someone to share the coming days with, to someday bring children into this world, to ... to stand against the darkness and the unknown." He broke off for a quick laugh. "Listen to me – I doubt I'm making any sense at all!"

"No, no – you're making perfect sense, more than I've been." Duncan sighed. "All I know is I can't do this much longer."

Colin nodded. "Well, of course you can't wait much longer! The inheritance–"

"No."

The interruption caught Colin up short. "Pardon?"

"Call me mad if you will, but this has nothing to do with the title or the inheritance. I must marry her, and soon, because of *her*. I have no idea why my need is so strong, but it's like a, a thirst that only she can quench. I must know she's mine, and that no one can ever take her from me."

They stood in silence for a minute. Finally Colin said, "Then let's make her your wife. We did invite the Rev. King, our beloved preacher, to the dance, did we not?"

Duncan's face seemed to come alight. "Indeed we did. Indeed we did."

"Let's to bed then," Colin said. "Tomorrow will be here soon enough."

"Yes, it will," Duncan agreed, then turned toward the barn.

"I say, whatever are you doing?"

"Going to bed."

"You have it *that* bad?"

"Yes, dear brother. Yes I do."

"Oh my," Colin said once more, shaking his head. "Well, you know what's best. Do you need a blanket?"

"Already have one." Duncan shrugged. "I brought it to the barn when I found out she was staying the night."

"Better safe than sorry?"

"Quite," Duncan replied pointedly.

"Well ... good evening, then." Colin turned to go back to the house.

"Good evening," Duncan echoed as he watched him go and noted the ladle in his belt. He laughed to himself, then sighed longingly. Maybe he should be the one with the ladle. Perhaps if he gave himself a few knocks to the head, it mightn't be such a long night.

# DAY 17

Duncan awoke to find Cozette already gone. He was puzzled about it, until Sadie told him that her father had come before sunrise and whisked her away to hunt. Everyone had a hard time envisioning the petite Cozette out hunting – everyone except Duncan, who'd seen her handle a pistol and had no trouble at all. But when she returned with her father later that day wearing new buckskins and toting a fresh kill, they were able to get a better grasp on the idea. Besides, she made the best venison stew any of them had ever tasted.

# DAY 18

There was still plenty of deer meat left, so Cozette made a roast from it. Though she did insist on cooking it over a fire outside – as she told the Cookes via note, *I don't know how to use the stove yet.* It was a reasonable explanation, and a delicious roast.

Duncan had already begun to realize what a prize she was, but this took it to a new level. It was all he could do pick her up, throw her over his shoulder and carry her off to the Rev. King and the chapel. But he settled for rarely letting her out of his sight.

# DAY 19

Belle had to practically pry Cozette away from Duncan for a cooking lesson with her Aunt Irene, who, pleased with their progress, only threatened to smack the girls with her ladle twice. The girls were grateful she hadn't brought her hatchet! And the bread, rolls, and pot roast they made were a huge hit with the customers at Mulligan's that day. Except with Duncan, who moped about while working the stock and whose mood had grown foul by sunset.

# DAY 20

Duncan didn't see Cozette all day, and became progressively crabbier. He couldn't eat, couldn't sleep soundly, and felt honestly ill. He knew he wanted to be with her, but now had the impression that if he wasn't, he would surely die! But that was mad; who'd ever heard of such a foolish thing?

# DAY 21

It didn't help when Duncan took a wild swing at Harrison for suggesting he was "heartsick." But what made it worse was that he had trouble keeping his balance afterward. Sadie suggested that perhaps he had eaten something that disagreed with him, but he insisted on going out and doing his share of the work. By the end of the day, though, he didn't even bother with dinner, and was barely able to get up the stairs and collapse into bed.

# DAY 22

There was a loud knock on the door. Cyrus Van Cleet looked at Polly as they sat at the kitchen table having breakfast. "Now, who could that be this early?" he wondered as he stood. He went to the door to answer it, but not before peeking out the nearby window to see who it was. "Good Lord!"

"Who is it, dear?" Polly asked.

Cyrus didn't answer, but hurried to the door. Duncan had slumped to the porch and all but fell across the door's threshold when Cyrus opened it. "Duncan, lad! What's happened?"

Duncan raised his head. He hadn't shaved for days and looked awful – skin pale, eyes sunken. Cyrus helped him to his feet and steered him toward the kitchen where he managed to deposit him in a chair at the table.

"Oh, my goodness!" Polly exclaimed. "What's wrong? Is he hurt? Has he been shot?"

Cyrus quickly examined him. "I don't see any wounds. And he isn't bleeding."

"Duncan?" Polly leaned over him, her voice pleading. "Talk to us! What happened?"

Duncan looked at them but didn't speak. His breathing was shallow, he looked as if he'd lost a lot of weight in the last few days, and he could barely hold his head up straight.

A sound suddenly caught his attention and he turned his head toward the kitchen doorway.

Cozette was standing there, staring at him, her eyes wide. Come to think of it, she looked a little peaked too ...

Cyrus and Polly watched both youngsters' eyes widen, and felt a strange sensation permeate the room, like the charge in the air before a lightning strike. And did it seem like Duncan's face was starting to get its color back? "Polly," Cyrus whispered.

"Yes, dear?"

"You remember how it was when we first met? Those weeks we were courting and thought we'd die without each other?"

Polly continued to watch as Cozette slowly walked toward the table. "I remember. I don't think it was this bad for us, though."

"Maybe it was and maybe it wasn't, but I think this is the same thing. I called it a miracle then, and I'll call it one now. These two are meant to be, Polly, sure as I'm standing here next to you."

"You didn't eat or sleep for days," she said, recalling. "Your mother thought you had the influenza."

"I thought I might die if I couldn't be with you. Could feel it in my bones, my heart. Everywhere ..."

Cozette sat at the table and took one of Duncan's hands in her own. His eyes softened at the contact and he managed a smile.

"I'd best get him some coffee," Polly said, and left. Cyrus sat across the table from the couple and continued to watch.

Cozette rubbed Duncan's hand as if it was terribly cold and looked straight into his eyes.

Cyrus nodded – this was all too familiar. It had been the same between Cyrus and Polly when they were young. He could see it plain as day: a soul-searing love that only happened once in a blue moon, a pairing of two people that, for whatever reason, the universe saw fit to join, not waiting for society or church or anything. And once done it could not be undone ... for if it were, death would surely follow. If he hadn't experienced it himself, he would never have believed such a thing existed. But he had. He still couldn't stand to be separated from Polly for any longer than a half-day. Not that he would ever want to.

Polly set a cup of coffee in front of Duncan. He looked at it numbly, picked it up with his free hand and took a small sip. Then a long swallow. Then he drained the cup and set it down on the table. "I'm sorry to barge in on you like this, Cyrus," he finally said, his voice a low rasp. "There is no excuse for my behavior. But I dare say, I don't know what's wrong with me."

Cyrus smiled. "No need to apologize, son – I remember what it was like when I was young. Had it as bad as you do. My, but I think we'd better plan for something more than a dance next week!"

Duncan looked at him, his eyes still glazed over. "I agree with you there, but as to my current condition, I ..." He trailed off.

Cyrus leaned toward him. "You what, son?"

Meanwhile, Cozette was looking Duncan over carefully, even going so far as to pry one eye open wider. She moved his head this way and that, then suddenly gasped and stood. She opened her mouth and tried to speak, but still couldn't manage it, finally banging her fist on the table in frustration.

"Cozette!" Polly exclaimed. "What is it?"

She found out soon enough – Duncan slumped to the side as his eyes rolled back, then fell out of his chair to land on the floor in a heap.

Cozette squeaked as she ran to him, Cyrus quickly joining her. Polly ran from the room, coming back with a piece of paper and a pen already dipped in ink. "Cozette, tell us!"

Cozette scribbled one word on the paper, never leaving Duncan's side.

"Poisoned?!" Polly exclaimed, and Cozette nodded. "Oh no! What should we do?"

Cozette began to write again. *Find my father! He knows what to do!*

"Cyrus?"

Cyrus had read it too. "Cozette, take Duncan's horse. "Tell your father what happened and bring him here."

Cozette nodded, took the pen and wrote once more. *Give him water.*

"We'll do that. Now hurry!"

He didn't have to tell her twice. Cozette hiked up her skirts and ran out of the house. She quickly untied Romeo from the hitching post, mounted and galloped off to find her father. She knew she had very little time to save Duncan Cooke's life. And if Duncan died, she would too – she knew in her heart that she couldn't live without him.

Anton crept along the ground, watching a rabbit come out of its hole. He lay perfectly still as he put the first traces of pressure on the trigger of his rifle. Perhaps he should find something bigger for dinner, but a rabbit stew would be nice for all of them that night.

The rabbit, suddenly alert, sat up a moment before it darted back into the hole. Something had startled it. Anton grunted in annoyance as he felt the ground vibrate beneath his belly. Then he heard the hoofbeats – one horse, coming fast. He rose to a sitting position to see who approached, prepared to give them a tongue-lashing for scaring off the game.

Wait – he recognized the big black horse as Duncan Cooke's Romeo! And the woman astride it – "Cozette!" he called out.

Cozette spotted him and turned the horse. Within seconds she came to a skidding stop before him and dismounted as best she could in a dress that really wasn't made for such a maneuver.

"Cozette, what is wrong? Has something happened to *Monsieur* Cooke?"

Cozette nodded, her eyes tearful and desperate.

"Calm down, *ma petite.* Tell your papa what has happened."

Cozette took a deep breath, and then another. She closed her eyes a moment, before starting a series of hand signals she'd learned during their years spent with the Indians.

"He is sick?" Her father asked.

Cozette shook her head and made more signs.

"*Sacre bleu* - he is poisoned?!"

She nodded rapidly

"Come. We must go!" He helped her re-mount, jumped up behind her, kicked the horse and they were off like a shot back to the Van Cleets'. Hopefully, they wouldn't be too late.

"I'm afraid you've got a problem, Mr. Cooke."

"Please, call me Harrison. I should think we're on a first-name basis by now." The two men had been out trying to locate missing stock all morning. So far, no luck.

"Looks like cattle rustling to me," Logan told him. "Seen it before. See how these tracks lead away from the herd? They were cut out of it and run off."

Harrison leaned on his saddle horn and sighed. "Lovely."

"Good news is they're all wearing the Big J brand," Logan began. "Shouldn't be too hard to track down. Problem is getting the word out. Who knows where the thieves have taken them, or if they've split them up yet."

"We'll get word out as best we can. The dance is in a few days, we can let most everyone know then. In the meantime, I'll tell Sheriff Hughes, and he'll find out if anyone's seen anything." He grunted in annoyance. "I thought this sort of thing was done with when Jack and Sam were locked away."

Logan shook his head. "Nah. Anytime you got cattle, someone'll be trying to rustle them, sure as ticks on a dog. Any strangers been seen around town lately?"

"Only some settlers camped south of town. But they're hardly the rustling type, I assure you."

"Well, you can never be too careful. Best get into town and let the sheriff know. I'll keep an eye on things here."

"Thank you, Logan. You've been a wonderful help these last few weeks. I don't know what we're going to do when you leave. You wouldn't consider staying on, would you, become the Triple-C's foreman?"

"Hmmm. Well, now there's something I haven't thought about. I'll consider it. But that being the case, I'd best keep calling you Mr. Cooke."

"If I'm your boss, I'll still want you to call me Harrison."

They both laughed just as Colin came riding up at a full gallop. "Harrison!"

"Good Lord! What is it?"

"It's Duncan! Anton and Cyrus just brought him home. He's in a bad way! You'd better come quickly!"

Colin didn't have to say more. Harrison kicked his mount and the two brothers started back to the house as fast as their horses could go.

Logan remained where he was to guard the stock. "That family sure has their fair share of trouble." He shook his head, turned his horse, and returned to work.

Harrison and Colin raced up to the house and jumped off their horses. One of the cowhands who'd stayed behind with Logan to help with the ranch took the horses and started for the barn. Harrison and Colin ran inside the house, quickly searched the first floor and, finding no one, hurried upstairs.

Duncan was in bed in his room, with Cozette sitting on one side and Doc Waller on the other. Sadie was gathering Duncan's clothes to carry them out. Doc had stripped their brother down, and they could see why – his forehead and chest were beaded in sweat, and the single sheet covering his body was already damp. His face held the pallor of death.

Harrison cringed at the sight. It was not the first time he'd seen it - his mother had looked the same, just before she died. "Doc?" he asked urgently.

Doc Waller slowly sighed and shook his head.

Harrison clenched a fist in anger. He turned toward the door, but Colin grabbed his shoulder to stop him. "Brother, don't."

Harrison stopped, his expression tight, and shook as if he were about to explode. "Bloody *hell*," he roared just as Anton Duprie entered the room. "What happened?!"

"We don't know, Harrison." Doc said solemnly. "We don't know anything except that ..."

Colin stepped forward, his face white. "Except that he's dying?"

Doc screwed up his face. "Except that he ate something he shouldn't have."

Anton bent over Duncan, a small vial in his hand. Cozette stood to give him better access.

"What is he doing?" Harrison demanded and lunged for the bed. Cozette blocked him to let her father help Duncan however he was able. Harrison grabbed her by the shoulders and tried to move her out of his way, but she held her ground. For a tiny thing, she was incredibly strong. "What is that? What's he giving him?"

Cozette put her hand in the middle of his chest and pushed him back a step, much to his surprise. Then she locked eyes with him and shook her head slowly in warning. *Let Papa do this. It is his only chance.*

"This will help. The Indians, they teach me," Anton explained. "There are only so many kinds of poison to kill a man. This will weaken it."

"He ... he'll live, then?" Colin asked hopefully as Belle entered the room and wrapped her arms around him from behind.

"*Oui,* if we are not too late. But it is too early to tell." Anton shrugged and stood. "I must make more medicine, but I need your help."

"What can we do?" Harrison asked.

Cozette went to her father's side, and he put a hand on her shoulder. "Guard him, *ma petite.* Keep him comfortable." He turned to the others. "There are plants on the prairie that I use to make the remedy. I show you what they look like. It would help, though, if we knew what was used to poison him."

"*Used* to poison him?" Belle gasped.

"Good Lord, man!" Harrison asked, aghast. "Are you saying ...?

"*Oui, Monsieur* Cooke. Someone has tried to kill your brother."

*You can't die, Duncan Cooke! I love you, do you hear me? You can't die!*

Cozette again dipped a cloth in cold water, wrung it out and placed it on Duncan's forehead. All color was gone from his face, his breathing had slowed to almost nothing. It was all Cozette could do to hold herself together as she watched him fight for every last inch of his life. And she knew he was fighting, could feel it as if they were one. How, she had no idea, but there it was.

A soft knock at the door, and Sadie entered. "Cozette," she began. "There are some people here who think they can help."

Cozette warily eyed the pair standing behind Sadie, a man and an incredibly beautiful woman. A chill went up her spine at the sight of them, and she shook it off as Sadie let them in.

"Hello, ma'am," the man said. "My name's Lany Moss. This is Mrs. MacDonald. We heard what happened. Some of us are helping look for the plants needed to counteract the poison."

"They're from the wagon train outside town," Sadie explained. "They came to see what they could do to help with the dance, and found out what happened. Mrs. MacDonald thinks she can help save Duncan."

Cozette stood as the settlers approached, and took a protective stance beside the bed.

"It's all right. We're not going to hurt him," Mrs. MacDonald said. Her voice was soft and soothing. Against her will, Cozette felt herself relax at the sound of it. The woman touched Cozette's arm to guide her out of the way, and an odd tingling coursed through her body at the contact. Should she let them near Duncan? Every fiber of her being was on alert at the thought of any more harm coming to the man on the bed. *Her* man.

The woman sat and examined the unconscious form. She removed the damp cloth, placed a hand on his forehead, and held it there a moment. "How long has he been like this?"

"Since they brought him here this morning," Sadie answered. "Can you help?"

"Mrs. MacDonald is, um ... a healer of sorts," Mr. Moss offered. "I'm sure she can."

"My husband is helping your father gather the plants," Mrs. MacDonald told Cozette. "I can give him something to slow the poison until they return. If we can slow it enough, he stands a good chance of recovering."

Cozette wanted to trust her, truly she did. But they were strangers, and her father had always warned her not to trust strangers. Then, he was allowing them to help him look for the plants he needed, so ... she took a deep breath and slowly nodded.

"Lany, go to the wagon and get my bag," Mrs. MacDonald told her companion, who nodded and left the room. "I will need some water," she then said to no one in particular.

Sadie plucked a pitcher off the table next to the bed and left to get fresh water.

Cozette stood and stared at the woman as she touched Duncan here and there, perhaps to gauge the fever. She placed one hand again on his forehead, the other on his belly, and began to hum. It was a pretty tune, and despite the gravity of the situation Cozette enjoyed the sound of it.

The woman continued to hum softly a moment before her voice grew a little louder. She then just as suddenly stopped. "Is he your husband?" she asked Cozette.

Cozette stared at her. She slowly shook her head, a tear in her eye.

"But he will be?"

Cozette smiled, sniffled, and clutched her hands to her chest. *I hope so.*

The woman smiled. "Well, I think he will live long enough so that he can be. The love in your eyes for him is hard to miss."

Cozette blushed. She hated that it was so obvious, but there was no denying it. If a perfect stranger could see it, then everyone else probably could too.

The woman went back to humming as she took up the cloth, dipped it in the basin of water, squeezed it out, then offered it to Cozette. "You should be doing this. We need to cool him down – he is too hot. Wipe his face first, then his arms and chest."

Cozette complied as Sadie and Mr. Moss returned. He handed Mrs. MacDonald the bag she sent him to fetch, then stood to one side.

"What else do you need?" Sadie asked her.

"Fill this with the water you brought." She held out a clear glass bottle she'd just pulled from the bag.

Sadie took it, carefully filled it from the pitcher and handed it to the woman. The woman dug through the doctor's bag and pulled out several more bottles. She sprinkled white powder out of two of them into the water, then corked it and shook it up.

Duncan moaned. Cozette immediately stopped her ministrations and looked at him.

"See if you can get him to drink this," Mrs. MacDonald told her, uncorking the water bottle. "Lany, help me to sit him up."

They went to work and got Duncan to a sitting position. The woman, who had gone to the other side of the bed, now sat and began to hum the same tune as before, while Cozette attempted to cradle Duncan's head with one arm and hold the bottle to his lips with the other.

"You might want to help her," Mrs. MacDonald told Sadie as she stood.

Sadie exchanged places with her and helped Cozette get the white liquid down. Duncan coughed and sputtered a few times but got most of it into him.

"We'll leave you now," Mr. Moss told them. "The others should be back soon. Between this and what Mr. Duprie is able to do, I think he'll make it."

"How can you be sure?" Sadie asked, her eyes pleading.

"I've seen Mrs. MacDonald work miracles," Mr. Moss said, without irony. "Trust me, she's handy to have around when you're crossing a continent."

Sadie smiled. "Understood." She knew that anyone well versed in doctoring was a godsend out on the prairie. Man or woman, it didn't matter in the wilderness so long as they got the job done. "Thank you."

Cozette continued to cradle Duncan's head against her chest. She looked toward the woman, tears in her eyes, and nodded her thanks.

"You are both very welcome," Mrs. MacDonald replied. "I am glad we could help. He will pull through – in fact, I am certain he will be asking you for a dance when the time comes," she added, smiling at Cozette. "But he will need to rest until then."

Cozette and Sadie both smiled back as the settlers quietly left.

A half hour later, Cozette heard heavy footsteps come running into the house. Her father, Harrison, Colin and Belle burst into the room and went straight to the bed. "Did she help? She knows the Indian ways better than I! *Le bon Dieu* has looked out for us this day!" Papa was clearly excited as he pulled the vial from his pocket and held it to Duncan's lips. "He will live, *ma petite*! I am sure of it!"

"I don't think I've ever prayed so hard," Colin said

"As long as the Good Lord heard, brother," Harrison added, staring intently at Duncan.

"The prayers of a righteous man availeth much," Belle whispered to herself.

Duncan coughed twice, groaned, then pulled away from Cozette and tried to take a swing at Anton.

"Oh, dear," Colin said. "Let me handle this." He went to the bed and drew Cozette out of Duncan's reach. She gave him a worried look but moved as he directed. He sat and took his brother's hand in his. "Duncan? Duncan, it's safe now."

Duncan's head turned toward Colin's voice. "They've gone?" he rasped.

Colin closed his eyes and sighed. "Yes. They've gone."

"Who'd they kill this time? Who'd we lose?"

Colin looked about the room and whispered, "Delirious. Thinks we're back in gaol."

Sadie and Harrison held onto each other, as Anton took Cozette in his arms.

"No one, Duncan," Colin continued. "We didn't lose a one."

Duncan visibly relaxed, then opened tear-filled eyes. "Won't let 'em hurt you again, Colin. I promise ..."

Colin swallowed and looked away. "I know. You've done a jolly good job of protecting all of us. You should be knighted."

The tears fell. "Didn't protect Tommy. I couldn't. What they did to him ... was heinous."

"Don't talk about it anymore. There was nothing any of us could do."

"He was just a boy."

"I know."

Duncan's head lolled to the side and he groaned again. "Co ... Cozette ..."

Cozette stood straight in her father's arms, but he didn't release her. Not yet.

"Where is my Cozette? *Mon bien précieux?*"

Now Anton let go, in surprise. But also in shock, she didn't move.

Colin smiled crookedly. "Where would you like her to be?" Harrison put a hand over his eyes and grimaced. Sadie only smiled.

"No games, man!" Duncan moaned and grabbed Colin by the shirt collar. "I want my wife! Bring me my wife!"

Colin tried to extricate himself from his brother's grasp. "I think you'll … have to remedy something first … before you carry on like that, old boy."

Duncan glared at him. "What?"

"You're not married yet," Colin said, trying his best not to laugh.

"Whaddaya mean I'm not married?" Duncan slurred. "Course I'm married."

"Good heavens!" Harrison said, looking at Anton. "Just what did you put in that concoction?"

The Frenchman shrugged. "I have never seen it affect a man this way. Maybe I give him too much?"

"It won't hurt him, will it?" Belle asked.

"I do not think so. What he needs is rest. We should leave him."

"Not before we get some clean sheets and make sure he's cooled down," said Sadie. "Belle, help me will you?" The two women left the room.

Cozette watched them go, then went to the bed and looked down at Duncan, her face flushed with embarrassment.

Colin smiled. "It seems he has a definite affection for you, my dear. I do hope you reciprocate."

She quickly looked between Colin and Duncan. *Recippa-what?*

"He's in love with you, Cozette. Do you feel the same way about him?" Harrison asked.

Tears in her eyes, she nodded.

"Good. Now that's settled, what say we get something to eat? Saving our brother's life has given me a terrible appetite! *Monsieur* Duprie, will you join us?"

Anton stepped behind his daughter and leaned down, and whispered in her ear. "He is a good match for you, *ma petite.* He will make you a fine husband and very happy." He kissed her on the cheek, then went over to the other men.

Colin held out his hand. "Thank you, *Monsieur.* You saved Duncan's life."

"I did what anyone would do. And the woman, she helped." They shook hands. "It took both of us."

"We can thank her at the dance – I'm sure they're still coming. In the meantime, we need to leave Duncan to his rest." Colin turned to Cozette. "He'll be all right now. Why don't you come downstairs and get something to eat?"

The look on Cozette's face was probably enough of an answer, but she still pointed at the patient on the bed: I'm staying here. With him.

Colin nodded in understanding.

"Good Lord!" Harrison suddenly said. "Doc Waller and Cyrus are still out looking for plants! They have no idea he's out of danger!"

Colin laughed. "Well, we'd best go find them first, then." He put his arm around Harrison and led him from the room.

Anton took Cozette by the hand and sat her on the bed next to Duncan. "Take good care of him, *ma petite.* I know you are not ready to leave him yet." He followed the other men out the door.

She watched his retreating back, tears in her eyes. *Oh Papa, you are so very right! I'll never leave him as long as I live ...*

# DAY 26

Duncan swung his legs over the side of the bed. He'd barely been out of it the last three days, and was determined not to spend another moment flat on his back if he could help it. At least he wasn't as dizzy as the day before when he tried this – he figured today he'd have better luck staying on his feet.

He slowly stood, balancing himself with his arms out, then let them fall to his sides and sighed. It felt good to stand. He slowly made his way to the window and looked outside. The Cooke women and several others were buzzing about, getting ready for tomorrow night's dance. He listened as Sadie barked orders with the efficiency of her father Horatio.

Smiling, he turned from the window and realized he was hungry.

Duncan found a pair of pants folded and placed on a chair. He pulled them on, then wandered out to the upstairs hall. But getting out of bed was one thing, getting down the stairs another. He gripped the stair rail and slowly began his decent, stopping twice to let waves of dizziness pass. Finally he reached the bottom. Who would have thought traversing a staircase would feel like such an accomplishment? But it did, and he smiled at his small triumph.

He made his way into the kitchen and stopped, his mouth dropping open. *Oh my ...*

Cozette was bending over to take something out of the oven. Her hair was pinned up, a sight he had never seen, and tiny strands had come loose to frame her face. She wore a white apron over her favorite pink dress, and the smatterings of this and that smeared on it told him she'd been busy.

She was beautiful, the most beautiful thing he'd ever seen. In fact, the whole tableau was intoxicating: the stove, Cozette, whatever confection filled the baking dish she'd started to pull out of the oven.

She caught sight of him and slowly stood, turning and placing the dish on top of the worktable behind her. She set down the hot pads she used, wiped her hands on her apron ... and uttered a delicate whimper, one so utterly female that Duncan felt his whole body tighten. *Uh-oh.* Perhaps he was feeling better than he first thought ...

Cozette walked toward him, then blushed and looked around the kitchen as if unsure of what to do. He wondered if she wasn't trying to look at anything *but* him.

It was then he remembered he wasn't even half-dressed. "Oh, I beg your pardon. I seem to be ... in a state of ... well ..." He crossed his arms over his chest in an attempt at modesty.

She smiled, perhaps at the knowledge she was not alone in her discomfort, and snuck a peek at his half-covered chest before backing away. She opened the back door and went out a moment, then returned with a clean shirt, crossing the kitchen and holding it out to him while trying to look at anything *but* him.

Unable to help himself, he chuckled.

She covered her embarrassed smile and turned her back to him.

He donned the shirt and began to button it up. "You're beautiful when you're blushing. Did you know that?" he whispered.

She looked shyly over her shoulder at him and shook her head.

He reached out, turned her toward him and drew her close. "Well, you are. So beautiful I could look at you forever."

She stared at him, her mouth half open as if to speak, but mouthed nothing. She instead looked down, a tear in her eye.

*Egads, not tears.* "What's the matter, *cherie?*" he asked gently. He placed a hand under her chin and lifted her face to his own. "Please don't cry. Tell me what it is? Has something happened?"

She slowly shook her head.

"Then what?"

She took a deep breath, as if to steel herself.

"Cozette?" he asked softly, so as not to frighten her. He had to know what was wrong.

She looked right into his eyes, blinked back her tears, and ever so slowly mouthed three simple words: *I. Love. You.*

Duncan let out a gasp in elation. "You did it! You used your mouth!" He wrapped her up in his arms and swung her in a complete circle, then stopped as a wave of dizziness took hold. It dragged him down to the floor, Cozette with him.

She pulled back a few inches and put her hand atop his head. *Are. You. All right?* she mouthed.

The room still spinning, he pulled her into his lap. "I'm fine – just a bit dizzy, that's all." Good Lord, but it felt good to be holding her like this! "I knew you could do it. You may not have made a sound, but it's a start."

She grinned and wriggled against him, seeming to enjoy being held. But he'd best get them off the floor before something let both of them know he was *definitely* feeling better. Reluctantly, he let her go.

She scrambled out of his lap, stood, then held out her hands to help him up.

"I think I'd better sit a moment. Bring a chair over here, will you?"

She went to the kitchen table and brought him the nearest chair. He used it to lever himself off the floor and sat in it. "Thank you," he said and held a hand out to her.

She looked at it tentatively then reached out, took it and slid into his lap again, putting an arm around his shoulder.

He could get used to this! "Thank you. Thank you for everything. You've hardly left my side these last few days. I don't know what to say."

She looked down at him and gently touched his lips. Her smile broadened.

"And what is that supposed to mean?" Duncan closed his eyes and groaned. "Oh. dear. Did I babble on that badly?"

She raised a single eyebrow and nodded.

"Oh. Did I incriminate myself horribly?"

She nodded again as the other brow went up.

"Ohhh ... the look on your face tells me this can't be good."

Her smile gentled and she slowly shook her head.

"But you're still here, so I can't have said anything too awful."

She stilled, an odd look on her face, then smiled again.

"Tell me, were we alone or were there witnesses?"

Her smile broadened.

"My brothers?" Oh no – now he could see her back molars! "Will any of it hold up in court?"

She threw her head back and laughed. *Really laughed.* An honest-to-goodness, out-loud, raspy guffaw!

"My God ... you... you... Cozette!"

She jumped up, eyes wide, her hands at her throat.

"Cozette!" He stood and grabbed her to him. "My sweet Cozette! This is wonderful!"

She stood in shock, not knowing what to do. This had never happened before – and it had happened without thinking, without trying! Without doing anything but what came naturally.

"Cozette," Duncan whispered as he hugged her. "Let's tell the others! I'll go get ..." He remembered the last dizzy spell. "... on second thought, could you fetch Sadie and Belle?"

She looked up at him, blinking rapidly.

Gently, he let her go. "They'll want to know – this is exciting news!"

Still shaking off her own surprise, she let her hands drop from her throat and slowly made her way across the kitchen to the door outside.

"Cozette!"

She turned back, her eyes moist.

Duncan smiled. He was staring at her with the most tender, understanding look he could muster. "Cozette ... I love you too."

Now the tears fell like the spring rain. He hadn't just heard that strangled laugh – he'd heard confession of love, even though it had been soundless. She'd said it with everything she had ... and he'd heard her wordless words! And he loved her too!

She ran across the kitchen and flung herself into his arms. She buried her face in his chest, her body heaving with sobs, and Duncan could feel her tears soak through the thin fabric of his shirt. But this time, he wasn't afraid of them – he knew they were born of happiness, and perhaps relief.

"My Cozette, my precious one, *mon bien précieux*," he told her, stroking her hair. "Of course I love you. And tomorrow night at the dance, I shall tell the entire world that I not only love you, but that you are to be my wife." He leaned down to kiss her gently, and with as much restraint as possible.

But Cozette wasn't interested in gentle restraint. Pulling him down, the future Duchess of Stantham gave the future Duke a kiss he would never forget!

# DAY 27

The morning of the dance dawned clear and bright. Sadie, Belle, Grandma and several women from the wagon train had decorated the barn beautifully. They'd worked hard the last few days, and would be working just as hard today preparing the food.

Two of the settlers helping out were a mother and daughter. The woman had lost her husband while traversing the mountain passes – not from sickness or injury, but a gunshot. Apparently the chap had a problem with stealing, and this time had tried to purloin another man's wife. Some ailments, even Mrs. MacDonald's healing abilities couldn't cure. Now the pair carried the shame of what their so-called loving husband and father had done. And one of the other families was holding a grudge, even though the women themselves were innocent.

Colin and Belle listened to Mr. Moss tell the whole story in the parlor after breakfast.

"I think it might do them well to settle here, rather than with the rest of the wagon train," Mr. Moss told Colin.

"I say, I can see why."

"They could stay with us until the hotel is built," offered Belle. "And I'm sure Mr. Van Cleet would employ them."

"I was hoping you'd say that. I think a fresh start in a small community would be better for them than going on to Oregon City."

"Sadie told me yesterday that Mrs. Van Zuyen is a school teacher," said Belle.

"In fact, she's more than that – she was a headmistress in a boarding school for young ladies in New York City. She worked with the daughters of many prominent families, and speaks several languages."

"How wonderful!" Belle exclaimed. "We'll be needing a schoolteacher soon! More and more families are settling here."

"Tell them they are more than welcome to stay on with us. I know Belle and Sadie could use the help around here and would appreciate having them," Colin said as he stood and offered Mr. Moss his hand.

"I'll let them know," said Mr. Moss as he gave Colin's hand a shake. "Now, if you'll excuse me, I think I'd better go help everyone get ready for a dance."

"We look forward to seeing you and the rest of your party tonight," Belle said before Colin walked him to the door and bid him goodbye.

"My, but our little town is growing! At this rate we'll have to elect a mayor!" Colin said as he re-entered the parlor.

"Oh? Are you going to put your name in?" asked Belle.

"Good heavens, no – I loathe politics. I'll stick to cattle ranching, if you don't mind." She smiled, kissed him, and, hand-in-hand, they went in search of the others to inform them of the news.

They found Duncan sulking at the kitchen table and picking at his breakfast. "I say, do try to eat more than three mouthfuls," Colin chided him. "You'll never get your strength back if you don't get something more in you than that."

Duncan sighed and slumped in his chair.

"What's the matter?" Belle asked. "You ate enough for three of us last night."

Duncan looked away and still said nothing.

"Ahhh, I think I know what it is," Colin said teasingly. "Cozette spent the night with the Van Cleets. She probably won't be here until much later. I say, we might as well have the Rev. King marry the two of you tonight! Everything's already here – the town, the food, the dance ..."

Belle looked at her husband, a wide smile on her face. "That's a great idea!"

Duncan suddenly sat up. "You ... you don't think it's too soon?"

"Yesterday, you told her you loved her, and said you were going to make an announcement to the rest of the town tonight," Belle reminded him. "Why not just marry her and have it over and done, with ... what, ten days to spare?"

"Eleven," Duncan said without thinking, then glared at Colin's Cheshire-cat grin.

Colin treated his look as mild and benign. "She's got you there, dear brother. You have to admit, you're cutting things rather close if you wait any longer. The timing couldn't be more perfect!"

"And *so* romantic!" Belle gushed. "Propose in front of the town, then marry her. Oh, this is wonderful – I must go tell Sadie–"

"Now, wait a minute!" Duncan protested. "What about Cozette? What if she doesn't like it being so public? And won't she want a special dress and flowers and, and all those things brides want with a wedding?"

Belle placed her hands on her hips. "Duncan Cooke! Trust me, I know what a woman likes. You can't get much more festive than Colin's and my wedding. In fact, if we use the dance, it *will* be bigger and better."

"Heaven knows we didn't have any dancing at our affair," Colin drawled. "Why was that anyway?"

"Henry Fig forgot his fiddle," Duncan commented.

"That's right. Thanks, Henry," Colin added sarcastically.

"Oh, will you two stop? This can't get any more perfect! And I'm sure Cozette will love it."

The brothers looked at Belle, then at each other. Colin shrugged. "I say do it. It really is the perfect setting – and, as Belle says, terribly romantic."

"Who am I to argue with romance? Someone best inform the Rev. King he's going to be performing a wedding ceremony tonight."

"I'll do it," Colin said. "Belle and I are heading to town to pick up some pies and a few other things Mrs. Dunnigan wanted to send out."

"Good," Duncan simply said, then sat up and began to poke at his food.

Colin sauntered over to the table. "Eat up, old boy," he whispered *sotto voce*. "If you're going to get married tonight, you'll need your strength for later."

Duncan resisted the temptation to stab his brother with a fork, and instead took a healthy bite of potatoes.

Just then, Harrison entered the kitchen. "Belle, Sadie needs you in the barn."

Belle nodded, kissed Colin and quickly left. Harrison watched her go then turned to his brothers. "We have something to discuss now that Duncan is feeling better."

"Oh, he's feeling more than just better!" Colin teased.

Harrison raised an eyebrow at the remark, then continued. "Whoever poisoned you is still at large. And seeing as how we haven't the aid of Scotland Yard out here, we're going to have to take our own precautions."

Colin sobered. "He's right, Duncan. And we can all guess who was behind it. No one's seen Thackary Holmes for days."

"What proof do we have?" Duncan asked.

"True. Not to mention, how did he do it?" Harrison added. "If he'd poisoned the well, we'd all have gotten sick. Same with the food."

"Indeed," Colin agreed. "So that leaves what? What would Duncan have access to that the rest of us wouldn't?"

Duncan suddenly sat up straight. "My canteen ..."

"Is in the barn!" Colin finished for him and ran out the kitchen's back door. Several moments later he hurried back in, Duncan's canteen in hand.

Duncan stood and took it from him. He shook it, heard the slosh of what water was left then unscrewed the top. He sniffed the contents a few times then shrugged. "Smells like plain water."

"And the inside of your canteen," Colin took it from him and poured a small amount into his hand. He set the canteen down, sniffed at the water in his palm, then gingerly tasted it.

Duncan cringed at the action but stayed put.

Colin held his hand out to Harrison, who also took a whiff. "It does smell odd."

"Tastes odd, too," Colin replied, then added, "and not just the way stagnant water does. There's something ... chemical about it."

Duncan picked up the canteen, examined it and found a small white fingerprint on the bottom. He displayed his find to his brothers. "It looks like he used a powder. But we can't be sure what it is."

"There's one thing we can be sure of," Harrison said. "Thackary Holmes will indubitably try again."

The night was warm, the moon was full, and a warm breeze blew across the prairie. Sadie, Belle, and the other ladies who'd helped with the preparations couldn't have been happier with how it had turned out. It was beautiful.

And, unbeknownst to most of them, the perfect setting for a wedding.

The women hurried to ready themselves. The Van Zuyen women were there, along with Grandma and Polly. Doc and Cyrus were out in the barn helping to set up tables for the food. They'd decided to hold the actual dance outside, in front of the barn, but have the food and tables inside. Wagons were already beginning to arrive.

"You have a lovely home," Mrs. Van Zuyen said. She had a beautiful accent, with a lilt that neither Belle nor Sadie could identify.

Finally Belle asked, "Where are you from, Mrs. Van Zuyen? I know Sadie meant to ask yesterday, but we were all so busy decorating."

"The Netherlands, my dear – Brabant, specifically, in the south of the country. My accent is not as pronounced as it once was – I have been too long in this country."

"And your daughter?" Sadie looked toward the pretty young blonde as she worked to put up her mother's golden brown hair.

"Madeline? My Maddie has no accent, at least not like mine. She was raised in this country. But one day I hope to take her to the Netherlands and show her where she comes from. There is much I wish her to learn about her country and its people."

The girl blushed as she put the final pins into her mother's hair. "There, Mama. How do you like it?"

"You are a true treasure, my dear. Now let us help our hostesses. They have enough to do without worrying about their hair."

Sadie and Belle happily sat just as Polly and Cozette entered Sadie's bedroom. "Land sakes, everything looks wonderful!" Polly exclaimed. "You girls have outdone yourselves!"

"We couldn't have done it without everyone's help," said Sadie. "Now let's finish getting ready. Cozette, I have your dress; it's hanging up behind the door."

Cozette nodded and went to the door. She was nervous about tonight, all the people and activity. But as she spied what was hanging on the back of the door, all her fears vanished ... along with her ability to breathe.

She found herself looking at a wedding dress.

She spun to look at the others, confusion written on her face as large as a newspaper headline.

"It was my mother's," Belle explained. "I thought you should wear it tonight. It's too short for me, but it would fit you perfectly."

"It *is* lovely," Mrs. Van Zuyen commented. "Are you getting married?"

Cozette immediately blushed.

Belle jumped in quickly. "Cozette needed a new dress for the dance, and I thought this would suit her. It'll look beautiful."

Cozette touched the pretty fabric. It was white with delicate pink flower petals sewn into the lace that covered much of the dress. It was the most beautiful thing she had ever seen.

"But is it proper to wear such a dress at a dance?" Mrs. Van Zuyen asked.

"Out here it doesn't really matter," Sadie told her. "Life on the frontier means making do with whatever we have. It's pretty, that's what counts."

"I see. I suppose we shall have to get used to the ways of country life," Mrs. Van Zuyen told her daughter.

"This isn't New York City, Mama."

"In that, my dear, you are correct. But I must admit, Clear Creek does have its charm." She smiled at the younger women. "Now, let's see about getting you ladies ready for a dance."

Cozette stood at the back door of the kitchen, unable to bring herself to leave the safe confines of the house. She'd thought she might faint when she saw herself in the mirror in Sadie's room. She was so beautiful she didn't even recognize the woman she saw – it felt like she was looking at someone else's reflection.

Wearing the dress made everything seem surreal, and the evening air felt charged. She fought to stay calm, wondering if she were in some sort of fairytale.

"You look like a princess," Mrs. Van Cleet told her. "I'm so proud of you. I know perhaps this sounds silly, but I've come to think of you like a daughter."

Cozette smiled, and impulsively kissed her on the cheek.

Mrs. Van Cleet smiled back, and took Cozette's arm. "Let's go, then. I'll hang onto you for support. I know this is a lot for you, but these people are all very nice. You'll be fine."

Cozette took a deep breath, and with Mrs. Van Cleet she stepped onto the back porch, and left the safety of the house behind. But she was still worried about the fairy-tale atmosphere. She'd read fairy tales, after all – and in addition to beautiful princesses and handsome princes, they also contained witches, and trolls, and dragons …

Duncan stood near the barn's wide entrance, sipping slowly from the glass of punch in his hand. Andel Berg, the new town blacksmith, stood next to him and spoke in low tones with the Scotsman Mr. MacDonald. The two giants were getting along famously.

Duncan began to wonder what they were talking about when he saw her – and dropped his glass. A chill went up his spine, and he fought for control.

Polly was escorting Cozette across the barnyard, past the dance floor and straight toward him.

"Good God," he whispered to himself. Good God indeed, for the Lord could not have made a better choice of wife for him. If he'd thought she was beautiful before, nothing compared to how she looked tonight. *Her wedding night ...*

"Laddie? I think ye dropped something." Mr. MacDonald picked up Duncan's glass and handed it to him. Thankfully it hadn't broken – it was from Honoria Cooke's favorite punch bowl set.

"Thank you," Duncan said without taking his eyes off Cozette – or taking the glass.

Mr. MacDonald looked from Duncan to Cozette and back again. "Dinna mention it." He took Duncan's left hand, put the glass into it, then snorted in amusement and slapped Mr. Berg on the back. Deciding they weren't needed there, the two big men headed into the barn and toward the food.

Cozette arrived in front of Duncan and attempted a curtsy. Polly silently slipped into the barn after the others.

Duncan took her hand in his. "You take my breath away," he whispered down at Cozette.

Cozette blushed, smiled and made a point of looking him up and down. He had on a dark suit, white shirt and black tie. His hair was combed back, he was clean-shaven, and he smelled heavenly. She fought the urge to bury her face in his chest and just inhale. *You don't look so bad yourself.*

They stood staring into each other's eyes for a minute before Duncan found his voice – or, rather, remembered to use hers. He held up the glass. *Would you like some punch?*

Cozette, still smiling, gave a slow nod, and he led her into the barn.

The women had decorated the barn in prairie flowers, augmented by linens and lace from their homes. It was beautiful and quaint. Mrs. Dunnigan was there and obviously in charge of all the food, waving her ladle as she fussed and ordered people into a single line.

Cozette squeezed Duncan's hand as her other hand came to her mouth to stifle her laughter. No noise – this time – but she was indeed laughing as she watched Mrs. Dunnigan give Mr. MacDonald and Mr. Berg a tongue-lashing for who knows what offense. From a distance, it looked like the two giants were restraining their mirth as well, despite being chastened like a couple of misbehaving schoolboys. But they still knew better than to defy her.

Duncan finally released a single snicker, kissed Cozette on the cheek, then led her to the punch bowl.

Just as they got some punch, the music started outside. A cheer went up as people began to head for the dance area.

"Would you do me the honor, Mademoiselle Duprie?" Duncan asked, setting down his glass and offering her his arm.

She stared at his arm in dread, and turned away.

"Here now, what's this?" he asked and turned her back around to face him.

Cozette looked from Duncan to the people gathering in the dance area. She shook her head, holding up her hands helplessly. *Oh, Duncan! I cannot dance!*

He tenderly cupped her face with his hand. "You needn't worry, sweetheart. For one, you've never seen any of *these* people dance."

Cozette cocked her head to one side at the remark. She looked past him, out the door of the barn to the dance area, and her eyes widened. He was right; she shouldn't be worried that she had never danced. From the looks of it, the townspeople of Clear Creek hadn't a clue how to dance either.

Not that it was stopping them. More men were participating than women, not just because men were a majority in Clear Creek, but because many of the women there were busy with the food. Wilfred Dunnigan was doing some sort of jig with Mr. Mulligan. The sheriff and Cyrus Van Cleet were trying to approximate a square dance with a couple of settler's children, whose idea of dancing was simply jumping about to the music. Mr. Moss was over to the side, swaying back and forth by himself. Sadie and Harrison were moving in a more civilized manner, as were Belle and Colin (well, Belle, at least). But otherwise there was no rhyme or reason to any of it. It all looked a bit ridiculous, but everyone was enjoying it.

Cozette physically relaxed at the chaotic sight. It didn't matter. All that did was the man leading her out to the dance area. A man she could spend the rest of her life with.

The evening happily wore on: the music, the incredible food (albeit at the cost of facing Mrs. Dunnigan), the townsfolk, and Duncan. Nothing could have been more wonderful. Nothing could have made Cozette any happier.

And just when she thought it couldn't get any better, it did.

Duncan picked her up and placed her in the back of the buckboard the fiddlers were using as a bandstand. They smiled at him and stopped their playing. "Can I have everyone's attention?" he called to the crowd.

The people stopped dancing and chattering and faced the buckboard.

"Quiet, please," Duncan called. "I want the lady to be able to hear what I have to say."

Smiles broke out, and some people elbowed others in the ribs. Cozette gathered that they knew what was coming. Perhaps she was the only one that didn't.

"Some of you already know what I have to say," Duncan announced.

"Tarnation, Duncan, I think we've *all* figured it out!" Sheriff Hughes yelled, and everyone laughed.

"Yes, but I'd appreciate it if you would keep it to yourselves until I tell the young lady standing before me."

"Stop the fancy talk and get on with it, then!" declared Wilfred. More laughter.

Duncan smiled, took Cozette's hands in his own, and went down on one knee.

Cozette gasped and quickly glanced around. All eyes were on her. A lump in her throat, she looked down at Duncan. *Could it be ...?*

"Cozette Duprie," he began. "You'd make me the happiest man in the territory if you'll say yes."

"Yes to what?" Doc Waller called. "You haven't asked her anything!" The townspeople roared.

"Shut up, all of you, and let him ask the question!" Mrs. Dunnigan snapped, waving her ladle at the crowd.

Immediate silence.

Duncan nodded in gratitude to Mrs. Dunnigan, then looked up at Cozette. "My precious one. My beautiful Cozette. Will you marry me?"

Cozette's knees gave way, and she collapsed into his arms. She'd imagined he would ask her to marry him in private, not in front of the entire town! But no matter how he'd done it, the answer would have been the same.

She pulled his head to hers and kissed him soundly, to the cheers of the crowd.

Duncan broke the kiss. "I'll take that as a yes?"

She smiled, nodded and kissed him again.

Another cheer. Cozette thought she heard someone yell, "Call for the preacher!"

"You two are supposed to wait to do that!" Grandma yelled. "Somebody find the Rev. King quick like before the evening plumb turns indecent!"

"I, er, believe he's in the privy!" Harrison called from the back of the crowd.

"Then you'd best retrieve him, lad!" called a voice, probably Patrick Mulligan's.

"You heard the man! Let's go get him!" Colin yelled.

Many of the men laughed and gathered around Colin, who quickly found himself the leader of the 'retrieval party.' Apparently, from the location of the privy, poor Josiah King wouldn't have heard all that was going on. The men planned to sneak up to it and surprise the new preacher.

Cozette slapped her hands on her thighs in amusement as every man quietly made their way into the darkness and the privy which lay beyond the lights of the dance area. She saw Colin signal to Henry Fig, who began playing his fiddle to make it sound like the party was continuing.

Some of the women followed, at least to the edge of the lantern light, and did their best to stifle their giggles. Cozette wanted to go with them, but Duncan had gone with the rest of the men. She didn't want to try to get off the back of the wagon without help and risk ripping her beautiful dress. But maybe there was an easier way to climb down. She turned around to look ...

... and, not for the first time in her life, wished she could scream. She opened her mouth, but nothing came out.

"Which one of you idiots brought this old crow along?" Jeb demanded as his men deposited their loads into the back of a wagon. The bed creaked loudly when a bound and gagged Irene Dunnigan was hefted into it next to the other women.

"But Jeb! She can cook like nobody's business!" one of the men insisted.

"Oh, for the love of ... you stupid mule, don't you realize she'll only slow us down?" Jeb hissed.

"We best make a run fer it before they discover they're missin'! Won't take 'em long to figger out!" Johnny pleaded.

Jeb sighed. "You're right. Let's go. How many we got?"

"The two ya wanted, plus two extra and the fat one."

A muffled grunt came from Mrs. Dunnigan.

"We'll have to share then," Jeb commented.

"I wanna know when I'm gonna get paid," one man asked.

"When we get 'em to the hideout. Then ya can take whichever one you want," Jeb told him.

"I didn't mean that! When you asked me and my cousin to help, you didn't say we was only takin' women. You said there'd be *gold* involved."

"And there will be," Jeb answered, sounding offended.

"No one broke into the house and got any," the outlaw's cousin argued. "We didn't rob no townsfolk." He spat on the ground. "Shoot, if all I wanted was a woman, I coulda bought one in Oregon City or Portland ..."

Jeb lit a match. "If you Randall boys had the good sense God gave a gopher, you'd know we got something worth more than a few coin purses off them townsfolk." He held the match up high enough to display their evening's catch: Cozette, Sadie and the two Van Zuyen women as well as Mrs. Dunnigan. "We got some of them Cooke women – one of which is the daughter of none other than Horatio Jones!"

"The cattle baron?" one man exclaimed.

"Yep." Jeb blew out the match. "And she'll bring more money'n any of us have ever seen. Now let's go."

"But Jeb, what about finishing the job for that Holmes fella?" Johnny asked.

"Forget about him. I met someone who convinced me this is better. Much better."

As the townsfolk of Clear Creek were busy poking fun at the preacher in the privy, the outlaw gang rode off with five of their women.

Cozette and Sadie, both tied up like the others, looked at each other in terror and had the same thought. Mrs. Dunnigan's trusty hatchet would sure come in mighty handy right about now.

"But where could she have gone?" Duncan asked as he searched around the buckboard for Cozette.

"Well, we know she didn't go to use the privy!" Colin laughed. Several other men around them laughed as well, including a rather disheveled-looking Rev. King.

"I say, has anyone seen Sadie?" Harrison asked. I can't find her."

"While you men were fetching the Reverend, she went into the barn with Aunt Irene to help get the cake ready," Belle told him.

"Very good, then. I'll see if Cozette is with her. In the meantime, dear brother, you had better run upstairs and get Mother's ring!"

Duncan slapped his hand against his forehead. "Gads! I forgot about the ring!" He took off toward the house at a fast walk. He wasn't quite strong enough to make it a run.

"I'd better go help with the cake and make more punch. We'll serve it right after the I-do's and the kiss," Belle said to Grandma, who stood nearby.

But she hadn't taken three steps when Harrison came walking toward her. "No one's in the barn. I can't understand why they aren't, though ..."

Belle looked around. "They must be in the kitchen, then. I'll go fetch them." She turned and started for the house.

By the time she entered the kitchen Duncan was just coming down the stairs. "I found it! I can't believe I forgot!" he told her as he made for the back door.

Belle laughed, then suddenly realized they were the only ones there. "Duncan, where's Sadie? Was she upstairs?"

"No. Why would she ...?" Duncan stopped dead in his tracks. He looked out into the barnyard at the people, the decorations, the barn itself. A cold dread suddenly gripped him, and he knew. Something terrible had happened ... and once again, he hadn't been there to stop it.

He burst out the back door and all but flew off the porch. "Harrison!"

Harrison came running, Colin close behind. Belle ran out the back door as Duncan again stopped and stilled himself, as if listening.

"She's gone," he whispered. "Something's happened to her." He looked Harrison right in the eye. "Where's Sadie?"

"I say, Duncan, you're beginning to scare me," Harrison told him.

Colin's eyes widened. He turned to the townsfolk and ran into their midst. He spoke in low tones to several men, who quickly began a search.

"Sarah!" Doc yelled as he looked for his wife. Other men began to call their wives to them, and soon all the women had been rounded up. All the ones that were still there, at least.

"Good Lord," Harrison breathed. "Where are they?"

"Who else is missing?" Duncan asked as Sheriff Hughes approached.

"Besides Miss Duprie and your sister-in-law, two of the settler women have disappeared," the sheriff reported.

"And my Irene," Wilfred Dunnigan added. He looked like he was about to faint.

"No!" Belle wailed, her eyes wide.

Sheriff Hughes didn't look too healthy either. "Well, don't this beat all," he said, scratching the back of his head. "Only one thing to do, though – let's go find 'em!"

"But Sheriff!" Belle began. "We don't even know where to look!"

Duncan's face had clenched like a fist. "I have a pretty good idea," he said, and stormed toward the barn where Thackary Holmes had just emerged, a glass of punch in his hand. He'd just managed to take a sip before Duncan's hand swung around and slapped him in the head. The blow knocked the smaller man to the dusty ground and sent the glass flying.

Harrison caught it before it could hit the dirt and shatter. The two brothers glanced at each other in triumph.

"You bloody well better have a good explanation for that, *Mister* Cooke!" Thackary spat.

Duncan bared his teeth. "The name is *Sayer*, and I bloody well *did* have a good reason for that. Where are they?"

"What are you talking about? Where is ... who?" Thackary asked as he picked himself up from the ground, scuttling back a few feet as he did.

Mr. Ashford suddenly appeared. "You struck him without proper cause. That's considered assault, you know."

"I didn't see anything," Sheriff Hughes, who'd caught up to the scene, told him. He crossed his arms over his chest.

"Shut up and stay out of this," Duncan told Ashford, then took a step forward and grabbed Holmes by his coat. "I said, where are they?"

"And *I said*, what are you talking about?"

"You good-for-nothing bloody bast–"

"Duncan! Harrison! Come quickly!" Colin yelled from inside the barn.

Duncan seethed, his eyes narrowed to slits. He turned to the nearest man, Mr. MacDonald. "Make sure he doesn't leave."

Dallan eyed Holmes as if amused. "Dinna worry, laddie. This *Sassanach* devil isna going anywhere." Much to Holmes' horror, the Scot grabbed him by the back of his collar and picked him up off the ground with one arm. Mr. Berg, standing behind him, smiled as he watched the dandy's feet helplessly dangle above the ground.

Duncan stormed into the barn followed by Harrison. Within moments, they both came back out and went straight to Thackary Holmes. "You worthless scum!" Duncan declared. "You're behind this!"

"Behind ... what?" Thackary choked out as he began to kick his feet in mid-air.

"This!" Duncan said and shoved a piece of paper in front of him.

"What does it ... say?" Thackary gasped.

"Read it!"

"I can't ... with this brute ... choking me!"

Duncan made a face and nodded to Mr. MacDonald. The big Scot shrugged and dropped Holmes, who landed on the ground in a coughing heap, then took the note from Duncan and read it aloud. "*Bring 100 pieces of gold to the old mining cave on the ridge in three days or we kill your women. Come by yourselves, or they're just as dead.*" He lowered the note and took in the shocked faces surrounding him. "Weel, now, that's a problem."

"Indeed," Duncan snarled.

"Kidnapped? I can't believe it!" Harrison said. "How? We had our backs turned for only moments. How could they have planned such a thing?"

"Ask *him*!" Duncan snapped and kicked at Holmes' leg.

"I hate to be the bearer of bad news, lads," Mr. MacDonald declared. "But I dinna think this one had anything to do wi' it."

"What? Of course he did!" Colin put in as he came out of the barn.

"I arrived just before you ruffians went to yank your preacher from the privy!" Holmes argued. "I got dragged along with the rest of you!"

"He's right. I saw him there," Doc Waller said, just now catching up to the group.

"But if he had nothing to do with it, what happened to our women?" Harrison asked as he seethed.

"Weel, lads, I suggest ye get yerselves up to that ridge and find out."

"Sheriff?" Harrison called.

The sheriff had been poking around by the barn. "Someone took them, all right. There's signs of a struggle near the other barn door."

"Harrison, Colin," Duncan began on a low hiss. "Saddle up. Let's go get our women back."

The townsfolk had never seen even one of the Cooke brothers truly angry. But that night they witnessed all three brothers not only angry, but ready to kill.

They saddled their horses. They checked their guns. They mounted up as one.

If Mrs. Dunnigan had been there, she might have swooned. Fanny Fig filled in, though.

The Cookes turned their horses and galloped away. But behind them others were getting ready to follow, including the two giants Mr. MacDonald and Mr. Berg, neither of whom looked any happier about the stolen women.

"C'mon, boys!" Sheriff Hughes called to his newly-formed posse. "Let's go hunt us some scum!"

Eleven men rode out after the sheriff, including Mr. MacDonald and Mr. Berg. Colin and Harrison were several lengths ahead of them, and in the lead was a very angry Duncan.

None of them noticed the three riders who brought up the rear. Mr. Moss was one, along with an elderly gentleman from the wagon train, a fidgety fellow named Angus. And behind them, Thackary Holmes.

Twenty men rode out that night. Jeb and his outlaw gang had no idea what was coming. But the men in hot pursuit of the outlaws had no idea what was waiting.

Cozette was sick to her stomach, and knew that if they didn't stop soon, she'd make a horrible mess. At least they hadn't gagged her – probably because it didn't take them long to figure out she was mute. But the other women hadn't fared as well; they had not only been individually gagged and bound, but lashed to one another by the ankles. Why she herself had been set apart she had no idea.

Looking at her companions, she realized Mrs. Dunnigan's stomach probably didn't feel any better than hers. The woman's face had a definite green tinge to it, which was only growing worse the longer she was jostled about.

The outlaws stopped at one point to steal horses from some poor, unsuspecting farmer, probably one who was at the Triple-C for the dance. A couple of hours later, they switched out the horses, then continued on. They didn't travel in a direct line to the hills, but cut diagonally across the prairie as if purposely taking the long way around. Even if they were heading for the hills, they were up against some mighty slow going – they wouldn't be able to get far with the wagon, and would be out of luck unless they planned on doubling up on the horses to transport their prisoners.

But eventually it became apparent they weren't going into the hills – at least not directly. Instead, they traveled along the tree line bordering the prairie until they came to where the incline became so steep it would be nearly impossible to climb, even on foot. A small creek flowed along the hillside's base, and they followed it upstream for a while before they finally came to a stop.

"Get 'em out and get 'em up!" Jeb ordered.

The men dismounted. One hopped into the wagon, grabbed Cozette and tossed her down to another man, then turned, cut Sadie loose from the other women and sent her down as well.

"Take the wagon inside and put the fat one to work," Jeb ordered. "I'm hungry."

Cozette and Sadie watched the wagon go around some trees, past a stand of brush and disappear.

Jeb leered at the two women. "You gals're gonna spend the night topside. Get 'em out of here, Johnny, an' stay with 'em." He grabbed the younger man by the shirt and pulled him closer. "Make sure those Randall boys don't touch 'em. 'Specially the quiet one – our new benefactor has plans for her."

"Er ... Jeb? What's a bennyfactor?"

"Someone who's gonna see to it we get mighty rich off these here gals."

Johnny scratched his head. "Well, if you say so." He motioned for two of the men to follow him. They carried the women in the same direction as the wagon, right into the brush.

Two more men rode up behind them. They dismounted, then proceeded to shove some of the bushes aside. Cozette heard Sadie moan through her gag. The bushes concealed a cave entrance, one big enough to get a wagon through.

Their captors carried them into the cave. Torches had just been lit and a fire was being built. Cozette caught the looks of fear of the remaining women as the men began to haul them out of the wagon.

Johnny grabbed a torch, and the scene quickly disappeared as Cozette and Sadie were carried into another cave. But this one was so dark and so large that the flame didn't give enough light to see anything but a big rock and part of the cave wall they were standing next to. Cozette and Sadie looked at one another. Just how big was this place?

Johnny led them along the rock wall. If Cozette was right, they were moving on a decline as they traversed deeper.

After about five minutes they reached what she hoped was the bottom. Johnny stuck his torch into a crevice in the rock wall, disappeared into the darkness a moment, then reappeared with more torches. He lit two and gave them to the men who had just set Cozette and Sadie on their feet. Bound as they were, they both collapsed onto the cold ground.

"Shoot, yew guys!" Johnny chided the other men. "C'mon, load 'em and head up," He turned and walked away, the light of his torch still only enough to light their immediate surroundings.

The enormous cavern stayed cold, mostly dark and deathly silent as the men picked Sadie and Cozette up, threw them over their shoulders and carried them deeper into the rock. When they finally stopped, Johnny fiddled with something ahead of them. It squeaked as if a big heavy bucket was being drawn up from a well. Then there was a loud *bang*, as something large hit the cave floor. The men carried the women to the sound, stepped onto something and set the women down, more carefully this time.

Cozette and Sadie were able to see what had made the noise. It was a small wooden platform, about four feet by six, that reminded Cozette of a raft she and her father had once built. Ropes were attached to all four corners by heavy metal rings which, in turn, were secured to large bolts that had been screwed into logs that were part of the wooden frame. Each line of rope was then attached to a large hook and pulley and more rope, which disappeared into the darkness far above them.

The women instinctively began to struggle. Who wouldn't, knowing they were about to be yanked high above the cave floor through pitch-blackness?

"Stop it!" Johnny warned. "You might tip us and get us all killed!" They stopped, their breathing panicked as the men positioned themselves to balance the platform. "Now I'd be real still-like if I were you, 'cause trust me, if'n you fall from this here lift, your lives won't be worth a plugged nickel."

Cozette and Sadie both froze as one of the men pulled on a rope the women hadn't noticed. A bell rang somewhere high above. Within seconds there was the sound of pulleys, and the platform began to rise. They closed their eyes in response as they traveled upward into the pitch darkness.

Cozette had dealt with wolf packs, had hunted bears and moose, had dodged rockslides and escaped bar fights. But she'd never been more frightened in her life than she was at that moment.

# DAY 28

The posse slowed as they reached the tree line. "Good Lord, Duncan!" Harrison said. "The horses need a rest, or they'll never make the climb."

His brother spun Romeo around to face him. "We stop for only a moment, do you hear?"

"Duncan, you need to rest too. You're not yourself with this nasty business, and you're still weak. You won't be able to rescue Sadie and Cozette and the other women if you're half dead!"

"Harrison's right," Colin added. "Slow down, man. They've not harmed them yet. There's been no time."

Duncan took a deep breath. "Sure of that, are you?"

"Look," Harrison began. "If anyone knows about this, it's me. I remember what it took to rescue Sadie from the same sort of business. It's my wife up there too, you know. And Colin's ... um ..." He and Duncan both looked at Colin.

Colin shrugged. "Well ... Mrs. Dunnigan *is* part of the family now, so to speak."

Duncan smiled and calmed somewhat. "You're right, of course. I apologize – my rash actions could have put us all in danger. Thank you for reminding me of my duty to you both."

Sheriff Hughes rode up. "What's the plan, gentlemen?"

"Now that we're here," said Duncan. "I suppose it's time to make one."

"How far up to the cave in question?" asked Colin.

"A few miles. Slow going, as I recall," said the sheriff.

"Ah, can I say something?" one of the nearby riders asked.

All heads turned in Mr. Moss' direction as he walked his horse forward. "What is it, son?" Sheriff Hughes asked.

Mr. Moss pulled out a pocket watch. "It seems to me that at the rate we've been traveling, given the time involved with any head start the kidnappers might have and the extra weight from the women their carrying ... well, shouldn't we have overtaken them a long time ago?"

Everyone stared at him a moment before his words sunk in.

"Er ... just a thought," Mr. Moss added.

"By Jove," Duncan began. "The man's right. As hard as we've been driving the horses we should have found them already!"

"Good Lord, have we been going in the wrong direction?" Harrison cried.

"This is my fault," Duncan said as he seethed. "Who knows where they are by now?"

Mr. MacDonald rode up to join them. "What if they cut across the prairie the opposite way? Seems to me 'tis what I would do if I wanted to send someone on a wild goose chase. Would buy me the time I needed to get away ye ken."

The Cookes and the sheriff looked at one another. "Boys, we've been hoodwinked!" Sheriff Hughes exclaimed. "Those fellas were counting on us to hightail it after 'em!"

"And in the wrong direction," Colin said.

"But the note said to bring the gold to the old mining cave on the ridge in three days," Harrison stated. "The only mining cave I know of is up this hill."

"Is there more than one cave?" Mr. Moss asked.

"This is the one everyone knows about, especially after what happened to Sadie," Harrison said. Then it hit him. "It's the cave we'd think of first ..."

"But there are others?" Mr. MacDonald asked.

"Yes," Sheriff Hughes admitted. "But no one goes there, on account of those mines are extremely dangerous. Folks have been known to go up there and never come back."

"Then I'd say it's a good bet," said Mr. Moss.

"If we head due east, we can reach them in a couple of hours," said Duncan.

"Maybe we should send a few men up this part of the ridge to check things out, just in case," Sheriff Hughes suggested.

"Good idea," agreed Duncan. "If they don't find anything, have them return to the Triple-C."

"Will do," Sheriff Hughes said, then called his men. Four went up the ridge to double-check, while the rest headed east. With any luck, they'd get there in time.

The men pushed on. What hope did the women have until they got there? Even though the men knew the outlaws wouldn't kill the women right away, who knew what other horrors they might suffer in the meantime?

It didn't bear thinking about. So they didn't.

"And another thing! You good-for-nothing, low-down, dirty, stinking, scumbag, cotton-eating imbeciles don't have any *salt!* If you want me to cook for ya, you'd better come up with some decent supplies!"

The outlaw gang stood in open-mouthed shock as Irene Dunnigan continued her tirade. A cookpot hung over an open fire, and one of them had been foolish enough to give her a ladle to stir the pot. That had been all the opening she'd needed.

"I can't make a decent pot roast without *salt*! What's the matter with you? Have you all got straw for brains? The very idea!"

Jeb came into the cave. "Will *somebody* shut her up?!"

"I'd rather die than make a pot roast without the proper seasonings!" She waved the ladle around threateningly.

Jeb pulled out his gun. "I'd be happy to arrange that."

"NO!" several of his men cried.

"What the Sam blazes do you mean, *no*? That harpy hasn't shut up since we took the gag off!"

"Jeb, you can't kill her!" one of the men pleaded.

Jeb cocked the gun and pointed it at the man's head. "Wanna tell me again what I can't do?"

"Well ... at least not until after dinner," he whimpered.

"No pot roast is worth all this," Jeb growled and stomped over to the Van Zuyen women. He grabbed Madeline and yanked her to her feet. Trussed up as she was, she had to rely on him to hold her up. Jeb held the gun to her temple. "Listen here, you cantankerous windbag! Make that pot roast and be quiet about it or I'm gonna shoot the little lady here!"

"Unhand her this instant!" Mrs. Dunnigan ordered. "And who are you calling me a *windbag*, you ... you possum-breathed THIEF!"

Jeb looked at his men, then back at Mrs. Dunnigan, he even looked at Madeline, who could only shrug. Finally he snarled at the ladle-wielding banshee, raised his gun, and aimed it at her. "Forget this – I'm gonna shoot her."

"Not until after dinner!" several men cried, and quickly formed a human shield to protect their new-found treasure.

Jeb's mouth fell open. "You mean, you're siding with that crotchety old crow?"

"Nossir, Jeb. We'd never side with no woman," one of his men assured him.

"Heck no!" another quickly added. "We're sidin' with the pot roast!"

"Oh, for the love of ..." He shoved Madeline to the ground. "Just cook, lady. Don't talk, just cook. Or I swear, I'm gonna shoot you the second that roast is done!"

Mrs. Dunnigan scrunched up her face, narrowed her eyes, and glared at him. "Where's the *salt?*"

"Somebody get this woman some salt," Jeb barely managed to growl, then left to go check on his other prisoners.

Cozette struggled against her bonds when the men weren't looking, but it was no use. Via the wooden platform, she and Sadie had been taken hundreds of feet up into another cave, through a hole in the upper cave's floor that was about eight feet across. Anyone who stumbled upon the upper cave and didn't know the hole was there would fall to their death – and over the years some probably had.

This cave obviously had an outside entrance, and from what Cozette gathered by watching and listening to the men going in and out, its entrance was also hidden by a lot of brush and branches. They must be at the top of the ridge. It also looked like there was another hole above them, with the rope and pulley system anchored outside the cave over their heads. Again, should someone be poking about above and not see the hole, they'd fall through the smaller hole into the upper cave and on through the larger hole to the enormous cavern below. She shuddered at the thought.

She noticed Sadie studying their surroundings and looking at the pulley system above their heads, probably coming to the same conclusions. She, too, shuddered and tried not to make any unnecessary movements.

Everyone had remained on the wooden platform, waiting. For what, the women didn't know.

"You have what I want?" they heard a distinctly English voice ask from the other side of a rock formation.

Cozette and Sadie both looked at one another. *Thackary Holmes?*

"They're in there, tied up. Whaddaya want me to do with 'em?" Jeb answered from somewhere else.

"Lay a trap. They're the bait. But I will take the one when I leave. I don't care what you do with the others. Just be sure you kill the males."

"You got it. I'll take my money now, if'n you don't mind."

The women listened to the distinct sound of heavy coins being counted out, then dropped in a bag. "Just be sure you kill all three of them. I'll not risk any of their line carrying on. I want the Sayer heirs wiped out."

"What about the one gal in there? Been married to one of them boys a while now – good chance she's carrying a brat at this point."

"Hmmm ... smart man. You could be right. Do away with her as well."

Sadie's eyes suddenly widened over her gag. She shook her head as tears formed in her eyes.

"Sure thing, but not 'til we've had a little fun first, if'n you know what I mean. Besides, she owes me a good time."

Cozette looked around and risked struggling against her bonds again. They had to get out of there! But how?

Duncan and his brothers signaled a halt. They'd ridden along the tree line for the last two hours and come to the edge of the ridge. At this point, the ridge itself became too steep to ride. They'd have to go up on foot.

"Where do you think they are? There's really no place for them to hide beyond this point," Sheriff Hughes lamented.

"Fetch me Duprie," Duncan told the nearest man.

Within moments, Anton was there. He dismounted and looked for any signs of the outlaws. "They were here. And they have a wagon. Must be at least six other horses, maybe more. I see tracks over there, as well. You were right, they came from a different direction."

"But where are they?" Harrison asked. "You don't think they climbed up to the top of the ridge from here with the women, do you?"

Anton looked up the ridge. "No. Too rough, too dark to take a woman up that."

"They especially wouldn't be able to drag Mrs. Dunnigan up there," Colin added.

"Precisely," Harrison agreed. "Which brings us back to my original question. Where *are* they?"

"Wait a minute. You smell that?" Sheriff Hughes asked.

"Smell what?" Duncan began, and then he picked it up. "A campfire?"

Anton Duprie sniffed the air. "Not only a campfire! I smell meat cooking!"

The men looked about and lowered their voices. "We'll split up and find them - they've got to be around here somewhere!" Sheriff Hughes said.

"Good heavens!" Colin suddenly blurted. "I know that smell!"

All eyes turned to him.

He shook his head and chuckled. "It's Aunt Irene's pot roast."

Sheriff Hughes smiled, then signaled the rest of the men to gather around. Once he had everyone's attention he gave the order. "Okay, men, split up. Find that pot roast!"

Duncan, Colin and Harrison dismounted and slipped in among the trees. The smell of Mrs. Dunnigan's legendary pot roast was getting stronger by the minute. They had to be practically right on top of the outlaws. But there was still no sign of them.

Mr. MacDonald and Mr. Berg crept up to join them. "Any luck, lads?" the Scot asked in a low voice.

"None. And you?" Duncan whispered.

"Nothing. But if my sense o' smell is correct, I'd say the source is coming from over there."

The men looked in the likely direction. There was nothing but a wall of brush against an extremely steep incline.

"Are you all thinking what I'm thinking?" Colin asked.

"I'd say we bloody well are, brother," Duncan told him.

Harrison looked at the ground. "And I say we've been so busy trying to sniff out a roast, we didn't look for the obvious." He pointed to the grass. Even in the moonlight, they could see the wagon tracks that led straight into the brush.

"Weel then, laddies, that solves the problem o' where they are. Now what?"

Duncan was about to comment when a woman's scream rent the air. But it hadn't come from the wall of brush – it came from somewhere above them.

Harrison stiffened. "That sounded like Sadie!"

"Bugger!" Duncan cursed. "They do have them up there!"

Another scream, only this one *did* come from behind the wall of brush.

"They've split them up!" Colin said.

"We'll handle things down here; you lads get up there," Mr. MacDonald told the three brothers. "Hurry!"

And they did.

"That's right, sweetheart, how 'bout another one?" Jeb said. "Make it a good scream this time so they can hear ya. Make it sound like you're in a bad way, and I'm sure they'll hurry along."

A bound Sadie sat precariously on a simple wooden bench, which was suspended over the huge gaping hole like a swing. And even though there was a makeshift backing of rope behind her, one wrong move, one slip, and she would fall to her death. Tears rolled down her cheeks as she looked, horrified, at Jeb and several of his men.

They seemed to be enjoying her discomfort immensely. One of them took a pole and pushed on the bench. She screamed in horror at the movement, and the men laughed.

Cozette lay bound beside a crate behind them, helplessly watching the men taunt her friend. When they'd reached the upper cave, men had come and placed planks across the hole so they could get everyone off the platform. They then slackened the ropes, pushed the platform away from the hole and leaned it against the cave wall. They'd lowered the bench, removed Sadie's gag and placed her on it. As soon as they had her there, they'd pulled the planks out from beneath her feet to expose the neverending blackness below, and she'd started screaming.

Cozette turned her face away. How horrible, how helpless she felt! If she could just ... get ... free!

"Now, you gals make yourselves comfortable," Jeb teased. "We'll be back with some folks just dyin' to keep you company." The men laughed and left the cave.

Sadie whimpered a moment, then looked to Cozette for comfort. "What are we going to do?" she whispered.

Cozette shook her head as she fought against tears. *I don't know!*

Both women froze as someone entered the cave and hurried around the rock formation into view. "Good God! What's going on here? Are you all right?"

Thackary Holmes was the last person either of them had expected! Sadie thought she was seeing things, and blinked a few times to clear her vision. But no, there he stood, looking as if he couldn't decide which one of them to rescue first. "Mr. Holmes! Help us, please! Get me off this thing!"

"Oh, dear me! You poor girl! Right away!" He turned to Cozette. "Oh! And look at you, Miss Duprie! Let me help you!" He got her up on her feet which were still bound, and scooped her up into his arms. "Don't worry, I'll take you to safety!"

"Mr. Holmes!" Sadie cried. "What are you doing? *Help* me!"

"One thing at a time, Mrs. Cooke! I must get Miss Duprie out of harm's way!" he said as he quickly left the cave.

"Come back here!" Sadie called after him.

But he never did.

"That's it, toss your guns over there or I shoot the lady." a voice hissed from behind. A woman's helpless whimper followed.

Duncan, Colin, and Harrison stood frozen in place a few seconds before they complied. They'd climbed up the ridge as fast as they could, and just as they reached the top Duncan nearly collapsed. They let him rest a moment then started for what looked like a triangle of logs lashed together on top of a small rise. It was then that they were ambushed from behind.

As soon as their guns hit the ground, they were set upon by men who quickly lashed their hands behind their backs. Their captors then spun them around to face their leader. Jeb stood next to a young man who continued to whimper like a frightened girl.

Duncan rolled his eyes, his jaw tight. Harrison could only stare. Colin's mouth dropped open in shock. "I can't believe we bloody well fell for that!"

Johnny batted his eyes, blew them a kiss, then broke into hysterics. "We got you good!"

Jeb slapped him on the back. "Good work. Now, let's finish this."

Andel Berg was, for the most part, a gentle man. But one thing he couldn't abide was seeing a helpless woman in trouble. And what he saw was making his blood boil.

He crouched behind a rock next to Mr. MacDonald and M. Duprie. They'd managed to find the entrance to the cave and sneak in unseen. The dozen or so men inside were too busy devouring Mrs. Dunnigan's cooking. But soon they'd finished, and were ready for dessert – namely, the Van Zuyen women.

"What'll it be, boys?" a man yelled as he pulled the bound women up from the ground. "Prime rib?" He gave Mrs. Van Zuyen a shake. "Or lamb chop?"

Mrs. Dunnigan quickly gauged the situation. "Stop! You filthy scum aren't going to touch either one of them!"

"Why not?" a man next to her drawled. "You volunteerin' to go first?"

Mrs. Dunnigan looked at him in shock and teetered a bit as if she were about to faint. But instead, she hit the scoundrel across the face with her ladle with enough force to send him sprawling.

The other men stared at her for a moment, then looked to their fallen comrade. They then burst into laughter and went for the Van Zuyen women. They cut their bonds at their feet, dragged them to a corner, threw them each on top of a wooden plank, and lashed them down by the waist. They then leaned the planks against a low rock formation. The men wouldn't even have to get on the ground to take what they wanted.

To Mr. Berg and the others, it was obvious the gang had done this sort of thing before. The men even formed two lines!

"Andel, wait!" Mr. MacDonald whispered to him before he could jump out from behind the rock. "Ye canna just run out there and open fire. One o' the women might get hurt."

"He's right," Anton added. "And they have fourteen guns to our three."

"Wait 'til they start dropping their gun belts, lad – then we'll take them." No sooner had Mr. MacDonald said it than the gun belts began to come off.

One of the first men in line took the gag off of Madeline. "I like it better when they scream."

Madeline took one look at him and the men lined up behind him, and did just that.

The entire atmosphere in the cave changed. Lust was indeed a powerful force. The rest of the men couldn't get their belts off fast enough.

"Seven for you, laddie, seven for me?" Mr. MacDonald whispered.

Andel Berg smiled.

"*Monsieur* Duprie, take care o' the women. Get them out as fast ye can." Mr. MacDonald paused. "Ready, gentlemen?"

They nodded.

"Good. Let's go!"

Chaos broke out as the two giants leapt over the rock, uttering the most bloodcurdling war cries the gang had ever heard. One would swear Mr. Berg was more of a Viking warrior than a blacksmith. And Mr. MacDonald fought like nothing any of them had ever seen. The two didn't even have to pull their guns. Even Irene Dunnigan gaped at the sight (in between clobbering men with her ladle when they came within range) and wondered where they'd learned to fight like that.

Anton, meanwhile, wormed his way through the chaotic mess, kicking gun belts aside as he did. A few men, deciding it was better to live to fight another day, were carrying off the Van Zuyen women, planks and all, toward the nearest exit. He redoubled his efforts, but one man took Mrs. Van Zuyen down one passage, while two more took young Madeline down another.

"*Monsieur* Berg!" Duprie cried as he pointed to the passage Madeline had been carried into.

"Go get the wee lassie, man – I'll take care o' the rest!" Mr. MacDonald told Andel as he expertly felled another man with one fist.

There were five men still left standing. But Andel knew that the Scotsman would have no problem with them. He nodded and took off down the passage to rescue young Madeline.

Mrs. Dunnigan watched as the big Scot decked the nearest outlaw, smiled, spit on his hands, then said, "Now, laddies, is that *really* all ye've got?"

She stood, ladle at the ready, to do her part.

"Good Lord, I feel like we're in one of Mother's penny dreadfuls!" Colin quipped.

Harrison had to concede Colin's point. They were tied hand and foot, crammed together on the swinging bench. The ropes holding it creaked from even the slightest movement, the device not made to hold the weight of three men.

"Colin, stop moving." Duncan pleaded.

"Sadie, are you hurt?" Harrison asked while trying to stay as still as possible.

She lay bound in the same spot Cozette had been earlier. The trap having been sprung, the outlaws had taken her off the bench, gagged her again, and set her where she was. But none of them said a word about the missing Cozette, which certainly indicated that Thackary Holmes was behind all of this and had hired the gang to do his dirty work. Why else wouldn't they mention a missing captive?

She shook her head, tears in her eyes – she was scared, but not actually injured. She was more worried about the men right now than she was herself. Not only did they have to maintain their balancing act, they had to pray that the ropes would hold their weight!

"Now ain't this a pretty sight?" Jeb asked as he entered the cave and went to stand at the edge of the hole.

All three Cookes narrowed their eyes at their captor. It was lucky for Jeb that the brothers were bound and hanging precariously as they were. Jeb knew it, too, and laughed as he grabbed the same pole that had been used to shove Sadie around.

Sadie began to struggle wildly and screamed into the gag. Jeb looked over his shoulder at her. "Now don't be wasting all your strength now, ya hear? You're gonna need it in a minute. Remember that good time you owe me?"

Sadie snarled as best she could.

"Hmmm, I bet the thought of someone like me having my way with this pretty little thing makes you boys mad as a rattler, don't it?" Jeb taunted.

Harrison seethed. "Don't you dare lay a hand on her!"

Jeb laughed. "You fellers are polite even when you make threats! Must be *your* wife, huh? Well, let's see how long you can stay up there while I collect what she owes me."

"Owes you? She owes you nothing, you cur!" Harrison spat.

"Oh, but she does. If it weren't for you, I'da had her a long time ago."

Harrison's face screwed up in confusion for a second, then comprehension dawned. His entire body tensed.

"Don't *move*, Harrison!" Duncan warned.

"It's all comin' back to you now, ain't it? Ya know yer stepbrothers were purty good at what they done when they worked for me. All that cattle rustling, and then the way they framed two o' you for it. I gotta admit, it was a reg'lar work o' art! It kinda upset me when I found out Jack an' Sam got themselves caught."

"You!" Colin began, then froze. The ropes creaked, and a tiny snapping sound could be heard somewhere above them. He stilled his breathing and tried again. "You were behind it all along!"

Jeb smiled. "Still am, boys, in a manner of speakin'. This time around I'm just the hired help. But it ain't without its perks." He set down the pole, reached for

Sadie and pulled her to her feet. "Now, let's see how still you boys can sit while you watch me collect my debt ..."

Cozette struggled against Holmes as he made his way down the other side of the ridge. The trail was faint, but easier going than how the others went when they'd heard Sadie scream. Besides, he knew of the trail – that traitor Jeb had told him about it when he drew him the layout of the caves at their last meeting. But the outlaws were supposed to steal enough of the Triple-C's cattle to cripple the ranch, so none of the brothers wanted to have anything to do with the title and estate and would hand it over to Holmes. They were to hide the ill-gotten herd in the caves. Kidnapping the women was *not* part of the plan.

But he'd deal with that later. In the meantime, he'd jumped at the chance to make himself the hero, get rid of the Cooke brothers, make off with a wife in the process and beat the old Duke's deadline. He'd heard Jeb and his men plan their ambush just outside the cave, then go in and get Sadie Cooke to scream enough to lure the Cookes up. A good plan. He should have thought of it himself. But right now he had other problems.

For one, he was getting tired. He stopped, his breathing heavy, and set Cozette down. "I'm terribly sorry, Miss Duprie. But even as slight a load as you are, I'm afraid you're going to have to run the rest of the way." He pulled a small knife out of his pocket and cut her bonds.

She immediately jumped to her feet and began to scramble back up the trail.

"Wait!" Thackary shouted after her. He dove, caught her around the waist and pulled her down. "Don't be a fool, Miss Duprie! Those outlaws will kill you the moment they see you! You must let me help you escape!"

She shook her head as he grabbed her by the wrist and pulled her to her feet. She struggled and again tried to head back the way they'd come.

"I understand your concern for Mrs. Cooke, but her husband will come to her aid. Now, stop it or I'll truss you up and carry you again if I have to!"

She stopped and looked his way, her eyes suddenly wide. It took a moment for him to realize she wasn't looking at him, but behind him.

Cozette's lovely face was the last thing Holmes saw before everything went black.

Jeb cut the rope binding Sadie's ankles, then dragged her over a few feet so Harrison and his brothers would have a better view. She screamed into the gag, cried, bucked and kicked at Jeb, but not for herself – she was more worried about her husband and brothers-in-law.

Jeb only laughed at her struggles.

"Stop it!" Harrison yelled as he began to pull at his bonds.

The ropes above them snapped again. The bench dropped an inch to one side. "Harrison, stop! There's nothing we can do!" Colin cried.

"*Sadie!*" he screeched in desperation. He was *not* going to sit there, watch his wife be raped before his eyes, and do nothing about it. There was a limit.

No amount of kicking and struggling helped, and Sadie quickly began to tire. He threw her to the ground and straddled her, a knee on either side of her hips. "I'm gonna enjoy this." He took off his gun belt, tossed it to the side, then began to take off his belt. "In fact, I think I'll enjoy you for Jack and Sam as well. How's that sound?"

"It sounds like I've heard enough." *Click!*

Everyone froze. From Sadie's vantage point all she could see was a gun barrel pointed at Jeb's head. She turned and looked at Harrison, Duncan, and Colin as they stared in open-mouthed shock.

It was then that Cozette ran into the cave. She took one look at the brothers and stopped short. Her entire body shuddered, her mouth opened, and ... "Dun...can!" It was a barely recognizable rasp. But she'd said it. She spoke his name.

"Cozette!" Duncan cried.

The rope snapped again. The bench dropped another couple of inches, causing the brothers to gasp.

"Cozette, take my gun. If this piece of filth moves ... shoot him dead." Jefferson Cooke handed her his pistol, then quickly looked around for whatever he could find to save his stepsons.

The rope snapped again, and the distinct sound of it rapidly unwinding could now be heard overhead. Jefferson threw one of the wooden planks across the hole, then another, just as the bench lurched to one side. Harrison and Colin managed to land on the boards, but Duncan had a harder time of it. He wobbled as his knees hit the planks, and it looked like he was going to lose his balance.

"Duncan!" Cozette screamed, clearer this time, as she used her free hand to pick up the pole Jeb had discarded earlier. She pushed Duncan with it enough to help him right himself. But in doing so, she took her eyes off of Jeb, who jumped up and ran.

Jefferson ignored him and carefully stepped onto the planks to help guide the brothers to safety. He pulled out a knife, cut the ropes that bound their ankles, then helped them up. "Easy now, boys. Let's get you on solid ground."

They stood carefully and inched their way off the planks and onto the dirt. Harrison tried to immediately go to Sadie, not caring that his hands were still bound behind his back.

Jefferson stopped him. "Can't hold your wife like that, can you?" He cut his wrists loose, then went to free the others.

Duncan was the last to be freed. He grabbed Cozette to him and held her close. Both of them shuddered at the contact. He then looked down at her, and without saying anything, kissed her with everything he had.

Colin stared at Jefferson, his mouth half open in shock. "I say, where did you come from?"

"I lit out with the rest of the posse. None of you took notice?" Jefferson said gruffly.

All three brothers stood and stared at their stepfather.

"What are you all looking at? Why wouldn't I come help? I'm a *Cooke,* ain't I?"

Colin was the first to say something, a tear in his eye. "Yes, you are. You most certainly are!" He grabbed his stepfather and hugged him fiercely. Duncan and Colin did the same, as Sadie and Cozette found and held onto each other, both still shaken from the whole ordeal.

"It seems I owe you boys an apology," Jefferson began. "All this time I thought it was you three that was messing things up. But it turns out it was Jack and Sam all along. Problem was, I was too plumb drunk, and bitter, to notice. Guess it took me drying out a little and ... well, letting myself feel something to be able to see the truth."

Sheriff Hughes suddenly ran into the cave. "Everything all right in here?"

"Fine," Jefferson said. "Everything's just fine now, ain't it, boys?"

Duncan, Colin and Harrison nodded solemnly as they continued to stare at Jefferson, his words still sinking in. At long last, it looked like they could be a family again.

"You get that fella that ran outta here?" Jefferson asked the sheriff.

"Him, and most of the rest of the gang. Seems they've got quite the operation. Found your missing cattle in a cave down below along with Mrs. Dunnigan. That MacDonald fella done rounded up most of the gang single-handed. I've never seen anything like it. He had them stripped to their underwear and trussed up like a bunch of rabbits! Funniest thing I ever saw."

"What about Mrs. Van Zuyen and Madeline?" Sadie asked. What happened to them?"

Sheriff Hughes suddenly looked horrified. "Good grief, I have no idea!"

If there was one thing Andel Berg loved, it was a good fight. If there was one thing Andel liked better than a good fight, it was the prize at the end. And over the years, Andel had won his fair share of prizes. Not that he always won; he didn't. But this fight, this particular prize, he had to win.

He was fighting for the life of a woman – and not just any woman.

Young Madeline Van Zuyen had to be no more than eighteen, if that. Her eyes were red and swollen from crying, her face bruised from where one of the men had struck her. They had her hands bound behind her back and a knife to her throat.

"We know you're out there!" the man holding her called into the darkness around them. They only had one torch which didn't come close to illuminating the vast darkness that had swallowed them up the moment they entered the cavern.

"Yeah!" the other man added. "Come any closer, we cut her throat, ya hear?" Their voices echoed eerily off the cavern walls. Andel searched the ground near his feet for something to use to take advantage of it.

"Looks like yer rescuer done left you to fend for yerself," the man holding the knife hissed. "Too bad for you – guess he figured ya weren't worth it. And after we're done with ya, you won't be."

"Unless of course you can cook like that one lady done! Woo·wee, that was something!" the other laughed.

"Can you cook, little lady? Can you make something hot and tasty?" He grabbed at her body.

Madeline cried out and instinctively kicked him.

He took the knife from her throat, spun her around and tried to kiss her. She struggled against him as he got a hand in her hair to keep her still. She cried out in frustration, which only served to make both men laugh at her futile attempts. They then began to tear at her clothing. Madeline screamed.

Then everything happened at once.

What sounded like a gunshot echoed through the cavern. But was it a gunshot? It didn't sound loud enough. But then another came, and another.

"What was that?" one of the men cried just before something came out of nowhere to hit him with rock-hard force. Or actually, a rock hitting him with the force of Andel Berg. It felled the man instantly.

The other looked around, then at the torch they'd stuck into a crevice – just in time to see something hit it and send it hurtling to the ground, dimming the light considerably. "Stay away!" he yelled, his voice shrill with panic. "Stay away or I'll kill her–"

But before he could move, let alone raise the knife to Madeline's throat, something struck him in the back of the head. The knife dropped out of his hand and he, too, was felled.

Madeline stood in the dim light, her dress torn in several places, her body shaking uncontrollably when he came out of the darkness. He was a giant of a man, but approached her as if she was a precious piece of china. He looked around to make sure there were no other men, glanced at the two on the cave floor, then looked right at her.

But it was what he spoke that almost sent Madeline into a faint. "Are you all right, Your Highness?"

*Your Highness?!* Did she hear him right?

"Don't be frightened. I know who you are – both you and your mother."

She was speechless a moment. What was he talking about? Not only that but where was he from? He had an accent much like her mother's. She shook her head in confusion.

He straightened as he carefully approached. Was he afraid she might disappear? "You don't know, do you? Your mother never told you?"

"Told me what? Who *are* you?"

The giant bowed deeply. "I'm Andel Berg, at your service, Your Highness. I was sent to this country to find you. But right now, I'm here to rescue you."

Madeline didn't know who he was or what he was talking about ... and a few seconds later, she was glad to fall into blissful unconsciousness.

# DAY 33

*Five days to spare before the Duke's
stipulated deadline:*

"I do."

They were only two words, but they were the loveliest Duncan had ever heard. And his precious Cozette had uttered them loud and clear, all on her own.

"I now pronounce you man and wife!" the Rev. King said loudly enough for everyone to hear. Then a little more softly, "You may kiss the bride." And Duncan did.

He would have liked to keep on kissing her, only everyone in the church started cheering and throwing hats in the air. Several gunshots sounded outside, which he took as his cue to lead his bride out to the wedding wagon.

As they ran beneath a cascade of flower petals and who knows what else, he briefly recalled the last time he'd approached the same wagon barely over a month ago. Who would have thought his life could change so dramatically in such a short time? Or that he would now be married to the woman of his dreams?

"Congratulations," Colin said, then bowed and added, "Your Grace."

And who would have thought he would become the next Duke of Stantham? But here he was. And while he knew he'd better get used to it, he still sighed. "Don't start. There will be enough of that later as it is."

"You might as well get in some practice, old boy," Harrison put in. "You'll be putting it to use soon enough."

"I have time. And Cozette's lessons come first."

Cozette smiled up at her new husband. "I ... look forward ... to them." Her speech was still strained, and occasionally her accent, stilted by a lifetime of French, made her hard to understand. But the words came more easily every day.

Duncan didn't care, as long as the words came out. Her voice was pure heaven, and soothed those around her much the same as Mrs. MacDonald's had. It was downright beautiful, and not just when she was speaking – when he'd heard her hum for the first time, he thought he'd go mad. It was a pity the MacDonalds and the other settlers hadn't stayed for the wedding. But once the supplies they needed came three days ago, they pushed on for Oregon City.

As far as the kidnappees from the night of the dance, all of them were fairly well recovered except for Madeline Van Zuyen. She'd had a harder time after the ordeal, was put on bed rest by her mother and had kept to herself since then, speaking to no one. For whatever reason, her rescuer, Andel Berg, was sulking as well – but he was also coming out to the Triple-C as often as he could to help out with the stock. Sadie and Belle, of course, were convinced he had an eye for Madeline, and perhaps they were right.

As for Mrs. Van Zuyen, Anton Duprie was the one to rescue her in the nick of time. Unlike her daughter, she'd been busy – helping Cozette regain her speech and preparing her for her new responsibilities. Having been a headmistress and well-educated in etiquette, she'd taken it upon herself to coach the erstwhile duchess in the social graces over the next few months before she and Duncan left for London. After all, it wouldn't do to present the new Duchess of Stantham as a stammering, buckskin-clad huntress with shoddy table manners.

Duncan was admittedly amused by the thought of taking her along in her full wilderness kit, just to see what kind of scandal would ensue in English high society. But Cozette vetoed the idea immediately. She was committed to her new life, and – while she would likely bring her buckskins, bow and arrows on the trip – she only figured on using them in the privacy of her own estate. Otherwise, gowns and a tiara were the order of the day.

And speaking of scandals, no one had seen hide nor hair of Thackary Holmes since Jefferson had sapped him in the back of the head with the butt of his gun before taking Cozette up the ridge to find his stepsons. Not even Mr. Ashford – the dandy had simply disappeared. Hopefully, all the trouble had disappeared with him.

Duncan helped Cozette up onto the wagon seat, jumped up beside her and waved at the townsfolk of Clear Creek. "Thank you all! I'm going to miss this place while I'm in London!"

"You ain't goin' for a few months! You can't start missin' us till then!" Wilfred shouted.

"And I'm not done giving your wife cooking lessons!" Mrs. Dunnigan added.

"My dear Mrs. Dunnigan, if you teach our wives nothing else, we ask that you teach them one thing!" Duncan called to her.

"What's that?" she asked, confused.

"The proper use of a ladle!" Duncan shouted.

The entire wedding party and their guests exploded into riotous laughter. Even Irene.

The new Duke and Duchess of Stantham kissed, and then, with a flick of the reins, started back to the Triple-C for the wedding supper. And this time, Duncan planned on eating until he could eat no more.

Captain Andel Berg, on the other hand, planned to continue the mission assigned him nearly a year ago: Find and retrieve Princess Madeleina Valenta at any cost and return her to her beloved country and her betrothed. The problem was, as much as Captain Berg loved his country, he despised the Princess's intended – the heartless fiend had forced the assignment on him by holding his father hostage. The longer Andel failed to return with the Princess in his possession, the more likely his father's life was forfeit.

Andel didn't know if his father was still alive now, but didn't want to risk it in case he was. He would do the work required of him, no matter what.

But the Princess Madeleina, going by the name Madeline Van Zuyen, had no idea who she was. She thought she was a simple girl from New York, crossing the prairie to settle in the tiny town of Clear Creek, and none of the townsfolk were the wiser. But Madeleina's mother, the Countess Van Zuyen, would have to have known that someone would catch up with them eventually and take them back to their homeland. And now that the King's youngest son had gotten himself shot, his daughter was the only living heir and would have to ascend the throne. With her betrothed at her side, of course – never mind that she'd never met him or even heard of him before. She was his ticket to the throne, and he'd stop at nothing to get her, including killing Andel's father.

But there was a new problem on top of that. Ever since Andel had rescued her from the cruelty of the outlaws, cradled her in his arms and carried her from that cave, he'd begun to have second thoughts about his mission. In fact, he was having thoughts he hadn't known he *could* have! His sense of duty to his position, his country, even his father became difficult to maintain whenever he remembered how her frightened eyes had filled with relief as he'd stepped into the dim light to rescue her. She was so beautiful – her blonde hair framing her face, her blue eyes seeking his comfort, his protection ...

Something had awakened within his heart that day. And Andel hadn't been able to quell it since, any more than he could make it rain.

He sighed, mounted his horse, and left for the wedding supper to continue to plan how he'd fulfill his assignment. But in addition to the questions of how and when was a new one: *should* he?

## The End

I hope you enjoyed reading Harrison, Colin, and Duncan's stories. The excitement continues with the next installments of the Prairie Bride series. Find out what happens next in:

**Her Prairie Viking** (Prairie Brides, Book Four)
**His Prairie Sweetheart** (Prairie Brides, Book Five)
**Her Prairie Outlaw** (Prairie Brides, Book Six)
**Christmas in Clear Creek** (Prairie Brides, Book Seven)

# ABOUT THE AUTHOR

Kit Morgan, aka Geralyn Beauchamp, loves a good Western. Her father loved them as well, and they watched their fair share together over the years. You can keep up-to-date on future books, fun contests and more at **Kit Morgan's Facebook page** or by checking out her blog at **www.authorkitmorgan.blogspot.com**. You can also find her hanging out at one of the best Facebook groups around: **Pioneer Hearts**

Made in the USA
Columbia, SC
04 February 2020